"Castille's debut is steamy."   —*Publishers Weekly*

"Hot, hot, hot."   —*Nocturne Romance Reads*

"Smart, sharp, sizzling and deliciously sexy . . . a knockout."
           —Alison Kent, bestselling author of *Unbreakable*

"There's plenty to keep readers coming back for more . . ."
           —*RT Book Reviews*

"It's a book that's gobbled up in giant bites"
           —*Dear Author*

"Powerful. Gritty. Heart wrenching. And sexy beyond belief. This book dragged me through an emotional wringer, bringing me to tears more than once. Sarah is a true master!"
           —Opal Carew, *New York Times* Best Selling Author

"Hilarious, hot, and occasionally heartbreaking. I loved it!"
           —*Maryse's Book Blog*

"Steamy and sexy, the characters and the story will have readers enthralled."
           —*Bookaholics Romance Book Club*

"Sexy . . . I love a good alpha-male!"
           —*About That Story*

Arianne paused midstep and shook her hand free. "Jag—"

"Shhhh."

Her eyes narrowed. "Did you just *shhhh* me?"

He cupped her jaw with his warm palm and tilted her head back, forcing her to meet his gaze. "This is the part where I'm protecting you, so you'll have to put up with bossy." He ran his thumb lightly over her mouth. "And I'll put up with your lip because—"

"Because my lips are telling you I'm heading out of town as soon as I find my brother," she said, cutting him off. "My lips are also telling you I didn't agree to your plan. I'm better off at Dawn's place. Why risk the repercussions of protecting me when I'm about to leave?"

His gaze, hot and heavy, fell to her mouth and then he leaned down and brushed his lips over hers in the softest kiss. "Say yes, lips." The soft yet commanding murmur of his voice turned her legs to jelly.

Arianne's brain fuzzed. Whether from the warm touch of his palm on her cheek, the arousal his kiss sparked in her blood, or the overwhelming desire to feel safe, even if only for a night, she didn't know. But she wanted to go with him.

★ ROUGH JUSTICE ★

Sinner's Tribe Motorcycle Club

SARAH CASTILLE

St. Martin's Paperbacks

This is a work of fiction. All of the characters, organizations, and events portrayed in this novel are either products of the author's imagination or are used fictitiously.

ROUGH JUSTICE

Copyright © 2015 by Sarah Castille.
Excerpt from *Beyond the Cut* copyright © 2015 by Sarah Castille.

For information address St. Martin's Press, 175 Fifth Avenue, New York, NY 10010.

ISBN: 978-1-250-05660-3

Printed in the United States of America

St. Martin's Paperbacks edition / February 2015

St. Martin's Paperbacks are published by St. Martin's Press, 175 Fifth Avenue, New York, NY 10010.

10 9 8 7 6 5 4 3 2

To my Harley man
Two bikes, two hearts, one journey

★ ACKNOWLEDGMENTS ★

To the bikers on the ferry between Harwich and Esbjerg for all the ideas, and my agent, Laura Bradford for knowing I was a biker chick at heart. And to my fabulous editor Monique Patterson for polishing my manuscript and making it shine, and her assistant Alexandra Sehulster for her patience with my questions about turtle soup. To Jill, Donna, and Bev for their sharp eyes and helpful insights. And always to my family, for their patience, understanding, and ability to act out even the most complicated fight scenes.

★ ONE ★

The name of the club shall be the Sinner's Tribe Motorcycle Club.

"*Christ.*"

Jagger skidded his sleek Harley chopper to a stop as incandescent chunks of steel arced across the night sky. Clouds of black smoke engulfed the flaming skeleton of what had once been his clubhouse, now a crumbling beacon at the edge of town.

"Looks like someone wants a war." Zane, his Vice President and closest friend, dropped the engine of his V-Rod Muscle to idle and pulled his .38 Special double-action revolver from inside his cut, the leather vest bearing the three-piece patch that identified him as a member of the Sinner's Tribe Motorcycle Club. "I know my fires—and that one was accelerated. Hope our arsonist is still around."

Not likely with fifty angry MC brothers buzzing around the fire. Jagger parked his bike curbside, and stepped onto the paved lot that surrounded the burning building, converted from a run-down garage into the heart of his outlaw MC. He drew his own weapon, gripping the handle so hard, his knuckles blazed under the streetlight, burning as fiercely as the rage pumping through his veins.

"I'll find him and bring him to you." Zane's words were a small comfort for Jagger's pain. If the arsonist were stupid enough to stick around and watch the fireworks, he'd never get away alive—not with Zane on his tail. Lean and dark, with the sharpest eyes this side of Montana's Bridger Mountains, Zane was the best tracker in the MC, with the uncanny ability to hunt down even the most elusive prey.

Glass shattered and the flames roared higher into the air, fanned by the dry autumn breeze. The converted warehouse had been a second home for many of Jagger's biker brethren, and its senseless destruction stirred a protective fury in him. As president, Jagger was responsible for his MC brothers. Their pain was his pain. Their loss was his loss. And their revenge . . . When it came, he would make sure it was the sweetest fucking revenge they'd ever tasted.

"Jag, over here, I found Gunner."

Jagger walked across the parking lot, following Wheels' voice through the thick, acrid smoke to the forest that bordered the east side of the clubhouse. He spotted the MC's newest prospect crouched under a tree, his golden-blond hair gleaming in the moonlight. The kid needed a haircut bad. Paired with that soft babyish face, the long fringe made Wheels look like a boy band singer instead of an MC pledge. Jagger already had doubts about whether the kid would survive the trials every prospect faced to prove worthy of wearing the Sinner's Tribe full-patch.

Propped up against the tree trunk, one leg stretched in front of him, Gunner grunted a greeting as Jagger squatted opposite Wheels. As a member of the MC's executive board, Gunner could have used his real name instead of the road name chosen by his brothers, but "Gunner" suited him so well he'd decided to keep it. A weapons expert, with detailed knowledge about the construction and use of almost every weapon legal or illegal, he never carried fewer than four guns at any time.

"Took one in the leg?" Jagger's field training kicked in as soon as he saw Gunner's blood-soaked jeans, and he tugged off his bandanna and twisted it into a makeshift bandage for his sergeant at arms.

"Just a flesh wound. Bullet tore the muscle when it grazed my calf. I've had worse. Just need a hand to my bike." Gunner took the bandanna and tied it around his leg. An inch taller than Jagger, and with a shaved head and pierced ear, Gunner was a slab of solid muscle with strength unmatched by any of the brothers in the club, making him a shoo-in for sergeant at arms at their biannual executive board elections. The man hadn't taken a bullet yet that could put him out of commission.

"What happened?" Jagger helped Gunner tighten the bandanna. *Damn lucky.* He'd seen men lose their legs from a bullet. Hell, he'd seen just about everything a bullet could do to a human body.

"We smelled smoke out back." Gunner bent his leg, testing his weight. "Cole went to investigate. I heard a coupla shots, so I ran out with a fucking AK-47. Couldn't find Cole, but I saw four guys in cuts in our yard—definitely bikers, but it was too dark to see their patches. One of them was carrying a gas can, and was pouring gasoline along the north wall of the clubhouse. Another was in the woods, and the other two were at the weapons shed unloading our new shipment of AKs into a truck."

"Fuck." Jagger scraped a hand through his hair. Could this night get any worse? Not only had they lost the clubhouse, they'd lost the weapons that would have cemented their new relationship with a powerful Mexican cartel who had been looking for an arms supplier in the northern states.

Dry leaves crackled under Gunner's hands as he tried to push himself up. "Yeah, I hear you, brother. And I did my fucking best to save those weapons. I headed into the trees, planning to come up behind the two at the shed. By that time, there was nothing I could do to save the clubhouse. The flames had already spread across the south and west walls. But damned if one of them heard me. He got me in the leg before I could get off a shot."

"They're gonna be dead twice over when we catch them." Wheels paled and checked himself when Jagger shot him a warning look.

"I mean you . . . Jagger . . . no . . . the Sinners. And me . . . I'll be doing what you tell me to do. For the club. Like always."

Jagger gritted his teeth against the urge to berate the hapless prospect, and gestured for Gunner to continue. Always enthusiastic and eager to please, Wheels had his strengths. Unfortunately, understanding the nuances of biker politics wasn't one of them.

With Jagger's help, Gunner stood, bearing most of his weight on his good leg. "The bastard near the clubhouse finished up with the gas can." He winced as he tried to take a step. "He was on his way to the truck when a dude on a piece-of-shit Kawasaki Ninja raced into the yard. I heard tires skidding, and then a crash near the weapons shed. I grabbed my gun and just fired blind in the direction of the noise. Then the truck blasted outta here."

Jagger sent Wheels to the shop to investigate, and then helped Gunner to his bike. The firefighters would be on their way soon, and the cops wouldn't be far behind. Although Jagger had the sheriff on his payroll, not all the local law enforcement were happy to have an outlaw MC in Conundrum. He had to get his men out of here.

Gunner's chromed-out Harley Softail Classic rumbled to life, and Jagger pulled Cade, the club treasurer, from the enraged crowd and told him to lead Gunner and the rest of the brothers to the club's emergency base, a run-down country house on the outskirts of town. From there, they would do a head count, reorganize, and start planning a counterstrike.

"Jag—Jag—Jag—" Wheels raced toward him, his pale face almost translucent in the semidarkness. "Half the weapons are gone, but they caught him. The guy on the Ninja. They're at the weapons shed. Zane's trying to stop Axle from shooting him in the head."

Fuck.

Fury coiled in his gut as he stalked toward the weapons shed, tucked away in a small copse of trees and far enough away from the heat of the flames that the remaining weapons weren't at risk. His ire wasn't directed just at the Ninja rider whose life he now held in his hands, but at that goddamned son-of-a-bitch, Axle.

He tensed, preparing for a battle that had been festering for over a year. After gaining the support of a small group of dissident brothers, Axle had made no effort to hide the fact that he wanted Jagger's position as president. The fact that he'd dared to draw his weapon on the arsonist, despite knowing Jagger was nearby, was a challenge to Jagger's authority, and even the legitimacy of Jagger's five year run as MC president.

Jagger rounded the corner of the small cinder block shed just as Axle wrenched himself away from an infuriated Zane. With a speed that belied his heavy frame, Axle vaulted across the pavement, skirted the fallen Kawasaki Ninja, and then ground to a halt beside a leather-clad figure sprawled unconscious on the cement.

"Bastard's gonna die." Axle pointed his .45 ACP semiautomatic Colt pistol at the motionless body and slid his finger through the trigger.

"Drop it." Rage tinted Jagger's vision red. "Now."

Axle didn't waver. Violent and vicious, with sharp features and dark eyes, he was a crack shot and always the first to draw his weapon in a fight. And although Jagger shared Axle's need for vengeance and retribution for the wrong done to the club, he couldn't in good conscience condone the execution of a man when there was, as yet, no evidence of his guilt.

"We have to make a statement." Axle's face twisted in a snarl, and he glanced over at the gathering crowd of angry bikers. "Everyone will expect it—our mother chapter, rival MCs, the Russians, the Mafia, the Mexican cartels, even the Triads. We do nothing, and they'll smell weakness. He's gotta pay a blood price for what he's done to our club, and I'm willing to collect it." He gave the unconscious biker a hard kick in the ribs, drawing murmurs of encouragement from the crowd.

Jagger cursed under his breath and holstered his weapon beneath his cut. He maintained his leadership position by using coercion and power to impose his will on his brothers. Drawing his weapon on Axle, as he was tempted to do, would suggest he could no longer control Axle by force of will alone—an admission of weakness that could cost him his presidency, even his life. He fisted his hand at his side and glared "My club. My call. If you shoot him, it'll be the last fucking thing you ever do."

Axle stood motionless above the fallen biker, sweat beading his brow as he toyed with his gun, no doubt weighing the chance to be the club hero against the very real possibility Jagger would make good his threat.

Jagger's pulse pounded out each second of delay. Axle had been a thorn in his side far too long, but until now, he'd been smart enough never to openly defy Jagger, preferring instead to skulk resentfully in the shadows, making underhanded attempts to erode Jagger's power base. Tonight, however, the emotionally charged situation was clearly an opportunity Axle couldn't pass up. He had finally shown his hand. But Jagger hadn't held the presidency for five years without knowing how to deal with snakes like Axle.

"Step away. I'll deal with him." Pointedly ignoring Axle's weapon, and without waiting for Axle's compliance, Jagger crouched down beside the unmoving figure. Small for a Ninja rider and thin . . . almost delicate. He carefully rolled the unconscious biker to the side, and his fists convulsed with suppressed rage when he saw the Black Jacks MC patch, a jack from a deck of playing cards with a skull for a face.

Zane muttered a curse. Wheels let out a long, low whistle. Even Jagger startled. The Black Jacks and the Sinner's Tribe had been engaged in a feud over territory for years. But two years ago, the high death toll had drawn the attention of federal authorities and the national media, driving away the illicit underground black market that was the bread and butter of Montana's outlaw MC operations. In the interest of self-preservation, Jagger and the Black Jacks president, Viper, had called an uneasy truce. The Black Jacks took control of Montana's drug trade, and the Sinner's Tribe took over the more lucrative contracts in illegal arms trafficking. With both clubs claiming dominance of the state, the occasional skirmish was unavoidable. But for the most part, the truce had held.

Until now.

Axle cocked his gun and gestured at the two-piece patch on the fallen biker's cut. "He's wearing fucking Jacks colors. Outta my way, Jagger. The feud is back on."

"He's not a full-patch brother." Wheels shot Axle a pleading look and then slid his gaze to Jagger. "He's missing the bottom rocker. He might only be a prospect doing what he was told to do. You can't just kill him." Wheels edged closer to the fallen biker. "We don't even know if he's the one who set the fire."

"We can do whatever the fuck we want." Axle shot Wheels an irritated glance. "The Sinners are one-percenters. You know what that means, prospect? It means we're the one percent of bikers who *don't* follow fucking civilian law. We make our own rules, follow our own codes, and administer our own justice. And the penalty for burning down our clubhouse is death."

Jagger pushed himself to his feet, taking advantage of his six-foot-two-inch frame as he loomed over Axle. "Last I heard, I was the president of the Sinner's Tribe. That means administering justice is my call. And after talking to Gunner, I'm not convinced the Ninja rider is the man who torched our clubhouse."

Axle's face lit with bitter triumph, and he offered his weapon to Jagger, an insulting gesture, since he knew Jagger was carrying a gun. "Doesn't matter. He's a Black Jack. In a matter of honor, one Jack is as good as the next. So do your duty. Give us justice. Revenge. Show us what you're made of, *Oh great leader.*"

Jagger took the offered weapon, removed the magazine, then stepped forward and smashed the butt of the gun into Axle's head. Axle dropped to his knees, then slumped on the ground.

"Zane, he's yours for tonight." Jagger's voice cracked through the silence. "But make sure he's fit to attend the executive board meeting in the morning to answer for his disrespect." He tossed Axle's gun to Zane and glowered at the crowd. "Anyone else got a problem?"

Without waiting for a response, he bent down and removed the fallen biker's helmet. Long, dark hair spilled over the pavement in a silken wave.

"Well, damn." Zane exhaled his words in a shocked whisper. "He's a she. We've been disrespected by a fucking girl."

No, not a girl. A woman. An angel. From Black Jack hell.

Jagger pressed his fingers to her neck, feeling for a pulse beneath her soft, cool skin. She moaned and her eyes fluttered open, startling him with an emerald-green brilliance like nothing he had ever seen before.

For an instant he couldn't speak, and then her thick, dark lashes drifted over creamy cheeks and her head drooped to the side. Beneath the pads of his fingers, her pulse beat steady but faint. Reassured, he removed his hand. Only then did he see her injuries—long, thick, finger-shaped bruises around her neck.

With a light touch, he traced along the fine line of her jaw. Mottled black-and-blue marks extended from her temple to her chin. His eyes slid to the helmet and then back to her pale face. Definitely not injuries from the accident. For some reason he couldn't name, he wanted to hunt down whoever had hurt her and pound him into the ground.

Ironic, really, since he might have to kill her.

★ TWO ★

Club first. Club only. Club always.

The dream was always the same: soft bed, dim light, fluffy pink duvet, homework on her desk.

Leo on top of her.

Screams and shouting. Her arms pinned. His hand yanking down her jeans. Her thrashing on the bed, a wail escaping her lips.

"Wake up." A rough hand stroked her cheek and wiped away a tear.

Arianne's eyes fluttered open and she squinted to adjust to the dim light, trying to make sense of her surroundings.

She tried to push herself up and then fell back on the pillow when her stomach heaved.

"Don't move."

Panicked, Arianne froze and peered in the direction of the deep, rich voice. She blinked to clear her vision and he came into view, leaning back on the chair beside her bed, long legs stretched out in front of him, thick arms covered with tats and folded over a massive chest. Under his cut, a Harley-Davidson T-shirt stretched taut over toned pecs and a washboard stomach. Black jeans hugged his narrow hips, and thick dark hair brushed the top of his wide shoulders. Rough and weathered, he sported at least a day's worth of beard over his square jaw.

Delicious.

His sheer presence drew her in. No. Not presence. *Power.* Raw and untamed.

"Who are you?" Her voice wavered despite her best efforts to slow her pounding heart. Running and screaming would do her little good if she knew nothing about her situation.

"Jagger."

"Jagger?" The name was familiar, but with her brain still fuzzy she couldn't place him. In fact, she couldn't place anything. Not even herself. She forced her mind backward, trying to pinpoint her last memory.

"Maybe this will help."

He removed his cut and spun it around, holding it up to give her a good view of the back. She recognized the three-piece patch at once: a winged skull set above flames, with two stars on either side and two curved rockers above and below, proclaiming the name of his club and the chapter.

THE SINNER'S TRIBE MC.

She was going to die.

And on the very day she had planned to escape this life forever. Gritting her teeth, Arianne forced back a whimper. She wouldn't give him the satisfaction of begging for her life. *Death with dignity.* She would make her mother proud. And her father, too, if he was even capable of that emotion.

Jagger grimaced and shrugged on the cut, his fingers brushing over the patch identifying him as president. "Looks like you know who we are."

Blood pounded in her throat and she dipped her chin. Who didn't know the Conundrum chapter of the Sinner's

Tribe, the dominant outlaw MC in Montana, and one of the top outlaw MCs in the country? The club boasted nine hundred members across the northern United States alone. Archenemies of the Black Jacks MC in which she had been born and raised, the Sinner's Tribe were unequaled in size or power in Montana. And Jagger was their king.

A sickening wave of terror cleared the fog from her brain. Everything came back in a rush. All her hard work to save enough money to procure false passports and new identities for her and Jeff. Favors pulled to arrange for them to get to Canada under the Black Jacks' radar. The excitement of knowing they would finally be free from their father, Viper; the Black Jacks; and the biker world. And then Jeff's text: he wasn't coming. Viper had caught him on his way out and sent him with a team of Jacks to torch the Sinner's Tribe's clubhouse and steal a shipment of weapons.

She swallowed dryly as she remembered racing through Conundrum on her Ninja, desperate to stop Jeff from making a mistake that could cost him his life. Hope and desolation. Flames flickering. The crack of a gun. And then darkness.

Jagger leaned forward, his hand outstretched as if to steady her. "You're lookin' very white. You gonna pass out?"

"No. I'm fine."

Fighting back an almost overwhelming urge to run, she made a quick assessment of the room: king-size bed, night table, and wooden chair. Bare and functional. Her .38, still in its leather calf holster, sat beside a black gym bag on a low, wide dresser. A window with no curtains. Moonlight casting shadows on the floor. Handsome-as-fuck executioner. No Jeff. *Small mercy.* Maybe he'd escaped.

Maybe she could escape, too. She had to escape. If Jagger found out her father was his mortal enemy, he would shoot her on the spot.

"Where are we?" Her voice was thin, almost unrecognizable, and raw in her throat.

Jagger tilted his head and gave her an amused smile. "Too far to run, if that's what you're thinking. We acquired this old house from a double-crossing dealer who thought he could play us. Nothing around for miles except mountains, trees, and the odd wolf. And if you did get it into your head to go for a hike, there are one hundred angry Sinners and support club members outside who think you burned down our clubhouse. They want blood. Right now, this is the safest place for you to be."

Okay. Not good odds. But staying here was certain death. Squaring her shoulders, she pushed herself to sitting, grimacing as pain sliced through her head.

With a soft, admonishing grumble, Jagger clasped her arm and helped her back down onto the pillow. "Doc said you had a concussion and shouldn't get out of bed for a coupla days."

She stared at him in surprise. "Why didn't you just kill me? Why bother with a doctor? Or do you like your prisoners healthy before you torture them?"

He shifted in his chair, and a shadow crossed his disturbingly attractive face. "Innocent until proven guilty. I added it to our bylaws. Keeps the boys from becoming vigilantes and delivering instant retribution for imagined slights."

"Maybe in your club. Not in mine."

She clamped her mouth shut. *Damn.* Even the smallest bit of information could reveal the identity of her father, although save for the dark hair, she and her father didn't look much alike. And despite the fact that she'd been wearing her Black Jacks cut, she wasn't a Jack. Not by a long shot.

Jagger studied her in silence, unnerving her with his steady stare. But damned if she would . . . could look away from those warm brown eyes. Deep. Fathomless. For a second her mind unmoored and she was floating in a chocolate sea.

Safe.

Protected.

What the hell was she doing? When had anyone ever protected her? And he was the enemy. Their clubs had been fighting over territory for years, trading brutalities the way young boys traded insults. Even the old ladies weren't safe.

Or their daughters . . .

She pushed the memory away. Her mother hadn't died because of the feud but because of the biker culture at the heart of it. A culture that considered women to be property and nothing more.

"You got a name?" He leaned back and spread his legs in the irritating way men often did, taking up the space of three people in an effort to exert dominance.

Except Jagger didn't really have to try. From the authority in his voice to the power oozing from his pores, he was every inch the dominant alpha male. A natural leader. She doubted anyone ever challenged him. And that traitorous lick of heat deep in her core? Simply an instinctive primal response. Easily rationalized away.

"Arianne." The name dropped from her lips before she could catch it. Almost immediately, she realized her mistake. She'd given him her real name. Her birth name. The name she hadn't used in the biker world since her mother died. What the hell was she thinking? "I mean, Vexy." She firmed her voice. "Vexy is my road name."

His rugged face softened. "Arianne is a pretty name. Soft. Suits you. Vexy, not so much. Makes me think of a sexy woman who's got a temper."

She gave an exasperated sigh. As if she didn't know what the word "vex" meant. But bikers didn't get to choose their road names; those names were bestowed by the club. And although women weren't allowed to be an official part of the Black Jacks, she had status, a road name, and a cut simply because of who she was.

Jagger lifted an eyebrow. "That you, Arianne? You got a temper?"

Her cheeks heated. Was he teasing her? With his face an impassive mask, and his tone cool and even, she couldn't tell. But she liked the sound of her name on his lips—his soft rumble over the second syllable—so much that she didn't correct him. The temper part, however . . . Folding her arms across her chest, she narrowed her eyes. "Try me."

Jagger tilted his head to the side. "I didn't see a property patch on your cut. You got someone to keep you in line? You a mama or a sweet butt? Or did the Black Jacks change the rules and allow women to ride in their club?"

Arianne glared. Nothing rankled her more than the misogyny that permeated the biker world. Wives and girlfriends were supposed to feel honored to be deemed a biker's "property" or "old lady," the equivalent of a civilian wife. "House mamas" and "sweet butts" who looked after the bikers' needs, both in and out of the bedroom, and took care of the clubhouse in return for housing and protection were considered communal property, but usually hooked up with one biker at a time. And the "hood rats," "hang-arounds," and "lays" who came for the parties and the thrill of a one-night stand with a badass biker were free for the taking.

"I'm nobody's property and I'm no sweet butt." She straightened her posture and met his gaze full-on. "I was born into the Jacks. My dad is . . . a biker." She caught herself just in time. What the hell was wrong with her? She wasn't a talkative person at the best of times, and now, when keeping her mouth shut mattered the most, she was about to tell him the one thing that could get her killed, no questions asked. And yet, perversely, there was something about Jagger that put her at ease. Maybe she'd hit her head harder than she thought.

"So, how is it you're patched?" He pointed to her cut, hanging off the footboard of her bed, the two-piece Black Jacks patch, missing the bottom rocker that only full patch members were permitted to wear, a reminder of her vulnerable position. She wore her cut only on club business, and she tried to do as little of that as possible.

She shrugged her answer, digging her nails into her palms. What was with all the questions? Either he was going to kill her or he wasn't, and odds favored the latter, since honor dictated that someone had to pay for the destruction of his clubhouse. So why didn't he just get on with it—or give her a chance to try to escape or die fighting instead of beguiling her with his winning personality, charm, and good looks?

"How about an easier question then." His face grew pensive. "Did you burn down my clubhouse?"

Emotion welled up in her throat, fed by fear and tension and a disconcerting attraction to the ridiculously handsome man who held her life in his hands. "No, it wasn't me."

"But it was the Black Jacks?"

Arianne fought to stay calm. Was there any point denying the Black Jacks were involved? No one else would have dared step foot on Sinners' property much less burn down the clubhouse. Or was this a test? Had a member of his club already identified the Jacks before they fled?

"Arianne?" He leaned forward, resting his elbows on his knees, his body tense.

She shook her head, wary of revealing too much. Although she hated the Jacks with a passion, she wasn't about to break the biker code of conduct that had been drilled into her since she could walk, especially when her brother's life was at risk. And the number-one rule was that club business stayed in the club. "You know I can't answer that question."

"Justice won't be served if I take an innocent life."

Her life. His not-so-subtle threat shattered her fantasy that he was just a normal man, and not the president of a vicious one-percenter outlaw motorcycle club, who handed out death sentences the way she handed out drinks at Banks bar. He had just claimed he wouldn't hurt her, and now he was threatening to take her life. Was this some sort of a game to him?

"But honor will be," she said. "Isn't that what you're getting at? Or are you saying I'm not innocent? Guilty by association?"

When his brows drew together, she tightened her grip on the sheet. *Bastard.* He was toying with her. Lulling her into a false sense of security before moving in for the kill. Well, he was about to discover she wasn't going down easy. Her father's cruelty seemed almost a kindness now: He'd made her strong. He'd forced her to learn how to survive.

Gritting her teeth against the dull ache in her head, she sat up again and shifted on the bed, swinging her legs over the side. Pain erupted in her ribs, so sharp and fierce, her hand flew to her side and she gasped.

Jagger hissed out a breath and his jaw tightened. "Axle kicked you when you were down. Doc said he bruised your ribs." He leaned over and brushed his fingers lightly down her neck, sending a pulse of heat through her body. "She also said you'd been badly beaten. She wanted to take you to the hospital to check for internal injuries, but I could go only so far." He trailed his fingers along her jaw and over the apple of her cheek, his touch so soothing that tears, unwanted and unexpected, welled in her eyes.

His voice dropped to a quiet murmur. "She said it wasn't the first time."

"Don't." She batted his hand away, confused by a kindness that belied the presidential patch on the front of his cut. And yet there was something different about Jagger. A calm confidence. A tempered edge.

His eyes glittered. "Did a Jack do this to you?"

She was saved from lying when the door opened, just a crack at first, and then wider. Deeply tanned fingers curled around the edge, pushing the door ajar.

But not wide enough for a clear run.

A tall, dark-haired man wearing a Sinner's Tribe cut stepped into the room, his broad shoulders and lean muscled body completely filling the doorway. Darkly sensual, with chiseled features and penetrating brown eyes, he swept his gaze over the stark space, pausing briefly on her and then locking on Jagger. "Need to speak to you."

With a sigh, Jagger stood. "Zane is VP of the Sinner's Tribe and my oldest friend. He's usually a little more polite with the ladies." Jagger's easy familiarity suggested he didn't consider Arianne a threat, but his friend clearly did.

"The ladies I know don't burn down buildings and kill our brothers."

Arianne cringed at Zane's venom-laced voice.

"Cole's dead?" A muscle worked in Jagger's jaw.

"We found him in the woods. Two bullets. One in the chest. The other went through his shoulder. Shooter used a .22. Woman's gun." Zane fixed Arianne with a frigid stare.

She gave a disdainful sniff. "Clearly, you don't know many women who shoot. I use a .38 unless I can't conceal the carry."

"She's telling the truth." Jagger pointed to the dresser

where her gun lay just out of reach. "Did you find anything else?"

Zane drew Jagger over to the window. Arianne's gaze slid to the slightly open door and then over to the two men who appeared to be engrossed in their conversation.

Gun or exit? And did she even dare? Her body ached, her ribs burned, her head throbbed, and she was wearing only an oversized T-shirt and her underwear. No doubt she'd been undressed for the doctor's examination, which is how they'd found her weapon.

Still, how could she not try? She knew better than anyone how their world worked: Club first. Club always. Regardless of Jagger's personal views, if her death was in the best interests of the club, then he would kill her without hesitation. Better to die trying to live than to sit passively awaiting her fate because of a few injuries or a reluctance to let anyone see her pink polka-dot panties.

She steeled herself against the pain, and placed her feet firmly on the floor. The exit was her safest bet. Chances were they would shoot her before she could grab and unholster her gun.

One . . . two . . . three . . . go. Launching herself forward, Arianne shot off the bed and threw herself at the opening in the door. But even as she flew across the room, her feet barely touching the wooden floor, she knew Jagger would catch her.

"*Christ.*" He grabbed her before she reached the hallway, one hand clasping her shoulder, the other around her waist. With a sharp jerk, he pulled her into his body, imprisoning her in the warm circle of his arms.

Be careful what you wish for.

Seconds passed. Neither of them moved. Chests heaved together. Hearts pounded in unison. She drew in a ragged gasp and inhaled his intoxicating scent of leather and whiskey; a rush of longing, almost visceral in its intensity, caught her off guard.

Jagger leaned forward, brushing his lips over her ear, and they both shuddered. "Why the fuck did you do that?"

"Wouldn't have been able to live with myself if I didn't try." A wave of dizziness hit her hard, almost overshadowing the pain from her ribs. *Damn betraying body.* She tried to wiggle free and her knees buckled.

"I've got you." His arms tightened around her, imprisonment becoming support, and she breathed out a small sigh.

"I'm okay." She made another half-hearted attempt to escape, but he simply held her closer to his body.

"Let me go." "I don't need your help."

With a snort of laughter, he lifted her easily in his arms. "Never met anyone who needed help as much as you."

He should be angry.

Hell, Zane was spitting bullets in the corner. Instead, Jagger was amused, impressed, and no small bit aroused by his sexy prisoner's attempt to escape. With her sweet warm body in his arms, her lush ass wiggling against his groin, he was reminded of just how long he had been without a woman—sweet butts and hood rats excluded, of course. Although the sweet butts were always happy to relieve the needs of his Sinner's Tribe brethren, they were a quick fix that always left him feeling unsatisfied.

She was tough—no doubt about that—but beneath her armor, he'd sensed fragility, and a quiet softness that did strange things to his stomach. Still, he couldn't let her actions go unpunished. Between Arianne and Axle, his authority had been challenged more tonight than it had been in years. Maybe the full moon was to blame.

While Zane stood guard, Jagger fished around in his

gym bag and pulled out a pair of handcuffs. Last time he'd used them, he was trunking with Cade and Gunner.

He smiled inwardly at the memory as he crossed over to the bed. Cade had snatched a dumb-ass, top-level drug dealer off the street and Jagger had cuffed him and stuffed him in the trunk of his black Chrysler 300C. Then they'd spent the next hour shooting the breeze and driving around Conundrum while Gunner negotiated with the dealer's family for his release. One hundred thousand dollars for two hours of work. And it all went into the club's already-overflowing coffers.

"Didn't want to do this, but I can't have you trying to escape again." He snapped one of the cuffs around her slender wrist. "Not only did the doctor say you have to stay in bed, but I wasn't kidding when I said everyone outside this room wants you dead. We wouldn't be having this conversation if you'd made it past the door."

Any other prisoner would've been shaking in the sheets, begging his forgiveness. Arianne glared. "Handcuffs? Seriously? Why don't you be honest? This isn't about me. It's about your big-ass ego. I almost got away. Now you feel the need to put me in my place. Reassert your dominant alpha-male status."

Stunned speechless, he just stared. *Hell*. Seriously injured, handcuffed to the bed, wolves at the door baying for her blood, and she was giving him attitude. Maybe she wasn't as soft or fragile as he'd thought. Still, he shouldn't be so surprised at her grit. She wore a Black Jack cut, and those colors weren't earned without blood or a piece of one's soul.

Zane smiled wickedly. "Careful, sweetheart, or Jagger'll be adding another blood patch to his cut sooner rather than later. I'm pretty sure a couple of the ones he's got on there are from killing Jacks who gave him lip."

Jagger bristled, curiously annoyed by Zane's reference

to his blood patches, one for every life he'd taken. He wasn't proud of those patches, but death was inevitable in their kill-or-be-killed world, and when his club or his men were under threat, he had no hesitation pulling the trigger.

He caught the flash of disapproval in her eyes before she sighed. "If you think that scares me, you're dead wrong. Except for the prospects, I don't think there are any Jacks without blood patches."

"What about you?"

Her eyes flashed, amused. "If I were the kind of woman who spent her time earning blood patches, you'd be the one in handcuffs, and your friend over there would be dead on the floor."

Laughter welled up in his chest, and he fought like hell to keep it back. *Damn.* This was the kind of woman who should be in his bed. Sassy, sensual, and full of fire. And with her wrist handcuffed above her head, her sweet body stretched out on the sheets and affording him a glimpse of her creamy thighs, his mouth watered at the thought of taming her.

Zane snorted in disbelief. "Given you were wearing riding leathers, drove a high-end Kawasaki into our yard, made a suicidal escape attempt, and then proceeded to give us lip, I'd say there is a strong possibility you might have earned a blood patch or two."

"Well, I haven't, but I'm happy to start with you." Her chin lifted. "Just toss over the key . . . unless, of course, you're afraid of me."

Of all the fucking cheek. Jagger couldn't help but admire her moxie, but he wasn't about to make the same mistake twice. "The cuff stays on. I don't want to worry you'll try to earn your patch at my expense while I'm asleep."

"I must have 'killer' written all over me," Arianne huffed.

This time he couldn't hold back the laughter. She was

many things—sexy, beautiful, and brave—but "killer" didn't fit. "Not anywhere I can see."

Color rose in her cheeks and she shifted on the bed, her shirt riding up almost to the juncture of her thighs. Jagger's groin tightened and he forced himself to look away. He should have given the doctor one of Gunner's oversize shirts, or sent Sherry, the house mama, to buy their captive something decent to wear. He couldn't afford to think of her as anything but a prisoner, an enemy. With a glare at Zane, who had also been studying her with interest, Jagger grabbed a blanket from the foot of the bed and covered her up.

"So . . . how *did* you get so many blood patches?" Her lips curled in disdain even as she tucked the blanket around her sides with her free hand. "Women? Families? Civilians?"

"You know better than to ask." Club business was never shared with outsiders, and yet her derision sliced through him, a knife in his gut.

What the hell? He barely knew her, and he was acting like her opinion mattered. Better she knew he was a happily blooded member of the MC than a man who regretted every life he'd had to take. Scowling, he spun away and stalked toward the door without a second glance at the woman on the bed. Regret was a weakness. As was compassion. And he'd extended too much of that already.

★ THREE ★

The mission of the club is to foster the ideals of honor, truth, loyalty, and brotherhood through a common interest in motorcycling.

Handcuffs.

Arianne pressed her lips together to keep her laughter in as she worked the lock with the underwire from her bra. How often had she and Jeff timed each other as they each took a turn escaping from her father's handcuffs? Biker kids didn't play with normal toys. They didn't learn normal skills. They were patched in at birth and expected to learn how to survive in the biker world. And she had taken those lessons to heart.

With a soft click, the lock gave way.

Free. Well, sort of. And it had taken her a disappointing hour and a half, according to her watch. Jeff would have laughed.

She tried the door first, but it was securely locked and bolted from the outside. The window yielded more success. After pushing it open, she looked out over the porch overhang, fighting back the memories of another night, another roof, and a fear so overwhelming, her knees shook. She could almost feel Jeff's small body shivering in her arms as they plastered themselves against the cold brick chimney, and prayed someone would hear the screams and yelling inside and call the police.

Yes, she could escape, but where would she go? Small perimeter lights revealed a vast overgrown lawn, dry flower beds, and a crumbling brick wall around the property. A moonlit forest stretched as far as she could see in front of her, and the shadows of the Bridger Mountains lay to her east. Isolated, as Jagger had said. Definitely miles from town. But at least she had her bearings. Conundrum and the highway lay to west.

Still, she couldn't see any city or traffic lights. She had no clothes, and although she could hot-wire a bike, the Sinners would be riding 1,200cc hogs, heavy to push, slow on the road, and hard to manage without shoes.

Drawing in a deep breath of crisp autumn air, she stared out into the night as a cloud passed over the moon. God, she hated the darkness. Almost as much as she hated her father.

"Looking for something?"

Panic shot through her and she whirled around to face the intruder. How had she not heard the door open? An unforgivable loss of concentration, and one that could have cost her life.

He flicked the light on and she blinked as her eyes adjusted. Young—maybe twenty-two or twenty-three—and handsome in a baby-faced way, the biker who stepped into the room had long blond hair cut to hang across his face, rock-star style. But with a gun in one hand and a girl tucked under his arm, he clearly wasn't there to entertain her.

"Name's Wheels." He motioned to the curvy redhead beside him. "And this here is Sherry. She's in charge of keeping house. I'm in charge of looking after bikes, guests, and doing whatever it is the bikers need doing. Jagger sent us up to make sure you were okay." He gestured to the cuffs still hanging on the bed. "Looks like you made yourself more comfortable."

Ah. He had to be a prospect. Only club pledges were given the menial task of looking after the club's bikes and doing the dirty jobs no one else wanted to do—like looking after prisoners—to earn the respect of the club and their full-patch status. And yet he didn't have the officious attitude the usual prospect showed when talking to someone from outside the club.

"I needed some air." She pressed her back to the window, wary of being alone with two strangers in the room, and disconcerted that she hadn't felt similarly cautious when she was alone with Jagger earlier.

"We're not going to hurt you." Sherry pulled away from Wheels and leaned against the now empty dresser. Zane had removed Arianne's gun and Jagger's gym bag on his way out.

"Jagger won't hurt you either," she said. "He doesn't hurt women."

"Unless they burn down our clubhouse and kill one of our brothers." Wheels scowled, but with his baby face, the scowl was more of a scrunch and just made him look cute.

"It wasn't me."

Sherry laughed. "I'd say that, too, if I were trapped in a rival MC's clubhouse with one hundred angry bikers downstairs calling for my head."

She must have paled, because Sherry was instantly contrite. "Hey, don't worry. I meant what I said about Jagger. I know him well . . . probably better than anyone here. He never takes a life unless it's justified."

Arianne grabbed the window ledge for support. He was the enemy—a ruthless, merciless biker who led the only MC in Montana her father considered a true threat—and she needed to keep that fact foremost in her mind.

"Well, that didn't reassure her," Wheels said. "Now she looks like she's about to faint."

"Kinda like you when Zane and Cade told you the Devil

Dog VP's old lady was a sweet butt who wanted into your pants."

"That wasn't funny." Wheels' nostrils flared. "I'd been a prospect for only a week. No one told me old ladies were totally off-limits, even to talk to. He almost killed me."

Sherry winked at Arianne, then looked up at Wheels. "I don't think it was the 'talking' part that pissed off the VP; it was when you put your hand up her skirt and pinched her ass right in front of him."

Arianne laughed, and her tension eased. Even the Black Jacks loved to haze their prospects. It was a favorite biker pastime.

"Who took off her handcuffs?" Jagger's deep voice cut through the laughter, and the room stilled. He braced one arm on the doorjamb and one overhead filling the doorway with his lean, muscular body.

"That would be me." She gave him a cool smile, amused by his assumption she'd required assistance to get free.

Jagger glared at Sherry and Wheels. "No one thought to put them back on her? After I told you only twenty minutes ago that she was a flight risk?" He crossed the room and slammed the window closed behind her, the loud bang shaking the glass panes. "And you're letting her stand by an open window no more than ten feet off the ground?"

Wheels and Sherry shared a terrified glance, and Arianne felt a twinge of annoyance. Despite her situation, she had to admit they'd been nothing but friendly. Not that she would jump to their defense. Political savvy had saved her neck time and again in the Black Jack clubhouse, and no one, but no one, challenged the president. At least, not in public.

Jagger dismissed Wheels and Sherry, waiting until the door closed before he circled Arianne's wrist with his thumb and forefinger, his voice dropping to a sensual growl. "When I cuff you to the bed, I expect you to stay there."

If his intent was to throw her off balance, it had worked. Mouth dry, every nerve in her body focused on the soft brush of his thumb over her skin, her body came alive with sensation. She toyed with the hem of her shirt as she tried to get herself together.

"I wasn't really in the mood to be restrained."

His eyes glittered, and electricity fired the air between them. "What were you in the mood for, little vixen?" He dropped his gaze to her lips, and for a second, she thought he might kiss her. Instead he tugged her in the direction of the bed.

"Escape. That's usually what people want when they've been captured."

"You think you're a prisoner?" He spun to face her, filling every inch of her personal space.

Arianne forced herself to look away from his broad chest and rippling abs. He had a warrior's body—taut, hard, and without an ounce of fat. "Can I leave?"

"No."

"Then, yes, I think I'm a prisoner." Arianne scowled, no longer flustered by the proximity of his body or by his direct stare. "Kinda fits the definition, since you're holding me here against my will." She stifled a curse and tried to shake off his hand. During her years with the Jacks, she'd learned the hard way how to stay cool around dangerous men. Problem was, except for her father, she'd never met a man so dangerously attractive as Jagger.

A high-pitched whine from the hallway broke the spell. Jagger released her wrist and crossed the room to open the door. With a sharp bark of delight, a midsize collie bounded into the room.

Jagger's face softened in an instant and he bent down and ruffled the collie's fur. "This is Max. We found him abandoned when we took over the property a few months ago. He's not supposed to be in the house, but tonight has been unsettling for everyone."

Arianne knelt down and held out her hand. After much sniffing, Max licked her palm. "He's beautiful."

"You like dogs?"

"We had a golden lab when I was growing up," she said wistfully. "If I didn't live in an apartment now, I would get another one. But they're big dogs. It wouldn't be fair."

"Dogs need their space." Jagger went thoughtful, staring at her, and Arianne tugged her shirt down over her knees, self-conscious about being hunkered on the floor beside Max, wearing only the oversized T-shirt and a pair of panties.

"Max and I come out here a coupla times a week to run." He patted Max's head. "Gives me time to check up on the property and we get some time away. The minute the vehicle stops, he's gone. Only way to get him back is to whistle. He can hear the sound almost a mile away." When he held two fingers up to his mouth, Arianne put up a warning hand.

"No need for a demo. I like my eardrums unbroken, thank you."

Jagger chuckled and held out a hand to help her up. The small courteous gesture sent a warm tingle through her body that turned into a full-on tidal wave when skin touched skin and he pulled her up.

For a moment, neither of them moved, and then Jagger dropped her hand. "Better get some sleep."

"Well . . . good night." She stood beside Max, waiting for Jagger to leave, but instead he sat on the bed and pulled off his boots.

Arianne's palms grew clammy. "You're sleeping here?"

He licked his lips and smiled. "Not many of the bedrooms are furnished, and since you clearly can't be trusted on your own, this is the only option. The bed is big enough for both of us, but I'm not planning to do anything more than sleep. It's been a helluva day."

"I'll sleep on the floor, then," she said. "Maybe Max can keep me company."

"Unacceptable. You're injured and a woman. You'll sleep in the bed."

Irritation chased the filaments of Arianne's fear away. "Women can sleep on floors."

"Not under my roof and not in my club." Jagger removed his cut and then stripped off his T-shirt.

Arianne's eyes widened and her jaw went slack. *Oh God.* Why did he have to do that? He had the kind of chest she'd seen only on billboards or in men's underwear ads. Well, except for the Sinner's Tribe tattoo that spanned his broad chest, the wings surrounding the skull reaching up and over his shoulders to join the intricate tat sleeves that covered his upper arms. But it was the scar down the center of his chest and not totally concealed by the tat that gave her pause. Not a knife scar—she was well acquainted with those—but something more precise. Surgical.

But she knew better than to ask. At least not right now. Her gaze slid down, over his washboard abs, following the dark silky shadow of hair leading below the belt. . . .

Jagger's hand dropped to his buckle, and her eyes widened. Did he know what she was thinking?

"Please." Beads of perspiration formed on her forehead. "At least keep your jeans on."

Seeming amused he unbuckled his belt and yanked it off with a loud crack. "If it'll make you more comfortable."

"It will." But likely not in the way he was thinking.

Hell came in many different forms: from trying to survive enemy fire in a sweltering desert to the mind-numbing pain of shrapnel piercing flesh, and from the helplessness of being intubated in a hospital bed, to burying the bodies of his biker brothers during the feud.

Jagger threw a stick for Max as he walked off their morning run, irritated that not even fresh air and exercise could calm the fire raging through his blood.

Last night had been a different type of hell altogether.

What had he been thinking? Lying beside Arianne all night was a torture worse than he could ever have imagined. With her silky hair strewn across the pillow, her face soft with sleep, lips so invitingly pink and plump, it was all he could do to stay on his side of the bed. And when she kicked off the covers, revealing just how high her shirt had ridden up, he almost lost it right then. God, she was beautiful. From her exquisite oval face to her softly rounded breasts, and from her graceful curves to her toned, lean legs, she was perfection with a kick-ass attitude.

His body had hardened when she moaned in her sleep and licked her lips, and it took every ounce of his self-control not to lean over and take her mouth in a deep, lingering kiss. But nothing could stop the throbbing in his groin when she curled up, treating him to an unimpeded view of her beautiful rounded cheeks covered in frilly pink polka dots.

Pink polka dots. He'd first caught a glimpse of her panties when she'd been cuffed to the bed, but he hadn't been in a mood to appreciate them. His prickly tough biker chick had a soft girly side. And seeing something he wasn't meant to see—hell, that did things to a man. Dangerous things. He'd been forced to go out and find her clothes, then shake her awake and make her get dressed.

He'd never reacted this way with any other women. Not even Christel. Although not his old lady, they'd been together long enough for everyone to treat her with similar respect. But then the Wolverines MC had found her. The upstart MC, hell-bent on challenging Sinner dominance in Montana, had used Christel against him. And when Jagger gave them what they'd wanted, they left her broken body outside his clubhouse and she'd died in his arms.

Destroying the Wolverines hadn't brought her back, nor had it eased the ache in his heart. Time was not the great healer so many claimed it to be. Instead, time had made him more set in his ways. Christel's fate was the reason he allowed himself only casual relationships. His enemies would find no weakness. His lovers and his heart would suffer no risk.

Max returned with the stick and Jagger threw it again, watching it disappear into the cool morning mist. The air was fragrant with the scent of rich earth, and dew clung to every leaf and blade of grass. Mornings were his favorite time. Quiet. Peaceful. With all the promise of the day ahead.

He looked up at the window to the bedroom he had shared with Arianne, half expecting to see her sliding down the roof. But with two guards outside her door and two more outside the building's entrance, she would be going nowhere fast. He chuckled as a memory tore through him: Arianne wearing only his T-shirt, shivering by the window, beguiled by the loquacious Wheels and the effervescent Sherry as they thwarted her attempt to escape.

He should have warned her that no one ever escaped from the Sinners.

Or from him.

The soft thud of footsteps on grass and the rustle of autumn leaves alerted him to Cade's presence well before his former army buddy joined him on the front lawn. As the MC's treasurer, Cade carried out his duties with ruthless efficiency, and like Zane, he always had Jagger's back.

Cade gave him a quick update on the status of the old clubhouse and the local authorities' investigation into the fire. Then he glanced up at Arianne's window, smirking at the guards stationed below. "So, what are you going to do with her?"

"I'm waiting to see the surveillance tapes," Jagger said. "Zane picked them up this morning from the off-site data-storage facility. If she's not directly involved, I'll let her go. I won't hold a woman responsible for the actions of her club."

Cade tunnelled his hand through his thick, blond hair, his brow creasing. "How do you know it was the Jacks?"

Jagger pulled out his phone and showed Cade a picture he'd received from his contact in the police department. Someone had spray painted a crude outline of the Black Jacks' patch on the side of the weapons shed that had been robbed. "They left a calling card. Most of the brothers who weren't drowning their sorrows in some sweet butt's arms last night have already been told."

Cade didn't react to the silent admonition. No doubt he'd spent the night just as Jagger had said. Cade was known for his ability to charm women into his bed. Sherry claimed his chick magnet appeal had to do with his appearance, likening him to some movie star who'd played the part of the Norse god, Thor. Jagger didn't have time for movies. Or movie stars. Or brothers who spent the night buried between some sweet butt's thighs instead of worrying about the loss of their clubhouse, the end of the feud, and a little Black Jack who couldn't be touched.

"Gotta get back." He gestured toward the house, and Cade fell into step, Max trotting beside them.

"I was wondering why Axle was gunning for Arianne to pay the price this morning," Cade said, oblivious to Jagger's annoyance. "Tensions are high right now and he's already got a lot of support. The fire hit too close to home."

"It *was* home." At least for him and Cade, and a few of

the unattached brothers who were out of work or needed a temporary place to stay.

"They need someone to blame." Cade hesitated. "If they don't get a focus for their anger, the club will explode."

Was he seriously suggesting offering Arianne up as a sacrificial lamb? "And it's Gunner's job to make sure that doesn't happen." A burst of protective anger caught him off guard. "She said she wasn't there to hurt anyone or cause any damage. I believe her."

Although ultimately evasive, Arianne's answer to that question had been delivered firmly and directly. No waver of the voice. No shifting of the eyes. He suspected deception wasn't in her nature. Hell, she'd given it to him straight when he cuffed her. His lips quivered with a repressed smile. When was the last time anyone had dared speak to him that way?

Cade rubbed the back of his neck. "Well, then I hope you have a plan for retribution that might ease the pain of just letting her go."

"I always have a plan." Jagger whistled for Max. "And you'll like this one. It involves runaway trucks, explosives, and destroying meth factories."

"You'll definitely need Axle on board, then. No one is better with explosives than him."

"Axle's done," Jagger said. "For the sake of appearances, I'll put the vote to the executive board later this morning, but as far as I'm concerned, he's out of the club. He's been pushing the boundaries ever since I took over as president, five years ago, and last night he went too far."

"Guess I'll let Zane know Axle won't be trunking with us tonight." Cade stopped walking before they came within earshot of the house. "You got a victim in mind?"

Jagger's tension eased. "Zane got the goods on a dealer who seems to have forgotten about our zero-tolerance policy for drugs in Conundrum." He finally allowed himself the luxury of a smile. "We'll have a little fun, raise some cash to fix this place up as our new clubhouse, and damage the Black Jack supply chain all at once."

"Almost as much fun as spending an evening with a coupla sweet butts in my lap." Cade twisted his lips to the side, considering. "Or maybe not."

"The feud is back on." Jagger slammed his fist into his palm. "We're gonna hit the Jacks hard and fast, and we're gonna make justice personal. The men who torched our old clubhouse and shot Cole and Gunner are first on our list after Cole's funeral. Then we hit the man who gave the order."

"Viper." Cade spat out the name. "And if the feud is back on, he'll be gunning for you."

"Not if I get to him first."

And his pretty little Black Jack might be just his ticket inside the Viper's den.

★ FOUR ★

Club rules and bylaws shall be strictly enforced.
Penalties for breaking the rules include a kick-out
or suspension, and always an ass-kicking.

"Up, bitch." A sharp tug on her hair startled Arianne from sleep. She turned but didn't recognize the man standing beside her bed. Although short in stature, he had a huge barrel chest and a belly to match.

"I said *up*." His hand in her hair, he yanked her off the bed. Arianne fell to her knees at his feet, getting a perfect view of the red patches lining the bottom of his cut. Her heart pumped spastically, and she looked quickly around the room. Where was Jagger?

"Let's go." With a snarl, he pulled her to her feet. Still shaking off the last vestiges of a deep, exhausted sleep, Arianne stumbled after him, thankful Jagger had insisted she put on her clothes in the middle of the night.

"You don't need to be so rough." She clamped her hand on her hair, lessening his pull. "It's not like I'm going anywhere."

"Shut the fuck up."

Curiously underwhelmed, she allowed him to pull her a few more steps, giving him a false sense of control. Like she hadn't lived through this scenario on a weekly basis at home. She waited until they were near the door, then put both her hands up to her head. Holding her hair, she twisted and spun out of his grip. Using her momentum, she ran back at him, head-butting him in the solar plexus and knocking him against the wall. He staggered, short-winded, but with breath enough to curse.

Arianne didn't wait to see the effects of her assault. Instead she ran at the open doorway—only to collide with a bony, redheaded biker with piercings in his nose and ears. He swore as he looked over her shoulder at the biker who lay groaning on the floor, but her attention was focused on his broad-shouldered companion who was wielding a knife six inches long.

She backed up and hit the wall as he advanced while regarding her with cool disdain. His face was thin and pale, but marred with recent cuts and bruises. Sharp, defined features were complemented by a thin, cruel slash of a mouth, and his dark hair was slicked back on his head, revealing a sharp widow's peak. Dark eyes, totally devoid of emotion, sent a chill up her spine. Had Jagger changed his mind and ordered her execution?

Without warning, his hand struck her left cheek and sent her reeling across the floor. Her head hit the bedpost, everything fading to gray. With a bark of derision, he slowly walked to where she lay and prodded her shoulder with the toe of his boot, forcing her onto her back. He didn't bother to crouch, merely towered over her, his face twisting in disgust. "Black Jack bitch. My name's Axle. Soon to be President Axle. Should have killed you when I had the chance, but I'm about to remedy that now."

With a jerk of his chin, he motioned for his pierced companion and his now-recovered friend to pick Arianne up off the floor.

Cheek stinging, still dazed from the fall, she didn't struggle when the two men clamped a hand around each of her arms and yanked her upright.

Choose your fights. The words of the old Black Jack road captain drifted through her mind as she contemplated how she could get free. He had sheltered Arianne and Jeff from the worst of their father's wrath, and it was because of him Arianne had developed her skills as a mechanic. She still took flowers to his grave, an unmarked mound north of town at the base of the Bridger Mountains.

But this was a fight she couldn't win. Not through physical force and not with the two bikers holding her arms so tight, she had to grit her teeth against the pain. And wouldn't her options be better downstairs?

"Does Jagger know about this?" She struggled to keep up with her captors as they dragged her down the hallway.

"He will soon enough." Axle smirked. "We're gonna take you to the meeting and give everyone a show they'll never forget."

Meeting? Her heart skipped a beat. Were they taking her to church? Outlaw MCs never allowed anyone other than full-patch brothers to attend "church," the monthly or extraordinary mandatory meetings required of club members. Bad enough dealing with these goons, but facing the entire full-patch contingent at once, knowing so many of them wanted her to pay for the attack——

She squared her shoulders and swallowed her fear as Axle preceded them down the stairs. If her father had taught her anything, it was that fear made people weak. And weak people couldn't fight.

Her captors were either stupid or desperate if they thought they could drag her into church without causing a minor riot. But at least Jagger would be there. Hopefully, he would keep her safe. If not, she'd be kicking ass and taking names. Today was not a good day to die.

They stopped outside a set of double doors, the paint chipped and cracked and the once gold-colored handles now blackened with age. The redhead with the piercings lightly slid a knife across her neck. "Be a good girl while the boys are talking."

Axle threw open the doors and her captor pushed her forward, the knife still at her throat.

"Justice for the Sinner's Tribe."

She had only a moment to take in the faded grandeur of what must once have been a massive living room, the sea of Sinner cuts, and Jagger sitting at the head of a table before the room exploded in chaos.

Justice?

Jagger grimaced as shouts and yells echoed around the room. Axle wasn't here for justice. He wanted Jagger's position, pure and simple, and knowing he was facing a possible dismissal, he'd decided to risk a stunt like this. Arianne was a pawn to him. Unnecessary. Expendable.

In danger.

He forced his gaze away from Arianne—the bright red mark on her cheek, the bruise on her temple, and the knife gleaming at her throat—and focused on the men seated at the table beside him. The executive board consisted of the president, vice president, secretary, treasurer, road captain, and sergeant at arms, as well as two members at large. He had served with the same board for five years, the only change being to the members-at-large, now Tank and Bandit. None of them would support Axle's bid for power. But he wasn't so sure that they were as convinced of Arianne's innocence as he was. All Axle needed was a seed of doubt to set in motion a chain of events that could topple Jagger from his throne.

A seed he wasn't going to sow on Jagger's watch.

Feigning weariness, Jagger raised his voice. "Stand down, Axle. Let her go."

"Someone's going down." Axle sneered and gestured to Arianne, who was standing stiff, the knife against her throat. "And it won't be me."

Rage pumped through Jagger's veins and every instinct screamed at him to protect her. But Christel's death had taught him to show no emotion when women were involved; reveal no weakness. So he focused his attention on the real threat: Axle. His eyes were bruised and swollen after the beating Zane had given him last night, but they gleamed victorious nonetheless. Not since Christel died, had he wanted to kill a man more.

"You do it or we do it," Axle shouted. "No more of this bullshit. The executive board will do what you tell them to do, but no one really wants to let her go. They're just afraid to tell you. Viper wants a war. Let's give it to him."

A few of the brothers dipped their chins in assent. Jagger leaned back in his chair, affecting an air of indifference while inside he seethed. Axle wasn't helping himself by making a mockery of their bylaws, despite the kernel of truth in his words. Cold, cruel, ruthless, and incredibly cunning, Viper wouldn't hesitate to kill Arianne if he were in Jagger's position, no matter that she was a woman.

Gunner pushed himself to his feet, wincing slightly as he stood. As sergeant at arms, he was responsible for keeping order in the meeting, and right now the room pulsed with tension, a powder keg ready to explode.

"Penalty for going against anything the board has voted on is suspension or dismissal." Gunner folded his thick arms and glared. "Penalty for disrupting a meeting is eviction. Penalty for bringing a woman and a non-patch member into a board meeting is suspension. Penalty for threatening a woman the board has just decided to release is a personal ass-kicking from me." He drew his Springfield XD-S .45ACP from its holster and placed it on the table in front of him. "You got a problem with any of that, Axle?"

Taking advantage of Gunner's diversion, Jagger rose slowly from his seat, his focus now back on Arianne. Her face was taut and her hands were fisted by her sides. But damned if she didn't look angry rather than afraid.

"Before this goes any further," Jagger said, struggling to keep his voice level. "The executive board reviewed the surveillance tapes before church began. We are satisfied that Vexy was not involved in the arson or the theft of the weapons. She arrived after the fire had started and Cole and Gunner were down. However, there are four Black Jacks whose lives are forfeit as soon as we identify them and all the Jacks will feel our wrath for what they have done."

The crowd cheered, but Axle cut them off with a bark of anger. "Why was she there? It's an obvious question that everyone seems afraid to answer. Was she too late to help out? Well, I've brought her to you. Ask her."

"Far as I can recall, you don't have the floor." Gunner thudded his fist on the table. "Penalty for talking without getting the floor from the president is eviction and an ass-kicking. Guess I get to take my boot to your ass more than once. I still got one good leg, and it packs a helluva kick"

"I'll accept the question." Lips pursed with suppressed fury, Jagger rounded the table and walked toward Arianne and her captor, a skinny rat of a man aptly nicknamed Weasel. "Vexy?"

She shot him a look of gratitude, which quickly faded into resignation. "I was trying to stop him . . . them." Her voice wavered. "But I got there too late. I saw the fire, drove to the back of the clubhouse, and then I don't know what happened. Next thing I remember, I was here." She narrowed her eyes and her features hardened. "And that's all you're getting from me."

"You got names for us?" Axle scowled.

"No."

Christ. She had more courage than most of the men in the room. No tears or sobs. No breaking down. No names.

Jagger didn't need to look around to know Zane and their road captain, Sparky, had left their seats, too. Cade reached for his weapon. The room, rank with the stench of too many bodies packed into too small a space, stilled.

"Not even to save your life?" Axle drew a line across his throat with his finger. Weasel's knife flashed. Arianne gaped, and blood trickled into the hollow at the base of her throat.

Jagger succumbed to the ferocity of his rage. Bloodlust that roared through his veins.

He charged, carrying Axle along the front of the table, through the crowd, and straight into the adjacent wall with the power of a linebacker. In a maddened frenzy of blows and kicks, he pummeled Axle until the man sank to the ground, the knife falling from his grasp. Turning, Jagger saw Arianne, now free and leaning against the back wall, her hand to her throat while Gunner wrestled with Weasel. Around them, Axle's supporters went down under the fists of his enraged executive board. Bones cracked. Shouts and yells. Someone screamed.

"You upset I damaged your fuck toy?" Axle panted against the baseboard and pushed himself to his feet.

Cade pressed the barrel of his gun to Axle's head and glanced over at Jagger. "You want him dead?"

Jagger's fist contacted Axle's jaw, sending Axle into the crowd. "He hasn't suffered enough yet."

Axle came up fighting, but in his current condition he

was no match for Jagger's speed and strength. Or his fury. Although he had restrained himself behind the old clubhouse, and told Zane not to work Axle over too hard last night, Jagger had no reason to hold back now. Axle's days in the club were over. If Jagger didn't deal most definitively with the man's blatant disrespect, his ability to lead the MC would be called into question. But more than that, a surge of possessiveness had gripped him by the throat alongside a desire to avenge the woman under his protection.

The room faded into silence as he knocked Axle to the ground. He lifted his boot for one last kick when Arianne placed a hand on his arm.

Shocked out of the haze of bloodlust, he stilled, expecting her to tell him to pull back and not kick a man when he was down. Instead, she gripped his sleeve, drew back her leg and growled, "Leave a piece of him for me."

Although she wasn't strong enough to do any serious damage, Arianne's kick ripped a harsh groan from Axle's lungs, and he rolled onto his back, clutching his side, a black stain on the threadbare carpet.

Damn. What a woman.

Jagger wiped his bloody hands on his shirt. "The meeting is adjourned. Axle and his supporters are hereby kicked out of the club on bad terms." He met the gaze of each member of the executive board, paying lip service to the bylaws, which required a general vote and unanimous consent of the board to terminate a membership. Right now he didn't give a fucking damn about the bylaws. If he didn't kick Axle out, he would kill Axle, and he didn't want Axle's blood on his hands. As expected, he was met with no dissent.

"Sparky, get the prospects to clean up the mess." He nodded at Axel's supporters on the floor. "Strip their colors, throw them into a van, and dump them at the side of the road. Their bikes stay with the club as compensation."

The traitors sucked in a collective breath. Taking away a man's bike was the ultimate humiliation, but under the bylaws of all outlaw clubs it was the appropriate penalty for members kicked out on bad terms.

"Out. Now." Heart hammering in his chest, muscles still twitching, Jagger grabbed Arianne's hand and dragged her from the room.

"Slow down." Arianne wriggled her wrist, trying to get free.

Jagger stalked across the grass, pulling her behind him as they headed toward the shimmering glow of motorcycles, parked in neat rows along the vast gravel drive.

"I need a minute to catch my breath. It's not every day someone yanks me out of bed, holds a knife to my throat, and then shoves me into the middle of a biker brawl."

But Jagger didn't stop, didn't speak. Nor did he slow down. Instead, he increased his pace until she was almost running behind him.

"Why didn't you just let me go last night? You must have known something like this would happen."

Her outburst was purely rhetorical, a vent for her adrenaline-enhanced anger and fear. In her experience, men with Jagger's power rarely explained their actions, and when they did, it wasn't because they'd been asked. So when he slowed his pace and looked over his shoulder at her, she was unprepared for his concession.

"It had to go to a vote. Otherwise, I'd be dealing with accusations that I wasn't prepared to take your life if the vote swung that way. I couldn't risk dissension in the club, nor did I want an entire MC of outlaw vigilantes bent on revenge hunting you down."

Arianne stopped in her tracks, forcing Jagger to slow

and release her wrist. "So you *were* prepared to kill me for something I didn't do? You took a gamble with my life? What if you didn't have surveillance tapes? What if they'd agreed with Axle?"

A spasm of irritation crossed Jagger's face and Arianne kicked herself for going too far. Why couldn't she rein herself in around him? She would never even have contemplated speaking to Viper this way, and from what she'd seen in her brief time with the Sinner's Tribe, Jagger was more than Viper's equal.

"I know my men. You weren't at risk. None of them would hurt a woman."

Unlike the Black Jacks. By the time she'd turned sixteen, even her father realized it wasn't safe for Arianne to be around the Jacks, despite the wall separating the clubhouse from their family home. But it had taken the biggest gamble of her life before he allowed her to move out, and even then he'd restricted her to Conundrum proper. She was a born a Black Jack, and he expected her to carry out her duties as a Black Jack whenever he called. But more than that, she belonged to him—his blood, his property—and there was no way Viper would ever let her go.

And yet she'd tried to run away—whether out of stubbornness, desperation, hope, or stupidity, she'd tried again and again. He'd caught her every time, and met her defiance with swift and brutal punishment.

"What about Axle?" She gestured toward the house. "What about the men who slapped me around and took me down to you at knifepoint? Weren't they your men? Did they not share your beliefs? Did you not patch them in?" Her throat constricted, and for a second she lost control of the fear she had been holding at bay. A violent tremble shook her body and she folded her arms to hide her shaking hands.

Jagger firmly clasped her shoulders, drawing her forward,

his eyes intent. She tensed, prepared for his anger. Viper would never have tolerated such an outburst.

"They will not harm you again, Arianne," he said, his voice low and even. "You have my word."

His word. A tremor went through her hands and her body slumped in relief. A biker's word was his bond, not given lightly, upheld as a matter of pride and respect and for the honor of the club.

"Okay." Her strangled whisper deepened his frown and he drew her closer, until she could feel the heat of his body, inhale the intoxicating scent of his cologne.

"They were patched in before my time," he continued, although he owed her no explanation. "Most of the brothers who didn't share my philosophy left the club when I became president. Axle and his supporters stayed, thinking my first term as president would be my last."

"They obviously didn't know you well."

His face softened at last and his lips quirked at the corners. He liked the flattery, she realized, even if it was tongue-in-cheek, and she enjoyed making him smile. Maybe too much.

"And you do?"

"I know men like you." And yet she'd never felt so at ease with a man as powerful and dominant as Jagger—not that many of those existed. She still couldn't believe the way she was speaking to him—challenging, sarcastic, teasing—and she marveled at the words that were coming out of her mouth.

Jagger gave her a slow, appraising glance and then turned away. "There are no men like me." He led her to a bike at the end of the row closest to the house, and pulled a small first aid kit from his saddlebag.

"Are you sure? You run this MC like every other outlaw club. There are only two penalties for breaking the rules: an ass-kicking or a kick-out with an ass-kicking on the side. You rule through violence and intimidation like any other MC president. The blood patches on your cut attest to that."

"Don't judge me, Arianne." His voice sharpened with warning. "If what you told me is true, and you grew up in this world, then you, of all people, should understand it. Maybe even better than me. Most of the Sinners are ex-military. They are violent men used to being led with a heavy hand. If I let one step out of line, I'll have a situation out of control. No law. No order. And that would put civilians at risk. I can't let that happen. Hell, it was the reason I became president in the first place."

"Not ambition and a burning need for power?" She gave him an incredulous look and Jagger laughed, defusing the tension.

"That, too." He opened a disinfectant wipe and gently patted the tiny cut on her throat. Disconcerted by the sudden change in his demeanor, she allowed him to minister to her, wincing at the sting when the disinfectant touched her open wound.

Jagger froze. "I'm hurting you."

"I find it hard to believe you'd be concerned about something like that after what you just did to Axle." She also found it hard to believe he would care enough to treat her wound personally. And how many MC presidents claimed they'd taken the throne to protect civilians?

He finished tending to her cut in silence. Arianne waved away the little bandage he produced from the kit. "It's just a scratch. I'll have a little scar to add to my collection as a memento of my visit."

Without a word, he cupped the back of her neck with one hand, holding her still, then carefully placed the bandage over the cut, overruling her objections. His breath was warm on her cheek, his lips so close, she had only to lean forward an inch to take a little lick.

He looked up from the dressing, caught her with his gaze, and the world faded away . . . She'd never been so utterly at a man's mercy, yet it wasn't fear that made her heart pound, but a primal, gut-wrenching desire for the one man she could never have.

"Jagger." She whispered his name. A plea. A request.

Spell broken, he released her, turning away too quickly for her to see his face. "Gotta get you outta here." He gestured to his bike and then packed the first aid kit in his saddlebag again. "Hop on."

"CVO Ultra Classic Electra Glide." Her voice came out in an awed gasp of appreciation as she tried not to drool over one of the most expensive Harley-Davidson motorcycles in production. "Nice bike, although I didn't take you for a touring man."

"I'm a collecting man." Jagger lifted an eyebrow as he pulled a bandanna from his jeans pocket—black with white skulls, of course, just like his patch—and tied it over his head. "You know your bikes."

God, the bandanna made him look even more handsome, the strong planes and angles of his jaw coming into sharp relief. She tore her gaze away and swung her leg over the seat. "I'm a journeyman mechanic. Bikes are my specialty." Even if she did manage to escape her father's stranglehold one day, she would never lose her fascination for the sleek design and powerful engines of the Harley-Davidson brand, or her need to make each one she touched run to smooth perfection.

Not that she had a bike to tinker with anymore. She briefly considered asking Jagger if his boys had retrieved her Ninja, but just as quickly dismissed the thought. Why would they bother, especially when they'd initially suspected she started the fire?

He shook his head and muttered, half to himself. "Of course you are."

"No passenger pegs or sissy bar on the back?" she said, as he settled on the bike in front of her. "You like your passengers holding on to you?"

"Never packed a passenger before."

"What? No old lady? No rides home for the sweet butts after a wild night on the town?" She cringed inwardly after she spoke. How juvenile. And yet, although she would never see this man again, some part of her still wanted to know if he was taken.

"No time to look after anyone else. Running the club and keeping the brothers in line are more than enough work." He looked back over his shoulder. "Where am I taking you?"

"Gas station on the corner of Eleventh and Main. I'll call a friend to pick me up. Don't want you to know where I live, in case you regret not killing me when you had the chance."

Jagger laughed, a warm deep chuckle that made her toes curl. "Never gonna happen. I make a decision, I stick to it."

She slid her arms around his waist, tucking her body against his, soothed by the familiar scent of leather and the less familiar scent of warm, musky male. "So, who looks after you while you're watching over everyone else?"

"I look after myself."

The motorcycle roared to life and Jagger peeled away from the sea of bikes. Arianne pressed her cheek against the cool leather of his cut and increased her grip around his waist.

"Me, too," she whispered.

He couldn't possibly have heard her over the roar of his engine, but when he reached back and gave her thigh a squeeze, tears prickled the backs of her eyes. Everything about Jagger confused her, from his gestures of respect to his unexpected kindness to his noticeable turmoil when she'd been in danger. Someone had forgotten to tell him this wasn't how outlaw MC presidents were supposed to behave.

Her body flamed as he slid his hand down her leg to rest it on her knee, his touch at once soothing and protective. When had any biker ever made her heart pound? Sure, she was comfortable in their world—she could talk the talk, joke with them, and even hold her own in the occasional fistfight. But regardless of such camaraderie, she was live to the underlying truth: In her world—this world—women were property or playthings, definitely not equals worthy of the respect she craved. Not once had she ever sought or wanted a biker's attention.

Until now.

He lifted his hand to grip the handlebars as they took a sharp turn. Arianne bemoaned the small loss of his warmth, the comfort of his strength, and the curious tingles that sizzled through her body from their brief contact.

After he dropped her off, she'd probably never see him again. She didn't frequent biker bars or hangouts, never even went to the Black Jack clubhouse unless her father specifically demanded her presence. She liked her quiet life, working at Banks's Bar, hanging with her best friend, Dawn, and occasionally helping out friends with their motorcycle troubles or working part-time at any garage with an opening for a journeyman mechanic. There were no crises. No wild parties. No crazy bikers doing crazy-biker things. No bloodshed. If not for her father dragging her out of bed in the middle of the night to help with club business from time to time, an outsider might've thought she led a normal life.

Jagger kicked up the accelerator. He had to be doing at least one hundred miles per hour, but no cop in Montana would dare stop a member of the Sinner's Tribe. A reluctant smile spread across Arianne's face. Fast as Jagger was, if she were on her Ninja right now, he would be eating her dust.

As they neared downtown, Arianne closed her eyes and took a mental snapshot of the ride: the cool wind in her clothes, the scent of Jagger's leather jacket, the sharp edge of his belt buckle digging into her palms, the warmth of his body, and the flutter in her belly whenever he reached back and patted her thigh to make sure she was okay. She couldn't remember the last time a man had cared enough to check up on her. But, to be fair, she never gave them that chance.

By the time they'd arrived at the gas station a few blocks from her apartment building on the west side of Conundrum, her heart was racing and a warm glow had settled in her body. Although she was glad to be away from the Sinner's Tribe clubhouse, she couldn't help feeling disappointed that the ride was over already.

The giant poplars lining the street cast long shadows in the afternoon sun. Jagger parked his bike at the side of the road and for a long moment, maybe too long, she stayed in her seat, arms around him, cheek pressed against his back, soaking up every last sensation.

"You okay?" He turned in his seat and she nodded, then quickly dismounted the bike, looking away from him to hide her burning cheeks.

What should she say? *Thanks for capturing me and leaving me at the mercy of your psychotic biker gang? Thanks for rescuing me? Thanks for taking off your shirt last night and giving me a year's worth of fantasies?*

"Well . . . good-bye. I'd say it's been fun, but except for the ride, it wasn't."

Jagger laughed. "You're a speed demon?"

"I have, on occasion, been known to go over the speed limit."

"I should have guessed." He slid off his bike. "It's a

good thing, then, we've got to say good-bye. I happen to like speed demons."

A firestorm of desire swept through her, sending her pulse into overdrive. "I have many unlikable traits. Consider yourself lucky you won't have a chance to discover what they are."

Jagger gave her a crooked smile and closed the distance between them. So close, she could feel his warmth through her cut. "Depends on how you define 'unlikable.' I also happen to enjoy the occasional challenge, being told off by a woman half my size, and discovering pink polka-dot panties under worn street leathers."

Was he flirting with her? Did she want him to stop?

"I knew you had a naughty streak," she brushed back the hair that had fallen over her face.

His gaze darkened, heated, until she thought she would burn in the sensual depths of his eyes. "You made it very difficult to look away."

Every nerve in her body fired at once. Definitely flirting. But why not? It was just a game. Neither of them had anything to lose, and they would never see each other again. Jacks and Sinners definitely didn't mix. She tilted her head and gave him what she hoped was a sultry smile. "You're a dangerous man, Jagger. I'm lucky to be getting away. Panties and all."

His shoulders shook with silent laughter. "I am a dangerous man. If you have any sense, sweetheart, you'll run down that road and never look back."

Sweetheart. The term of endearment did strange, fluttery things to her stomach, and she wished it was something more than a casual throwaway expression.

With great reluctance, she took one step back and then another, her eyes drinking in their last fill of the man who awakened desires she had long thought dead.

"Wait."

Arianne halted her steps, then relaxed when Jagger pulled her gun and holster from his saddlebag. "You might need these."

His fingers brushed over hers when she took them from his outstretched hand. Her blood sizzled. No doubt about it, Jagger tripped every hormone in her body in a way no man ever had.

"Especially with dangerous men like you around." A smile tugged at her lips.

"Where do I find you if I need to talk to you again?"

Her heart quickened. "Are you asking so you can come and kill me if your brothers decide to exact vengeance on me after all?"

"I'm asking in case someone in the club gets it in his head to act without my authority and I need to warn you."

Her desire faded beneath the very real chance he was right. She knew the biker culture as well as he did. "You think that's a possibility?"

"You know this world. Everything is a possibility."

She weighed the risk of letting him know where she lived versus the risk of one of his men—Axle, most likely—coming after her on his own. Although the risks on both sides were considerable, part of her trusted Jagger. He'd acted with honor, a quality lacking in pretty much every Black Jack biker she knew. The situation could have gone an entirely different way if not for him.

She gave herself a mental slap. Was she really considering giving her personal details to a member of the Sinner's Tribe? Rubbing her hand through her hair in distraction, she turned and walked down the sidewalk. "I'll take the risk."

"Arianne." His deep, husky voice stopped her in her tracks, and she looked back over her shoulder. He hadn't moved, and it was the hint that maybe there was more to his flirting that loosened her tongue.

"Banks Bar, west end of Villard Street." The words tumbled out before she could stop them. "I work the bar Tuesday to Saturday. And Mondays if there's a game on. If you're in the neighborhood for reasons other than killing me or warning me about being killed, I'll buy you a drink. Say thanks for saving me." *Should be safe enough.* She'd be working at Banks Bar only a few more days, maybe a week or two at the most. Once she got her fake passport from Jeff, she'd be leaving Conundrum behind.

"Thought you were a mechanic."

"I was . . . am. But I quit when I thought I was leaving and my boss hired my replacement before my last day so I could show him the ropes. Banks, my boss, wouldn't accept my resignation. He didn't believe I'd leave. Good thing, too. It means I can make some extra cash before I go."

"Got it."

When Jagger didn't say anything else, she stared down at her hands. *Stupid. Stupid. Stupid.* Why had she invited him for a drink? He was being courteous, not coming on to her.

Cheeks burning, she cleared her throat and gave him a weak smile. "Okay, then. Well . . . say bye to Max for me."

Then she turned and walked away.

★ FIVE ★

Respect must be shown, in order of importance, to your colors, bike, executive board, club members, clubhouse, other patch holders, prisoners, and chicks.

Flavio Fuentes screamed when Zane pointed the gun at his head.

He apologized for all the people he'd killed, the women he'd abused, and the children who'd suffered when their drug-addicted parents overdosed. He promised to go to church every Sunday, live clean, and give to charity. He would disband the cartel and leave Montana. Hell, he would even stop dealing with the Black Jacks. Anything but get into the trunk of Zane's Chrysler 300C. He'd heard about trunking, and although he was confident someone would pay his ransom before he ran out of air, he had suffered from claustrophobia since childhood. Surely the Sinners had mercy. Maybe Jagger and his men would like a couple of lines of speed on the house instead? Good-quality stuff.

"I want the location of the Jacks' icehouse." Jagger tapped Fuentes on the head with the barrel of his gun to get the drug lord's attention. The Black Jacks were making a fortune by producing their own crystal meth locally and avoiding the transport costs charged by the Mexican cartels. "Give me an address and you can steer clear of a cruise around the city in my trunk."

"I don't know. I don't know." Fuentes trembled. "I meet with the Jacks. They give me the stuff. I don't know where it comes from."

Zane shook his head. "He's lying."

Jagger thought so, too. He also thought it odd that a grown man would hug himself as if overcome with remorse. Too late, he realized that T-Rex, the club's most senior prospect, and Bandit, their newest full-patch, had missed a weapon the drug lord was hiding down the back of his pants.

Fuentes's gun flashed in the moonlight. Jagger dodged to the side, and the bullet skimmed past him. Zane fired next. Fuentes screamed and dropped his gun, both hands flying to hold his leg.

"Fuck." Cade rubbed his brow. "Why did you have to go and shoot him? He was worth at least two hundred grand alive, and now we have no lead on the location of the Black Jack icehouse."

"I shot him in the *leg*." Zane gave Cade an affronted glare. "And it's just a flesh wound. If we bandage him right, and his people pay the price, he'll live to deal drugs another day. You should be praising me for my accuracy, something you can never hope to achieve, since you shoot like a fucking girl."

"Like you need another pat on the back." Cade shot Zane a scathing look as he reached for Fuentes's arm and yanked him to his feet. "Your ego is so big, I have to step around it."

"Look who's talking." Zane grabbed Fuentes's other arm, and together he and Cade dragged the moaning drug lord to the vehicle. "You have women falling at your feet. We go out to a bar, and I know I'll be drinking alone because thirty seconds in the door, you'll have picked up some chick who can't keep her hands off you."

After bandaging Fuentes's leg, they opened the trunk of the vehicle and heaved Fuentes into it, raising their voices to be heard over his screams. "What can I say?" Cade grinned. "Women love me for my pretty face and my huge—"

"Cade." Jagger cut him off with a sharp bark. "How about a little professionalism? We're trunking, not comparing dick sizes. Call Fuentes's people and tell them he has only a few hours to live and the price just went up. I want five hundred grand and the location of the icehouse in a bag in the Dumpster outside Mountain Grill's on Ferguson just off the 191—otherwise, the trunk becomes his permanent home." He glared at Bandit and T-Rex, who were quivering in the shadows. "I should throw you in there with him. There's no excuse for missing that weapon."

Tall, blond, and built like a football linebacker, T-Rex whimpered. His dark-haired companion, Bandit, paled. *Good.* Jagger wanted them scared and thinking about the screwup for the rest of the night. He'd had closer calls, but regardless, he needed to be able to trust his men not to make the kinds of mistakes that could cost lives.

They drove around for an hour while Fuentes shouted and banged on the trunk. Zane shared a few stories about his years as a firefighter, and Cade talked about his women. Jagger tuned them out. There was only one woman he wanted to think about. A woman who hid a soft vulnerability behind a tough exterior. Strong. Brave. Beautiful. And totally off-limits, not just because she was the enemy, but also because he'd put her in danger once already, and it damn well wouldn't happen again.

The phone rang, and Cade confirmed Fuentes's people had agreed to the terms. Cheers and laughter all around. The money would help renovate the new clubhouse and finance the imminent destruction of the icehouse, which would put a severe dent in the Black Jacks' financial operations.

Twenty minutes later, they dragged an enraged, groaning Fuentes from the trunk and dumped him on the ground. T-Rex retrieved a sports bag from the Dumpster and fished out a piece of paper, holding it up for Fuentes to see before handing it to Jagger.

"There's an address on the piece of paper," Jagger said to Fuentes. "You're going to give me the address of the icehouse. If it matches, then you're free to go. If your people have given me the wrong address, you'll pay the price."

Fuentes's face grew chalky. Clearly he was worried his people would stab him in the back. Not something Jagger ever worried about—not even Axle would have dared to try to take him out. From here on, however, Jagger had no doubt Axle would be gunning for him. *Well, stand in line.*

Fuentes rattled off an address in a barely audible whisper. Jagger confirmed the match with a nod. Five minutes after that, they were headed back to the emergency base, which the board had just agreed would be renovated to become their new clubhouse, five hundred grand richer and set to blow the Jacks' icehouse sky high.

"This stays between us," Jagger cautioned as he drove through the darkened streets. "No one else in the club hears about the plan. I don't want to risk a leak."

"Good thing, then, you got rid of that pretty little Black Jack." Bandit gave an obsequious laugh, clearly trying to make up for his massive screwup with Fuentes and totally unaware he was just digging himself in deeper. But that was Bandit. Loyal, honest, but a total knucklehead when it came to social relations.

"She's one hot little piece of ass," he continued. "Maybe Cade should've worked her up for some Jack intel. The way he tells it, there isn't a woman alive who doesn't want in his pants."

Jagger gripped the steering wheel so hard, his knuckles whitened. Then, without warning, or even a word, he reached over the seat, grabbed Bandit by the collar, and smashed his face into the back of the headrest. He made a turn, righted the steering wheel, and kept driving.

Zane looked over from the passenger seat and dropped his voice to a low murmur only Jagger could hear. "What's eating you? We're supposed to be celebrating."

"Fucking hate cages." Jagger blew out a long breath and shifted his weight. He wasn't lying. Cages brought back memories of the months he'd spent intubated as he recovered from the rocket strike while on tour in Afghanistan. Unable to shake the residual claustrophobia and the memories of pain and utter helplessness, Jagger could no longer ride in a cage unless he was driving and all the windows were down. And no way would he have been able to handle what they'd just put Fuentes through. PTSD was the military psychologist's diagnosis. Jagger just called it a need to be in control.

"Unfortunately, my charm doesn't work on hard-core biker chicks." Cade folded his arms behind his head, forcing Bandit and T-Rex to move toward the side doors. "Too much life experience too young makes 'em sharp and savvy, not innocent, the way I like 'em. Plus they're hard to control, hard to manage, and—"

"You mean they see through your bullshit." Zane laughed and glanced over at Jagger. "She had balls, though, and one helluva kick."

Jagger stared straight ahead. Zane was entirely too perceptive. Although Jagger never discussed his PTSD, Zane, who knew him best, had been quick to pick up on his triggers. He was the one who'd insisted they ride with the windows down, and when it came time to drive, he'd tossed Jagger his keys.

"What's on for tomorrow?" He pointedly ignored Zane's not-so-subtle attempt to feel him out about Arianne, because Zane clearly knew what he thought already, and the fact that he'd picked up on Jagger's interest in the fiery brunette irked him even more than Bandit's disrespect.

"Devil Dogs MC are good to meet tomorrow," Cade said. "They're so desperate for a patch-over, I think they'd lick our boots if we asked. I've already placed the order for new cuts with our patches on them. They've passed all the tests. If you approve, I think they'd be a welcome addition to the club."

He'd been thinking the same thing. While the truce with the Black Jacks had held and they weren't losing brothers left, right, and center, Jagger had been reluctant to bring smaller biker clubs into the fold because the resources required to keep them in line and protect them were substantial. But now that the feud was back on, the Sinner's Tribe would need to aggressively expand to keep their numbers up and protect their territory. And if his ultimate goal was to maintain their status as the dominant club in the state, he would need to patch in new clubs.

Cade leaned over the seat. "You want them to come to the new clubhouse?"

"We still don't have full security in place," Jagger said. "And I want to meet them on neutral ground." His pulse kicked up a notch, and then the words spilled out before he could catch them. "There's a bar on the West Side, just off the 191. We'll meet them there. It's called Banks Bar."

Arianne parked her car in the dimly lit parking lot behind Banks Bar and reached down to check the LadySmith .38 Special in her lower calf holster.

He was coming for her. She knew it from the pounding of her heart and the sick feeling that hadn't disappeared since Jagger dropped her off five days ago. If she could only get home to collect the rest of her weapons inventory: a 9 mm Glock 26, usually holstered under her shirt when on

Black Jack business, and a .22 she carried in her purse when she wore a skirt or dress. But she'd been in such a hurry to get to Jeff the night of the fire, she hadn't had time to get them, and since then she hadn't been able to go home to retrieve them. Hell, she hadn't even been able to collect clean clothes, knowing that the minute she stepped into her apartment, she would be snatched up and dragged back to face Viper's wrath.

But that was the biker way. A price would have to be paid for her interference with the raid on the Sinner clubhouse, especially since Jeff hadn't managed to steal all the guns from the weapons shed out back, and there were only two possible punishments. Since she could never be kicked out of the club, she would have to pay in blood and bruises, and she hadn't yet recovered from the last beating.

Arianne took one last glance in the rearview mirror before turning off her vehicle. She'd managed to hide at Dawn's place for the last week. Her best friend and co-worker was always more than happy to give up her spare room when Arianne needed a place to stay, and had even cleared out a space in her wardrobe so Arianne could store emergency clothes. But after five days of sneaking out in disguise to search for Jeff, and with her savings depleted, Arianne had to break cover.

Her father would've anticipated her eventual emergence. Waited. When it served his needs, Viper had infinite patience, and when it didn't, he let loose a temper that had spilled the blood of some of the strongest men she knew.

And women.

Even after so many years, she was still afraid of him. Not that she would ever let him know it. Fear was a weakness, and Viper, president of the Black Jacks MC, didn't tolerate weakness. Not in himself. And certainly not in his daughter.

With one hand on the door handle, she made a slow,

thorough check of the area for Black Jacks before sliding out of the vehicle, and racing to the back door of the bar. The night was crisp and cold. A harsh breeze sent leaves scurrying across the pavement. She fumbled with the key, and caught a whiff of piss and stale beer, and . . . leather.

No.

She wrenched open the door and threw herself into the warm, dimly lit stockroom, where her Dawn was counting bottles with their boss, Joe Banks aka Banks.

"You okay?" His eyebrows furrowed. "Someone outside bothering you?"

"No. Just . . . looking forward to work." She turned around and worked the dead bolt with a firm click.

"Really?" The bar's owner and manager straightened and glared at the door as if he could see through the steel and into the night. Standing just over six feet tall, he was muscular but not bulky, his forearms covered with tats from the year he'd spent in prison. The soft fuzz on his head—usually shaved to a number 2—contrasted with piercing steel-blue eyes that could warm to a deep azure in an instant. He wore his usual uniform of black heavy metal band T-shirt, khakis, and an ancient pair of kicks.

"Yeah. I'm good." She held her voice firm, knowing even the slightest hitch would send him charging into the parking lot in an overprotective frenzy, ready to pound on anyone who dared mess with his staff.

Dawn brushed back her soft blond curls with one hand and gave her a questioning look. Small and curvy with a pixie face and big green eyes, she was the yin to Banks's yang. Soft where he was hard, sweet where he was bitter, she could cajole their boss to do almost anything except leave her unattended on the floor. Banks had hired a new bouncer, ostensibly to tighten up security, but in reality to keep roaming hands off Dawn's ass. Little did he know,

Dawn's seemingly delicate fists packed a dangerous punch. She'd once been a biker's old lady and could still hold her own.

"You're looking kinda pale." Dawn stared at her intently. "Even paler than when I saw you this morning."

"Seriously." Arianne told her. "Just jumpy tonight."

Banks huffed and then gave Arianne a slow perusal, from her dark chestnut hair swept into a high ponytail to her plain black tank top and her tight jeans to her ballet flats. "Your top is too low, your jeans are too tight, and you're wearing too much lipstick to work the bar tonight. Unless you want me to pull security from the door to watch you, I'd suggest you put on one of my T-shirts."

A smile curled her lips, and for the first time in a week, she felt as close to safe as she ever got. No one messed with Banks, and that meant no one messed with her. "You say that all the time, and yet I do just fine on my own."

He gave an exasperated grunt. "Last week you were wearing too much blush."

"You sound like someone's dad." Dawn pressed her lips together to keep her laughter in. "You gotta get a handle on that protective streak, Banks. What are you gonna do when you finally stop working so hard and get yourself a girlfriend? Wrap her up in tissue and keep her in the house? Or spend your evenings beating on anyone who dares look in her direction? I'll tell you right now, those are big relationship killers."

Banks scowled. "Fired."

Dawn laughed, her throaty voice warming the room. "Seeing as you fire me at least three times a night, honey, I'll just keep countin' bottles and get ready for work."

Arianne's tension eased with their familiar banter. She grabbed her apron off its hook and tied it firmly around her waist. "For the record, I don't wear blush. Blows off when I'm riding." Banks knew about her bike but not about her biker family. No one knew about them. Not her friends or coworkers. No one except Dawn.

But Dawn hadn't been so forthcoming about her own past, the night Arianne shared her story. Whatever pulled Dawn into the biker world had scarred her so deep, she refused to talk about it.

"Good thing. Got enough trouble with the guys drooling over you two." Banks hoisted a crate onto a nearby shelf and then stepped to the side to let Arianne pass.

She leaned up and pressed a kiss to his cheek as she reached for the door to the bar. "Thanks for giving me the week off. And for caring."

"I don't care." He turned and shoved the crate to the back of the shelf. "Just need to make sure my girls aren't being harassed. Got a business to run, and now I got a fucking motorcycle club breathing down my neck, demanding protection money."

Arianne stopped short, her hand on the door. She had taken the job at Banks Bar for the simple reason that it was one of the few bars in Conundrum not owned, managed, or under the "protection" of any gang or motorcycle club. Banks was tough enough to keep those wolves at bay.

"Which club?"

He pried the lid off another crate. "Don't know. They're all the same to me. They came in here this morning when I was taking a delivery. One of them pulled a gun on me while the others cased the joint. I told them where to go, but these guys were different from the usual suspects. They asked for the protection money as an afterthought, and when I told them to go fuck themselves, they went."

Arianne's pulse kicked up a notch. Good thing she was leaving anyway. If one of the MCs decided to shake down Banks, she would have had to quit. She couldn't take the risk of being recognized by any of the Black Jacks' enemies. "Do you think they'll be back?"

"They didn't say." Banks scowled. "But I do know I'm not playing that game. They come back, I'll burn down the bar, take the insurance money, and start up somewhere else. I don't have a sentimental attachment to this place. Won it from a guy in a poker game my first night out of the joint."

"Well, if that happens, you won't have to worry about staff. As long as I'm in town, I'll follow you wherever you go. And I know Dawn and the other staff will, too."

His face hardened with emotion. "Don't know if I'll need a bartender who wears too much lipstick."

"And I don't know if I'd follow a guy who fires me at least three times a night." Dawn gave him a warm smile.

"You two don't get onto the floor right away, you'll both be fired." Banks turned away, his voice rough. "Doors open in ten minutes."

"Hey, sugar. You okay?" Sherry smoothed her hands over Jagger's shoulders, her breasts brushing against his sweat-slicked back. "The boys said you were all wound up. You want me to take care of you?"

Jagger's muscles bunched at her touch. Axle and his supporters had declared a vendetta against the Sinners and, according to new intel, were trying to patch over to a midsized rival club to get support to carry the vendetta through. *As if having to deal with the Black Jacks wasn't enough.*

After an afternoon closeted with the executive board, discussing whether to strike first or wait it out, and a long run through the forest with Max, his body still thrummed with anger. The last thing he needed right now was having to deal with Sherry's attempts to get back together. "Not now, Sherry."

She backed off, her voice wavering. "Sorry, Jag. I just thought . . . you know . . . maybe I could help. It's been such a long time. . . ."

Instantly contrite, he motioned for her to sit on the front

step beside him. Yes, he'd cut her loose. Although Sherry didn't spark his heart, she was warm and sweet, and it had become too easy to fall into bed with her. But when people started treating her like his old lady, he'd had to draw the line. He was not willing to go down that path again, and even if he were, it wouldn't be with a woman who needed his constant attention. He didn't have the time or the energy to deal with someone who couldn't stand on her own two feet.

"Got a lot on my mind."

"Sure." She settled beside him and Jagger bit back a sigh. She just didn't get it. Sherry lacked the political savvy necessary for the role of a president's old lady. Jagger couldn't afford to indulge in the usual give-and-take or friendly banter that were a natural part of a normal relationship. He couldn't be questioned or challenged in public. Perception was everything. His power must appear absolute. A public disagreement, a sarcastic remark, or even disobeying an order, if done in public, could erode the foundation of a president's power. And that was something he could never allow.

"Do you miss me?" She propped her chin up with her elbows, her question confirming yet again that he'd made the right decision to let her go.

"It was too easy between us, babe. And you know how I feel about getting seriously involved. Too much of a risk for you, for me, and for the club."

She shot him a sideways glance. "You're still not over her, are you?"

Jagger huffed his annoyance. Sherry knew better than to bring up Christel. He would carry the guilt of her death for the rest of his life. Atonement lay in ensuring it never happened again. "Don't go there."

"If not me, who else?" She curled her hand around his arm and scooted over the worn wooden step, closer to him.

"You don't talk about her. You don't let anyone else talk about her. And ever since she died, you don't let anyone in. I know I'm not her, but we were good together. I can make you happy. Lord knows you need a little happiness in your life."

He gently detached her hand from his arm and stood, putting some distance between them. "What did I just say?"

"Don't go there."

"And what did you do?"

"I went there."

Jagger ran his hand through his hair "And that is the reason it wouldn't work. Aside from the fact that my position as president would put you in danger, you don't seem to understand our politics: You don't challenge me. You don't question me. You don't disobey me. And you sure as hell don't presume to tell me what I need, even if it is coming from a good place. What I *need* is someone who can navigate the politics and work with me, not against me. You need to find someone who can look after you, make you happy, and keep you safe."

"I thought that was you."

Jagger inwardly cursed himself for not ending it sooner with her. He'd known from the start Sherry wasn't right for him, but loneliness had driven him to take what she offered until he realized too late that she'd given him everything.

He remained standing in silence watching Wheels play Frisbee with Max on the front lawn. Another problem he would have to deal with. Wheels was a competent prospect and well-liked by the brothers, but something about him didn't sit right. Sometimes he was too well spoken for someone who claimed only a high school education. Other times he seemed almost too well informed about the biker scene in Conundrum. And although he was always sociable, he never revealed much about himself.

Not that Jagger was a big talker, but usually this far into a prospect's year, he had the measure of the man. Wheels, however, was still an enigma.

"You seemed pretty sweet on that Black Jack girl you let get away." Sherry's soft voice derailed his train of thought. "Vexy."

"You're just determined to go all the places you shouldn't go." Jagger tempered his anger by holding out a hand and helping her to her feet. They'd had some good times together and she'd been genuine in her affections. But he needed to end this now, before she read anything into this brief encounter.

"Axle thinks you don't have what it takes to lead anymore." She followed him down the stairs. "He said if you'd made her pay for what the Black Jacks did, we would be the dominant club in Montana. No one, not even the Black Jacks, would mess with us, because they would know we had no limits when it came to revenge. He says he would have done it for the club." She cocked her head to the side. "Of course, maybe I misheard. It was . . . you know . . . pillow talk."

If she thought to make him jealous, she was on the wrong track. He didn't do jealous. He'd never cared enough to be jealous, except maybe with Christel. If a woman he was with wanted to be with someone else, he had no problem letting her go. Everyone deserved to find their little piece of happiness. But not by fraternizing with the enemy.

"First, Sherry, we *are* the dominant club in Montana." He stopped and turned to face her. "Despite what the Jacks say. And second—" His brows drew together. "—what the fuck are you doing with Axle? He's out on bad terms, dead to the club. If you're with him, then you're not with us."

Sherry paled. "Not now. It was before you kicked him out. The night of the fire. I was looking after him after Zane beat him up."

"Better be." Jagger's face hardened. "If I find out you're with him, or passing on information—"

"I'm not." She held up her hands palms forward. "I'm loyal to the Sinners. I have been for five years. That isn't going to change just because you and I aren't together. It's just . . . you know Axle, sometimes he doesn't think before he acts."

Mollified, he grunted. "Stay away from him. A man who would take the life of an innocent woman would have no qualms about hurting one either."

"Maybe she's not so innocent." Sherry paused midstep. "Maybe she's setting you up. What if the fire was a diversion and the Black Jacks' real goal was to get her into the clubhouse, maybe into your heart? She certainly caught your attention."

Jagger folded his arms as an unfamiliar swell of emotion threatened his control. "She's gone. So, whether she's playing me or not is irrelevant."

Gone, but not forgotten.

Gone, but soon to be seen.

What the hell was he doing holding a meeting in her bar? The Sinner's Tribe owned four bars and two strip clubs in Conundrum, and if he'd really wanted neutral ground, he could have met the Devil Dogs MC at any civilian bar in the city. But the answer came in a heartbeat. He wanted to see her again. *No.* He *had* to see her again. And hell, she'd as good as given him an invitation. He didn't want to be impolite and turn it down.

He turned and walked away, knowing he'd been too harsh. Sherry had been with the club for five years, and never once had she given him cause to doubt her loyalty. His anger was directed at himself and not her. And yet, despite all the reasons not to go, nothing could keep him away from Banks Bar tonight. He needed to see Arianne again. He needed to know if he was well and truly fucked.

★ SIX ★

*Don't mess with a brother's old lady or other
patch holders' chicks*

"Hey, baby. You gonna give me a little sugar with that whiskey?"

Arianne groaned when the inebriated trucker leaned across the bar and motioned her forward with a thick finger. Every weekend was the same. As the evening progressed, the happy drunks became lusty drunks, and trapped behind the bar, she was fair game. But she was safer than Dawn. At least she had the counter to keep their hands away.

Dodging to the side, she slammed his whiskey down and gave him a cold smile. "Only sugar on offer is in the little white packets at the end of the counter. Why don't you head down there and get one?"

He held out his hands, palms up as if to ward off a blow. "Hey, baby. I was just being friendly. No need to get uptight." He slid off his seat with a huff, no doubt to return to his friends and tell them about the bitch behind the bar.

And "bitch" was the right word. But her prickly shell had helped her survive after her mother died. She fingered the ring she always wore, her mother's last gift. Not a day went by that she didn't miss her. Not a day went by that she didn't long to escape the biker world that had been responsible for her mother's death. But Viper would never allow it. Especially when there was work to be done and few he trusted to do it. One week she was sent to procure weapons from soldiers at a local military base. Before that, she'd been a midnight drug mule. Last month had been intelligence gathering from city hall to find out who had dared purchase the plot of land beside the Black Jack clubhouse.

The front door opened and her head jerked up as it had a hundred times that night, her heart hammering in dread anticipation of seeing a Black Jack patch. Adrenaline surged through her body until the crowds parted to reveal a couple of middle-aged bikers, balding and wearing patch-free leather jackets. *Weekend warriors.* She saw them all the time. Business types who wheeled out their bikes only on evenings and sunny weekends. She sagged against the counter in relief.

"You worried about the Jacks?" Dawn hoisted her tray of empties onto the bar. "You've been watching that door all night, and since you aren't interested in dating, I know it isn't because of a guy."

Was she that obvious? Turning to hide her disquiet, Arianne said, "I was safe at your place, but I got a bad feeling the minute I pulled into the parking lot outside. I need to be ready to hit the door running because I'm not up for a Viper-style interrogation right now. I still have bruises from being knocked off my bike."

"Fucking bastard." Dawn pressed a fist to her mouth. "Wish I still had the kind of contacts I did when I was with Jimmy. I'd so like to kick me some nasty Viper ass, and then I'd . . ." Her voice trailed off when the front door banged shut again. Arianne followed Dawn's gaze to the group of bikers walking through the bar, her heart slowing only when she spotted Devil Dogs MC patches on their cuts. Relieved, she turned away, only to look back when Dawn whispered.

"Well . . . hellooo, baby."

Arianne looked up and her heart seized in her chest.

Jagger.

What the hell was he doing here?

Her body heated in an instant, a blush burning her cheeks as she cast a surreptitious glance at Jagger from beneath her lashes. Conundrum had more than its fair share of bars, and the Sinners owned Riders and had recently carved out Sixty-Nine Bar on the east side of town as their turf.

Three Sinners followed Jagger as he wove his way through the tables toward the Devil Dogs, who were in the process of clearing everyone out of the back corner. Dawn's eyes widened when they rushed to seat Jagger at the end of the table, his back to the wall, giving him a clear view of the bar.

"He's someone important, that's for sure. I would need to see the patches on his cut—"

"Jagger."

Dawn startled. "Jagger, the president-of-Sinner's-Tribe-who-kidnapped-you-then-let-you-go-and-now-you're-hot-for-him-although-you-shouldn't-be Jagger?" Her voice rose above Motörhead's "Ace of Spades," blasting through the speakers. No easy feat.

"Well, look at him. He's devastatingly gorgeous. I mean, how many bikers look like that? And he was different from the bikers I know. He cleaned up the knife wound on my throat."

"You do understand how absolutely inane that sounds," Dawn said. "His friend sliced you with a knife, but he's a nice biker because he cleaned you up."

Heart thudding, she looked over at the corner table. Jagger caught her with his gaze, giving her no time to stifle her blush. A thrill of excitement shot through her veins.

Oh God. It was like high school all over again, except he had come to her bar and not her locker, and he was the bad-ass president of a rival MC and not the grungy lead singer of a high school metal band she had been panting after for two years.

Still, her body reacted to his unexpected presence exactly the same way—stomach churning, body heating, nipples hardening—although this time with an intensity that stole her breath away.

"Cool it with the doe eyes and dreamy smile." Dawn reached over the bar and pinched Arianne's arm. "You've spent your life trying to get away from bikers. Just ignore him and he'll go away."

"I don't think he's the kind of man who just goes away."

"Maybe not." Dawn licked her lips. "He's got the 'king of the castle' thing goin' on there. Lookit those Devil Dogs fawning over him. I wouldn't be surprised if they drop to the floor and lick his—" She cut herself off with a gasp. "Sweet mother of hotness. It's Thor." Dawn gestured to a tall biker with shoulder-length blond hair walking toward the table. "Maybe I spoke too soon. In fact, I did speak too soon. You should definitely go and talk to him, and while you're there, you can find out who his friend is. The blond with the body made for sin. That boy could turn a good girl bad."

"I saw him at the meeting," Arianne said. She'd told Dawn about everything except Jeff's possible involvement in burning down the clubhouse. "He's on the executive board, but I didn't catch his name."

"Well, we're gonna catch it right now." Dawn grabbed her tray. "You talk. I'll take orders and drool. And to think I wasted time on a man like Eugene."

"Eugene?" Arianne tried, but failed to keep a straight face. "Your dating website disaster? You texted me from the restaurant for an emergency call thirty seconds after you sat down, and I picked you up ten minutes later. There wasn't much time wasted that evening."

Dawn shuddered. "That ten minutes felt like ten years. He brayed when he laughed. And his lips peeled back. Did I tell you he had horse teeth?"

"You Instagrammed his teeth, so everyone knew."

"But it was okay." Dawn had the good grace to blush. "He wasn't into social media. He had no friends, so he couldn't be embarrassed, and I didn't use his real name. Just his teeth."

"That's right." Laughter bubbled in her chest. "You nicknamed him 'the Italian Stallion.'"

Her tension eased momentarily as they shared a laugh, but when she caught Jagger watching them, a delicious shiver wound up her spine. Why did he have to be a biker?

"I'm not paying you two to laugh." Banks joined them at the bar and scowled. "Dawn, I need you at the table near the dance floor. And Arianne, looks like we got some thirsty bikers in the corner. Get over there and take their orders. I'll watch the bar till you're back. Daisy went home 'cause she wasn't feeling well, so we're short-staffed tonight."

Arianne's pulse kicked up a notch. Aside from taking Jagger's order, what was she going to say? *Fancy meeting you here? Planning to kidnap me again? Nice to see you took me up on my invitation?*

"What if they're here because they figured out who I am?" She kept her voice low as she fished under the counter for a notepad.

"They don't know who you are?" Dawn gave her an incredulous glance. "No wonder they let you go."

"Exactly."

Dawn's gaze flicked to the bikers and then back to Arianne. "They don't seem to be in a kidnapping kinda mood. My guess is the Dogs want to patch over, and they're meeting the Sinners to hash over the details. Only time you ever see that kinda boot-licking going on."

"You're probably right." Arianne had seen dozens of clubs come begging for Viper's protection and the power of his patch, but he was discriminating to a fault, preferring to grow the club organically rather than inherit men who didn't make the cut. The Devil Dogs had the same hungry look as the prospecting clubs that had come to visit the Jacks, but unlike the Jacks, the Sinners would likely patch them over.

"What's the worst that can happen?" Dawn said. "It's not like you don't know your way around bikers. Or dangerous men. Or biker presidents who are the epitome of dangerous men."

Maybe so, but she sure as hell didn't know her way around men so utterly compelling as Jagger. She'd always kept her relationships safe, dating easygoing, eager-to-please beta males. Men she could control. And strictly civilians. She had no interest in getting involved with a biker. Ever. So why drag her feet when she had a job to do?

"Fine. I'll go." Arianne flipped open her notepad and navigated her way through the bar to the now rowdy tables in the corner.

She didn't have to look up to know Jagger was watching her. She could feel his gaze burning into her skin, but instead of intimidating her, his frank interest made her bold. Lifting her head, she shook off her fear, and met his stare full-on, smiling before she dropped her gaze. Confident, not challenging. That was the key.

And from the smile that spread across his lips when she reached the table, she could tell she'd played it just right.

"Vexy." The deep rumble of his voice vibrated through her body, sending a rush of heat straight to her core. He'd remembered to use her road name.

"Nice to see you again." And she meant it. She'd been

fantasizing about him all week, mentally stripping off his clothes, running her hands over the breadth of his shoulders, his massive chest, those taut abs, and then lower, tugging off his belt, her own heat rising as she ripped open his fly. Power, barely contained, beneath her, above her. Inside—

Jagger gave a satisfied rumble, as if her words—or her face—had settled something in his mind.

"What can I get you?"

"I'll start with some of this." The Devil Dog seated beside Jagger pinched Arianne's ass.

Without hesitation, Arianne grabbed his wrist and twisted his arm behind his back. "I'm afraid my ass isn't on the menu."

Wham. Jagger thudded a knife on the table between the outstretched fingers of the biker's free hand. "You don't fucking touch her. You don't talk to her. You don't look at her. And you sure as fuck don't disrespect her."

The table stilled. If he had been any other man, she might have thanked him verbally, or she might have pointed out that his actions were dramatic and unnecessary, since she had the situation in hand. But he wasn't just any man. He was an outlaw biker president, and his actions weren't directed solely at saving her ass from a squeeze. In that brief exchange, he'd laid down the law for the bikers on both sides of the table. First, he was in charge. And second, Arianne belonged to him.

So she gave him a simple nod of thanks. Her response seemed to please him. His face softened almost imperceptibly as he unclasped her hand from the Devil Dog's wrist, then tugged until she released her captive. Her skin tingled at his touch, and when he rubbed this thumb lightly over her knuckles, she felt each stroke as a throb deep in her core.

Still holding her hand, he retrieved his knife and then

leaned back in his chair, his icy glare fixed on the now quivering Devil Dog who had no doubt pinched his very last ass.

"Sinners don't disrespect women. You want to patch over, you adjust the attitude."

The Devil Dog, his face red, sweat beading on his brow at the possibility his behavior might have just lost his club the protection they clearly needed, apologized profusely to Arianne. Then he apologized to Jagger and each of the Sinners at the table. When he was done, he started again, but Arianne held up her free hand.

"Apology accepted. Now, let's get some drinks on the table. Jagger, you want to start?"

"You already started something." Jagger's voice dropped to a low, husky rasp, and he squeezed her hand, sending all the wrong messages to all the right parts of her body.

"Question is . . . do I want to finish it?"

She couldn't tell if he was flirting with her or threatening to beat on the Devil Dog, so she threw the question back at him. "Question is, what do you want to drink?"

"Pad." He released his grip and held out his hand. Arianne gave him the pen and pad and he scrawled on the paper, then handed it back to her.

Sexy. As. Fuck.

Biting her lip to stifle a laugh, she tucked the notepad in her pocket. "So, our best whiskey and enough glasses to go round?"

Satisfaction glittered in his eyes as he confirmed his assent with the briefest dip of his chin. For a heartbeat, she wondered if he'd been testing her. But did he really think she would give the game away?

Relieved to have an excuse to get away from Jagger's distracting charm and good looks, she headed back to the stockroom. What the hell was she thinking? Not only was she about to leave Conundrum, but he was exactly the kind of man she'd spent a lifetime trying to avoid: Too powerful. Too confident. Too violent. Too masculine. With the quiet kind of arrogance that came from being in command.

And, of course, he had to be a biker.

She searched the shelves for Banks's twenty-one-year-old Redbreast. Although not a whiskey drinker—vodka was more her style—but she figured that at $180 a bottle, the selection would satisfy even the most discerning palate. Spotting the yellow label at the back of the shelf, she stretched up and reached for the green glass bottle.

"Hello, Vexy." Low and rough with an unmistakable drawl, the voice in her ear sent a wave of cockroaches skittering beneath her skin, but not so much as the hand sliding over her hip.

Danger. The warning spiked through her mind, bringing with it fleeting images from the nightmares that haunted her sleep. *Dark room, torn clothing, fingers around her throat. Her body pinned to the bed. Helpless.* Arianne drew in a ragged breath and tried to stem the flow, but the dam was broken. More images flashed. *The thud of a door. Cool, sweet air in her lungs. A roar. The crack of bone. Jeff's scream. And then Viper.*

Gritting her teeth, she forced the memories away. "Leo." She spat out his name, her nose wrinkling when he pulled her hard against his body. "How did you get in here? Get the hell off me."

"I'll get off on you, babe. How would you like that?" He ground his hips into her ass and she almost heaved.

"You're disgusting." She grabbed the bottle from the shelf and slid past him, then headed for the door. Last thing she wanted was to be trapped in a room with Viper's VP.

"And you're coming with me when you're done work," Leo said, following her into the main room. "Viper wants to see you, but he's tied up till later, so there's time for a drink."

He rounded the bar and settled himself on a barstool. Almost immediately, the couple at the end of the bar vacated their seats. But then, Leo always had that effect on people. With his sharp, angular features, unnaturally pale skin, cruel slash of a mouth, and pitch black hair cut long on top, he almost had the look of a comic book villain. But there was nothing comical about her father's VP. Not even the bulky hoodie he wore under his leather cut could hide the enormous, cruel power of his muscular body.

Arianne didn't dare look at the Sinners in the corner as she filled a tray with whiskey glasses. Leo had to have come in through the back door leading to the parking lot. He would never have risked a public meeting with the Sinners this soon after the fire. Would Jagger think she was still with the Jacks? How could he not, with her pouring drinks and chatting with Leo at the bar?

Still, she could hardly wait until Jagger saw Leo's cut. The Sinners were the dominant presence in the bar, which meant no other bikers were welcome tonight. She had no love for Leo, and he deserved what was coming to him.

"Sure." She opened and closed cupboards on the pretense of looking for more glasses. For the first time ever, she considered not answering Viper's summons. Usually he sent Leo when she'd done something wrong. This time she'd done something unforgivable, and it wasn't just her at risk, but Jeff, too.

"What does Viper want with me?" Still playing for time—what the hell was taking those Sinners so long to notice the Black Jack sitting at the bar?—she added a few more glasses to the tray and placed the whiskey bottle in the center. Then, to keep Leo distracted, she threw a few ice cubes into a glass and shoved it across the counter.

"What do you think he wants?" Leo's eyes narrowed in contempt. "He wants to know what the fuck you were doing at the Sinner's Tribe clubhouse, fucking up Jeff's job.

The truck came back half empty, and Jeff has disappeared. The Triad is riding Viper something fierce 'cause he made them pay in advance for those weapons." Leo leaned toward her, his body thrumming with menace. "Viper's wondering if you and Jeff got together and decided to do a little business on the side. And even if you didn't, you know how it works: Someone has to take the fall—and he's decided on you."

"He can get more damn guns." She dropped her hand to the counter, just above the hidden emergency call button. She'd seen Leo angry and agitated, but never like this. Viper must have blamed him in some way for what happened.

Leo's mouth crimped in annoyance. "There are no more AK-47s in any of the four neighboring states, and he can't take the risk of bringing them direct from Mexico. He's so fucking pissed, Vexy, he's destroyed half the clubhouse and put the three men who went with Jeff in the hospital."

Arianne rearranged the glassware beneath the counter to hide her trembling hands, but she couldn't stop a shudder from coursing up her spine.

"Yeah." Leo's gaze crawled over her. "You know what I'm talking about. This time when you go back to the clubhouse, you won't be coming out again. At least not in one piece." His lips twisted in a cold leer of a smile. "Not unless you ask me for help. And you know the price."

Not a price she was prepared to pay. Arianne stared down the tray and then over at the rowdy group of bikers. Should she bring the tray over and ask for help? Technically she was a Black Jack and MCs as a rule didn't interfere with the business of other clubs. Given Jagger's duty was first and foremost to the Sinners, a request for assistance might put him in a difficult position, and her, if he refused.

And since when had she ever needed help? Arianne

grabbed a bottle of Scotch and poured it into Leo's glass. She still had the .38 strapped to her leg, and Banks kept a .45 in the drawer under the cash register in case of emergency, which this was. Still, Leo wouldn't have come alone, and if she drew a weapon, civilians might get hurt.

"At least you remember my favorite drink," Leo said, after his first sip.

As if she could forget—the smell of Scotch on his breath as he threw her on the bed that awful night had ruined her for Scotch forever.

Leo turned thoughtful as he threw back the rest of his drink and shoved toward her. "Viper's looking for Jeff, too. He might show you some mercy if you give him up. You know where he's at?"

"I haven't seen him, and I have nothing to say to Viper." A sliver of relief shot through her heart. At least Jeff had the sense to stay hidden. She held up the bottle, offering a refill. Maybe if he was drunk, he wouldn't notice when she slipped out of the bar. "I got there after the fire started. Then someone knocked me off my bike. The Sinners took me. They let me go. End of story."

"You forget how well I know you." Leo reached across the counter and squeezed her fingers around the bottle so hard her eyes watered. "And I can tell when you're lying." He released her with a satisfied smirk. "You always thought you were better than me, Vexy. That was always your problem. Too much thinking, not enough fucking."

She didn't know why she felt so bold. Maybe it was because she knew that within the next few days she would be leaving Conundrum for good. Or maybe it was because Jagger was in the corner and he'd almost sliced off a Devil Dog's fingers for pinching her ass. Whatever the reason, she met his gaze full-on. "I fuck, Leo. Just not with you."

Even as the words left her mouth, she knew she would

pay a heavy price. And she did. He backhanded her so fast she didn't have time to defend herself. She staggered back, her head hitting the shelf so hard, bottles crashed to the ground, splintering on the wooden floor in a cacophony of sound.

"Fucking bitch. I was trying to be nice, letting you finish your shift, having a little talk. But clearly I was wasting my time. Just 'cause you don't ride with the Jacks doesn't mean you aren't bound by the rules. You're coming with me now, even if I have to drag you out of here, screaming your little ass off—"

And then he was gone.

Arianne blinked, trying to clear her vision as people scattered—Was that . . . Jagger with his hand around Leo's neck? Pounding Leo's head on the counter?

"Fucking cowardly piece of shit, beating on a woman." Jagger's deep growl reverberated through her body. "Let's see how you like it."

Wham. Wham. Wham.

"Coupla Jacks on their way over." The heavily muscled blond biker helped Arianne up, then gestured toward the door. "They seem to be takin' offense to the way you're treating Leo."

Arianne wasn't surprised they knew who Leo was. The top brass of all the clubs knew each other, if not by sight, then at least by name.

Jagger scowled. "Clear the bar, Cade. I'm not done yet, and the civilians will go crazy when they see blood." With one hand still around Leo's neck, he wrenched a .45 from the holster under his cut, then waved over a tall biker with thick chestnut hair and eyes a deep, almost azure blue. Arianne recognized him from the meeting, too. Did the Sinners have a good-looks requirement for patching in new members?

"Sparky, go help Cade get the customers outta here. Pay

off the manager for the rest of the evening. Me 'n' Leo need a little alone time." Jagger thumped Leo's head on the counter again and then jerked him to standing.

"Heads up." Cade shouted from beside the window. "It's a fucking ambush. Jacks comin' in from the front. I count at least ten bikes. They got a support club with 'em too."

The front door slammed open. People screamed. Pulse racing, Arianne edged toward the till as the bar erupted into chaos around them.

Banks and the mouth-watering Sparky wove their way through the tables, yanking people from their seats and herding them out the side door to the beat of Jay-Z's "On the Run." Shouts and the tinkle of broken glass peppered the air. Sinners and Devil Dogs launched themselves at the Jacks who had come in the front door, heedless of the customers racing for the exit. Dawn shot her a worried glance, then held up her keys and mouthed "outside" before Banks hustled her through a fire exit.

Arianne reached for the drawer beneath the till, and Jagger froze her with a glare. "Don't even think about it."

"I'm not with them. I left the Jacks a long time ago." She held up her hands so he could see she wasn't armed, and he nodded, his free hand still pinning Leo, cheek to the bar.

"So . . . did you wind up here by chance, or because I invited you?" Heart hammering in her chest, Arianne contemplated her escape route as she tried to keep Jagger distracted. Her safest bet was the stockroom exit to the parking lot, but with a biker brawl on the premises and Jacks no doubt on patrol outside, she couldn't risk going unarmed. She still had the gun she'd strapped to her leg, but it wasn't so easy to retrieve in a pinch. The gun under the till was her best option. But if she had to pull the gun on Jagger, was she prepared to use it?

"Man rescues a woman, usually expects a little gratitude before being interrogated. But since I'm in a good

mood, I'll let it slide. You owe me a drink, sweetheart."
He casually banged Leo's head again, and Leo slumped
forward on the counter.

"A drink?" She waved her hand vaguely around the bar,
where the Jacks and Sinners were now engaged in a full-
out brawl. "Didn't you notice there's a fight going on? Or
that there is a very dangerous man attached to your hand?"

And then, because Leo was semiconscious and no one
was within hearing distance, she leaned forward and
said what she'd wanted to say when the Devil Dog had
pawed her ass. "I had the situation under control. Am I supposed to be grateful you caused a scene, terrified the customers, and started a wholesale destruction of the bar?"

Jagger's eyes narrowed. "Yeah, sweetheart. You had it
under control. I picked that up when he sent you flying into
the cabinet." He reached out with his free hand and ran his
finger lightly over her cheek, his touch lingering on her
skin. "You're hurt."

Coming from a man who had almost just cracked open
Leo's head, Jagger's concern unnerved her, as did his sudden switch from fierce to kind. Pulse racing, she dropped
her hand back to the till. "You didn't answer my question.
Why are you here?"

"Had a meeting. Needed neutral ground. Couldn't get
your pretty face outta my head, and since you invited me,
I brought everyone here." He glanced down at Leo, who
was moaning on the counter and a muscle twitched in his
jaw. "You with him?"

"Will he live if I say no?" Arianne's fingers curled
around the bottom drawer, and she tugged on it ever so
slowly.

Jagger's eyes glittered fever bright. "You want him to
live?"

Did she want Leo to live? She'd wanted him to die since
the night he'd tried to rape her. She'd dreamt of his death

every time he looked at her or touched her since. Sometimes she even fantasized about pulling the trigger. But she had no doubt if she said yes, Jagger would kill him, and she couldn't live with his death on her conscience.

The lie dropped from her tongue. "Yes."

"Then he'll live."

She couldn't help but smile, not just because he was being perversely sweet, but because her fingers had finally touched cold steel. "Thank you."

"Pleasure, sweetheart. But I should let you know, he will suffer. I have zero tolerance for violence against women."

Too late, she saw the danger in their intimate exchange.

Leo pushed himself up, dislodging Jagger's hand, his eyes narrowed and his face twisted into a mask of fury. "What the fuck? What. The. Fuck? You got something going on with the fucking president of the enemy, Vexy? You would dare betray Viper and the Jacks?"

Arianne wrapped her hand around the grip of the gun and gritted her teeth. "There's nothing between us, Leo."

"Doesn't look like nothing to me." He wrenched himself away from Jagger, then staggered back, out of reach. "Daughter or not, Viper's gonna show you no fucking mercy. Nothing he hates more than betrayal, and you've dished him up a double dose."

"Daughter?" Jagger stilled, his face smoothing to an expressionless mask. "You're Viper's daughter?"

"Unfortunately." Arianne slid her finger through the trigger, her gaze now fixed on the bigger threat—the man who had gone from kind to killer in a heartbeat.

"No fucking way in hell."

"You got the 'hell' part right," she said.

"Wait until Viper hears about this." Leo cast a quick glance behind him, where the Jacks now outnumbered the Sinners two to one, then turned back to Arianne, his eyes black with rage. "All that fuss about putting out for me, and after one night, you're spreading your legs for the damn Sinners."

Arianne's lips curled in disgust. He felt no remorse for what he'd done to an innocent sixteen-year old girl, only regret that he hadn't finished the job. Her free hand closed around an empty glass, and in one swift movement, she lifted it and threw it at his head. "Go to hell."

And he almost did. With a bellow of rage, Jagger let loose. He smashed his fist into Leo's face, and within minutes, they had joined the brawl.

Wood cracked and glass shattered. Chairs and tables splintered under heavy bodies. Jacks and Sinners fought without restraint and totally without mercy. *Poor Banks.* He'd only just finished with the renovations. This was all because of her.

Another crash. A scream. A mug sailed across the bar. *Goddamn outlaw bikers.* No respect for people or property. She'd managed to live almost a normal life for the last three years, and suddenly she was in the thick of it again—all because she'd tried to stop Jeff from making the biggest mistake of his life. And failed.

Through the frenzy of fists and the maelstrom of violence, she could feel Jagger's gaze on her, whether out of concern or anger she didn't know. But she couldn't stay. Not now. Not when Leo thought she'd betrayed the Black Jacks. Not when Jagger knew the truth about who she was and would likely try to capture her again.

For the briefest time, desire, so fleeting, had danced on the tip of her tongue. Hope had burned bright in her soul. She should have known it wouldn't last. Her father's taint destroyed everything good in her life. Even the promise of something that could never be.

She yanked the gun from the drawer and backed up to the stockroom door. Then she turned and ran.

★ SEVEN ★

*The president is the sole representative of the club
in all matters of public relations.*

Fuck. Jagger caught sight of the swinging stockroom door just as Leo charged.

He easily sidestepped the assault and retaliated with a left uppercut. The back of Leo's head slammed into the wall and blood sprayed from his nose. More satisfying, however, was the pleasing crunch of cartilage under Jagger's knuckles.

Leo howled. "You'll fucking pay for this."

Undeterred, Jagger continued to pummel the bastard. What had he done to Arianne? Whatever it was, his brave vixen had turned sheet white, her reaction triggering his protective instincts and calling forth the darkness that he always kept tightly leashed. Now that side of him thirsted for the chance to exact vengeance on someone who deserved what was coming to him. It had been too long.

Just as the last five days had been too long.

Despite his best efforts, long runs with Max, and even longer workouts in the gym, Jagger hadn't been able to get the little temptress out of his head. The meeting with the Devil Dogs had been a perfect excuse. Who would have known it would turn into a test of their courage and loyalty?

Leo struggled to his feet, and Jagger stared at the swinging door. *Viper's daughter?* He turned the words over in his mind, but he couldn't reconcile the woman he'd dropped off at the West Side gas station less than a week ago as the daughter of the vicious, bloodthirsty self-styled biker king of Montana.

Where the fuck had she gone? He'd come over to the bar to protect her, and instead he'd allowed himself to be pulled into a fight with Leo. So unlike him. Still, she wasn't the kind of woman to stand around, waiting to be rescued. As she'd told him before, she could take care of herself.

He turned to finish off his prisoner, only to realize Leo had slipped away in his moment of self-reflection. *Christ.* Arianne was beyond distracting. When had he ever lost focus in a fight? He headed around the bar to check out the stockroom, pulling up short when Zane called his name.

"Wheels just got here." Zane joined him at the door. "He brought reinforcements, but he spotted another bunch of Black Jacks heading this way." Zane hesitated. "And something else you're not gonna want to hear . . ."

"Spit it out." He needed to get to Arianne. Protect her in case there were Jacks outside. Zane, Cade, and Sparky could organize the Sinners who had since joined the fight.

"It's Axle. He and his boys are out looking for Vexy. Weasel tipped off Tank, hoping to win his way back into the club. He told Tank that Axle blames Vexy for getting him kicked out of the club. Axle still thinks if he offs her, the brothers will kick you out and vote him in as president."

"Jesus fucking Christ." Jagger pounded his fist on the counter. "Does Axle seriously think the Jacks would vote him in? Or that I would ever let him get his hands on her?" He glanced around the bar. With many bikers now lying on the floor groaning, the fight had lost steam, and no doubt the police would be on their way.

"Have you seen her? She'll need protection until we deal with Axle."

"Wheels saw her getting into a cage out back."

Jagger holstered his weapon and made a mental note to reconsider his reservations about Wheels. Damn prospect was everywhere.

"Tell Gunner to clear our people out of the bar, then meet me out back with Cade. We'll have to find her. She's got fucking Black Jacks after her, too." He paused, reluctant to share her secret, but he'd given in to desire one too many times in the last week—from defending Arianne when he wasn't certain of her innocence to holding his meeting at her bar—and duty reared its ugly head. " 'Course if Axle hurts her, he won't have just me to deal with. She's Viper's daughter."

"Viper's daughter? And we let her go?" Zane's lips pressed thin. "So are we gonna catch her and hold her hostage this time? Maybe get some of the Jacks' secrets out of her?"

Jagger gave an irritated huff as he rounded the bar and headed toward the stockroom door. "Axle's actions are our responsibility, and until we deal with him, she's under our protection. We'll take her somewhere safe."

"So now we're protecting Jacks?"

"Zane . . ." He paused in front of the door. One word was all the warning he usually needed. Jagger's best friend since they were five years old, and fiercely protective of those closest to him, Zane was the only person allowed to challenge him, but only when they were alone and only if he thought Jagger had overlooked something fundamentally important.

Which was the case now, apparently, since he kept right on talking.

"What if she's a plant and the whole thing is a setup?" Zane threw open his hands. "I mean, how did it happen that a bunch of Black Jacks showed up when we were here?" He sidestepped to avoid a pair of grappling bikers as they fell against the bar. "Seems like too much of a co-incidence. Maybe she called them. Staged a little drama to see what you're made of." He gritted his teeth and his voice came out harsh with emotion, flavored with bitter-ness. "Women don't think like we do. They're conniving and manipulative and can twist a fucking guy in knots without feeling any sort of remorse."

Jagger slammed open the door, his face hot and pinched with annoyance. "One day, you're gonna have to tell me what happened to you after I left for the army—'cause those years changed you, made you bitter as hell. Not all women are the same. And this situation has fuck all to do with the fact she's a woman. We owe her our protection. You've overstepped. There's nothing more to say." He brushed past Zane and stormed through the stockroom toward the back exit.

"Where do you want to take her?" Zane followed him, seemingly unperturbed by Jagger's reprimand or his quick dismissal of Zane's concerns. But that had always been Zane's way. Even when they were kids, Jagger had never known what Zane was thinking or how he was feeling unless Zane chose to share, which he almost never did.

"We'll put her in the safe house above Sparky's shop until we've dealt with Axle and figured out where she stands with the Jacks." He opened the back door, and a cool breeze ruffled his hair. He didn't ask Zane if he was com-ing. Except for the years they'd been apart, Zane always had his back, and he returned the favor. That's what best friends did.

"Viper's gonna be fucking pissed when he finds out you've got his daughter. What if she doesn't want to get on her daddy's bad side?" Zane followed him into the parking lot.

"She doesn't have to agree."

"She'll agree." A slow smile spread across Zane's face. "Never met a woman who could resist your charm."

"Faster, Dawn." Arianne's chest pounded as the bikers rapidly closed the distance between them. Dawn's Ford Fiesta was no match for 1,500 cc's of raw Harley horsepower, but maybe they could find somewhere to hide.

"My foot is down to the floor." Dawn gripped the steering wheel so hard, her knuckles turned white. "My Fiesta is a good car for safe city driving, not for high-speed getaways. If I'd known y'all were going to be chased by crazed bikers, I would've brought something sportier. Maybe you should give me a set of your keys so that next time we have to make an escape, we can take your car, although I doubt even your ancient Mustang convertible could outrun these guys."

"I'm so sorry about this." She reached over and squeezed Dawn's arm. "I should have just gone with Leo. Then none of this would have happened. You'd be safe. Banks would be safe. The bar wouldn't have been trashed." She scrubbed her hands over her face. "God, what have I done? I've never defied Viper like this before. I don't know why I ran."

She looked back at the string of motorcycle headlights and groaned. "I'm sure that's Leo and the Jacks. Maybe you should pull over and let me out. He won't hurt you, because it's me he wants."

Dawn gave an exasperated snort. "I saw what he did to you tonight. And I've seen you come back from the Black Jack clubhouse covered in bruises. I'm not leaving you to their mercy, because I know exactly what that means. You were so close to getting out this time. I'll keep you hidden until you find Jeff and get your passport."

Arianne checked the rearview mirror and her mouth went dry. "They're almost on top of us. I thought at first there were only two, but a third one just came out of nowhere."

One of the choppers accelerated and pulled up beside them. The driver motioned to the shoulder of the road, his face obscured by the glare of headlights.

"Oh damn." Dawn's shoulders sagged. "That's it. I gotta pull over, honey. They're gonna run me off the road."

"And scratch their paint?" Arianne barked a laugh. "Not likely. But pull over. This is my fight. I shouldn't have taken the ride."

Dawn pulled the Fiesta onto the gravel, and the bikers parked around them, one on each side and one in back. All too soon, a leather-clad fist pounded on Arianne's window.

"Bastard." Dawn lowered her window. "We hear you. But I'm telling you now, you touch my girl, and it'll be the last fucking thing you ever do."

"Dawn, no. I don't want you to get involved. I'm going out." Arianne reached for the handle, but before she had a firm grip, the door swung open, and she was yanked out of the car.

"Jagger." His name came out with her breath as she hit his rock-hard chest.

He stared down at her, his body vibrating as if he might fly apart any moment, eyes blazing with sensual fire. She could almost feel the blood pounding through his veins and when she placed a hand on his chest, his heart hammered against her palm.

"Get on my bike."

She stepped back, startled by his abrupt tone. "I'm going home with Dawn."

"You gonna put her in danger?" He stroked his hand down her hair and bowed his head briefly, as if relieved. But why would he be? He'd just found out she was Viper's daughter. More likely he and his men were going to imprison her again, this time for real.

"Leo doesn't know where she lives."

"And if you're wrong about that?" He dropped his hand to her shoulder. "He gonna treat you to more of the same if you go to the Jacks' clubhouse?"

"Actually, Viper's the one who beats on her at the clubhouse." Dawn stepped out of the vehicle with a can of pepper spray in her hand. "Leo just gets to shove her around outside."

"Dawn. No."

Dawn rounded the vehicle, holding the pepper spray aloft. "Y'all planning to kidnap my girl again? 'Cause I'm telling you now, it ain't gonna happen."

Almost immediately, two shadows emerged from the darkness: Cade, and the darkly sensual Zane, whom Arianne recognized from the clubhouse.

Dawn took a brazen step toward them and then faltered when she caught sight of Cade. "Got you covered, honey. Anyone tries anything, I'm taking them down. I don't care how hot they are. Nothing's hotter than pepper spray."

"Save your pepper spray for the Black Jacks," Arianne said. "I don't think these guys are here to hurt us." She gave Jagger a half-hearted smile. "Thanks for checking up on us, but we need to get going before Leo—"

With slow, deliberate steps, he backed her up to the vehicle, stopping only when her ass pressed tight against the cool metal. His gaze locked with hers, and he thudded one hand on the roof on either side of her head, caging her with his body. "Easy, sweetheart. I need you to listen." His breath was warm against her ear, his body heat beating away the chill of the night. She gritted her teeth and tried to push him away, but he had her well and truly pinned.

"I can listen from a distance." She looked around for Dawn and her handy canister of pepper spray, but her faithless friend was deep in conversation with Cade and Zane and unaware Arianne was having an inappropriate response to being trapped against her car by a sexy biker who smelled like heaven and looked like sin.

"Leo's not the only one looking for you," he said. "Axle blames you for his expulsion from the club, and wants his revenge. I can keep you safe." He moved closer, his chest brushing against her breasts, his thick thigh sliding between her legs.

Her breath left her in a rush. Part of her wanted nothing more than to accept his offer, climb on the back of his bike, wrap her arms around him and race away into the night. But her survival instinct was too strong, her independence too hard fought, and she'd seen firsthand what happened to people who defied Viper in order to help her.

"Thanks, but I can take care of myself. And to be honest, I'm not feeling very safe with you right now. In fact, I'd have to say this position is mildly threatening and—" Her voice caught. "—a little too dominant alpha male."

"Always with the lip." Although his words came out in a husky rumble, his eyes were warm, amused.

"Always with the bossiness." She wriggled against him, pleased when he edged away the tiniest bit.

"Only when I'm trying to protect you."

She caught the slight irritation in his tone, but she was too far gone to stop her mouth from running on. "So you've been trying to protect me every minute since we've met?" Liquid heat pooled between her thighs when she felt the hard press of his erection against her stomach. Damn. Her escape attempt had inflamed them both.

"It seems so."

"Have you forgotten I'm Viper's daughter? You should be running in the other direction, or tying me up and holding me for ransom." There. She'd said it. Might as well get it out in the open and discover his true intentions.

His face softened and his gaze slid to her mouth. "I haven't forgotten a single thing about you, Arianne. Not since the minute we met."

Enfolded in the semidarkness, his hot, hard body pressed against her, Arianne trembled. As if sensing her arousal, he bent his head and touched his mouth to her cheek, a whisper of lips so fleeting, she wondered if she'd imagined it.

"Come with me."

She ached to go with him. Wanted him in that moment almost as desperately as she wanted out of Conundrum. But how could she trust her father's worst enemy when he was bound always to do what was in the best interests of his club? And if that meant sacrificing her, he would. Regardless of his feelings.

"You'll probably torture me for his secrets."

"You have my word you'll be safe with me. No one will hurt you."

She threw out another objection, something he couldn't ignore. "You're putting your club at risk."

He tucked a strand of hair behind her ear. "No more than it is already. Viper reignited the feud, burned down my clubhouse, and killed one of my men. He knows I'll seek retribution. Giving sanctuary to Viper's daughter, helps me further that goal. And I'm duty-bound to protect you from Axle."

Duty. Not desire. But how could it be otherwise? They barely knew each other.

"Viper will go crazy looking for me." She tapped her right cheekbone. "The last time I defied him, and it was nothing compared to this, he left me with this scar."

Jagger stilled, his eyes burning into her cheek like laser beams. Then, as if she'd already agreed, he backed away, clasped her hand, and tugged her toward his bike. "We're going to the clubhouse."

"What about the safe house?" Zane's deep voice cut into the silence. "I told Wheels to go get it ready just before we left the bar."

Jagger squeezed Arianne's hand. "She's coming with us tonight. I'll take her to Sparky's tomorrow."

Arianne paused midstep and shook her hand free. "Jag—"

"Shhhh."

Her eyes narrowed. "Did you just *shhhh* me?"

He cupped her jaw with his warm palm and tilted her head back, forcing her to meet his gaze. "This is the part where I'm protecting you, so you'll have to put up with bossy." He ran his thumb lightly over her mouth. "And I'll put up with your lip because—"

"Because my lips are telling you I'm heading out of town as soon as I find my brother," she said, cutting him off. "My lips are also telling you I didn't agree to your plan. I'm better off at Dawn's place. Why risk the repercussions of protecting me when I'm about to leave?"

His gaze, hot and heavy, fell to her mouth and then he leaned down and brushed his lips over hers in the softest kiss. "Say yes, lips." The soft yet commanding murmur of his voice turned her legs to jelly.

Arianne's brain fuzzed. Whether from the warm touch of his palm on her cheek, the arousal his kiss sparked in her blood, or the overwhelming desire to feel safe, even if only for a night, she didn't know. But she wanted to go with him. Wanted it almost as much as she wanted to be free. And yet—

A growling roar in the distance drew Arianne's attention. But before she had even processed the fact that the faint lights were from motorcycles, Jagger, Cade, and Zane were already on the move.

"Leave the car." Cade gestured Dawn to his bike. "You'll

never outrun them. I'll take you home and send a coupla
prospects to pick up your vehicle when it's safe."

Dawn gazed Arianne a questioning look and Arianne
shrugged. Although she felt safe with Jagger, she didn't
know Cade and couldn't give her bestie the assurance she
sought. These men were bikers, after all.

But then, so was Dawn. Once.

With a light laugh, Dawn swung her leg over Cade's pillion seat. "Rock 'n' ride, baby. And if you hurt a hair on
my golden head, you'll be gettin' a face full of pepper spray.
I might be small, but I pack a punch."

Arianne took one last, lingering look at Dawn's car and
then turned to Jagger. Her heart pounded as the roar of the
motorcycles on the highway grew louder. Zane and Cade
started their engines, but still she couldn't move. Everyone she'd trusted in her life had let her down, and now the
one person who she should trust the least was asking her
to trust him the most.

Seemingly unconcerned by the approaching motorcycles, Jagger squeezed her hand. "You'll be safe with me,
Arianne."

For an instant she didn't move. Wanting. Hoping. Then
she swung her leg over the back of his bike. "If you're lying to me, Jagger, I'll put a knife through your heart."

"Sweetheart, you already did."

He wanted to fuck her.

Heart still thrumming from the adrenaline rush of the
pursuit, Jagger gripped his handlebars so hard, his fingers
almost went through his leather riding gloves. For a man
who rigidly controlled every aspect of his world, the un-
certainty involved in every encounter with Arianne both
inflamed and exhausted him. She couldn't be cajoled or en-
ticed, controlled or dominated. She did what she wanted

to do when she wanted to do it, and he had never been so damned aroused in his entire life.

Vexy. Vixen. He'd been wrong before. Her road name suited her to a T.

And yet, here she was. Tucked up against him as they raced through the night. Masculine pride suffused his body as if he had just single-handedly conquered an army. Her acceptance of his protection roused an almost primal sense of satisfaction in him, and a desire so fierce and sharp, it took his breath away.

Worthy.

He grunted his approval when she locked her arms around him in anticipation of a sharp curve, and not just because she fit so perfectly against him. She knew how to ride pillion. Hell, if he hadn't been so attuned to her body—the soft swell of her breasts pressed against his back, firm hips tucked against his ass, her sweet thighs parted around him—he would barely have known she was there.

As if that were a possibility.

He glanced quickly over his shoulder, catching her gaze to make sure she could handle the speed. He would have preferred her to wear a helmet for safety, but since Montana was one of the few states without a helmet law, he didn't carry one. Damn, she was beautiful. Her hair, tousled by the wind, framed the perfect oval of her face, and her eyes, green and liquid, sparkled with the thrill of the ride. Speed demon. Just like him. And yet when he saw the scar on her cheek, his body tensed. No wonder she found it hard to trust anyone.

She licked her plump lips, and he felt an almost overwhelming urge to pull over and savor her mouth, drink until he was drunk with her pleasure. But he'd only just saved himself from making that mistake at the roadside, pulling away before he had really sampled the sweet promise of those lips. He had no doubt, one taste of Arianne wouldn't be enough.

One taste.

One. Fucking. Taste.

Unable to stop himself, he turned onto a side road and drove until he found a secluded copse of trees. Then he killed the engine.

"Something wrong with your bike?"

Arianne slid off the seat. Her hair fanned over her shoulders in a silken wave, and Jagger's blood pulsed through his veins. Even in the thin light of the moon, he imagined he could see the flush on her cheeks, her lips plump and glistening, and the glow that came only with the exhilaration of speed.

Every muscle in his body tensed as she squatted down beside the bike, her head level with the part of his body that had led him here.

"I spent a lot of time with our road captain fixing bikes in the Jacks' shop, and after I left, I apprenticed as a mechanic at Liam's Garage." She looked up at him, green eyes sparkling under the light of the moon. "If you want to get off, I can take a look."

Hell, yeah, he wanted to get off. But as she stood, arms folded, waiting for him to dismount, instinct told him he'd made a mistake bringing her here. A full frontal assault would likely be met with an equally forceful rejection. If he had to put a finger on the quality that distinguished her from the women who frequented the clubhouse—old ladies excepted, of course—it was class. Ironic, given who her father was.

With a heavy sigh, he swung his leg over the seat and stepped onto the ground, leaves crunching under his boots. He would have to gain her trust for a true taste of those lush lips. She wasn't a woman for a quick fix, but a slow, sensuous seduction, and when he finally breached her walls, he knew it would be worth the wait.

"Turn it on." She gestured to the engine, and Jagger lifted an eyebrow. He strictly enforced the hierarchy in the club, and the concomitant levels of respect. And that meant no one told Jagger what to do.

Except, apparently, Viper's daughter.

But only in private. Her political savvy, both in the club-house and in the bar, had impressed him. She had an innate understanding of the nuances of biker culture. Although she had disagreed with him, she never directly challenged him in public. And when he'd reprimanded the Devil Dog, her reaction made it clear she'd understood the power play, and the fact he had claimed her for the night.

"We'll take it to Sparky. He's my road captain." Heart heavy with regret, Jagger took his seat and gestured for her to join him.

"You don't think I can fix your bike?"

"Pretty hard to do in the dark without tools." He patted the leather pillion seat behind him.

"Then why did you stop here?"

Jagger gritted his teeth. For the first time, he wished he were more adept at lying, but military families prided themselves on bringing up children steeped in honor, discipline, loyalty and honesty, and his family was military three generations back. Evasion, on the other hand, was part and parcel of being an outlaw. "On the bike, Arianne."

If he were a man with even an ounce less self-control, her amused smile would have been enough to have him twining that shimmering hair around his fist and hauling her to his lips for a sweet taste of her honey. And when she brushed a kiss over his cheek before settling on the seat behind him, he almost did.

"Well, now that our romantic rendezvous in the moonlight is over, let's get going." She settled herself behind him, wrapping her arms around his body. "I have a bike to fix." She pressed herself against his back and whispered her lips in his ear. "Or not."

His body reacted as if he'd been shot with adrenaline, his groin tightening, heart thudding in his chest, desire thickening his veins. To hell with the slow sensuous seduction. He wanted her. Now. And damned if he would wait another minute to have her after that invitation.

"Off the bike."

Arianne sighed as she slid to the ground. "Seriously, Jagger. This is getting . . ."

Her voice trailed off when he turned and lifted her, helping her straddle the seat in front him, her hips only inches away from his cock, which was rock hard and pressing painfully against his fly.

One taste. Just one taste.

Arianne tilted her head back, looking up at him through the curtain of her lashes, a smile playing across her lips as she cupped his jaw and stroked her thumb over his cheek. "Well . . . this promises to be more interesting than taking apart your engine in the dark."

Fuck. Could she be any more perfect? No screams or giggles. No dissembling or games. She wanted him, and she wasn't afraid to let him know it.

He tugged her hand away and pressed his lips against the sensitive underside of her wrist. *Control.* He needed control. His body thrummed with the need to take her, an overpowering primal urge like nothing he'd felt before. But if he gave in to instinct, he'd hurt her, and from what little he knew of her life, she'd suffered enough.

"Jagger?" Her voice caught, broke, and when he looked up, he saw the heat in her eyes.

Fucking irresistible.

Sliding one arm around her waist, he pulled her against

him and covered her mouth with his own. Soft. Sweet. Her lips parted and he swept his tongue inside, tasting, exploring, feeding the desire that even now threatened to overwhelm him. Arianne softened against him, her tongue tangling with his as she returned his kiss with a passion he wanted desperately to unleash.

But not here. Not now. The brothers would be waiting for them. But more than that, he wanted to savor her, strip off her clothes until she lay naked and trembling beneath him. His for the taking.

Just a taste.

Deepening the kiss, he cupped her breast and let the soft weight settle in his palm. He kneaded her soft flesh and she moaned, a soft guttural sound that made his cock throb.

"So fucking sexy." He broke away and feathered kisses along her jaw and down the slender column of her neck, delighted when her head dropped to the side to give him better access. She tasted of sunshine and flowers, perfumed with sex and sin.

"You ever fuck on your bike, Jagger?" The throaty rasp of her voice slid through his body like a silken ribbon, tying itself around his cock until he had to grit his teeth against the pain. Wary of the soft press of her hips against his thighs and the potential for a touch that might set him off, he cupped the back of her head with his hand, holding her still. Then he kissed and licked with abandon, as images of her naked and straddling his lap assailed his mind.

Get a fucking grip. He was goddamn MC president, not a horny teenager at a drive-through. And yet he couldn't remember ever being so hard or wanting a woman as much as he wanted Arianne right now.

"When I fuck you the first time, sweetheart," he murmured, nuzzling her neck, "we're gonna need a bed, 'cause I want to take it slow. So slow that by the time I slide my cock inside you, there won't be an inch of your body I haven't claimed. And when I make you come, you'll be so fucking wet and ready, you're gonna scream my name." He pulled away and fisted her hair, testing her response to his dominance. "I want to hear that scream, Arianne."

She groaned and her head fell back, exposing the delectable hollow at the base of her throat. Jagger kissed her lightly, enjoying the rapid flutter of her pulse against his lips. Aroused. Like him.

"Tease."

"Fact," he said, although he had serious doubts he'd be able to hold out long enough to do what he'd said.

"What about the second time?" She licked her lips, not submitting to his hold, but not fighting it either. *How far would she let him go?*

"The second time, you'll be on your knees and I'm gonna watch those sweet lips slide up and down my cock."

She slid her hands up his chest, twining them around his neck. "You've got a dirty mouth, Mr. President."

"Dirty mouth for a dirty girl."

Arianne laughed. "You think I'm a dirty girl?"

He traced his finger down her throat to the V of her shirt, then tugged the garment, exposing the crescent of her breasts. "You're here with me. Wantin' to fuck on my bike. Makes you a dirty girl."

She leaned up and nuzzled his neck. "I think you like dirty girls."

"The third time," he said, reluctant to admit to having any feelings for her beyond lust, "I'll give it to you the way you want it."

Arianne stilled. "Hard?"

"Very hard."

"Hot?"

"Scorching."

"Wild?"

His pulse kicked up a notch. *Jesus Christ*. He had to get things under control or he'd be ripping off her clothes and giving her "wild" over the back of his bike. "We gotta go." He gritted his teeth as he pulled away. "Boys will be wondering what happened to us, and with the Jacks and Axle on the road, they'll come looking."

"Too bad." She leaned against him, her cheek pressed against his chest. "I never fucked on a bike before."

He had no idea how he managed to start the engine after she switched back to the pillion seat, and when his bike roared to life and Arianne firmed her grip, he decided even a run through enemy fire would have been easier to endure. He shifted uncomfortably as they pulled out onto the road, self-adjustment out of the question. Served him right. Although when he contemplated the distance he would have to ride and then walk before he could hit a cold shower, the punishment seemed disproportionate to the crime.

As if sensing his discomfort, Arianne lowered her hands until they dangled below his belt. He glanced at his mirror, hoping for some telltale sign that would let him know if she was purposely torturing him or unaware of the situation, but she ducked her head behind his back, depriving him of even that small pleasure.

"C'mon, Jagger." Her voice rose above the wind. "Stop puttering around like an old man. Let's see what this baby's got."

Energized by her excitement, intoxicated by the feel of the bike between his thighs and the beautiful woman pressed against his back, the cool night air whistling through his hair, he flicked the throttle, and the bike leaped forward with a deep, throaty rumble that echoed into the night.

"Faster." Her eyes glittered with an inner light, and he stared at the rear view mirror as she leaned to the side and gave him a wink.

Christ, he had it bad. He'd never realized what he was looking for in a woman until he met Arianne, but she pressed all his buttons. Beautiful, confident, challenging, independent, and with enough cheek to make him laugh. A woman who wasn't afraid of who he was and wanted nothing from him. A woman who could tease him and walk away. A woman who shared his passions and understood the politics of biker culture and the tightrope he had to walk to maintain control of the club.

And yet their circumstances precluded any interaction beyond the immediate need to keep her safe. What had happened back there shouldn't have happened. For so many reasons. He couldn't endanger her life further by allowing her close to him. Nor could he put his club at risk. Not that it mattered, since she wasn't planning to stick around.

Maybe that was a good thing after all.

★ EIGHT ★

Old ladies, house mamas, sweet butts, hood rats,
and lays are allowed in the clubhouse
only if escorted. No loose chicks.

Arianne chewed her lip as she contemplated the king-size bed in front of her.

After their intense encounter, she'd expected to be dragged up to the bedroom for some hot biker sex, but by the time they reached the new clubhouse, Jagger's passion had cooled.

While Sinners partied around them, they'd spent an hour chatting about motorcycles in the clubhouse kitchen over warm beer and stale tacos as if they hadn't almost just torn off each other's clothes and had wild sex on his bike. And when the beer had run out, Jagger sent her upstairs with nothing more than, "I'll see you in the morning."

I'll see you in the morning. The old love 'em and leave 'em routine, except she hadn't had much lovin' at all. She couldn't decide whether he'd backed off because of her actions, something she'd said, or because he regretted what they'd done.

Which wasn't a hell of a lot, as far as she was concerned. She'd been with other men. But none of them had fired her blood or made her heart pound. And she couldn't imagine any of them hauling her onto a motorcycle and kissing her breathless. Jagger was a force of nature. Fierce. Unyielding. Utterly dominant. Her mouth watered at the thought of spending a night with him in bed.

The door opened behind her, and in that second she thought dreams could come true.

"Nowhere else to sleep." Jagger banged the door shut behind him. "Got a full house tonight."

Without waiting for her reply, Jagger stripped off his shirt, baring the broad, mouth-watering expanse of his chest, then climbed onto the bed. Arianne couldn't move, couldn't speak. He was simply the most magnificent man she had ever seen. She tried not to notice the way the muscles of his chest rippled as he settled himself on the bedspread, or how his abs tightened into stark relief when he raked a hand through his damp hair, sending a trickle of water down his neck. He must have just had a shower. She fought back a fierce desire to lick the water droplets away and willed him to take his perfect body out the door.

"You comin' to bed?" He lay back on the pillow, his arms folded behind his head, legs spread, taking up three quarters of the damn space. The quintessential alpha male.

"You mind telling me what's going on? The whole hot-and-cold thing is—"

"Done." He patted the bed beside him. "Shouldn't have happened. Won't happen again."

Her heart squeezed in her chest. Well, that was for the best. She was leaving Conundrum and she was pretty damn sure Jagger wouldn't be an easy one-night stand to forget.

"Fine." She considered crashing on the couch downstairs, or even on the floor, but he wasn't interested anymore, so why the hell not get a good night's sleep? She walked toward the bed, tugging down the hem of the T-shirt she'd appropriated from the dresser drawer. "At least I know you'll behave."

"When have I ever misbehaved?"

"Oh, I don't know. On the roadside? Possibly in those woods?"

"I was a perfect gentleman."

Arianne scoffed. "Perfect gentlemen don't stop their bikes in a copse of trees, pretending to have bike trouble, and then try to seduce a journeyman mechanic who knows a smooth running bike when she hears it."

"Who seduced whom?" He rolled to his side, propping his head up with his elbow, and twirled a strand of her hair around his finger. "I heard you say 'or not' after you kissed me."

Mimicking his position, her body only inches away from his, she placed a tentative hand on his chest, enjoying the ripple of powerful muscle beneath the pads of her fingers. "I was referring to fixing your bike. And I didn't kiss you. My lips were near your ear so you could hear me over the roar of your perfectly-tuned engine."

With a low growl, he released her hair and tucked it behind her shoulder, his fingers lingering on her skin. Arianne's body flamed in an instant. Caught by the dark intensity of his sensual gaze, she couldn't tear her eyes away.

"You kissed me." His hand slid to the back of her neck, his thumb tracing the line of her jaw, sending sizzles of white lightning through her veins. His deep gaze, his gentle touch, his body, hard against hers, electrified her senses, and desire gripped her so hard, her knees trembled.

"So arrogant." Bolder now, she caressed his chest, tracing the planes and angles of his pecs, and then ever so lightly she stroked a finger along his scar. But if he understood her silent question, he wasn't about to answer it, so she continued her downward journey, following the soft trail of hair to his belt. "You probably think all women want to kiss you."

"They do." He rasped his breaths, his body burning beneath her touch.

Intoxicated by the feel of taut skin over rock-hard muscle, his scent of leather and body wash, and the crisp autumn breeze, she tried to ignore the warning niggle at the back of her mind—the feeling that started when she'd first walked into the clubhouse, and everyone turned and stared. Whispers had followed her through the living room to the kitchen. Jagger must have taken her hostage. Why else would he bring the Black Jack back onto Sinner turf?

Although Jagger had given his word she wouldn't be harmed, she would be a fool to ignore the possibility he might succumb to the temptation to use her as a weapon against Viper, and more of a fool to forget that her goal was and always had been escaping Conundrum. Her energy should be directed at finding Jeff, not indulging her torrid fantasies with her father's greatest enemy. Even for one night.

Heart racing, she tried to pull away, only to have him draw her so close, she could feel his breath on her cheek.

"You like my arrogance," he whispered. "Or you wouldn't have kissed me."

"If it was a kiss—" She struggled to resist the fever of desire raging through her blood. "—and I'm not admitting it was, then it was a lapse in judgment brought on by your ill-conceived and transparent attempt to seduce me in the moonlight. And the fact you kissed me first."

Jagger threw back his head and laughed. "I'm a man, sweetheart. And I don't know many men who could resist a beautiful, sexy biker chick tucked up against them, her eyes glittering with excitement when my bike hit a speed that would make other women scream."

Her pulse leaped when he tightened his grip, sending an erotic shiver down her spine. God, when had she ever been so fiercely attracted to a man? So deeply aroused, she almost didn't care if he decided to hold her for ransom. "I don't scream."

His low guttural groan inflamed her, but not as much as his impassioned promise. "You would scream for me."

She almost came right then.

With a low groan, he pulled her against him, crushing her breasts against his chest as he threaded one hand through her hair. His lips were so close, full and sensuous. Maybe she should take that kiss, after all.

Without warning, her mind slid back to her first kiss, her first love. At fifteen years old, she'd fallen hard for the bad boy of her high school, an eighteen-year-old wannabe rock star named Slick. On a grassy field under the beauty of Fourth of July fireworks, when he'd leaned over and pressed his lips against hers, she discovered Slick wasn't a bad boy after all. He had a soft side, a tenderness he hid from the world, a misguided chivalry that had cost him his fingers and nearly his life courtesy of Leo's blade.

Arianne's blood chilled. This was wrong for so many reasons, not the least of which was the fact she was putting them both at risk. And for what? A night of passion? They had no possible future together, and she couldn't afford to get emotionally involved.

She pulled away, then slowly peeled his hand off her hip. "I can't do this. You were right when you said it shouldn't have happened and won't happen again." After slipping on her shoes, she headed for the door. Surely there was somewhere she would sleep downstairs. If not, she could crash on the couch and watch TV.

"Arianne."

She looked back when her name dropped softly from his lips. His face held neither censure nor derision. Disappointment, maybe. Curiosity, certainly. And possibly . . . understanding? "Once I lay down the law, you'll be as safe with the brothers as you are with me, but until that happens, it's better if you stay here and I go."

A sliver of guilt speared through her chest. "I don't want to kick you out of your room."

"And I never meant for things to go as far as they have." Seemingly unabashed, he pushed himself off the bed in one lithe, easy movement. "I promised you would be safe with me. I said you could trust me, but—"

Arianne's heart sank as he grabbed his shirt and tugged it on. For the price of a kiss, she could have spent the night in his arms. But the risk was simply too high.

"I couldn't resist," he continued. "You threaten my control like no one else."

"All other reasons aside, Viper would kill you," she said. "Without hesitation."

"You're afraid for me?" Incredulity flickered across his face.

"And me." She twisted her mother's ring around her finger. "You don't understand. He has no limits. There is nothing he won't do, no one who is untouchable—women, children, innocent citizens—"

"You?"

Her hand flew to her cheek, tracing the old scar, and then she wrapped her arms around herself. "Yes, me."

He tilted his head to the side, considering. "And yet you came here."

"You make me feel safe." Her voice quavered. "I've never felt safe before. Even when my mother was alive, we were never safe. But when I'm with you . . . I'm not constantly looking over my shoulder. It's an intoxicating feeling."

"You *are* safe." He closed the distance between them and wrapped his arms around her. "You'll always be safe with me."

Stunned that he would comfort and reassure her only moments after she had rejected him, awed by his strength, she accepted the gift of his understanding, leaning into his warmth with a shuddered sigh.

"After my mother died, the Jacks moved to a new clubhouse with a house attached to it. Our place had a separate entrance and separate yard, but invariably we would wind up at the clubhouse. Jeff and I watched out for each other, and I learned pretty fast how to take care of myself, but sometimes there's only so much a kid can do. Even now . . ."

Jagger's body tensed, his muscles quivering as if he were about to punch someone. "Never again."

Drawing back, she stroked a finger along his rigid jaw, soothing, connecting. "I appreciate the sentiment, but it's not your fight. And really, Jeff had it worse than me. He inherited our mother's genes, so he's thin and slight, sensitive, and artistically inclined. Not the rough-and-tumble son Viper wanted. Jeff was desperate for Viper's approval, but Viper never thought he was good enough. I think that's why Jeff turned to drugs. It's part of the reason I wanted to leave. I thought I could get him into rehab once we were away from Viper and Jeff could be the artist he's meant to be."

"Might not be that easy," Jagger warned. "We've had brothers hooked on speed, and they couldn't shake it, even when we threatened to kick them out of the club. Drugs change people, change their priorities. . . ."

Arianne felt a tug at her heart. Maybe she was talking too much, revealing too much. But the cozy intimacy of the bedroom, his warmth and understanding, and his fierce protective instinct had lowered her defenses. "I have to try. When he's not using, he's the kindest, sweetest, most caring person I know. He sat with me through flus and breakups; he helped me decorate my apartment; he was there every time I had to go to the hospital, and the pictures he draws . . . he has real talent. I worked and saved for two years to get fake Canadian passports so we could get away and start a new life in Canada. Jeff picked them up the day . . . of the fire, and we were supposed to leave that night."

"What happened?"

She looked away, not wanting to lie and yet not able to tell him the whole truth. "Viper caught him trying to sneak out. Sent him out on a job. Offered him something he wanted more than freedom—full-patch status, and Viper's approval." She skipped over the events at the clubhouse: Seeing Jeff loading weapons into the truck; the gun in his hand; her heart sinking with the knowledge she had finally lost him to Viper.

Jagger covered her hand with his own, trapping her palm against his warm cheek. "So, you're just going to give up your life in Conundrum?"

"I want a better life. A life where I don't live in fear. Where I'm not pulled out of bed in the middle of the night and forced to be a drug mule, or where I'm not chased down and beaten for disobeying the rules. I want a life where I'm not property. I'm going to be happy. And free. I'm going to find someone who cares whether I live or die; some-one Viper can't touch. I'll do what it takes to make that happen."

"So fierce." He brushed a kiss over her forehead. "So determined. I don't think I've ever met anyone with as much passion."

She blushed. "Desperation. Not passion."

"Beautiful."

A wave of longing swept over her, making her tremble. How could he be so wrong for her and yet so right? A threat and a savior. An enemy and a protector. She allowed her-self a brief moment to imagine what would have happened if she'd met him before . . . when the door wasn't stand-ing open . . . when she had no options. She imagined his warmth beside her in bed, his strength keeping her safe. And then she imagined succumbing to the desire that threatened to overwhelm her anytime he was near. Before she could stop herself, she leaned up and kissed him.

And then he had her in his arms, his mouth covering her own, his tongue searching, diving deep, his need drinking her dry.

A soft moan escaped her lips and she melted against him, her hands sliding over his broad chest and around his neck, pulling him down for more. God, he even *felt* safe, warm skin over rock-hard muscle, firm and unyielding. She threaded her fingers through his hair, soft and silky, just brushing the top of his cut. Then she licked her way up his neck, tasting the salt on his skin and feeling the pulse of his arousal against her lips.

"Arianne . . ." He pulled away, his chest heaving, body shaking as if he was fighting for control.

"Go," she said. Because if he didn't leave, she wouldn't be able to turn him away.

Within a heartbeat, he was gone.

He was already on edge when she came down the stairs the next morning and entered.

Lack of sleep, thwarted desire, and the imminent bombing of the Black Jacks' ice house had wound him up tight. But nothing had caused him more emotional disquiet than the memory of Arianne's soft, sweet body in his arms, her warm lips pressed against his own. He ached with wanting her, a longing so fierce, he'd had to force himself to walk away. He knew the moment she kissed him, that he had to have her. And once he had her, he would never let her go. He had almost laughed at the paradox. Keeping her meant endangering her, and after Christel, that was a risk he couldn't take.

She descended the staircase, thick, dark hair fanned out over her shoulders, every curve of her lush body hugged by her skin-tight jeans and even tighter T-shirt, the swell of her breasts visible above the low, scooped neck. Jagger hissed out a long low breath and every sense he had sharpened as he walked across the now partially furnished living room to greet her.

Wheels tore his attention away from the football game on television and wolf-whistled. Gunner, seated beside him on the worn, brown couch, cuffed him on the head. "She's a guest. Have some fucking respect."

"I thought she was a hostage."

"Guest. Hostage." Gunner grinned. "Same difference."

"Go easy on him." Sparky looked up from the table the executive board had used in their last church meeting. He had taken apart his Ruger MK III and was trying to beat Zane's time for reassembly. Zane leaned against the wall, arms crossed. He held the record for weapon reassembly in the club and from his bored expression, he clearly didn't think Sparky was a threat to his title.

"Coffee's in the kitchen." Jagger gestured Arianne to the door behind them. "I made bacon and eggs. They're in the pan on the stove."

"He cooks, too." Arianne lifted an eyebrow. "Is there no end to your talent?"

Jagger chuckled. "He does many things. And I have talents I have yet to reveal."

"But don't try to talk to him until he's had his first cup of coffee," Sparky said. "Unless you want to be chewed out for doing fucking-dick-all."

"Sparky. Language." Jagger scowled. "We have a guest."

Sparky threw up his hands in mock defeat. "For doing fucking nothing at all."

"Better."

Arianne smiled at their banter, then turned to Jagger. "Did you manage to save my bike?"

"It's at Sparky's shop. He'll take you there after breakfast. The safe house is in the apartment upstairs." He hoped she understood his meaning. Once she went to the safe house, she wouldn't be leaving until he'd dealt with Axle.

"How bad is it?"

"Fairing is pretty badly damaged," Sparky said, "but I didn't see any obvious mechanical problems. Course, I didn't give it a thorough check, but I could look at it—"

"I can do it." Her eyes lit up, and Jagger fought back the urge to knock Sparky around the room. Arianne should be looking at him like that. She should sparkle for him and no one else.

"I've got my journeyman certificate, and if the fairing needs to be replaced, I can ride it naked."

"Fuck. I want to see that." Wheels jumped to his feet. "Do you ride naked all the time?"

"Wheels." Jagger gritted his teeth against the mental picture of Arianne naked on her bike. Damn Wheels for putting the image in his head. "She's talking about riding without fairing. How about you go out and polish all the bikes so you learn something about them, and after you're done, you can draw a picture of your bike naked and label all the parts."

Wheels paled. "I didn't know—"

"Even Arianne knew what it meant," Zane admonished. "Now so do you. And after today, you'll never forget it."

"*Even* Arianne?" Her hands found her hips.

Zane shrugged, stepping away from the wall. "You're a girl."

"I'm not a girl. I'm a woman. And you think women don't know anything about motorcycles?"

"Generally, no." He shot Jagger a puzzled look. "If you're telling the truth, you're an exception."

She walked toward him and glared. "What else? I'll bet you think women are weak and in need of protection."

Seemingly oblivious to Sparky's violent head shaking, Zane continued. "Generally, yes. Women need protecting. You needed protecting last night."

Gunner gave a loud, indiscreet cough that sounded suspiciously like "shut the fuck up" or maybe it was "run away." Jill and Tanya, two new sweet butts, emerged from the kitchen, drawn by the raised voices. Jagger vaguely recalled seeing them at the party last night. They must have spent the night with two of the brothers. No wonder there hadn't been a spare room to crash.

"I needed protecting?" Arianne's voice rose in pitch, and Jagger folded his arms, amused. The boys had never encountered a woman in the clubhouse who stood up to them as an equal. Not only that, she wasn't the least bit intimidated or afraid, although all three men stood at least five inches taller than her. She may have had a tough life with Viper, but it had given her the kind of backbone he wished he could see in the prospects that came knocking at the door. Wheels included.

"I didn't need protecting last night," she said. "I had successfully evaded Leo, and Dawn and I were headed to her place. I also had a .45 in my jacket, and this." She bent down and pulled up her jeans, revealing a holstered Lady-Smith .38.

"Christ." Gunner licked his lips. "She rides, she fixes bikes, she's hot, and she's packing. She's every biker's wet dream."

"She's also Viper's fucking daughter." Zane's lips curled in disgust, giving Jagger a first insight into his odd behavior. "What do you think Daddy Dearest would do if he caught someone playing hide the salami with his little princess? I'm guessing he'd slice off the guy's balls. Maybe make a sandwich for lunch."

"Ouch." Sparky grimaced. "Don't hold back there, Zane. Lay it on the line."

Zane folded his arms and stared at Arianne. "Just sayin' . . . girls who carry usually do it just for show. Or did your daddy teach you something other than trying to wiggle your way into a man's bed?"

Jagger was across the room before he even realized he had moved, momentum carrying him forward until he had Zane by the collar. With a growl, he slammed Zane back against the wall. "You are so fucking out of line, I don't even know where to begin."

"Well, I'll tell you where's it's gonna end," Zane muttered, his voice so low only Jagger could hear. "With you bleeding in a fucking ditch. And I won't stand around and watch it happen. She's the enemy. Plain and simple. We can't—"

Jagger cut him off with a glare and the word, "Don't."

They stared at each other, eyes locked, and then Zane looked away. "Whatever happens, you know I've got your back. But it would be better if I didn't have to be there."

Christ. He couldn't fucking hit him now. But shoving Zane against the wall wasn't enough punishment for his disrespect. Everyone was watching, waiting to see what Jagger would do, but he didn't want to strain their friendship. He'd never hit Zane before, and he had no idea how his friend would react.

"Do I get a chance to defend my honor?" Arianne placed a cool hand on his arm.

Her touch calmed him, grounded him. His mind cleared and he released Zane and rasped in a breath.

"What are you talking about?"

Arianne stepped closer to him, angling her body between him and Zane. "Viper didn't care much for me, but he taught me the three things he thought were most important in a biker's life: how to fix a bike, how to shoot pool and how to fire a gun. And when Viper teaches a lesson, you don't forget it. Zane accused me of packing for show. I'd like the chance to prove him wrong. Could be he apologizes and this all goes away."

Words failed him. In a few short minutes, she had neatly defused the tension, saved a friendship, and helped him save face. Did Viper realize what an incredible asset he'd lost when he alienated his daughter?

With a curt grunt of assent, he turned to Zane. "Your call."

"Let's see what she's got."

Jill and Tanya swooped in on Arianne as they traipsed outside. Women were few and far between at the club, and they tended to stick together. He rounded the corner and caught up to Zane as he mused over what the females might be talking about. Arianne didn't seem the type who would be into the usual girly stuff.

Zane looked over at Arianne and twisted his lips to the side. "Smart."

"Very."

"Don't know if we would have survived that punch," Zane said quietly.

Jagger's throat constricted. "I would have found another way."

"You always do, but this time you had help."

They walked through the overgrown grass, skirting around bushes badly in need of pruning, until they reached the vast expanse of the back lawn. Jagger filled his lungs with fresh air and exhaled his tension. He only ever felt relaxed outdoors, and at this property there was more than enough space for his rapidly expanding club.

"Got word back from our men on the street early this morning," Zane said. "Rumors are goin' around that we snatched Viper's daughter in retaliation for the fire. It's given us some serious street cred. We might be able to secure a coupla contracts we couldn't get before, make some of the gangs think twice before messing with us."

Jagger bristled. "She's not a prisoner this time."

"No one knows that but us."

They stopped in the middle of the lawn and Zane looked over at Wheels, dutifully polishing the bikes at the side of the house. "Might as well have some fun with this."

"You wouldn't."

"I'm in that kind of mood." Zane waved at Wheels and yelled. "Prospect. Under that tree. Now."

Ever the obedient prospect, Wheels jumped up and ran toward the large fir tree at the edge of the forest, about twenty yards away.

"You got a nasty streak, Zane." Jagger fought back a smile as he glanced over at the shivering prospect. "Think he'll piss himself?"

"Nah. I'm beginning to think a lot of his bumbling around is an act. When the chips are down, he outperforms even some of the senior patch. He's got balls; he just doesn't want anyone to know."

"What do you want me to do?" Wheels' quavering voice betrayed his anxiety.

Zane raised his weapon and pointed it at the trembling prospect. "Stay still. Arianne and I are having a shoot-out, and we need a target."

Jill and Tanya shrieked, but Arianne only rolled her eyes. Jagger chuckled. Although he could never fully participate in the high jinks, he enjoyed prospect hazing as much as his men did.

Zane grabbed a stick and threw it on the ground as a marker. Arianne stepped behind it and made a show of positioning her weapon. Jagger almost felt sorry for Wheels, but the kid would be asked to do worse things than act as a living target during his prospect year. And he should know by now that Jagger wouldn't let anyone hurt him.

"Smile, Wheels." Arianne pointed her gun at Wheels, and he squeezed his eyes shut and let out a thin whine.

"Wait." Arianne dropped her gun. "He's too white. The glare is throwing me off. You want to draw some circles on his face, or should we use a target instead?"

Everyone laughed. Gunner led a shaken Wheels away, and Arianne and Zane took turns shooting a makeshift target Sparky quickly fashioned from an old dartboard. Jagger leaned against a tree, entranced by Arianne and her ability to shoot. Most of the old ladies in the club knew how to use a gun, but none could handle a weapon with such ease, or skill. She radiated confidence and calm as she squeezed the trigger again and again, hitting the target every time.

Jagger wondered if he could make the shower any colder than it had been this morning. And when she walked over to him, all sexy confidence and cheeky smiles after Zane had offered a stilted apology, he wondered if a man could die from being too hard.

"Good shooting." He drew her around the west corner of the house, out of sight of his brothers, desperate to touch her but painfully aware that a show of affection would be inappropriate, especially if he wanted to foster the rumors she was there against her will.

"I held back. Didn't want to show Zane up." She looked up at him from beneath her lashes, her eyes glittering with satisfaction. Before he could stop himself, he cupped her jaw and traced the curve of her plump lips with his thumb. "Never seen you smile like this."

Her smile broadened and his heart surged in response.

"Bikers are a discriminatory bunch," she said. "Nothing

I like better than to show them how wrong they are when it comes to their attitudes about women."

His fingers tightened, the pressure forcing her to open her mouth, and he eased his thumb inside, stroking over the softness of her tongue.

Dominant, yes. Possessive, definitely. And yet he wasn't trying to take away from what she'd accomplished. Far from it. Her power drew him in, intoxicated him; he wanted it as he wanted her.

Arianne met his gaze, her green eyes heated, intense. She licked his thumb, working it with long strokes of her little pink tongue until all his blood had rushed to his groin and he was so hard, he had to grit his teeth against the pain.

And then she turned her head, loosening his grip, and pulled away.

"I'd better get going. I've got a bike to fix so I can go looking for Jeff and get to work this evening."

His mind still fuzzed with lust, it took him a moment to process her words. "You won't be going to work. You'll stay in the safe house until we've dealt with Axle."

"I thought I was a guest this time, not a prisoner." She wet her lips, and he felt every stroke of her tongue in his groin.

"And I've just shown you I can look after myself. No one will catch me on my bike, and I'll be safe at work with Banks and the bouncers."

Tension curled in the space between them, replacing their heat with fire. He was acutely aware of the steady thud of his heart, the rustle of leaves, and the rapid rise and fall of his chest, but even more aware of the fury in her emerald-green eyes. "I promised to protect you. I'm a man of my word. Means I'll do what it takes to fulfill that promise."

Arianne glared and Jagger silently willed her not to

challenge him further, for the sole reason that he didn't know what he would do. Her willingness to stand up to him, without hesitation or fear, was even more an aphrodisiac than watching her shoot.

"What if I don't want your protection anymore?"

Then she would leave. He might never see her again. She could fall prey to Axle or that piece-of-shit Leo. Get hurt. Maybe killed. *Unacceptable.*

"You made that choice on the side of the road last night," he said. "You accepted my protection, and you will have it on my terms until you're no longer in danger."

Her eyes flashed with annoyance. "So I *am* a prisoner."

"You're mine," he said simply. "Until I let you go."

He expected some kind of outburst; a sarcastic comment, or even Arianne walking away. Instead, she snaked her arms around his neck, pulled him close, and ground her hip into the erection still straining against his fly.

"Let me go, Jagger," she whispered.

"No."

"I'll take a guard with me." She nuzzled his neck, her breasts pressing against his chest, and his body flamed, tightened in response. He could feel his control slipping, giving way to a fierce, primal urge to rip off her clothes and take her against the cold brick wall—to fully possess the woman who challenged him on every level and whom he wanted with every cell in his body. He wanted to hear her scream in passion; he wanted his name on her lips when she lost control; he wanted her body under his when he plunged his cock deep inside her and claimed her as his own.

What if I don't want your protection anymore? What if she walked away?

"Four."

She slid her tongue along the seam of his lips, then kissed him when he opened his mouth, her lips soft and sweet, tasting faintly of mint. "Two. And I'll text you every hour."

He kissed her hard, bruising her lips, sharing the pain of his desire. "Every half hour."

"And when I see you again?" She rubbed up against him, a cat in heat, and he groaned, wondering how the hell he would make it through the day with a hard-on that just wouldn't quit.

"Your sweet body just made me a promise. And I intend to collect."

★ NINE ★

*All debts owing to the club will be secured by collateral
and can be discharged only by the president.*

Out of the frying pan . . .

Arianne's lips pursed with suppressed fury as Sparky
pulled his bike into the parking lot of a small warehouse
at the edge of Conundrum's commercial district, still seeth-
ing over Jagger's words: *You're mine. Until I let you go.*

Who did he think he was? Only one person spoke to her
like that—claimed her like a piece of property—and only
because she was powerless to stop him. In many ways,
Jagger and Viper were very much alike.

Too much alike.

Powerful and in control, dominant and unyielding, Viper
wanted nothing more than her complete and utter obedience. She had never been able to get under his skin. But
Jagger . . . she'd rattled him with a kiss. Maybe she should
rattle him some more. She'd never find Jeff if she had Tank
and Wheels flanking her wherever she went. Her brother
was clearly in hiding, afraid to face the consequences for
the botched raid on the Sinner weapons shed. And likely
he'd stay hidden until he could salvage the situation by producing the missing weapons before Viper found him.

Weapons that were now locked in the shed behind Sparky's shop, or so she'd overheard.

She followed Sparky across the gravel and waited as he unlocked the door.

"Here she is." He stepped to the side to let Arianne enter.

After her eyes adjusted to the light, she inhaled the familiar scents of grease and diesel, then looked over a shining sea of chrome, and smiled. "Nice shop."

"Yeah, it's like a second home." Sparky led her through a row of bikes while Wheels made himself comfortable on a worn couch in the corner. Tank stood guard at the door.

"Got something over here I think you'll appreciate." Sparky whipped a drop cloth off a bike in the corner and grinned.

Arianne gasped. "That's not—"

"My secret project. A Ducati 1098S. One of the fastest motorcycles in the world and manufactured only from 2007 to 2009. This one crashed in the Superbike World Championship in 2008, and the owner wanted to offload it for cheap. Didn't take long to replace and fix up the fairing, but the engine is still running rough. It's supposed to be able to do zero to sixty miles per hour in under three seconds and hit a top speed of a hundred eighty miles per hour, but I haven't been able to get it anywhere near that."

Arianne crouched beside the bike. "They have a few known problems like stalling on idle and leaking gaskets. And did you check the gas tank? The plastic one leaked ethanol, and the replacement is covered under warranty."

Sparky grinned. "Feel free to tinker with it if you want a break from your Ninja. I'll take it up to the work bay."

Sparky's shop was clearly the hub for club-related gossip, and over the course of the afternoon, at least a dozen bikers came in ostensibly to chat about mechanical problems, but for the most part to catch up on what was going on. No one seemed to notice Arianne in her coveralls, fixing up her Ninja in the corner.

So she heard about the two sweet butts Bandit took up to his room and how disappointed he was to find out they weren't sisters after all. And that Axle had been getting it on with Gunner's old lady before he'd been kicked out of the club. And how Cole's funeral had been especially heartbreaking because, save for the brothers, he had no one to mourn his death.

Tank reported that Dex, the reclusive club torturer, had sneaked some weed into a party the other night but was caught by Zane. No one had seen Dex since. Did anyone try the weed? T-Rex had, and it was good-quality stuff. He thought Zane had kept it to smoke in his room.

A heated discussion ensued about whether Zane was the kind of guy to smoke weed. They concluded that a guy as reserved as Zane wouldn't smoke weed, and how much did anyone really know about him aside from the fact he was Jagger's best friend? Bandit and Wheels didn't trust him. T-Rex wondered what it would be like to be Jagger's best friend and whether it would be fun. Bandit didn't think so. After all, Jagger rarely smiled or relaxed. Show of hands, anyone who had ever seen Jagger drunk or stoned. No hands went up. What about getting it on with the sweet butts during a party? Still no hands. Dancing or kicking back? Nope. Definitely not fun to be his friend.

Arianne dipped her head to hide her smile. She couldn't imagine Jagger losing control, either through drugs or alcohol or even letting loose at a party. She'd never met anyone as self-contained. What would Jagger think if he knew they were gossiping about him like this? He'd probably think it was a good thing no one thought he'd be a fun friend. Leadership was lonely, as Viper had told her on numerous occasions. A leader couldn't afford to be a friend, because someone close enough to know your mind was also close enough to stab you in the heart. Deep concepts for a ten-year-old girl to hear, but even then she'd gotten the message.

Getting serious now, Tank needed some advice. He'd met a girl. Not his usual type: college grad, rich parents, fancy clothes. But he thought she was sweet. Did she want him because he was a badass dangerous biker or did she just want him for his body? Sparky threw an empty soda can at his head and told him he was the least dangerous biker he'd ever met, and had the personality of a wet fish, so she must have been after his chunky, unwashed body. Wheels suggested he get a girl's advice. Why not ask Arianne?

Suddenly under scrutiny, Arianne froze, a piece of broken fairing in her hand. "What do you want to know?"

Tank stroked his chin. "What do women go for: body, brains, or biker?"

Arianne glared at Wheels for dragging her into the discussion and then said, "Confidence."

Confidence? No one understood. Arianne was asked to come out from behind the bike and explain herself. After several failed attempts, she lost her patience. She told them she'd meant women always checked out the package. The bigger, the better. Jill, who had come on Tank's bike, agreed. Much package checking and comparison ensued. Bandit told Tank he might as well forget about ever getting laid for the rest of his life. Tank took offense and punched Bandit in the nose. Sparky pointed to the door and told them to take it outside. His eyes widened. Everyone turned around.

Arianne's heart skipped a beat when she saw Jagger in the doorway, leaning against the doorjamb as if he'd been there for a long time.

He surveyed the room, his gaze stopping at each of the miscreants now terrified into silence. "I thought we had a clubhouse to rebuild, businesses to run, and contracts to fulfill."

The room sobered in an instant.

"Like I said"—Bandit brushed past Arianne on his way out—"no fun."

Over the next few days, Arianne worked on her Ninja and helped Sparky with the repairs to the members' bikes. She was drawn into more than one relationship discussion with the Sinners and quickly got to know them. Right away, she'd recognized that T-Rex, the club's senior prospect, was definitely full-patch material, but she still wasn't sure about Wheels. Although he was always pleasant enough, he was very careful when he spoke and self-aware to the point where she wondered if he was hiding something.

On her fourth day at the safe house, her phone buzzed in her pocket. Assuming it was Dawn, who had been calling to check up on her at least five times a day, she excused herself to go to the washroom and then took the call after she closed the door.

"Ari. You okay? I heard the Sinners got you."

She sucked in a sharp breath at the sound of Jeff's voice, and then choked on the cloying fetid scent. The first time she'd asked about the ladies' room, Sparky had laughed and pointed to the dingy door at the end of the hall. Apparently ladies rarely visited the shop, so no point wasting space for a separate bathroom. And he'd given her fair warning; it was only ever cleaned when the sweet butts came to visit, which was almost never.

Still, she was relieved to know Jeff was okay. She'd called in every favor and asked every friend she knew to check out Jeff's regular haunts for her. Maybe someone had flushed him out.

"No. It's okay. I'm good." She explained about Axle and how Jagger felt duty-bound to keep her safe until he had hunted Axle down.

"So you can leave?"

She gritted her teeth. Jagger's edict that she was not allowed to leave the safe house without guards still grated on her, but except for that one afternoon when he stopped by to make sure she'd made it to the shop, she hadn't seen him. She spent her days in the shop and her nights in the small one-bedroom apartment upstairs. Basic, functional, and decorated in stark white and blue, it was cold and lonely, and she often found herself back downstairs chatting with the bikers Jagger had posted as guards for the night.

"Not alone."

"Fuck." Jeff grunted, and she heard the thud of his fist against the wall. Oh God. Was he high? He was violent only when he was high or tweaking on crank.

"I need the rest of those guns, Ari. If I show up at the Black Jacks clubhouse without them, Viper's gonna kill me. And it's all your fault. If you hadn't shown up that night, I would have had time to take them all."

Arianne bristled. "If you'd just come with me when I showed up, you wouldn't need the guns. We'd be in Canada starting a new life, where we wouldn't be worried about Viper. You could have gone to rehab. It's what we always wanted, and—"

"It's what *you* always wanted." He cut her off abruptly. "And I went with you every time, not because I really wanted to leave, but because I love you and I wanted to keep you safe. I didn't want you going to a strange city or country alone. But Viper finally offered me what I always wanted the night of the fire. He said he'd patch me into the Jacks if I did a good job. I could have made him proud. I was going to bring you the passport when I was done. I thought you'd understand, but you messed it up."

A sudden coldness hit at her core. But really, was she surprised? If she was honest with herself, she'd sensed his lack of commitment from the start, but she just couldn't bring herself to believe he wanted to stay with Viper. Endure Viper's abuse. Join the biker gang that had been the cause of such heartache in their lives.

"I know you want the passport," he said. "And I need those guns. So here's the deal: You find out where they are and how to get in. Provide a distraction. I'll be in and out before those damn Sinners know what hit them. You do that, I'll leave the passport with Dawn and you can go have your happy Canadian life. I'm sorry I can't go with you, but I'll be a Black Jack, Ari. A full-patch. I'll be the son Viper always wanted."

Arianne sagged against the door of the filthy bathroom. How could she betray the Sinners after all Jagger had done for her? "Don't ask me to do this."

"Please help me," he pleaded. "You know what Viper will do to me if I show up without the weapons. I just want to make him proud. It's all I ever wanted, and he finally gave me a chance. Once I have that patch, I know I'll be able to kick the drugs because I'll know I'm not a failure."

"The patch won't solve the problem." Arianne scrubbed her free hand over her face. "You need rehab, therapy, someone who can figure out why you started in the first place and why you can't quit. And you need to get away from Viper. You're an artist, not a biker."

Jeff huffed his annoyance. "I need guns, and if you aren't going to help me take them from the Sinners, then you'll need to go see Bunny. He works out of his pool hall at the corner of Forty-seventh and Main. He's a man who can get things, but he charges a premium and he only deals in person. I can't break cover to meet him, 'cause Viper's got spies everywhere."

"What about payment?" Jeff had no job. No source of income other than what he earned working for the Jacks. How the hell would he finance the purchase?

"I'll come up with something."

"Fine," she said in a resigned monotone. "I'll see what I can do." *Meet with Bunny or steal from Jagger?* Her only other option was to work and save for a year to buy another passport. But a year was a long time to wait when she wanted to start her new life now. Sure, she could cross the border as a tourist, but eventually the immigration authorities would find her and kick her out. She wanted everything legit and the passport would allow her to live and work without fear of having her new life ripped away.

"Whatever you do, make sure it's fast." Jeff's voice rose in warning. "Viper's coming for me—and if he finds me, it won't be pretty."

After ending the call, Arianne sank to the floor, heedless of the filth around her, and buried her head in her arms. For a long time, she just stared at the dusty grey tiles. Her insides churned, her head throbbed, and a black hole had opened in the center of her chest. She wanted to call Dawn, but it was three o'clock and she knew her bestie never answered her phone between three and four in the afternoon and eight and nine in the morning. Her "sacred hours," as she called them.

What the hell was she going to do?

Bang.

The door bowed with the force of a blow, and her brain finally registered that the thumps and shouting outside had been going on for a while. Before she could get up, the door splintered and crashed to the ground.

"What's going on?" Jagger stood in the doorway, the scowl on his face softening into concern when he met her gaze. Sparky, Tank, and Wheels stood behind him. She tried to imagine how she looked, curled up in the corner of a filthy bathroom in her coveralls, tears and grease streaking her face.

"Nothing." Thoughts scrambling, she pushed herself to

standing. One thing she'd learned from Viper was never to show her weakness, and right now, it was all hanging out. "I'm good. Just taking a break." She brushed past him and stepped into the hallway, but before she could walk away, he grabbed her shoulder and waved the brothers away.

"I'll ask again. What's going on?"

"And I'll say again," she said. "Nothing. Now, if you'll excuse me, I have a bike to fix."

He wiped a tear off her cheek with his thumb. "This isn't nothing. I heard you talking. Who was on the phone?"

"Why the fuck do you care?" She snapped at him, mindful of keeping her voice low, but needing an outlet for her frustration. "I haven't seen you for four days. No one will tell me what's going on, whether you found Axle, or how long you expect me to stay here. I have a life to get on with. I have a job. Banks has been understanding, but—"

He cut her off with a kiss, soft and sweet. The tears she'd been holding back leaked from her eyes and she pulled away. "Don't."

But he didn't listen. Instead he wrapped his arms around her and kissed her again, this time starting with the tears.

"Jagger." And then she was kissing him back with four days' worth of longing, and half an hour of heartbreak, tasting the salt on his skin and the coffee on his lips, soaking in the heat of his strong body, wishing she could drown in him until all the pain went away.

"Been thinking about you every minute of every day since I dropped you off." He backed her up to the wall, leaning his forearms on either side of her head. "I just spent the afternoon beating the crap outta one of Axle's men, and I couldn't get you out of my mind."

"That's sweet in a twisted, outlaw-biker kinda way." She slid her hands over his broad chest, placing them on his shoulders. "Did you catch Axle?"

"No, but we know where he is."

She leaned up to nuzzle his neck, inhaling the sharp tang of his cologne and the earthy scent of leather. Always leather. "Shouldn't you be out there, chasing after him?"

Jagger growled, the sound vibrating through her body. "No. I should be here, stripping off your clothes and running my hands over your body, worshipping you with my mouth, and fucking you till you scream." He curled his upper lip, baring his teeth. "But we got a bigger problem than Axle, which is why I came. Viper knows you're here."

A wave of dizziness struck her and her legs trembled. *Of course he knew.* No matter where she went or what she did, he knew. It was why she'd never been able to run away. Somehow he always found out where she was going before she even arrived.

She pushed Jagger away and headed out into the shop. "My bike isn't looking pretty, but I think it's mechanically sound. I'd better get going." Her phone buzzed in her jeans pocket, and she reached for the zipper on her coveralls just as Jagger held up his hand.

"He's offered a trade to get you back."

Shock fuzzed her brain. Viper didn't trade or negotiate or even ask. He took. "What did he offer you?"

Jagger stiffened, and for the first time, she noticed the determined set of his mouth and the creases in his forehead. Wary, she bit her lip and took a step back. Her phone buzzed again.

"He offered me the guy who burned down the clubhouse and killed Cole."

Arianne grabbed the handlebar of the nearest bike to steady herself. *Jeff?* Had Viper found him? She immediately dismissed the idea that Viper would offer him up. For all that Jeff was a disappointment to Viper, he was still Viper's son. His possession. His property. No way would Viper hand him over to the Sinners. Which meant it was a trap.

"You okay?" Jagger took a step toward her, but Arianne waved him away.

"I'm fine. Just . . . surprised he found me so fast. Or, maybe not." Part of her wanted to warn him, and yet, how could she betray the Jacks or give Jeff up? Although she had turned her back on the club, the biker ethos stayed with her—duty, honor and loyalty. And fear. Always, the fear. "What are you going to do?"

Jagger scraped his hand through his hair. "I have a duty to find Cole's killer and the arsonist and obtain justice for the club."

"You're handing me over?"

"I didn't say I was handing you over." He scowled, deepening his tone. "I made a promise to keep you safe, and protect you. I'll find a way to meet both obligations."

"Seriously?" Arianne couldn't hide the bitterness in her voice. "There is no way to get what you want without handing me over. I know how it works: Club first, club last, club always. You're stuck, Jagger, and there's no way I'm offering myself up like a lamb for slaughter. I just need to stay off his radar for a few more days, take care of a little business, then I'm gone." She unzipped her coveralls and shrugged them off, then walked over to her bike. She hadn't had time to test out the engine on the road, but anything was better than staying here.

"Arianne . . ."

As she made one last quick check of her bike, she marveled at Viper's genius. No doubt whomever he handed over would be so badly beaten, he wouldn't be able to tell the Sinners they had the wrong man, and whoever he was, Viper wanted rid of him. So he saved himself the time and energy of killing the poor soul while forcing Jagger to give her up because he would know Jagger would choose the club over anything else.

"I know the biker culture, probably better than you." She

ran her hand over the recently repaired fairing. "But I also know something else: Unless you're prepared to tie me up and hand me over to him, I have a choice. And if I didn't believe that, I'd still be at home, being beaten by Viper and molested by the Jacks because that is the lot of women in the club."

"Not here," Jagger began, but Arianne held up a hand to stop him as the words poured out of her.

"When I was sixteen, I made a choice. I wanted safety. I wanted happiness. I wanted freedom. I wanted to give my body, not have it taken. So I put a gun to my head and told Viper if he didn't agree to let me leave, I'd kill myself. And you know what? He let me go because he knew I would do it. I left with only the clothes on my back and got a room in a house with an old lady who waived the rent in exchange for the company and some chores."

"Jesus Christ. I'm gonna fucking kill him." Jagger took a step toward her, but stopped when she backed away. "We're not Jacks, Arianne. Yes, the club is first, but that doesn't mean there isn't another solution."

Instinct screamed at her to run. Jagger was just throwing words around. In the end, his choice was no choice at all. Her phone buzzed yet again, and she pulled it out of her pocket, hoping it was Jeff. But the moment she looked at the text from Viper, she knew she'd been trumped.

He'd sent her a picture. A man. So badly beaten, she couldn't make out a single distinguishing feature on his face. And a message. *Time to come home.*

Sweat beaded on her forehead and a tremor coursed through her body. He knew her that well. If she didn't go back, he'd kill the patsy he'd picked up to take Jeff's place. Her shoulders slumped in defeat. "Guess I'll make it easy for you," she said. "I'll go."

Jagger's brow wrinkled. "What was that message?"

"Family business."

"Family business mean you're gonna get hurt?"

She turned away. "Why do you care? You were going to hand me over even if I didn't want to go."

Her heart sank when he didn't refute her words. She'd been wrong about Jagger. He wasn't *like* Viper. He was Viper. All over again.

★ TEN ★

★ TEN ★

The club will defend its own.

He couldn't keep his eyes on the damn road.

Instead, all he could see was Arianne's sweet ass as she bent low over her Ninja, burning up the road like she was desperate to get to the meet. Damn, that woman could ride. No fear. No hesitation. If she really wanted to get away, she could, and he almost wished she would just break and run. He still hadn't thought of a way to uphold the honor of the club and protect her at the same time. And although she'd agreed to the exchange, there was no damn way he was letting her go.

Lost in thought, torn between duty and desire and the unfamiliarity of remorse, Jagger almost missed the turn-off to the vacant lot in the run-down north end of town.

He signaled to the brothers behind him to form a perimeter in case of trouble, and sent the second wave ahead of them to form a smaller circle around the meet site. Sparky was already in the parking lot with the cage, ready to take back the civilian Viper thought to pawn off on him. He'd already sniffed out the trap. Hell, he would have done exactly the same thing. No biker president would voluntarily give up one of his own men, and especially not for a woman. "Club first" meant brothers first.

Arianne slowed for directions and he motioned her toward the parking lot. She hadn't spoken to him since they left the shop. Did she think he would have handed her over if she hadn't volunteered to go? Despite his decision to become an outlaw, he was a man of honor. He'd said he would protect her, and he would. But he still had to put the club first. An impossible dilemma.

He pulled up beside Arianne and gave her the details of the meet. Three men to a side, unarmed, one hostage each. He'd laughed at Viper's terms. As if either of them would send in a single unarmed man or show up without as many brothers as they could round up on short notice.

"He won't be there." Arianne combed her fingers through her hair. "He'll send Leo or Bear, his sergeant-at-arms. He never shows at things like this."

Jagger frowned. "You're his daughter."

"I'm a woman." She didn't need to explain. Misogyny was pervasive in the outlaw MCs, with women usually ranking lower than bikes, clubhouses, and sometimes pets.

But damnit, he didn't need a reminder. Didn't want to think about her soft curves beneath his hands, the brush of her lips, her sweet 'n' sassy mouth. His protective instincts were already stretched to breaking, and it was everything he could do not to bundle her up and hide her away where no one would hurt her ever again.

Damn. Damn. Damn. This was exactly why he preferred simple hookups to serious relationships. This is what he feared; the real reason he had stayed away from the safe house for four long days, although he ached every night to hold Arianne in his arms. He'd put her in danger, just as he'd put Christel in danger. And like Christel, Arianne would pay the price. He should have just let her go. But instead, he went on instinct. And instinct was telling him to keep her close.

With the perimeter established, Jagger signaled to Zane

and Gunner to cover his back as he walked with Arianne
through the garbage-strewn grass. A soft breeze ruffled the
tendrils of Arianne's hair, and he had to clench his fist
against the urge to run his fingers through those silky
strands just in case he didn't get another chance.

By the time they reached the meet point, the lot had
filled with bikes and bikers, primed and ready to fight if
the handover didn't go as planned. Leo was already waiting for him near a pile of rubble, accompanied by a huge
bear of a man who had at least three inches on Jagger in
height and maybe one hundred pounds in weight.

"Bear." Arianne muttered under her breath. "Viper's
sergeant-at-arms. He almost never leaves Viper's side. He's
Viper's shadow, except he's all brawn, no brains, and no
mercy."

Jagger swallowed a laugh. He doubted he'd ever heard
a more suitable road name. With the dark, full beard, short
curly hair, and thick furry forearms, Bear was a bear indeed. But it was clear from Bear's posture and his position slightly back from the group that he wasn't the one in
charge.

A murmur rippled through the crowd of Black Jacks,
and the temperature dipped as a cloud drifted in front of
the sun. Half-lit in the gloaming, a towering man stalked
toward them. Black Jacks scattered, deferential even as they
stumbled away.

"Viper." Arianne's hand flew to her parted lips. "I can't
believe he's here."

He stalked directly to them, his cut worn and heavy with
patches, swaying slightly over his barrel chest. His hair was
black, fading to gray, and long, just brushing the top of his
cut. A thick salt-and-pepper beard shadowed his jaw. Taller
than Jagger. Wider than Bear. His arms were thick with
ropy muscles, and covered in colorful tats. When the Black
Jack president swaggered to a stop, Jagger counted six gold

rings, three on each hand, the largest a snake's head with ruby eyes.

Up close, Viper's face was broad and scarred, his nose crooked and his expression one of pure brutality. Cold, dark eyes fixed on Jagger, showing no glimmer of emotion. Fierce and formidable, yes, but aging, too, as borne out by the lines of hard living etched into his face, and the slight rounding of his broad shoulders. And yet his sheer palpable presence cowed even the men standing closest to him. Power radiated off him, a storm, barely contained.

They studied each other, eyes locked on each other, neither willing to cede the power position by being the first to speak.

Finally, Viper gave an exasperated sigh. "Jagger."

"Viper."

"You got something belongs to me."

Jagger could almost feel the cords twanging in his neck. "You got the bastard who burned down my clubhouse and shot my brother?"

Viper looked back over his shoulder. "Bring the fucking prisoner."

Motionless by Jagger's elbow, Arianne sucked in a sharp breath. Although curious about her reaction, Jagger didn't dare take his gaze off Viper. This was a game he was playing to win.

A few minutes later, a young blond biker joined them, his cut worn but patch-free and hanging off his rail-thin body. His face was a mess of cuts and bruises, his bottom lip split, one eye swollen shut, and his left ear swathed in bandages. He carried himself awkwardly, as if every breath pained him, and from the beating he clearly had taken, maybe it did.

Viper dropped his gaze to the blond biker, and his lip curled in a snarl. "I told you to bring the fucking prisoner."

"He can't walk."

Viper cuffed the lad and he staggered to the side, stumbling over a discarded soda can. Arianne growled—a sound so soft, only Jagger could hear it. Was that her brother? He looked nothing like Arianne and bore no resemblance to Viper either.

"Bring him *anyway*. Leo, give him a hand."

They waited in silence until Leo and the blond dude returned, dragging a man behind them, his face badly battered and his thick red hair matted with blood. Arianne's barely audible sigh of relief gave Jagger pause, but this wasn't the time for questions.

"There you go," Leo said as they lowered the unconscious man on the ground.

"This the guy who torched our clubhouse?"

"This is him," Bear interjected, his voice thick with derision. "Acted without authorization. You can see what Viper thought of that."

"Did he shrink over the last few weeks?" Scenting victory, Jagger licked his lips.

A puzzled Bear shot a glance at Viper and then his lips pressed into a white slash. "What the fuck?"

Jagger's hand slid into his cut, and his fingers closed over cold steel. "We have video surveillance. Not great, but he doesn't resemble any of the men we caught on camera."

"This is fucking bullshit. We held up our end of the bargain." Leo gestured to Arianne. "Hand over Viper's property."

Arianne bristled. "I'm not property. I don't belong to anyone."

Viper's eyes glittered with malice as they slid to Arianne. "You belong to me."

Christ. Jagger couldn't imagine a young girl growing up with a father like Viper. Or a boy, for that matter. At the very least, the children would be starved for affection, and at most . . . well, he'd seen her scars. Some of them.

"You don't accept him?" Viper gestured to the prisoner on the ground, and Jagger's throat constricted. The man was in serious need of medical attention, but Jagger couldn't take him when he clearly wasn't the perpetrator of the crime. To so do would make him look weak not just to the Jacks, but to his own men as well. No doubt Viper would abandon him here, and they could call an ambulance after everyone had gone.

Jagger barked a laugh. "Some random dude who's likely pissed you off? No."

"Jeff." Viper's bark drew the blond biker to his side. So this *was* Arianne's brother. She hadn't lied when she said he was the opposite of Viper, nor had she lied about the drugs. He had the same sunken eyes and gaunt look he'd seen in the brothers he'd kicked out when they hadn't been able to beat their addiction.

"Kill him."

Jeff blanched and his voice rose to a whine. "You told me I just had to beat him up."

"Now I'm telling you to kill him." Viper gave an irritated snarl "We have no use for him. Sinners don't want him."

"Jeff. No." Arianne stepped forward. "You're not a killer. You don't have to do this. Once you cross that line—"

"Shut it, girl." Viper cut her off, then glared at Jeff. "You wanna be a Jack? Then act like one. Not one of my boys would hesitate to pull the trigger. Hell, your sister would do it. Wouldn't blink an eye. You ever wonder why she got patches and you didn't? 'Cause you don't have her balls. Show me you're better than a fucking girl. Make me proud. Earn your colors, or prove you really are the pussy I always thought you were."

"But . . ." His pleading glance sliced through Jagger's heart, but Viper was unmoved.

"Pussy."

Jagger's skin crawled with loathing as Jeff raised his weapon with a shaking hand. Fucking bastard goading his own son. And the innocent on the ground. . . . But what could he do? He had rejected the prisoner, so by rights the man belonged to Viper. What happened to him was Black Jack business, and if Jagger got involved, the Jacks could retaliate. With everyone armed and already on edge, interference on his part could lead to a fucking disaster. He would be putting his men at risk.

Viper snarled. "Three seconds, boy, or you'll never get those colors."

Fuck. Fuck. Fuck. He couldn't let an innocent man die. Jagger drew his weapon and pointed it at Jeff. "Let him—"

Crack. The sound of the bullet tore through the silence, sending crows squawking and flapping in the air. Jeff's hand dropped, the gun hanging from his finger, his face contorted in anguished despair.

"*No.*" Arianne shrieked and took a step forward, but Jagger held her back. *Too late.* They were both too late. And if she went to Viper now, the poor soul on the grass would have died for nothing.

"Problem solved." Viper glanced over at Arianne. "Come, girl." He snapped his fingers and pointed at the ground beside him.

Arianne didn't move, her gaze fixed on Jeff, her face reflecting his despair.

"Jesus, bitch. You never listen." Viper took two quick strides toward Arianne, fingers outstretched as if to grab her. Arianne stepped back, closer to Jagger, her hand flying to Jagger's arm to rest at the crook of his elbow.

And in that second, everything changed.

Mine.

Her small, unconscious gesture, a statement of trust that he would keep his word, keep her safe, roused in him a protectiveness so fierce, he was powerless to stop his reaction. Shifting his stance, he positioned himself between Arianne and Viper, shielding her with his body as he met Viper's furious glare.

"Black Jacks broke the truce," Jagger snapped. "I lost a clubhouse *and* a good man." He looked back over his shoulder and lifted his chin in Arianne's direction. "Now I got compensation. Since she's your daughter, I'll call it even. I claim her as the blood price for the debt you owe us."

Beside him, Zane hissed his disapproval, but Jagger had made his decision. He had, in fact, made the decision when he'd first received the call from Viper about the meet. But the part of him that put duty above everything else, coupled with Arianne's insistence that she was going to the exchange, had almost convinced him he would be able to give her up.

Growls and a buzz of anger rippled through the Black Jacks.

Leo's brow furrowed and he scratched his head. "Viper's daughter?"

"Yes."

"You're taking *Viper's daughter* as a blood price?" His voice rose in disbelief. "You gonna kill her?"

"She's mine. If I want to kill her, I will. If I want to keep her as a house mama, I'll do that, instead." And then, because he knew Leo wanted Arianne, and Viper was already bearing down on him, he said, "And if I want to use her, I'll keep her chained to my bed."

Arianne clutched his arm, anger radiating off her in waves, but she stayed silent. Jagger let out the breath he hadn't realized he was holding. She understood he was saving her from whatever punishment lay in store if Viper thought she'd gone with him of her own volition. And he was giving her a way out. They had both been aware of the risk that night on the roadside. As she'd said, she had a choice. And she'd chosen him.

"Take her." He shoved her back toward Gunner and was ready when Viper struck. He had already braced himself for the blow. But he hadn't anticipated the flickblade Viper had concealed in his palm. The blade sliced through the front of his shirt, leaving a gash four inches across. Jagger grunted at the pain in his chest and grabbed Viper's wrist, twisting it back and away until the knife dropped and they faced each other man-to-man.

"She's dead to you." Jagger spat out the words as Sinners and Jacks threw themselves into the fray. "You don't touch her. You don't look at her. You don't call her. You don't hunt her. She belongs to me."

Viper jeered. "You're thinking with your dick, boy. Are the lives of your men worth a bit of pussy?"

Shaking with rage, Jagger slammed his fist into Viper's face, following the punch with a kick that sent his opponent staggering back.

In the distance a siren wailed. The shrill sound of a whistle cut through the smack of flesh on flesh, grunts and groans, and the crack of bone. A warning.

"Jag, gotta go." Zane raced toward him, his cheek cut and bruised. "Wheels is on lookout. He says there's at least ten cop cars on the way. Maybe more. Not sure how they found us. None of our lookouts reported cars or people in the area, and I'm sure the Jacks had lookouts of their own."

Gritting his teeth, Jagger turned back to his opponent, but Viper was already on the move, the Jacks swarming around him as they headed for their bikes.

"Arianne."

"Over there." Zane pointed to the pile of rubble where Arianne knelt beside the fallen man.

"Grab Gunner and go round up the stragglers." Jagger said, as he raced over to join her. Arianne looked up when he knelt down beside her.

"He's still alive."

"We gotta go." Jagger tugged on her arm. "Cops are on the way."

She pulled away. "I can feel his pulse. We need to call an ambulance, and his family . . ."

Still alive. Jagger's head fell back in relief. "The police are only minutes away. They'll take care of him. There's nothing you can do."

"I don't want to leave him alone." She looked up, her eyes glittering with tears. "He's hurt because of me."

Jagger stood, tugging her to her feet. "He must have done something pretty bad to the Jacks or they wouldn't have caught him in the first place. And it was Jeff who hurt him and Viper who pulled the strings. Not you." He kissed her lightly on the forehead, puzzled when she pulled away. "You know what happens if the cops catch you here," he continued. "Either you walk or I'll carry you, but you're coming now. We can watch from the hill, where it's safe, to make sure they find him."

She hesitated, then pushed to her feet, refusing his outstretched hand. "Okay."

Still curious about her rejection, Jagger tried to catch her gaze as they jogged across the lot, but her eyes were firmly fixed on the road ahead.

"You're on my bike." He pointed to the pillion seat. "We're meeting at Sparky's shop. One of the prospects will bring your Ninja. Can't risk losing you now."

Not now. Not when she was finally his.

Jagger's heart pounded as she mounted the seat behind him. He had claimed her under the biker code. Arianne belonged to him. No one would ever touch her again. No one would hurt her. And she wouldn't run away. An almost primitive joy suffused his body, and a fierce primal instinct to claim her in the most carnal way tightened his groin.

Mine.

★ ELEVEN ★

*What belongs to the club, belongs to the brothers unless
the president says otherwise.*

She'd known he would come.

While her fingers stayed busy, twisting bolts and pulling wires on her Ninja, and her mind tried to sort through
her tangled emotions, her body remained tense, alert, every
sense heightened by the knowledge that you did not turn
your back on a man like Jagger and walk away without
paying a price.

And she had turned her back. After he accepted the
cheers and commendations from his men for snatching Viper's prize from under his nose, he'd dismissed her enraged
declaration that she was nobody's property with a simple,
"You're mine."

Well . . . not so simple. He'd curled his hand around her
neck, dragging her toward him, plastering her body against
his. Then he had pressed his lips to her ear, his voice dropping to a low, threatening growl, and repeated the word that
set her teeth on edge: "Mine."

So she'd walked away. The alternative was to slap him,
and although she longed to do so, she couldn't bring herself to challenge him in front of his men. Her lessons in

respecting the authority of the president were too ingrained. Inside and out.

The door closed and she tensed when the dead bolt snapped into place. Still, she didn't bother to turn around. Instead she carefully positioned the repaired fairing on her Ninja and inspected the result. *Damn.* The lacquer hadn't dried evenly. She'd have to start again.

A draft of cool air made her shiver despite the coveralls she had thrown over her clothes, but not so much as the shadow she glimpsed out of the corner of her eye. The shadow of a man who had defied Viper. A man who had protected her. The man who now called her "mine."

"Leave me alone." She swiped a grease-covered hand over her nose and grabbed a socket wrench from the set beside her. "I have nothing to say to you."

"How about thank you?"

She pushed herself to standing and whirled around to face him. Jagger leaned against the tool bench, thick arms folded over his cut. Her gaze traveled down his muscular body, to the hand-tooled leather belt and the Harley-Davidson buckle shining in the last rays of the afternoon sun, which streamed through the window. And then her focus slid below his belt to the powerful thighs and the prominent bulge at his groin. Her cheeks heated and she looked away.

Mind out of the gutter.

"For what? For doing to me what Viper did? For treating me like a piece of property? You can't own me." Her voice rose in pitch and her body shook with the effort to contain her emotion. "This is the twenty-first century. It's against the law."

"Since when do one-percenters obey the law?" Although his voice was calm and even, there was no mistaking his tone. This wasn't a discussion. It was a *fait accompli.*

Arianne shuddered. In the short time she'd known Jagger, she had come to realize he was far more dangerous than any of the Jacks, maybe even more dangerous than Viper. So cool. So calm. So utterly in control of everything and everyone around him. Nothing surprised him. He seemed to plan every move at least three steps ahead, enforcing his will before ever making a demand.

"What are you saying?" She squeezed her wrench so hard, her knuckles whitened. "I've paid for my life with my freedom? And now that you own me, you expect me to do your bidding?"

He held up his hands palms forward. "You're upset. I understand that. But stop right there before you say something we'll both regret."

But she couldn't stop. A lifetime of anger, pain, and humiliation bubbled over in her utter despair at letting her guard down only to see there was nothing on the other side except more of the same. She had trusted Jagger despite herself, only to have the freedom that had almost been within her grasp snatched away.

In frustration, she threw the small wrench at him and reached down to pick up another as he dodged her throw. "It's not going to happen. I'm not property. Not for Viper. Not for Leo. Not for you. Not for anyone." Her voice rose, to a shout. "How could you do this to me? All I ever wanted was to be free."

"Stop." Louder now, his voice cut through her rant but not through her rage.

"I'm leaving. If not on my bike, then on someone else's, and if I don't have a bike, I'll damn well walk." She threw another wrench and Jagger stalked toward her, ducking to the right to avoid the flying tool.

Her third wrench went wide, but by the time she picked up a fourth, he was bearing down on her too fast, an unstoppable force. She took one step back and then another, but he kept coming and coming until her back hit the wall and his hand clasped firmly around her wrist. Arianne turned her head to the side, squeezed her eyes, and steeled herself for his fist.

"Drop it." His forceful tone left no room for argument.

She dropped the wrench. But when he released her wrist, and the strike didn't come, she slapped at his chest in a frenzy of blows. "Get away from me. You treated me no better than Viper ever did." She cut herself off and glared. "This is why I hate bikers. I hate being part of this world where women are nothing but pawns in a game, property to be traded and used and abused and cast aside. The only way I ever got any respect was to be as good as or better at what they did. So I learned to shoot better and ride better and play pool better. And yet in the end, I'm still nothing. I'm a 'girl.' I'm the prize you snatched from Viper."

Her chest heaved as she rasped her breaths, her breasts brushing against his cut. But when she looked up, she saw neither anger nor scorn in the depths of his eyes. Instead she saw concern, sympathy . . . and goddamn unyielding determination.

He hugged her face with his warm hands, even as he trapped her with his body. "The things that happened to you—and one day I want to hear everything—don't happen in my club. I won't deny that misogyny exists, or that women take on roles that might be looked down on generally by civilians, but in return for what they do for the club, they are given respect and protection and they know they won't be harmed."

"Why would you care what happened to me? That's all in the past."

Jagger bent down and touched his forehead to hers. "Because you're *mine*. And 'mine' means you have my protection. 'Mine' means I'll look after you. It means nothing happens you don't want to happen and no one touches you without your consent. It means your life is in my hands and I will do everything in my power to ensure you are safe and secure and your needs are met. It means something happened to you that twisted your perception so bad, you look at us and you see only them. I'll make that right. I'll give you justice. I'll give you back whatever was taken from you."

"Respect?"

His face softened and his lips quirked at the corners. "I remember someone telling me respect has to be earned."

A violent, desperate tremble shook her body as she struggled against a deep-seated longing for what he offered. A gift she could never accept because the price was simply too high—freedom and control, the two things she had fought for all her life. "You can never give it back." She pushed him away. "What I lost is gone forever."

His hands slid to her shoulders and he pulled her toward him, his intoxicating scent of leather and autumn leaves confusing her senses.

"'Mine' means I'll find a way, Arianne. It means I will do everything I can to make you happy, give you as much freedom as I can. But always, you will belong to me."

"Please." She twisted out of his grasp. "Don't do this. You did what you had to do for the club. I get that. You get justice and a reputation as a kickass MC president for taking Viper's daughter. And you could rationalize it on the basis you were helping me by sending a message to Viper that I wasn't here by choice. It was a win–win situation, and we both received a benefit. But that's it. There's nothing else. There is no protecting me or looking after me or fixing a past that can never be fixed. There is no giving me back my life. There is no *mine*, Jagger. There's only you, president of the MC, who lives and breathes for the club. And there is me, who lives and breathes for the day I get out of Conundrum forever."

"There was no way in hell I was letting you go." He

leaned so close, her head dropped back, her mouth only inches from his.

"Do you understand?" His hand curled around the back of her neck. "This evening in that vacant lot. There was no way in hell I was letting you go. I will never let you go." He threaded the fingers of his free hand through hers, joining them palm to palm.

Tears of frustration welled in her eyes. "What does that mean? Are you saying you want me to be your old lady? Because I won't do it. I don't want to be a biker's old lady. I don't want to be a biker's anything."

"I want you, Arianne." His voice dropped to a husky rumble. "More than anything I have ever wanted in my life. And no, not as an old lady. I won't subject you to that kind of risk. So if this is the only way I can have you, then this is how it will be."

He wanted her. Just as much as she wanted him. And although she hated him for what he had done, the part of her that understood wanted to take what he offered, even if just this one time.

"I want you to be mine in every sense of the word." Stepping closer, he raised their twined hands and then thudded them against the wall above her head, pinning her in place.

Far from eliciting a fear response, his dominance aroused her. Her body arched to accommodate the stretch of her arms, her breasts pressing against his chest as he firmed his grip around her neck. Unable to stop herself, she tipped her head back and parted her lips in silent invitation.

Demanding, hot and hungry, his lips moved over hers, forcing her mouth open for the determined thrust of his tongue. Possessive. Dominant. Ruthless.

And then he was everywhere, searching and claiming, his hands sliding down her body, fingers digging into soft flesh, pressing her against the steel of his erection. Passion suffused his kiss, desire and need.

Arianne melted against him with a soft groan that only seemed to inflame him. His arms wrapped around her, their bodies so close, she could feel his heart pound against her ribs. Giving in to the tension that had been building since the day they met, she slid her hands over the broad expanse of his chest, and then froze when cotton gave way to flesh.

"You're hurt."

"Just a scratch."

She circled a finger lightly over the wound, which was still raw and caked with dried blood. "It needs to be tended to."

"I got something else needing tending that hurts a hell of a lot more."

Arianne twined her arms around his neck, then pulled him toward her, the last of her inhibitions drifting away. "Ah, the dirty mouth again. Say something else. Your dirty talk makes me wet."

"*Christ.*" He strained against her grip. "Don't tease, sweetheart. I won't be able to stop."

"I don't want you to stop." She leaned up and nipped his neck, then licked the wound, sliding her tongue down to the hollow at the base of his throat as his taste, hot musky male, seared across her tongue.

"Arianne . . ." His protest went unheeded as she ground against his hardened length.

"Take me," she whispered. "I don't want to think. I don't want to feel. I don't want to see, smell, touch, taste, or hear anything but you. I want to pretend this evening never happened and just for now that this is real . . . that I'm yours and you're mine and that I'm safe and happy and no one is going to take it away."

"You are mine." He unzipped her coveralls and shoved them down to her waist. "You are safe. And no one will take anything away." Without pause, he lifted her shirt, reaching around to flick the catch on her bra. Her breasts spilled into his waiting palms and he cupped them, squeezing gently as he brushed his thumbs over her nipples until they hardened into peaks.

"So beautiful."

Arianne trembled, arching into his touch. "More."

He obliged by bending down and drawing her nipple into his mouth, hot, wet, and warm. He nipped and teased, flicking his tongue back and forth until her head fell back and she groaned his name.

"Say it again." His deep rumble reverberated through her body. "I want to hear my name on your lips and nothing else."

"Jagger."

He knelt in front of her, first sliding her coveralls down, then opening the button on her jeans and easing them slowly over her hips. Arianne sifted her hands through his hair, letting the silky strands slip through her fingers.

"Like these." He traced the lace along the edge of her red silk panties, following the crease of her thigh. So close, but not close enough to where she wanted him to go.

She moaned softly and he looked up and smiled. "Been waiting a long time to have you, sweetheart. I'm not gonna rush. I want to enjoy your body."

"My body would be more enjoyable if you finished taking off my clothes."

He laughed and steadied her while she kicked the clothes away, but he wouldn't let her remove her panties.

"You take those off, and it ends right now." He cupped her sex with his hand, pressing his palm firmly on the silk barrier covering her clit, and every nerve in her body flared in response. "When I take you, sweetheart, I want you so wet and so ready, you're gonna come fast and you're gonna come hard and you're gonna squeeze me so I'm coming with you." He splayed his fingers, forcing her legs apart. "Open for me. Let me play."

Arianne yielded to the pressure, parting her legs as the warmth of his hand soaked through her panties and she thought she'd combust from the heat raging within her.

"Don't I get to play, too?" She nuzzled his neck and then lightly nipped his skin, delighting when he growled. Her biker liked it rough.

"You want my cock?"

She smiled and licked her lips. "Yes, baby, I want your cock." The term of endearment slipped out too fast for her to catch it. But it felt right, and from the warmth in his eyes, it felt right to him, too.

"Have at it. I did promise to give you what you want." He stepped back, releasing her and she instantly felt bereft.

Hands trembling, Arianne stripped off his cut. Desperate to touch his bare skin, she was tempted to toss it to the side so she could get her hands under his shirt, but a biker's cut was his heart, and although she was more determined than ever to leave this world after the encounter with Viper today, she couldn't bring herself to throw Jagger's heart on the floor.

Folding it carefully, she placed it on the seat of the bike nearest her and then looked up as she reached for his shirt. Jagger's eyes flicked to his cut and back to her. Then his gaze softened and he nodded, his silent appreciation sending a warm tingle through her body.

Within seconds she had his shirt off, and her hands on his magnificent body. She traced her fingers over his massive chest, a perfect canvas for the Sinner's Tribe tattoo, marred only slightly by that long scar, and then down over the ridges of his abs.

"Very nice." Her voice came out in a husky rasp that made Jagger chuckle.

"Glad you approve."

By the time she reached his buckle, she had lost patience with the game. Without hesitation, she tugged open his belt and undid his fly. Hands trembling, she shoved his jeans and boxers down, freeing his cock from its restraint.

Huge and heavy, his shaft bounced in her direction.

"Touch me." His voice came out in a strangled groan and Arianne wrapped her hand around him. So hot. So hard. But the skin over his shaft was soft and smooth as silk. She gripped him firmly, stroking down his length and then back up, ripping a second groan from his throat.

"Faster."

"What happened to taking our time?" She quickened her strokes, cupping his balls with her free hand and giving them a squeeze.

"Time's up. Fuck . . . gotta stop." He clasped her wrist, drawing her hand away from his thick shaft, then reached between her legs and shoved her panties to the side. Before Arianne's lust-soaked brain could process his intentions, he had thrust a thick finger into her sex. She gasped and stiffened at the delicious intrusion.

"Christ, you're so wet, sweetheart. So fucking tight. We'll have to take it slow. I don't want to hurt you."

He added a second finger, stretching her, filling her, making her shudder with need. She gripped his shoulder with her free hand and reached for his cock again, stroking him faster than before.

"Panties gotta go." With a sharp yank, Jagger tore her panties away, discarding them over his shoulder.

"I liked those." Arianne firmed her grip on his shaft. "Now you'll have to pay."

He jerked his hips, rocking into her palm as his fingers thrust deep inside her, gliding along her sensitive tissue. Arianne dug her nails into his shoulder determined not to give in to the raging need building inside her.

At least not before him.

"Enough." He slid his fingers from her pussy, then tugged her hand away. "I want to come inside you. I want to fuck you hard and fuck you deep and fuck you until you come all over my cock."

Arianne groaned. "Now would be a good time. There's a condom in my purse."

Jagger stilled. "Why? You gotta man?"

"You're asking me now if I have a man?" Her voice rose in pitch. "First, I'm leaving town, so why would I get involved? Second, it's called safe sex. And if you haven't heard of it, then this is as far as we go."

A pained expression crossed his face—so fleeting, she wondered if she'd imagined it—and then he scowled. "I don't share, Arianne. Anyone touches you, tries to lay claim to you, he'll answer to me."

Her lips curled in a bemused smile. "Lucky for you, I broke up with my last boyfriend months ago."

"Lucky for him."

Jagger retrieved the condom and sheathed himself, but when he returned, something had changed. He seemed pensive, brooding, and more intense than he had been moments ago, all traces of his good humor gone. And when he kissed her, his lips were hard, firm, unyielding, as if he had a message he couldn't say in words.

"Jagger?" Was it the mention of other guys that was bothering him? The condom? Or was it the fact she was leaving town?

He lifted her, his fingers digging into her ass, his cock pressed against her sex. Arianne wrapped her legs around his waist and gripped his shoulders as he backed her up against the wall.

"Say something," she whispered.

Jagger bent down and drew her nipple between his teeth, sucking and nipping until she was writhing against him.

His hand slid down, skimming over her clit to stroke along her folds.

"Are you ready for me?" There was an edge to his voice that made her heart skip a beat, and she briefly considered slowing things down, finding out the reasons for his sudden fierce intensity, but her core ached and her clit throbbed and she was close—so close, she could almost taste the oblivion of release.

"Yeah, baby. I'm ready for you."

Jagger closed his eyes, buried his face in her neck, and groaned. "Fuck, sweetheart. Just . . . fuck."

Impatient, she shifted against him, levering herself up to position herself where she wanted him to go. Jagger took over in an instant, pressing the head of his cock against her entrance.

"Relax for me."

She gritted her teeth and locked her legs around his hips, forcing him in farther. "Relaxing is not what I want to do right now. It's been a while, but I'm not going to break."

With a low moan, he thrust inside her, his size, the sense of fullness, the erotic sensation of being stretched to the point of discomfort so intense she shuddered with desire.

"You promised me hard and fast." Her breaths came in short pants and Jagger gave her a slow, sensual smile.

"Yes, I did."

Then he lifted her and thrust in deep, withdrawing and then pounding into her sending her arousal skyrocketing. When Arianne moaned, he slid one hand between them and spread her moisture up and around her clit. Awash with sensation, the tang of his blood on her tongue, she was totally unprepared when he pinched her clit and sent her over the edge.

Her orgasm hit in a fierce, violent wave of intensity, crashing through her body and rippling out to her fingers and toes. As she throbbed and pulsed around him, Jagger hammered into her, finally coming with a roar, the heated jerks of his cock against her sensitive inner walls sending a shock wave through her body as she writhed against him.

"I think we skipped numbers one and two from your list and jumped to number three." She leaned against him, feeling the steady beat of his heart against her chest, as she came down from the ride.

"Lots of time for one and two," he murmured.

"But—"

Jagger pulled away abruptly before she could tell him again she was leaving, easing her to the floor before he went to dispose of the condom. By the time he returned, Arianne had put on her clothes and hidden her torn panties in the pocket of her coveralls. She ran her hands through her hair, smoothing down the loose strands. Why was he being so cold?

His eyes hardened when he saw her dressed. Without a word, he tugged on his jeans and reached for his shirt.

"Jagger? What's wrong?"

He looked back over his shoulder and yanked on his shirt, heedless of the laceration on his chest. "You're mine," he said simply.

"Okay."

"Not okay." Jagger whirled to face her, then closed the distance between them in two long strides. "You don't get it."

The skin on the back of her neck prickled in warning, but she pushed on. "Then explain it to me."

He twined her hair in his hand and tugged her head back, forcing her to meet his gaze. "You aren't leaving Conundrum. I claimed you."

A chill shot down Arianne's spine. "I thought you claimed me to help me get away from Viper and for all the political reasons that go with it. Not for real. Not for—"

"Yes, for real." He cut her off so abruptly, she startled.

"I claimed you as a biker and now I claimed you as a man. You are mine, Arianne. No one will fuck you but me. No one will touch you but me. I'll kill any man who hurts you and hurt anyone who makes you cry. If you need something, I'll get it for you. If you're sad, I'll make you happy. If you want to go out, you ask. Every night you will sleep in my bed. And you will not leave Conundrum."

Shocked, speechless, she could only stare. "Seriously?" Her hand flew to her chest. "Do you seriously think I belong to you because we had sex? Or that you can stop me from leaving if that's what I want to do?"

"Yes."

"It doesn't work that way," she said, her heart stuttering in her chest. "Not with me. I fought too hard for too long to wind up in the exact same situation I was trying to escape."

Gravel crunched outside, and Jagger released Arianne, spinning to hide her as she zipped up her coveralls. She had just smoothed down her hair when the door opened and Sparky stepped inside.

"We've got a lead on Axle. He knows she's here and he's in the neighborhood, likely at one of the local bars."

Jagger waved him back. "Gimme five."

"What's out there for you?" Jagger pulled on his cut after the door closed. "Aside from just getting away from Viper, what is it you're looking for?"

"Happiness is out there." She tried to keep her voice even despite the ache in her throat. "Normal is out there. I'll have a normal life, where every day I get to decide how to live. No one will get shot or threaten to kill me. No one will hold a knife to my throat or claim me as a blood price. I'll feel safe when I go to bed and safe when I walk out the door. I'll be a person and not a piece of property. I'll have a house and a husband and kids and a dog and a nine-to-five job and—"

"You gonna trade the Ninja in for a minivan?" He gave her an incredulous look. "Drive the speed limit down the highway? You gonna tone down the attitude that makes a man so hard, he can't think straight?"

"Some things will stay the same."

"Is that really what you want?" He softened his tone. "You're not normal, and you never will be. You were born into this world. You adapted, survived. The skills you have, you don't need out there. But the skills you need out there, you don't have."

"There won't be any bikers around. That's all I need to be happy."

"Happiness is in here." He tapped her chest just above her heart. "Not out there."

Arianne brushed his hand away. "There's nothing left in there. Everyone I loved is gone, and everyone I trusted betrayed me. And now Jeff . . ." Her throat constricted, cutting off her words. "But I'll find it again once I leave Conundrum. I know I will, and I won't let anyone stop me—not Viper, not Leo . . . not you. I don't give up when I want something. Even at the worst of times, I never gave up. "

"Neither do I."

"Jagger—"

"Later." And then he turned and walked away.

The Sinners found Axle at a bar only a few blocks away, and sharing a table with Mac "the Blade" Lombardo, one of Montana's most infamous hit men. While Cade and Sparky took the Blade outside for a "chat" and Zane cleared out the civilians, Jagger settled himself at Axle's table and sent Wheels to scrounge up a couple of drinks.

He said nothing while the bar was being locked down, the owner paid off, and the lights dimmed, enjoying Axle's increasing discomfort and the fear only silence could bring. Instead, he checked out the pictures on the walls:

Harleys mostly, and women, and women on Harleys, so scantily clad, his mind wandered to the little Black Jack he'd left behind in Sparky's shop.

Arianne. On his bike. Naked. Now that was something to lighten his dark mood.

The bar was small—fifteen worn wooden tables—and narrow, smelling of yeast and stale beer. Just enough room for Cade and Sparky to walk on either side of the Blade as they dragged him to the back door. The bar counter was scratched and the walls covered in Giants' pennants. But that's what happened when you lived in a state with no professional sports teams.

By the time Wheels returned with the drinks, the civilians were gone, and sweat beaded on Axle's brow. Axle reached up to take the beer from Wheels, and his trembling hand made Jagger smile. He could see Axle's fear, smell Axle's guilt, and by the time the night was over, his knife would taste Axle's blood. But first, a little fun.

"Wheels, we need some tunes for this happy occasion." Jagger forced a smile. "Not every day we meet up with a long-lost ex brother." He took a beer from Wheels' outstretched hand, and motioned to the speakers in the corners. "Find the sound system. Put on something fitting."

Ever the obedient prospect, Wheels headed for the back while Tank and Gunner took up guard positions near the doors. Zane joined Jagger at the table, a smirk on his face. He loved interrogations. Maybe too much.

"Heard you'd issued a vendetta against me." Jagger took a long sip from his bottle then reached behind his hip and pulled his knife from its sheath. "And against Vexy." He toyed with the knife, holding it up as if inspecting the blade under the light.

"Don't know anything about a vendetta." Axle's voice rose in pitch as he stared at the knife. "Never made any threats against you or that little Black Jack wh—"

Jagger slammed his knife through Axle's hand, pinning it to the table just as George Thorogood's "Bad to the Bone," blasted through the speakers. He folded his arms and leaned back in his chair, waiting for Axle's screams to die down.

"Also heard you were looking to patch in to a new club."

Axle gritted his teeth, his entire focus on the knife in his hand. He would be desperate to remove it, but he knew if he touched it before Jagger gave him permission, the consequences would be severe. "You kicked me out, so there's no reason I can't patch in to a new club." He grimaced and looked up. "Who's been talking about me?"

One thing about Axle, he'd never lacked balls. Not many men would be throwing questions back at him, but Jagger, now secure in his claim over Arianne, was in a mellow mood.

"Weasel. True to his name."

"Fucking bastard." Axle balled his free hand into a fist. "I don't know why he would fucking lie, but since he's a disloyal, dishonorable, lying *scumbag,* I'm not surprised. If you want to have a talk with him, he's staying with his mom. Blue house on Fir Street."

"Not interested in Weasel right now." Jagger took another swig of his beer. "I'm interested in you and only you."

Axle shuddered. Clearly, he knew what was coming. He'd been with the Sinners before Jagger had joined the club. And he'd seen just how ruthless Jagger could be.

"Look, Jag. You know Weasel. Never said an honest word since the day he was born. I was always about the club. What happened at that meeting, I was doing it for the club."

"You were doing it for yourself." Jagger placed his index finger on top of the knife, and Axle stilled.

"No man." He whined. "I'm still about the club. I got a

good thing going now. Cock fighting. Easy money. I'll let the club in on it, just to prove it to you. The brothers are still my brothers."

Jagger briefly rocked the knife, and Axle shrieked. Sweat trickled down his temples, and his complexion turned three different shades of green.

"Club's got enough money." Jagger flicked the knife again. "But what we don't have is information. For example, I'm interested to know why you're having a drink with the Blade only three blocks from Sparky's shop."

Axle's voice dropped to a pathetic whimper. "Just a casual acquaintance. Bumped into him when I stopped in for a drink."

"Really?" Cade appeared at Jagger's side and tossed a cell phone on the table, then leaned down to wipe away a drop of fresh blood from the screen. "The Blade offered to give us his phone. He's got something on there that makes me think Axle's not telling us the truth."

Now standing behind Axle, Zane leaned over and stared at the screen. "Well, isn't this a coincidence? The Blade knows Vexy. Even has a picture of her working at Banks's Bar." He wrapped his arm in a stranglehold around Axle's neck. "How did the Blade know where she worked?"

"Don't know." Axle's eyes bulged as he struggled for breath.

"You knew she worked there." Zane tightened his grip. "You were coming for her the night the Jacks were there."

Axle clawed at Zane's arm with his free hand. "Yeah, I knew she worked there."

"So maybe you set the Blade on her? Told him to go check her out, maybe make your job easier when you got to the bar."

"No." Axle's rasped, his face turning purple.

Jagger took the phone from Cade and stared at the picture of Arianne. She was smiling at someone, clearly unaware of the threat only a few feet away. His stomach lurched and it was all he could do not to pull out the knife and drive it into Axle's heart.

But that would be too easy.

"Axle's looking a little pale, Zane. Let him go. I'm thinking he needs some air." Jagger yanked his knife from Axle's hand. Axle wheezed in a breath and slumped in his chair.

"Up and at 'em, cowboy." Cade tugged on Axle's shirt to help him up and then gawked in mock disbelief. "Uh-oh. Someone forgot to remove his Sinner's Tribe tattoo."

Jagger fixed Axle with a frigid stare. Kick-outs had seven days to remove their tattoos and hand in anything bearing the Sinner's Tribe mark. Although he had intended simply to teach Axle a lesson about making threats against club members, his flagrant breach of the rules of his banishment was a much more serious matter.

"I'm sorry." Axle babbled as Zane and Cade pulled him out of his chair. "I meant to have it covered, but the guy in my local shop was booked solid. He said he could do it next week."

"Lucky for you, I'm in a good mood." Jagger finished his beer and thumped the bottle on the table. "I'll just remove it for you myself. There's a room in the basement of the new clubhouse. No windows. Nice and quiet. You can choose . . . fire or acid. No one will hear you scream."

★ TWELVE ★

*Members are responsible for their own property.
This includes chicks.*

"So, how'd she take it?" Zane stretched out in his chair in the "reserved" corner of Riders Bar and tipped back his beer bottle.

They'd spent a night and a day extracting information from their prisoner. Finally, after burning away Axle's tattoo with a blowtorch, they'd dropped him off at a local hospital, and adjourned to the bar for a little celebration. Cade had promised to join them when he finished shaking down some locals who didn't think they needed Sinner protection. And Sparky had one more bike to finish up before he was done for the day.

"What?" Jagger drummed his thumb on the table. He hadn't seen Arianne since leaving her in Sparky's shop yesterday, and although he needed this drink after dealing with Axle, he wanted to talk to her, try to smooth things out. In retrospect, he might have been a bit insensitive with regard to her past, but when she'd made it clear that despite what they'd shared together, she was still planning to leave Conundrum, his possessive instinct had risen to the fore, and all he could think was *No*.

"Claiming her as a blood price."

"Not so good." Jagger took a sip of whiskey, grimacing at what was clearly a watered-down inferior brand.

Zane smirked. "I can imagine. What are you gonna do?"

"Keep her."

"You can't keep a woman like that." Zane brushed back his hair. He alternated growing it long with shaving it all off. Right now it was as long as Jagger had ever seen it, straight, and edging past his shoulders.

"She'll stay if she wants to stay and go if she wants to go." He lifted a casual shoulder. "Nothing you can do to stop her, short of tying her up."

Or locking her up.

Jagger gripped the glass. He'd meant it when he told her she wouldn't be leaving Conundrum. But he hadn't realized until this moment just how far he would go to keep her or how important she'd become in his life. Hell. It made no sense. He barely knew her. They'd never had anything close to a normal date. They'd fucked once, and although he'd never wanted a woman so bad or come so hard in his life, it was, as she'd said, just sex, without the kind of intimacy on which a lasting bond could be built.

So why did it feel like something more? And why did he want it to be? He had created the perfect situation: The biker world would now see her as property of the Sinners. The Sinners knew she belonged to him. He could keep her without exposing her to the risk of being the old lady of the president. She wouldn't suffer the way Christel had suffered, or become a target.

She would be his.

"If that's what it takes." He spoke with a conviction he didn't feel. Wouldn't it be better to prove he could protect her? Convince, rather than force her to stay?

"You're fucked, man." Zane leaned back in his chair and propped his foot up on the table brace. "She's got you by the balls. Only woman I've ever met who is worthy of you is the only woman who doesn't want what you have to offer." He chuckled and gestured to the dance floor, which was packed with biker chicks. "Any one of those women would fall over herself to be the old lady of the president of the Sinner's Tribe Motorcycle Club. You could take any one of them home with you right now, and she'd be on her fucking knees begging to please you. But that Vexy chick you just claimed—"

Jagger bristled. "Arianne."

"Arianne. Vexy. Whatever." Zane gave a curt laugh. "My guess is she's sitting at Sparky's, plotting a way to escape—if she's not gone already. And I gotta respect that. She doesn't play games or lead a man on. She doesn't twist a man's nuts while she's stabbing him in the back, or sleep with the first dick that walks in the door—"

"Zane."

"There's no deceit in her. You're not gonna love her all your days only to have her betray you, rip out your heart, and stomp it on the fucking ground. She's not gonna tell you she loves you and that she's gonna wait for you forever, and then the minute you're gone, she's fucking anything that—"

Jagger cut him off mid rant. "What's riding your ass?"

Zane took a long swig of his beer. "Nothin'."

He almost pushed. Zane had never shared this much about what happened in the years they'd been apart. He'd always suspected Zane had been burned by a woman, but now he wondered if the answer lay closer to home.

"She's not at Sparky's," he said, not wanting to risk Zane shutting him out. "She texted this afternoon and asked if she could go shoot stick with her friend Dawn. Since we had Axle and she belongs to us now, I let her go, but I sent Wheels and T-Rex with them."

"You shoulda sent Cade," Zane grinned, his momentary lapse seemingly forgotten. "He's been panting after her friend since they met at Banks Bar. He took her to his place for a drink, and they wound up in bed together, but she left in the middle of the night. Drove him crazy. He's never had a woman walk out on him." He pulled out his phone and tapped the screen. "I'm gonna tell him where she's at, just for kicks. What's the address?"

"Pool hall at Forty-seventh and Main. I think it's called Sticky's."

"Forty-seventh and Main?" Zane tilted his head to the side and the skin on the back of Jagger's neck prickled.

"Yeah."

"Isn't that Bunny's new place?"

Blood pounded in Jagger's throat. A notorious underworld kingpin player, Bunny had connections that made him untouchable even to the Sinners and the Jacks. You wanted something—anything—Bunny could provide, but the price was high and always involved laying down a mark that meant he owned a piece of your soul. Bunny also had a habit of taking things without asking. Pretty things. Things other people wanted.

"Bunny's working out of a pool hall now?" Heart thumping, he threw a wad of cash on the table and pushed his chair away.

"Feds broke up his last human trafficking ring, so he had to move house. Last I heard he'd bought that pool hall and was back in business: drugs, arms, human trafficking . . . the works."

"Fuck." Jagger stalked through the bar, shoving tables and chairs aside in his haste to get out. "Of all the pool halls in Conundrum, why the hell did she pick that one?"

Sticky's was heaving for a Thursday night. The smoky pool hall in the basement of an ancient brick building at the edge of Conundrum was known for its watered-down beer, old-fashioned jukeboxes, sticky floors, and pristine pool tables.

"You boys want a drink?" Arianne gestured to a table and T-Rex and Wheels took their seats, clearly uncertain about the protocol involved in babysitting the president's blood price.

Wheels looked over at T-Rex and shrugged. T-Rex made a show of checking out the pool hall and then nodded. "Sure. Beer's good. You want us to get the drinks?"

"We'll get them." Dawn grabbed Arianne's hand and tugged her away from the table. "After all, you deserve a reward after keeping up with Arianne's bike on the way over here."

Biting back a laugh, Arianne followed Dawn through the bar at the end of a low row of pool tables, wrinkling her nose at the acrid scent of smoke mixed with stale beer. Lynyrd Skynyrd's "Free Bird" played in the background, and the clack of billiard balls filled the air.

"We've got a few minutes to ourselves." Arianne checked over her shoulder at the prospects, now busy talking to each other. "I'll ask the bartender to send a chatty waitress over to keep them distracted. Hopefully we can be in and out of Bunny's office before they realize we're gone."

Dawn laughed. "If there is one thing I miss about my biker days, it's abusing the prospects."

They skirted around the edge of the hall and made their way to the bar in the far corner. "Thanks for coming with me," Arianne said. "Bunny didn't sound like the kind of man I would want to meet alone."

Dawn looked back over her shoulder. "You know you can always count on me. But seriously, usually when you ask your bestie to be your wingman for the night, it's usually because you're planning to hook up with some hot guy in a bar, not shake down a dangerous underworld kingpin at the back of a pool hall."

"I'm not shaking him down. I'm asking him if he's got weapons for sale. And with you there, it should be a civilized conversation. From what Jeff said, Bunny doesn't like to get involved with civilians or draw the attention of the police."

They grabbed two seats at the bar, and Dawn waved the bartender over with a flip of her long blond hair and the kind of wink that sent Banks's male customers to their knees.

"Ladies. You here to play or just watching your men?" The bartender's eyes dropped to Dawn's cleavage, and she looked over at Arianne and rolled her eyes.

"We're looking for a talkative waitress to keep the two bikers near the front door busy." Dawn handed him two crisp twenty dollar bills. "They're drinking draft."

He took the money and lifted an eyebrow. "Anything for you?"

"We're looking for Bunny," Dawn said.

The bartender tensed and glanced around the pool hall. "Don't know anyone named Bunny."

"We heard he's a man who can get things, and there are things we want." Dawn leaned forward, giving the bartender a better view, and smiled. "Tell him Dee wants to see him. I'll make it worth your time." She whacked Arianne's leg under the counter and then tugged on Arianne's purse.

"Uh . . . yeah . . . here." Arianne pulled out a handful of bills and tossed them on the counter.

The bartender stuffed the money in his apron. "I might have seen him around." He disappeared into the stockroom, and Arianne stared at her friend. "Tell him Dee wants to see him? You're Dee? And you act like you bribe bartenders every day? Who are you and what did you do with my best friend?"

Dawn stared down at her hands. "I had a very different life when I was with Jimmy. The stuff we did together . . . Not something I'm proud of and not something I go out of my way to revisit. But if you've got the skills—"

"I can't believe we've been friends for so long and there's so much about your life you've never told me." Arianne raised her voice over the music. "I would never have asked you to help me if I knew you'd be going back to something you left behind."

"And right there is the reason I didn't," Dawn said in a quiet tone. "Yeah, you grew up in the Black Jack clubhouse, but you got a soft heart. Same as Jeff when he's not high or tweaking on drugs. That time he came to help you look after my girls when I was stuck at work, and he let them dress him up and pretend to be their daddy—" Her voice caught and she looked away. Dawn's twin girls were the joy and sorrow of her life, and she rarely talked about them.

Pool cues clacked behind them. Someone laughed. The music segued into AC/DC's "Overdose." Arianne inhaled the thick acrid smoke and coughed. "Jeff changed. Viper changed him. I'm not sure I really know him anymore."

"And I'm not sure I know you anymore." Dawn fiddled with her watch. "From what you said on the phone, it sounds like you've broken all your dating rules with Jagger, and you guys are—"

"Nothing."

"Seriously?" Dawn raised her eyebrow. "You told me it was the best sex you ever had."

"It was the most intense sex I've ever had. With the most intense man I've ever met. He seems to think his 'blood price' claim means he owns me body and soul. He said he'd never let me leave Conundrum."

Dawn twirled a strand of hair around her finger. "Maybe that's his way of saying he doesn't *want* you to leave. Most bikers I know aren't good with expressing emotion."

Arianne snorted. "What's so hard about saying, 'Hey, we had great sex. I like you. Don't leave'? Why all the drama and scowling and stomping around growling 'mine'?"

"I don't know." Dawn's lips curled in a smile. "What's so hard about saying, 'Hey, we had great sex. I like you. I'll stay'?"

"Because I don't know if I can stay."

"Do you want to stay?"

"I want the option." Arianne twisted her mother's ring around her finger. "Before I arranged to buy the passports, I had no option. I ran because the alternative was unbearable, but I always knew he would find me and bring me back. But once I have the passport, I'll know that if I leave, it will be forever. I want that choice. A real choice. Then I'll be able to think clearly. I won't be afraid to make the wrong choice, because I'll know I have an out if I do."

Dawn's face softened. "You must really like him. A few weeks ago, you wouldn't even have talked about options. You were going. End of story."

Arianne's cheeks flushed. "I feel like I know him, understand him. He's Viper, but with heart, soul, and the kind of body you just want to lick all over."

The bartender returned with a pretty, red-headed waitress who promised to keep Wheels and T-Rex entertained and well supplied with drinks. After she reached the prospects' table, the bartender motioned to them to follow, and they quickly rounded the bar, then walked single file down a narrow hallway to a small room at the end of the corridor.

The infamous Bunny—a pasty-faced, middle-aged man with a good-sized paunch and a receding hairline—gestured them inside from behind a wooden desk. If not for the two burly bodyguards standing on either side of him, the Beretta on the table, and the coldest, darkest eyes Arianne had ever seen outside the Black Jack clubhouse, he could have been anyone's dad.

Bunny's gaze flicked from Dawn to Arianne and then back to Dawn. "You."

"Me."

"You back in the game?"

Dawn lifted a cool shoulder. "Just helping out a friend. My girl's looking to buy some guns for a customer of yours. Jeff Wilder."

Arianne poked Dawn in the side and glared. "You know Bunny? Why didn't you tell me you knew him?"

Bunny leaned back in his chair and crossed his arms behind his head, his gaze raking over Arianne's body, leaving a bitter tang in her mouth. "'Cause she doesn't want to know me. Bad things happen to people who know me. Like that piece of scum, Jeff. How are you involved with him?"

"He's my brother."

Dawn hissed a warning a second too late. Bunny's ears perked up and his brow furrowed. "Viper's daughter. Interesting. Never knew he had a daughter. I've had enough problems dealing with your brother. Not so sure I want to double my risk and deal with you, too. What's it worth to you?"

"What do you want?"

"You. On your knees. Between my legs to start. Dee can stay and watch. She likes that kind of thing."

Dawn bristled. "Fuck you, Bunny."

He cocked his head to the side and leered. "You want in on the action, Dee, just say the word. I'll take you both at the same time."

Arianne's throat burned. "How about we stick with cash?"

"Got enough cash. Don't got enough pussy. Maybe if I had enough pussy, I'd remember if I had any weapons lying around."

Vile, disgusting, lecherous bastard. But she'd known men like him—the Jacks seemed to attract the lowest of the low—and she knew how to handle his unwanted advances, his pathetic attempts to shock her. At heart, men like Bunny wanted a challenge. She only had to threaten him to gain his respect.

Steeling herself to keep her face impassive and her voice calm, she said, "Maybe Viper would like to know that you're supplying Jeff under the table."

His face hardened, but she caught a glimmer of interest in his eyes. "He tell you that?"

She bit back a smile. "Jeff does what Viper tells him to do. Only thing he does on his own is drugs, and they're always in short supply. Since you're the man who can get anything, I figured he'd go to you."

Bunny scowled. "Maybe you'd like to use that smart mouth to pay off the five grand your brother owes me so I don't break his legs next time I see him. Once he and I are square, then we can talk weapons."

"Gimme a couple of hours on your tables, and I'll have your money."

Bunny cocked his head to the side, considering. "You shoot pool?"

"Viper might have taught me a thing or two."

"Still want that fucking honey sweet mouth of yours, so how about you play my boy Peter? You win, I give you the contact details of someone who can supply your brother. Guaranteed. You lose, and you spend the rest of the night with those sweet lips wrapped around my dick."

Arianne looked over at Dawn and got a vehement head shake despite the fact that Dawn had seen her play. Arianne had no idea how good Peter was, but as she'd told Jagger, when Viper taught a lesson, you never forgot it.

"I've been saving this mouth for someone special." She licked her lips for effect. "So if I win, Jeff's debt is erased *and* you give me the details."

Bunny huffed. "Definitely Viper's daughter. We got a deal. But I have to warn you, my boy's been playing since he was five years old."

Arianne laughed. "Then he started three years too late."

"Nononononononono."

Arianne ignored Dawn's moan and kept her focus on the striped ball on the pool table in front of her. Bunny hadn't lied. His son, Peter, was good. Damn good. But he'd missed a shot early on, and now she had control of the table. She took her shot, and the ball bounced off the bumper, knocking two striped balls into their pockets before spinning into the corner. Peter exhaled an irritated breath and headed over to his table at the back of their section, calling for his friends to pour him a drink.

"What's wrong?" Arianne chalked the cue as she considered the table. She was up by two now with only two to go, but if she missed, she just might be handing the game to Peter, who was now glowering at her from the corner.

"It's Cade."

Arianne's hand clenched around the cue. Had the Sinners come for her? Jagger had let her go out with Dawn after she'd swallowed her pride and asked permission. Even teenagers were allowed to stay out until midnight, and she still had her chaperones leaning against the wall, sweating because she'd refused to leave when they asked.

She lowered her voice, although Peter and his friends were far enough away, there was little chance they could overhear. "Is he alone?"

"So far. I think he's scouting. Damn. I thought I'd never see him again. I mean, that night we had together after the bar fight was hot, but I'm not looking for anything more than a one-night stand. Don't need another man in my life bossing me around."

Arianne glanced up just as Cade spotted them. "You could have done a lot worse for a one-night stand. He's pretty damn easy on the eyes. I mean, if he wasn't a biker, he could have been a movie star or a model—the angry, sullen type."

Cade barked a few words into his phone and headed

toward them, quickly eating up the distance with easy strides of his long, lean legs. T-Rex detached himself from the wall and walked over to greet him.

"Awkward." Dawn moaned again. "What am I going to say to him? I kinda ran out that night when he was asleep."

Arianne bit back a laugh before leaning over the table. "Tell him you had to get to work."

"It was Sunday morning."

"Church?"

Dawn snorted. "Not if I want to go up in flames. I mean, seriously, the things we did . . . That man is kink on a stick."

"Jogging?"

"With these?" She cupped her breasts. "I'd probably fall over or knock myself out."

"Not a problem I can sympathize with." Arianne mentally calculated angles and trajectories as Dawn fidgeted beside the table. If she wanted to win the game, she would need to keep control right until the end.

Dawn twisted her lips to the side and leaned against the table. "I was a coward and now I gotta pay the price. Just never thought I'd see him again."

"You talking or are you playing?" Peter shouted. He drained his glass and scowled. Tall and thin where Bunny was short and round, he had the same cold eyes and giant hook of a nose as his father. His posse of inebriated friends laughed.

"She knows she's gonna lose," one of them shouted. "She's trying to distract you with that sweet ass so she can play with your balls."

More laughter. Snickers. Arianne focused on the table and ignored the immature comments. "I don't know why you're complaining," she whispered to Dawn. "You had a good time. He had a good time. No strings attached. You're both adults."

"I'm not complaining. I'm embarrassed." Dawn plastered a smile on her face just as Cade reached their corner. "I've never had to face down a one-night stand who wanted more than one night."

Cade stopped in front of them, giving Dawn a curt, cold nod of greeting before turning to Arianne. "Jagger's looking for you."

She made her shot, sinking the ball in the corner pocket. "Here I am. But you'll have to excuse me, 'cause I'm in the middle of a game."

"He doesn't like you being here."

Arianne sidestepped him and considered the table, pulling her cloak of false bravado tight around her. She'd managed to hold her own with Bunny; she could handle Cade. "Then he shouldn't have said I could come."

Cade grunted. "You belong to the club. Club protects you. But we can't do that if you put yourself in danger."

"Only danger I'm facing is losing the game because you won't stop talking." She took another shot, slamming the ball into the side pocket, and Peter shouted a curse. Cade's head jerked around and he glared.

"You with him?"

"Seriously?" Arianne rolled her eyes. "I like 'em sweet but I don't like 'em young."

Cade gave a warning grunt. "Better watch that mouth around Jagger. He's fucking pissed, and Wheels and T-Rex are gonna suffer the most for not getting you back to the clubhouse on time."

"Jagger likes my mouth." Arianne met his gaze, her tension easing when she saw amusement flicker in his eyes. "And no one told me I had a curfew. To be fair, though, they might have suggested at one point that it would be a good idea to leave. And I might have suggested that the way club politics works is that you do what the president's blood price wants you to do 'cause if the blood price is happy, the president will be happy, and if he's happy, you might get home without any broken limbs."

Cade gave her a bemused smile. "Christ. Don't know how he manages you, but I'm gonna wait right here until he comes. This is gonna be a show I don't want to miss."

He turned to talk to Dawn, and Arianne walked to the far end of the table and bent low to eye the ball. A draft of cool air brushed her hair. The cacophony of voices and the clack of billiard balls quieted and the first few notes of AC/DC's "Hells Bells" filled the hall. She didn't need to hear the soft rattle of his belt chain to know he was there. His presence radiated through the entire hall.

Jagger.

A thrill of fear shot through her blood. Pulse racing, she focused on the table, trying to ignore the thud of footsteps, the hushed murmur of an intimidated crowd, and the soft creak of riding leathers. Taking a deep breath, she lifted her cue and slid it into position between her first two knuckles.

His steps didn't hesitate when he reached the table, and even though she had only to lift her head to meet his gaze, Arianne kept her focus on the ball. This game was too important for distractions. And Jagger was the biggest distraction of all.

Out of the corner of her eye she caught a flash of leather and the glitter of the chain that hung off his belt. Her body trembled as he neared her, so hot, sweat beaded on her brow.

And then his hand was on her ass.

Broad and warm, his palm cupped her right cheek, fingers splayed over the sensitive crease between her thigh and buttock, thumb brushing over the rise. No words. No greeting. No permission.

See your blood price. Grab her ass. Send her a message she'll never forget.

Utterly primitive, wholly possessive, his touch awakened something deep inside her, sweeping away civilized notions of self-respect and independence and awakening a deep primal desire to submit to his unspoken demand.

But when he squeezed her ass, punctuating the possessive move with a satisfied grunt, desire gave way to being really pissed off. Clearly his fancy speech about respecting women was baloney.

Steeling herself to control her shaking hands, she looked back over her shoulder and glared. "Why don't you just stamp 'Keep Off' on my ass? Save yourself some time."

His gaze met hers, hot, sensual, and unyielding, sparking a firestorm in her blood so intense, she thought she might combust.

"I just did." He smoothed his hand over the curve of her buttock, his fingers perilously close to the seam. "If anyone is unclear about my meaning, I'll kill them."

"Caveman." She muttered the word under her breath, never thinking he would hear.

Jagger's hand tightened, his fingers digging into her soft flesh, a pleasure pain that made her mouth water.

"I walked in here, and every man in front of you was looking down your shirt and every man behind you was staring at your ass." He smoothed his hand over her buttock, rubbing away the pain. "It took every bit of my self-control not to pound all their fucking heads in because I knew what they were thinking."

"What were they thinking?"

He slid one hand around her waist, pulling her up and against his rock-hard chest, the bulge in his jeans pressed firmly against her rear. "They wanna be the one with their hand on your ass, telling you 'later' has come and it's time to go."

Sweat trickled between her breasts and her mouth went dry, but as menacing as he was, the fate she might suffer at his hands couldn't compare to what faced her if she lost the match. "I'm in the middle of a game. I'm up three to two in a best of three."

"It's over."

Damnit to hell. With his men watching and the civilians shooting surreptitious glances their way, she couldn't tell him to back off and let her finish the game. He'd likely just throw her over his shoulder and storm out the door, and any hope of inveigling him in the future would be lost. No, this called for a subtler approach.

She wiggled free, then leaned over and took her shot, just scraping the outer edge of the ball, making it spin and then curve into the side pocket. A trick shot. Risky, but she needed to make a point.

Jagger grunted. "Impressive."

"I have five grand riding on this game." She kept her voice low. "I'm here for business, not pleasure."

Jagger twisted his hand through her hair, tugging her head back until she was looking up at him over her shoulder. Then he leaned down and brushed his lips over her ear. "I don't think you understand what it means to be mine."

She nuzzled her nose against the deliciously rough bristles of his cheek, inhaling his scent of leather and musky male, hoping to distract him. "And I don't think you understand who you think you've claimed."

He growled, a low, possessive, entirely thrilling sound. "Don't push me, sweetheart. This is as far as I go."

Her heart pounded in time to ZZ Top's "I'm Bad, I'm Nationwide now playing through the speakers. Over in the corner, she spotted Peter waving his pool cue and gesturing at her while T-Rex and Wheels held him back.

"I have only two balls left and then a quick meet with Bunny and I'm free to go. I get where you're coming from, but this is important to me. I need to finish playing, and I need to win."

Jagger reacted as if she'd slapped him, his body jerking back. He grabbed her shoulder, pulling her up and spinning her to face him. "That's why you came here? You're involved with fucking Bunny?"

She bit her lip but held his gaze. "We have a business arrangement, but first there was a matter of a debt to clear. If I win, the debt goes and we deal. I gave my word."

His face contorted into a fierce scowl. "And if you lose?"

I have to suck his dick. The words danced on the tip of her tongue and she amused herself, imagining what would happen if she told him. But that wouldn't be fair to Bunny. He didn't deserve to die tonight. Instead, she said, "That's between him and me."

Wrong thing to say, judging from Jagger's scowl. So she turned her back, lifted her cue, and made her call. It wasn't going to be easy. The cue ball lay over a ball, and she would have to shoot the length of the table off angle. "One ball in the corner pocket."

Jagger's eyes widened. "You got a jacked-up shot there. You really think you can shoot off angle?"

Seizing on his curiosity, she smiled. "Watch."

Her shot was perfect. The one ball slammed home and Cade whistled in appreciation.

Jagger curled his hand around her neck and pulled her close. "You're mine means you don't need to meet with people like Bunny. But you made a deal and you gave your word, so I'll respect that. Finish your game. But I handle Bunny. He owes you, I collect. You owe him, I shoot him between the fucking eyes. Not doing this because I don't think you can handle him. I know you can. But Bunny needs to understand we got your back."

Every inch of her body protested his intent to take control of the situation, but she bit back her words, gritted her teeth, and nodded her agreement. Jagger wasn't an ordinary man who might be cajoled or persuaded. Just like

Viper, he was a king, used to giving orders and having them followed without question. She'd wrung a concession from him that Viper would never have given, and if she wanted to maintain her advantage, she would have to play the game.

"I like the part about shooting him between the eyes," she said lightly, trying to hide the quaver in her voice. "Because I have a feeling, deal or no deal, word or not, you won't be down with what I agreed to do if I lose."

He brushed his knuckles over her cheek, and pleasure rippled down her spine. "Like it when you play nice, but don't think for a second I wouldn't drag you out of here and throw you on my bike if that's what I want to do." He held her gaze, his dark eyes burning into her soul. "I have reasons for letting you stay that have nothing to do with that smart sassy mouth."

"You're just dying to see me make the next shot."

Jagger laughed and released her, then settled himself on a chair at the end of the pool table, legs spread, arms folded across his chest. All alpha. All the time.

Arianne looked over her shoulder and bit her lip. "What are you doing?"

"Watchin' what's mine."

"This isn't your ass, Jagger."

The look he gave her, sensual, sinful, sent a wave of molten lava pounding through her veins. "You are mine, Arianne. And later, I'm gonna make sure you understand just what that means."

★ THIRTEEN ★

*Members may not involve old ladies in club
business without prior consent of the
president or they will get an ass-kicking.*

Two nights after the incident at the pool hall, Jagger got a
call that put an end to his plan to spend yet another night
showing Arianne what it meant to be his.

Raw instinct burned inside him as he watched her
fueling his bike. He'd been hard since met her at Banks
Bar and treated her to a preview of what was to come
against the brick wall at the back of the bar.

Entirely her fault. Usually he had no problem exercis-
ing restraint, but when his little minx had whispered in his
ear all the naughty things she'd been fantasizing about all
day and then let him feel just how wet those fantasies had
made her, he had to have her right then. Up went the skirt.
Off went the panties. Pop went the buttons on her blouse.
And he'd taken her as rough and hard as she'd begged him
to do. Yeah, he liked it dirty, but nothing turned him on
more than a woman who knew what she wanted and wasn't
afraid to tell him.

She'd also let him know what she thought of his plan to
let the prospects take her vehicle home from the parking lot
behind Banks Bar, but he would only yield so far. He wanted

her on his bike, her soft body tucked up against him. Safe from Viper and Axle, but not safe from him.

A truck rumbled by and he walked away from the pumps so he didn't miss anything Gunner had to say. He knew the news would have to be bad for Gunner to call, but he wasn't prepared for a total disaster.

A panicked Gunner gave him the details. The team was at the Black Jacks ice house. Everything was prepped and ready to go, but Bandit had let them down. Axle's protégé hadn't been able to set the explosives, and now they were sitting ducks, up on a hillside, with a stolen truck that was supposed to be rigged to blow. They needed Axle. Or someone with his expertise, and they needed him now. The window of opportunity between shift changes was closing. What did Jagger want him to do?

Jagger scrubbed a hand over his face. He couldn't remember the last time he'd reneged on a promise. And certainly not a promise to fuck a woman senseless. Nor could he remember a time he'd wanted a woman so bad, he'd been tempted to put aside his duty to the club and indulge himself simply so he could think straight again.

But he had to go. He had enough munitions experience to rig the truck. Problem was, he would need to take Arianne with him. He had just picked her up from work, and they were only twenty minutes from the ice house. No time to take her back to Sparky's place and no fucking way was he leaving her alone in the seedy East side of Conundrum.

He assured Gunner he was on his way, then tucked his phone into the pocket of his cut. *Later* was going to be even later than he'd planned. As always, duty would have to win out over desire.

"We gotta make a quick detour," he said when he returned to his bike. "Job's gone bad. Should only take a few minutes."

Arianne slid onto the seat behind him. "I'll entertain myself by thinking naughty thoughts."

Christ! As if he weren't hard already. "How 'bout you think about telling me what was on that piece of paper Bunny gave you the other night?"

After Arianne had sunk the eight ball, Bunny handed over a piece of paper with the greatest reluctance—and only after Jagger and Cade had disarmed his bodyguards and left them moaning on the floor. Clearly Bunny never intended to give Arianne the information he had been forced to hand over at gunpoint. Jagger didn't want to think about what Bunny had planned for her, but he'd left a few of the brothers behind to make sure Bunny got the message that Arianne was now under Sinner protection.

He'd fully expected Arianne to tell him why she'd gone to Bunny in the first place. But she'd tucked the paper away, and every time he raised the question, she gave him that cool smile he had come to realize meant the subject was closed for discussion. He'd indulged her for two days now, and this would be the last time he'd ask . . . nicely.

Twenty minutes later, they joined Gunner and his team at the top of a grassy hill overlooking the Black Jacks' darkened warehouse. Although she stopped mid-stride when she saw the ice house in the distance, and the truck set to blow it sky high, Arianne made no comment other than that it might be better if she stayed with the bikes. A sound decision, given the questioning glances being exchanged between the brothers on the job.

It took him less than five minutes to diagnose the problem and thirty seconds to rewire the explosives. Bandit apologized profusely, but Jagger held only himself to blame. Bandit had worked with Axle on only a handful of jobs, and he should have known better than to send out his brother with no mentor to guide him.

"You ready for the block?" Gunner lifted a concrete slab from the back of the cage, and Jagger nodded. They had only to drop the block on the accelerator, lock the steering wheel, and let the truck fly.

"Where the fuck is Cade?" Gunner grunted as he walked the block over to the truck. "He's supposed to be sharing the load."

Zane looked up and grinned, his teeth shining white in the semidarkness. "I'll bet he's banging Arianne's friend again."

"Jesus Christ." Sparky closed the truck's hood. "Has there ever been a day he wasn't banging some chick? I swear, the minute he walks into a room, they're all over him."

Gunner heaved the block into the truck. "They're not all over me, and I'm just as good-lookin' as him."

"Except you have no hair," Wheels called out from his vantage position on the rise.

"And you're missing a coupla teeth." Sparky chortled.

"But he does have a few extra rolls."

"And a few less smarts."

"Can it." Jagger cut them off with a growl, hoping to stop the conversation from degenerating any further before Arianne heard them. "Too much noise. He's with T-Rex, doing a last perimeter check."

"It's ready." Zane yanked on the doors and then pounded twice to let Gunner know to lock the steering wheel in place and get the block into position, while they waited for Bandit's signal down by the warehouse.

"Can't believe you brought her to watch us blow up her daddy's ice house." Zane joined Jagger at the top of the rise.

"We were close by. Couldn't just leave her on the street." Jagger folded his arms and turned to face his oldest friend. "You got something to say, Zane? I'm here, putting her in danger, because, as always, it is 'club first.' That a problem for you?"

Zane held up his hands, palms forward. "Just sayin' a job like this is no place for a woman. And bringing her here sends a message the boys won't forget. Just want to make sure it's the right message goin' around and not that she's got you so twisted around her finger, you can't do what a man's gotta do without having her by your side."

"If you weren't my oldest friend, I'd kick you out of the club for that kind of disrespect."

Zane laughed. "If you kicked me out every time I said something you didn't want to hear, I'd have an ass the size of Montana."

"Clear." Gunner's voice carried through the darkness, and Wheels and Bandit scurried back to the field. At Jagger's nod, Gunner turned on the engine and put the truck in neutral. With the wheel locked in place, the truck took off down the slope, gathering speed as it neared the warehouse.

Jagger felt an unwelcome, familiar heaviness in his chest when the truck slammed through the barbed wire fence and hit the front of the building. A fireball consumed the vehicle, then sheeted over the warehouse, lighting up the darkness. Filled with flammable chemicals, the warehouse didn't take long to ignite, and within minutes the acrid scent of smoke clouded the air around them.

"Jagger. Look out!" Arianne's voice rang in the silence, just as the beam of a flashlight cut through the shadows.

Jagger dived behind a bush as the light skimmed over the plateau. Heart pounding, he drew his weapon and rolled back into the bush. More flashlights. Footsteps. He estimated at least ten men. Where had they come from? The rocky outcropping that concealed them from the road and warehouse below would have made them invisible to everyone except those who knew their exact location. And where the fuck was Arianne?

"Find 'em. Kill 'em. If you see Jagger, leave him to me." The unmistakable rumble of Bear's deep voice echoed in the darkness.

Rage pumped hot through Jagger's veins. Was there a rat in the club? Wouldn't be hard to find out who it was, because the only people who knew about the job were the men with him now. And one woman. A Black Jack woman.

No. From what he knew of Arianne, she wasn't deceitful. And yet . . . Bunny . . . and the paper—

A shot rang out, pinging off the rocks. A scream. Wheels?

He lay flat, heart thudding in his chest, trying to fight back the memories of another ambush, a hot desert, an enemy that felt they had nothing to lose with a fierce, open attack. Taking stock, he noted the positions of his men around the small plateau, concealed in the shadows as the Jacks hunted them blind. There had been no cover for his men in Afghanistan. Nowhere to run. Nowhere to hide. Darkness was their savior, along with the hope the retrieval copter would take out the enemy before they all died.

He caught a flash in the darkness and then another. Someone was foolish enough to run, making himself a moving target silhouetted by the inferno raging below.

Bandit. Damnit. Too green. Too young. Too scared.

"After him." The shout came from the darkness.

"No." Arianne exploded from her hiding spot near Jagger's bike and shot at the Jacks chasing after Bandit.

Jagger took advantage of their confusion, leaping up and shooting into the shadows. From the other side of the clearing, Zane did the same.

He spotted Bear only moments after Bear recognized him. Too late. Pain seared across his arm and he stumbled, dropping to his knee. But when Bear took a step toward

him, a bullet shattered the rock beside his feet. Bear turned
with a roar.

"Vexy. You betraying little bitch. Thought you were
claimed by the Sinners, made a prisoner, but it looks like
it was all a fucking setup. You were with them all along.
Well, no more."

A shot. A thud. A whimper. Jagger's heart skipped a
beat and he pushed himself up, searching in the shadows.

Doors slammed. Feet thudded. He heard Cade shout and
then the rapid fire of automatic weapons. Cade and T-Rex
had come well-armed. Screams in the darkness, and then
the Black Jacks beat a hasty retreat.

He found her lying near a rocky outcropping. Motionless. Her gun still in her outstretched hand. For a moment he couldn't move, couldn't breathe. Sweat beaded
on his forehead and his heart pounded in his chest. If
she was dead . . . dead like Christel . . . dead because
of him . . . because he hadn't learned his lesson the first
time . . .

"She all right?" Zane clasped his shoulder and knelt
down beside him. He knew. Zane always seemed to know
when the PTSD kicked in and Jagger lost himself to the
ghosts of his past.

Jagger knelt beside her, placing his fingers lightly on
the artery in her neck, praying he would feel her pulse.

"I'm alive." She turned to look at them, her eyes bright in
the darkness. "Just hit my head kinda hard, so I thought I'd
lie here for a few minutes until I stopped seeing stars. But
it's night. So maybe that's why the stars aren't going away."

Words failed him, so instead he lifted her into his arms,
wincing when her shoulder brushed against his wound.

"I'll take her," Zane said. "We'd be at least two men
down if not for her, and you need to get that arm checked."

Arianne twisted to look at his injury, but he passed her
over to Zane and headed for his bike.

"Jagger? Where are you going?"

He kept walking. Zane would explain without giving too much away, and he would look after Arianne. No doubt he would also check her phone. If Jagger had suspicions now, then Zane would have had them from the start.

Jagger mounted his bike and started the engine. He needed to clear his head before returning to the clubhouse for the party that would invariably follow the successful operation.

Before ending it with Arianne.

And it had to end. By bringing her with him tonight, he had not only broken a club rule about involving women and outsiders in club business, but he had also put her in danger.

Unforgivable and totally unacceptable. There was no reason for her to be there. He could have dropped her off, called a cab, or sent one of the brothers to pick her up, but he hadn't been thinking straight.

He had wanted her with him every minute of every day, in part because she had been so adamant about leaving, but mostly because he enjoyed her company. She was smart, sharp, and savvy with a dry sense of humor and good sense of fun. They'd gone to the shooting range together, shot some stick at Riders Bar, and spent an afternoon racing through the mountain pass. For the first time in his life, he'd let his guard down. And now he had to pay the price.

Frustration speared through his heart as he peeled away from the hill. He was supposed to be holding her in his arms, stroking her sweet curves, burying himself deep inside her, listening to her moan as he made her his in every sense of the word. Instead, he was driving through the dark streets of Conundrum. Alone. Wondering how the hell he would let her go.

The party was just getting started.

While Wheels and T-Rex hauled crates of beer into the kitchen, telling the story about the ice house explosion yet again, Arianne helped Jill and Tanya unload the snacks from the cage. She'd assured Zane she was fine except for a headache, and although reluctant, he'd agreed not to call the club doctor who had been out of town the night she'd been knocked off her motorcycle.

When the beer had been opened and the snacks laid out, everyone gathered in the living room for a toast. First, they toasted Bandit, who had taken one in the ass when he panicked and ran and had to be saved by a girl. With all due respect to Arianne and no offense intended, of course.

Then they toasted Sparky and Cade, who had taken Bandit to the hospital. They toasted Zane for staying outside to guard so they could party without his wet blanket presence, and Gunner for going out to find them some girls. Again, no offense to the ladies, but it was a party and there wasn't enough pussy to go around.

Only slightly offended, Arianne joined Jill and Tanya on the porch while the inebriated bikers texted Gunner with their specific requests.

"So, how do you like being a blood price?" Tanya handed Arianne a beer and grinned. Her golden-brown hair swung over her shoulder as she settled on the porch steps beside Jill.

Small and slender, with a heart-shaped face and wide green eyes, Tanya had quickly established herself as the dominant sweet butt in the club, with a mouth unfettered by social norms of politeness. Her friend Jill, a tall Nordic blonde, was more reserved, and unlike any of the sweet butts Arianne had ever met at the Black Jack clubhouse, who were all gregarious by nature.

"I'm no one's property." She sipped the beer, cringing as the bitter liquid slid over her tongue. Part of her wanted to belong to Jagger, but only in the same way he would belong to her.

"Seriously?" Tanya's eyes widened. "If Jagger wanted me, I'd be over the moon. He's sex on a stick, and president of the MC, although he's pretty damn terrifying. Except for Sherry, he's always been a one-night-stand kinda guy, probably because he scares most of the girls away. At least, that's how it's been since I joined the club."

"How did you wind up here?" Arianne couldn't hold back her curiosity. What kept the sweet butts coming back, aside from the promise of power and prestige if they were chosen as a biker's old lady?

Tanya looked past them and down the driveway to where Zane stood, keeping watch. "I was married. My ex was abusive. I ran away but he kept finding me. One night I was at a bar and I saw the Sinners beating up some guy 'cause he'd tried to rough up one of their sweet butts. They were real good to her after, and I decided I wanted some of that. So I started hanging around. Did some things I wasn't proud of, but generally tried to be helpful, if you know what I mean. Eventually, Jagger said I could stay."

"I get it." Arianne said softly. The Jacks had had a revolving door of women that turned so fast, she hadn't even bothered to learn their names. Had any of them been like Tanya—just needing a safe haven? She hoped not because they would have found themselves in hell.

"Most of the other sweet butts want to be a biker's old lady." Tanya gave her a shy smile. "Me? I'm just happy to be safe. No way will my ex be able to touch me now. And the guys here are fun and good to us. Suits me fine."

"How about you, Jill? Did you—?" She turned to Jill, but cut herself off when Jill's eyes teared and she looked away.

"I'm so sorry. I shouldn't have asked." Arianne reached

out and squeezed Jill's hand. Tanya leaned in, scooting closer.

"She just can't talk about it. Jagger found her beat up in an alley outside a bar one night. Took her to the hospital, but she wouldn't go in 'cause she had no insurance. He got the club doctor to look after her and found out she had no place to go and no one to look after her." Tanya put an arm around Jill's shoulders. "So, here she is. Our little stray."

Jill laughed and wiped away a tear. "I'm not a stray."

"You looked like one that night he brought you in." Tanya winked, and the tension between them eased. Arianne smiled. The Jacks' sweet butts were constantly infighting, trying to show each other up. But Tanya and Jill clearly had a close friendship, one that warmed Arianne's heart.

Gunner showed up with a van full of women, and they all headed inside to join the party. Arianne had never socialized with the Black Jacks, never chatted with the house mamas or sweet butts, never been accepted as a member of the club. But the Sinner's Tribe welcomed her as one of their own. Gunner introduced her around as the "girl who saved Bandit's ass," T-Rex kept her glass refilled, and Wheels shadowed her wherever she went.

Not that she needed a minder. As far as the Sinners were concerned, she belonged to Jagger, and that was enough to ensure they kept their distance. So she wasn't pinched or petted or stroked. No one joked with her or made suggestive remarks. Wheels even urged her to put on his hoodie when she stripped down to a T-shirt because of the heat. Having had no respect in the Jacks' clubhouse, she found their deference stifling, and she almost wished someone would slap her ass just so she wouldn't feel like a pariah.

Still, she'd never really felt like she had a family after

her mother died. Certainly not with the Jacks and not with Viper and Jeff. The bonds of brotherhood that held the Sinners together meant they were never alone. They were there for each other through thick and thin. "Club first" meant brothers first.

And that was the problem.

Although the Sinners were a different breed of biker than the Jacks, in their attitude toward women, they were all the same. Women were house mamas, sweet butts, hood rats, lays, or old ladies. Not equals. And when she had imagined her life outside Conundrum, equality had always been part of her dream.

★ FOURTEEN ★

Do as you say or walk away.

An angel in the darkness.

Jagger slowed his steps as he approached the clubhouse, his resolve to release Arianne from his claim waning when he saw her on the porch.

Leaning against a pillar at the top of the steps, a blanket wrapped around her shoulders, Max's head in her lap, she hadn't noticed his approach. From his vantage point in the shadows, he could see her face clearly in the moonlight, soft, unguarded, vulnerable.

Arianne without the armor. So beautiful, he was transfixed, an agony of desire coursing through his body.

Ever alert, Max looked up and Jagger was sure the damn dog smiled when she stroked his head. He couldn't begrudge Max her touch, but his hackles rose just the same. Until that moment, he had never realized how desperately he longed for that easy intimacy—the unguarded softness she tried so desperately to hide.

Gravel crunched under his feet as he drew near, barely audible as The Sheepdogs' "Feeling Good" blasted through the windows. The party was going strong. So why was Arianne outside?

Her head lifted and her lips pressed together as he

approached. He could almost see the walls slamming into place, her vulnerability hidden behind an iron fortress.

"You're back."

He sat down beside her. "You shouldn't be out here. You'll get cold."

"Max is keeping me warm, and I'm partied out. I should have paced myself. I didn't realize the Sinner celebration would go on all night."

"An ice house for a clubhouse. And justice is always worth celebrating."

"I thought *I* was the price for your clubhouse."

The skin on the back of his neck prickled in warning. "You're the price for Cole. A life for a life."

"So you have my life," she said, her voice deceptively mild. "What are you planning to do with it?" She toyed with a piece of paper in her hand—the paper Bunny had given her. It was everything he could do not to snatch it from her hand.

Jagger's pulse kicked up a notch. Give him a shoot-out or a fistfight any day, but trying to figure out where she was going with this conversation was like walking through a maze of thorns. She didn't seem angry or resigned, merely curious.

"Treasure it." He lifted her hand and kissed her palm. He should tell her now he wasn't going to do anything except let her go, but selfish bastard that he was, he couldn't do it. Arianne was no victim. And knowing she would never go down without a fight just made him want her even more.

"Is that your way of being evasive?" She leaned over and ran her tongue along the seam of his lips, then dipped it into his mouth. His cock stiffened and he fisted her hair. *Fuck.* He wanted her so bad, he didn't know if he could actually let her go.

"Only when there is a question for which there is no right answer." He ran his thumb back and forth over her knuckles, his anxiety fading as her warmth seeped into his palm.

"My mother used to do that," she said. "Usually when we were watching TV or just hanging out and she was thinking about something. I always found it soothing, although I think she did it to soothe herself."

He drank in the tidbit of information about her life, adding it to the puzzle, wondering if he would ever be able to fill in the rest. He wanted to know everything about her, from the first thing she remembered until the day they met.

"I don't remember much of my mother." He squeezed her hand needing her touch as he dredged up long-buried memories. "She walked out on us when I was seven. My father was an army man. Strict. Cold. Disciplined. My mom was the opposite. She was warm and passionate about the arts. She loved to sing and dance. My father cared for her deeply but he never let her see it, and I think one day it became too much. She packed her bag, kissed me on the cheek, and walked away. I never saw or heard from her again."

Arianne's faced creased in sympathy. "I know what it's like to grow up without a mom, but I can't imagine what you went through when she left you like that."

He gritted his teeth against the pain of that loss, the bewilderment of a seven-year-old boy who had lost his mother, believing every day she was going to come home, thinking he was to blame and wishing there was something he could do to bring her back.

So goddamn helpless. Never again.

"My dad eased up on me after that." He let go a ragged breath. "Made an effort to spend time with me because there was no one else. Didn't keep me from getting into trouble, though. I think he worried for my entire adolescence."

"Viper didn't give a damn about us so long as we were available to run his drugs across town or entertain his guests, hack into computer databases and wheedle information out of people who didn't want to give it up."

"You don't have to worry about him anymore."

"Not if I'm gone."

Jagger closed his eyes and leaned his forehead against her temple, inhaling the scent of her hair, wildflowers and autumn leaves. He didn't want to think about her gone. He wanted her to stay. Not by force, but by choice. He wanted her to want him the way he wanted her, with a fierce inexplicable desire that consumed him.

"You aren't leaving." He covered her hand with his, crushing the paper into her palm.

"Because you claimed me?"

"Because I want you."

He could feel her smile, her cheek lifting, brushing against his. "You want me?"

With a light tap, he dislodged Max, then pulled Arianne onto his lap facing him, her knees astride his hips. "You're all I thought about when I was out riding."

"Why do you want me?"

His arms slid around her and he pulled her close—so close, his erection ground against her hips in a pleasure-pain that almost sent him over the edge. "You make me feel calm, grounded. You make me laugh. You have courage, strength, and determination like no one I have ever met. You let nothing stand in the way of what you want. You frustrate the hell out me, and irritate me beyond belief. You aren't afraid to challenge me, but you have the political savvy to know when not to do it. You're a kick-ass mechanic, a fine shooter, and a hell of a pool player. And the sass that comes out of your mouth . . ."

Arianne blushed. "I thought you were going to say you liked my tits or my ass. You are a biker, after all."

He cupped her soft breast in his palm and bit back a groan. "I like all of you, sweetheart: your curves, your beautiful face, your smile, and especially your hair." He twined his hand through her silken waves and tugged her head back, baring her throat to his hungry mouth.

She moaned, arched under his touch, rocking against him until he thought he'd go mad if he couldn't get under her clothes, touch her, feel her against him, around him. God, he wanted her so badly, he fucking ached everywhere, inside and out. He'd never known want like this, lust driving him out of his mind.

"I want you," she whispered. "I want this. Not because I'm yours, but because you're mine. Even if it's just for tonight."

He didn't want to hear about "just tonight." He wanted to hear that she cared about him, that she trusted him to protect her, and that she wanted to stay. But later. Because goddamnit, after hearing she wanted him, if he didn't have her now, he would explode.

With his free hand he unclipped her bra and shoved up her clothes, baring her to his sight. A whimper escaped her lips as he tugged harder on her hair, pulling her head back making her arch for him, offering up her breasts for his licking pleasure.

A door slammed. Laughter carried through a window. Jagger growled low in his throat. "We'd better stop."

Stop? No stop. Bad stop. Whether it was the remnants of fear that something had happened to him, or the pent-up frustration of being denied, she wanted him so badly she burned inside. Leaning closer, brushing her lips over his, she murmured, "I thought I made myself clear. I want you. Here. Now."

He hesitated then cupped her breast and ran his thumb over her nipple. "Then stop talking, 'cause I'm going to take that sweet mouth of yours, and then I'm going to give you what you want."

She tilted her head and looked up into his eyes, as dark and stormy as the ocean. "My Jagger's back."

"I never left."

Arianne laughed and reached for her shirt, then paused. "What if someone comes out?"

"I'll shoot them."

"So romantic. I've always wanted to have sex on a porch with a man who said he'd shoot anyone who interrupts us."

A fierce groan broke from his chest. "This isn't about romance. It's about me putting my hands, my mouth, and my cock everywhere on or in your beautiful body and fucking you until I'm so deep you forget your own name."

"You sure know how to make a girl wet." She tongued his ear, delighting when his entire body tensed and his arms became steel cords around her. "You know what would make me wetter? My hands. My mouth. Your cock."

A raw, guttural groan tore from his throat. "Sweetheart, do not—and I repeat, do not—dirty talk me, because, Christ, I won't be able to hold back."

A thrill of fear shot through her veins, but she didn't heed the warning in the rapid beat of the pulse in his throat, or the demanding kisses that scattered her thoughts. Intoxicated by his scent of leather and soap, the promise of hard muscles rippling beneath his thin cotton T-shirt, she slid her hands around his waist and lifted his shirt, her fingers tracing over the taut lines and ridges of his magnificent torso.

Muscles wracked, he shuddered beneath her touch, but when her thumbs brushed over his nipples, Jagger ripped the shirt and cut over his head.

"Fuck." He buried his face in her neck and his hoarse exhalations fanned her desire.

"Yes." She smoothed her hands over his rock-hard biceps, her body heating at the raw power simmering beneath his skin. "Here. Now. On the porch. In the dark. Where anyone could see us. And I want to hear more things you're going to do to me. I want to hear more things that make me wet."

Jagger's muscles tensed beneath her palms and he rasped out his words. "Not slow and easy. Not this time. Need you too much. Gonna rip off your clothes, pull you onto my lap, go deep and hard, and watch you ride me until you're begging to come."

Arousal streamed through her veins like molten lava. She boldly slid her hand over his fly and stroked along the steel of his erection. "I like that talk. Maybe you should have a reward."

He didn't lose control. Instead, he took it, crushing her to him, his tongue invading her mouth, possessing, demanding, leaving nothing untouched.

"I wanted you from the moment I saw you." Still holding her head back, he slid his lips over her throat and down to the crescent of her breasts.

"I wanted you when you ran from me."

She tensed as he cupped her left breast in his palm, and then his mouth, hot, wet, and wicked was on her nipple, and her brain fuzzed with lust.

"I wanted you when there was a knife at your throat and you showed more courage than most of the men I know."

She whimpered as he licked and sucked, drawing her nipple into a hard peak before he turned to torture the other one. And although she ached to touch him, run her hands over the broad expanse of his back, undo his belt and hold the promise she'd felt beneath her palm, she let him take the lead. She'd pushed him as far as he would go. A man like Jagger needed to be in control, and she had the power to give it to him.

"Damn it, Arianne. Every time I see you, I want you. Every time you smile, you take my breath away. Every time you laugh, all I can think about is how to make you laugh again."

And, oh God, did he take control. Helpless in a way she'd never been before, Arianne succumbed to Jagger's touch. Her knees trembled when he undid her jeans and then helped her to her feet so he could pull them over her hips. With a soft exhale, he traced his finger up the sensitive skin of her inner thigh to the edge of her lacy pink panties.

"Never would have thought I'd see these under your leathers." He ran his finger inside the soft elastic edging. "Makes me fucking hot to think you're hiding a soft, girly side."

She leaned up to lick his Adam's apple and shuddered as his taste burst across her tongue, salt and sweat and the essence of him. "I'm hiding something else." She guided his hand up to the top of her panties, tracing his finger along the edge of elastic, just above her mound.

Jagger gave a satisfied grunt and eased her legs apart. "Open for me, sweetheart."

Heart pounding, she did as he asked, following the firm press of his hands on her inner thighs until he grunted in satisfaction. But when he cupped the curve of her sex, she couldn't hold back a moan.

"So fucking hot." With a firm touch, he shoved her panties aside and slid his thick finger along her soaked folds, then thrust it into her throbbing center. Her inner walls clenched around him and it was all she could do to stay standing.

Need him now.

Hand dropping to Jagger's belt, Arianne managed to get

the buckle undone before he shook his head and pulled away, leaving her bereft.

"That's the only thing stopping me from taking you right now. Hard and fast. One hand in your hair so I can watch your back arch and your beautiful breasts riding high, and one hand on your hip so I can fuck you so deep and hard you won't be able to leave my bed after we're done. I wanna pleasure you slow, sweetheart. I wanna watch you come. But if you go any further, that's just not gonna happen."

Without taking her gaze off his, Arianne ripped open his fly.

Good as his word, there was no more foreplay. He swung her up in his arms and carried her to the shadowed corner of the porch, then settled her on the edge of the cedar patio table. And with one quick motion, he shoved his jeans over his hips.

Arianne's mouth went dry as his erection, engorged and heavy, strained for her touch. Impulses warred within her. She wanted to grip him hard and run her tongue along his length. She wanted him to thrust his shaft inside her, soothing the ache in her sex. She wanted to take him into her mouth, wrap her lips around him and suck until he lost control.

Focus.

She stroked down and then up, watching him thicken in her hand as she bent her head and licked her lips.

"Christ, sweetheart." He groaned as he fumbled in his pocket. "Gimme a break."

"I hope you're reaching for a condom." Her words came out in a throaty rasp. "I only carry them when I'm trawling the bars, looking for a good time."

Jagger glared. "No. Just. No. Don't—"

Arianne laughed lightly and drew him closer. "Just teasing."

His lips curved into a sly smile and he slid another

finger through her wetness and then up and around her throbbing nub. Arianne moaned and tilted her hips, trying to get more of the pleasure he offered, but Jagger just grinned and pulled away.

"Just teasing."

"Beast." Arianne slapped at his chest and Jagger grabbed her wrist, trapping her hand against his tat. "Next time, I'm gonna restrain you. Hold you down so you can do nothing but feel me, take the pleasure I want to give."

Fear and arousal blended into a cocktail of desire so potent, she could no longer keep hold of the threads of rational thought. A soft moan escaped her lips, and Jagger's eyes darkened.

"Maybe I'll do it now." He released her hand and tugged off his belt with a sharp crack. "Hands over your head."

Memories assailed her. *Leo whipping off his belt, kneeling astride her on the bed as he wound the cold leather around her wrists* . . . Adrenaline spiked through her veins and she threw up her hands in a warding gesture, her voice rising in pitch. "No."

Jagger jerked back, the belt in his hand. His face creased in consternation, and then he dropped the belt and pulled her into his chest, enfolding her in his arms. "Shhhh, sweetheart. I would never do anything you don't want me to do."

She buried her face in his shoulder, gulping in her breaths as she tried to slow her hammering pulse. "I didn't know I didn't want you to do it until you did."

He stroked her hair, soothing her fear, but not her fire. "You've never been restrained before?"

"Not with a belt."

"I'll make sure to cross that one off the list."

She looked up and smiled, her panic fading in the face of his humor. "You have a list?"

"A long one. I add to it every day. It's called, 'Things I want to do to Arianne.'"

Her smile broadened. "What else is on the list?"

He kissed her, then caressed her breasts, rolling and pinching her tender nipples until the last vestiges of her fear had disappeared beneath a need made more fierce for having been denied for even those few minutes.

"Tasting you." He leaned down and took her nipple between his teeth. "Licking you till you come in my mouth. You want my mouth, Arianne?"

Arianne cried out softly as his heat burned her tender flesh, her core tightening with every rasp of his tongue. "Oh, God. Yes."

"Good girl. Like to hear those words." He tugged the shirt over his head, and she leaned forward and kissed his scar.

"Do I get to find out what this is from?" She smoothed her fingers over his naked torso.

"You gonna tell me why the belt made you panic?"

"No." She bit her lip as her cheeks flushed.

"Then we'll both keep our secrets a little bit longer."

The heat in his eyes made her smolder inside. Every minute she spent with him made it harder to imagine walking away.

He eased her back on the rough wooden surface of the table, positioning her feet on the lip, then slid his hands along her inner thighs. "Spread your legs for me."

Her mouth went dry. *Too intimate. Too vulnerable.* "Someone might come out."

"Texted Wheels when I got here." He settled in the chair in front of her. "Told him to make sure no one comes out. And Zane's at the front gate. He knows no one comes in. No one will bother us."

She pushed herself up on her elbows. "Why didn't you just tell them you were planning to seduce me and fuck me on the porch?"

"Not their business. They do what I tell them to do.

Now, relax, sweetheart. I want this. I want you. And I want to hear you come." Pressing her legs apart, he leaned in and licked along her folds.

Arianne groaned and fell back on the table as he tortured and teased. Any hesitation she might have felt disappeared. Every flick of his tongue heightened her need until her thighs trembled beneath his palms. "Can I scream now?"

"Soon." His tongue slid inside her as he parted her labia and stroked his thumbs along her sensitive inner walls. Her hips bucked against him and she cried out at the intense sensation.

"I love your body," he murmured. "Wanted to taste you this way since the day we met." He lapped at her clit as his thumbs stroked deeper, drawing her closer and closer to her peak. She'd never known pleasure like this, never been with a man who understood her body and could give her what she needed.

A cool breeze ruffled her hair, soothed her burning skin, and a bird chirped overhead. She felt at once cherished and dirty, outside in the dark, spread open on the rough wood surface, with his mouth licking her pussy as his brothers partied only a few meters away.

He alternated soft flicks of his tongue on her clit with the firm pressure of his thumbs against her sensitive tissue until she was coiled so tight, her body shook with need. Threading her fingers through his hair, she pressed his head down and moaned. "Make me come."

It took only one more lick. Arianne covered her mouth to stifle her scream as she arched off the table, her orgasm zinging through her body, making every nerve ending overload. But he didn't stop. He lapped at her clit and thrust two fingers deep inside her, curling them to press against her sensitive spot, a relentless stroking that made her buck and writhe on the table. She didn't know whether to plead for him to continue or push him away.

"I want you inside me." She panted her breaths, only a heartbeat shy of begging.

"And I want to watch you come again." His eyes glittered in the dim light. "Come all over my hand, and you can have my cock." He bent down and drew her clit between his teeth, nipping with the lightest pressure.

She almost forgot to stifle her moan, covering her mouth seconds after the orgasm hit, a deep pulsating sensation unlike anything she had experienced before.

With his gaze firmly fixed on her, Jagger grabbed a condom from his pocket and sheathed himself. "Gonna fuck you now," he said. "Hard and fast over the table while I imagine my mark—the Sinner mark—tattooed above your ass."

Her brain still fuzzy with lust, she didn't catch his meaning until he helped her off the table, only to spin her around and press her back down on the wooden surface, still warm from her body.

"Open." He kicked her legs apart and held her down with his broad palm against her lower back.

And then he was inside her, driving deep in one fierce thrust, filling her so completely, her eyes watered at the delicious sensation.

"Oh God." Arianne braced herself against the table, the worn cedar planks scraping over her hardened nipples and sending tiny darts of pain straight to her clit.

He took her exactly as he had promised. One hand twined through her hair, pulling her head back until she arched against him, the other on her hip, holding her still as he pounded into her with a raw animal need. Dirty, rough, and wild. His total control of her body sent her over the edge, and she let go, rapturous pleasure searing her veins.

"Jesus, Arianne. You feel like heaven." He fucked her hard, driving her hips into the edge of the table with each forceful thrust. She'd never been so hot, never imagined she would be overcome by such a deep-seated visceral need to be taken, dominated.

And yet he was there for her even as his control cracked, angling himself to hit her most sensitive tissue, tugging her head to the side so he could kiss her even as he pumped deeper and harder inside her. "I've never been so hard. I want to sink into your pussy so deep, you can't let me go."

He grunted dirty words, filthy words, putting images in her head that sent her arousal spiraling out of control. Her back was slicked in sweat, every nerve alive with the erotic sensation of Jagger sliding over her skin. Finally she peaked, gripping the table when she climaxed, hard, fast, and with shocking intensity.

"Yes. Fuck. Squeeze me, sweetheart." His fingers dug into her hips, making her eyes tear, and then he hammered her until he stiffened and came, his shaft thickening and pulsing inside her.

"Oh my god," she whispered, as he collapsed on top of her, taking his weight on his hands. "That was hands-down the best sex I've ever had."

"What about last time?" Jagger panted his breaths against her back.

Arianne laughed. "Last time was good. This time was better."

He pushed himself up, taking her with him, enfolding her in his body to beat away the chill. "Gimme a minute, and I'll show you best."

"Only a minute?"

Jagger clasped her hand and slid it down between them, folding her fingers around his semi-erect cock. "Maybe less than a minute."

"Impressive." She looked up at him over her shoulder, and he bent down to give her a kiss.

"You do that to me. Even if you're across the room."

He held her until even his warmth couldn't beat away the chill. And then he reluctantly drew away, settling her on the bench as he gathered up their clothes.

She watched him as he dressed, drinking in his powerful thighs and the mouth-watering cuts of his hip bones, unaware of his intentions until he held out his hand.

"What about me?" Arianne pointed to her clothing bunched in his other hand.

"No point puttin' on your clothes when all that's going to happen when we get upstairs is me taking them off you."

"Is that supposed to be romantic?"

Jagger chuckled. "No, sweetheart. It's efficient. Also saves me from tearing your clothes to shreds 'cause I'm ready for you all over again." He grabbed a blanket from the railing and wrapped it around her, then lifted her in his arms and walked across the porch.

"Um." She tensed in his arms as he neared the front entrance. "How are we going to get upstairs without anyone seeing us?"

Jagger kicked the door open and stepped inside. "We won't."

★ FIFTEEN ★

Every member of the Sinner's Tribe MC must ride an American bike.

The nightmare tormented her. Lucid dreaming, imprisoning her between sleep and wakefulness. Her heart pounded wildly as she tried to rouse herself, but her body was pinned to the bed, a heavy weight on top of her.

Can't move. Can't breathe. She heard a scream and realized it was her.

"Arianne."

The weight disappeared. Free. She rolled out of bed, her stomach heaving. In the back of her mind, she knew that voice. Safe. Warm. Not Leo's voice. But still she needed to get away.

Goose bumps pricked her skin, and she grabbed a blanket and wrapped it around her, quickly crossing the room until she reached the window. With one shove, she pushed it open and leaned out, breathing in the cool, crisp air.

"What's wrong?" Jagger followed her to the window, pulling his shirt over his head.

"Just a nightmare."

He brushed his hand over her cheek. "I was holding you. Was I holding too tight?"

She raised her gaze to meet his. "No. It's not a big deal. Same nightmare I have all the time. I'll be fine."

"Tell me about it."

Arianne bit her bottom lip. "I can't."

Hands on her shoulders, he turned her to face him. "I can't help you if you don't let me in."

Her tension eased under his firm grip. "I don't need your help."

"Talk to me, Arianne. Trust me."

Warmth spread through her body. No one had ever wanted to help her, Viper's daughter. Not when the risks of incurring his wrath were so high. But Jagger neither feared nor cared about Viper's wrath, and that made him a man to be reckoned with. A man she could trust. And she wanted to tell him. The only person who knew the story was Dawn, and Arianne had given her the version with the worst parts left out.

"When I turned sixteen, Viper threw me a birthday party." A shiver slid down her spine, and Jagger turned to close the window, then pulled her into his arms.

"Keep going. I'm here."

She buried her face in his chest and wrapped her arms around his waist, holding on as if the past might carry her away. "I hadn't had a party since my mother died. I was beyond excited. I thought it meant maybe Viper cared after all." Even now she couldn't believe she'd been so stupid, so naive, so trusting of a man who had done nothing to earn her trust.

"After the party," she continued, "he told me my present was waiting for me in my bedroom. I ran upstairs. He'd never bought me a present before." She squeezed her eyes shut and tried to pull away as the memories assailed her. "This is pathetic. I'm not looking for sympathy, Jagger, and I'm not looking for solutions. I'm over it."

"Apparently not, or we'd be fucking in the bed instead of freezing by the window."

She glanced up to see if he was joking, and her heart melted at his warm smile. "Fine. Okay. Well . . . Leo was there. He closed the door and told me he'd been waiting for me since I turned twelve."

Jagger jerked, his body going rigid in her arms. She wondered if he'd already guessed, but if he had, he wasn't letting on.

"He'd done something for Viper in the past. Something that indebted Viper to him. I don't know what it was, but it must have been pretty big, because Viper never puts himself in the position of owing anyone anything. Anyway, he said I was the reward. My virginity. All those years, I'd thought Viper was being a semi-normal dad, keeping the boys away, but in fact, he was just making sure Leo got what he was promised."

Jagger's hands clenched into fists against her back. She could feel his heart pounding against his ribs.

"What happened?"

"I couldn't believe that I had been given over like a piece of property, and the only thing I truly owned, the one thing I had thought I would save for the person I loved, was going to be taken from me. And I had trusted Leo. He was only twenty-two or twenty-three, and he was an outrageous flirt. I'd had a crush on him for years. I was so shocked I don't think I really understood what he was saying, so when he kissed me, I kissed him back." Bile rose in her throat at the memory of his cold, hard lips.

"He took that as a sign to go ahead, and he started pulling off my clothes. I pushed him away, told him I wasn't ready. He got angry. Threw me on the bed. He said I was his to do with as he pleased, and although the deal was only for a night, he would make it so I would want more."

A growl started low in Jagger's chest, rising until it became a bark of anger, but his arms around her were tender, and the lips that brushed her forehead were soft and reassuring.

"I screamed and fought," she said. "God, did I fight. I punched and scratched and kicked and bit. And I hurt him. Very badly. So he kneeled over me and pulled off his belt and wrapped it around my wrists, and then he tied them to the bed with my scarf. My legs were free and I kept kicking him and then he hit me so hard, I lost my breath. I thought that was it . . . and then Jeff burst into the room." She held on to Jagger as years of anguish spilled out, her body shaking in his arms as he pressed his lips to her temple and murmured soothing words in her ear.

"Jeff was only twelve, and small for his age, but very protective of me. He knocked Leo away with a steel pipe. He must have known he had no hope of winning that fight, but the odds didn't stop him. Leo went crazy. He grabbed the pipe and almost beat Jeff to death. Viper finally came upstairs and knocked Leo off him. Jeff was in the hospital for weeks. Because of me. I always thought I should have fought harder—"

"You were only sixteen, and Leo's not a small man."

"Still . . ." She looked up at him through lashes wet with tears. "If I'd been able to get him off me, Jeff wouldn't have been hurt."

"If he was only twelve and in the hospital, didn't social services get involved?" Jagger's nostrils flared. "The police?"

"Yes, they got involved," she said. "On behalf of both of us. I was injured, too, and they kept me in the hospital a few days. But Viper has a long reach and a lot of money and influence. Reports were misfiled, people paid off. The social worker disappeared. Viper went to the hospital and made a big show of being a caring dad. In the end, no one could save us."

Jagger pulled away and looked down at her, aghast. "So you went back?"

When she finally had herself under control, she tilted her chin up and met his gaze. "The day I was discharged from the hospital was the day I put a gun to my head and he let me go. But not Jeff. He said he'd kill Jeff before he let him leave with me."

"And Leo?"

She gripped his T-shirt, afraid she'd lose herself in the memories if she didn't have an anchor. "He never gave up. He stalked me for a while, beating up the guys I was dating. But when I got my first gun and threatened him after he broke my boyfriend's fingers, he backed off. He still harasses me, but not so much."

"And the nightmares?"

She shuddered. "It's always the same. Dark. Pinned to the bed. Can't move or breathe. Might be better if you didn't hold me. The first night we slept together was the first night I didn't have a nightmare."

Jagger hugged her face between his hands. "Do you like to be held?"

"Yes." More than anything. But only in *his* arms. She'd never felt as safe as when Jagger held her as she drifted off to sleep.

"Then I'll hold you. You deserve to be held. Not just tonight but every night."

"Maybe," she whispered. Just a few hours ago, she'd been happy, content, satisfied in a way she'd never been before, and now everything was an emotional tangle. Maybe one day when Conundrum was just a distant memory, someone would hold her every night and she would no longer feel afraid.

"No party." Jagger slammed his coffee cup on the worn, wooden kitchen table.

"It's Dawn's birthday. I'm not going to miss it."

Jagger stared at the infuriating woman in front of him and tried to think his way through the impasse. But quietly. Although they were the only people in the clubhouse kitchen, he had no idea who was outside.

"I don't want you going to some sleazy bar and dancing with men who have only one thought on their minds. Viper is still a threat. Axle is hurt, which makes him more dangerous, and we might have a rat in the club. There's no way the Jacks just found us at that hill above the ice house. Tell Dawn to come here." He gave himself a mental pat on the back for coming up with a perfect solution. None of the brothers would dare touch Arianne, and he'd be able to keep an eye on her. Plus he would be saved the hassle of beating up strangers who touched what was his.

"I thought we had an understanding: You pretend to own me. And I pretend I believe it."

His eyes narrowed. "There is no pretending. Especially after you told me you were going to meet Jeff and trade that piece of paper in your pocket for a passport outta town. There is no way I'm letting you meet him alone. I don't trust him. Viper's influence over him is pervasive. He goaded Jeff into shooting that civilian. Who know what else he'll make him do?"

Arianne gripped her coffee cup, her knuckles whitening, and cut him off with a huff. "This isn't about Jeff and the passport. It's about Dawn. I'm not going to sit around locked up at the clubhouse on my best friend's birthday, especially since it might be the last one we celebrate together."

Two steps forward. One step back. Last night she'd confided in him, accepted his comfort and protection. He'd held her as she slept in his arms, soothing her when he thought she might be distressed. He'd thought that would be the end of any talk about leaving Conundrum, and then she'd pulled out that damned piece of paper. Totally ruined his morning. And all before he'd had his first cup of coffee, which was rapidly cooling as they spoke.

"I can't keep you safe in a crowded bar."

"I know how to keep myself safe." Her eyes gleamed as she pushed her chair away from the table. The skin on the back of Jagger's neck prickled in warning, but by the time he was live to the danger, she was sitting on the table in front of him, a feast of curves to sate even the hungriest appetite.

She lifted one long, beautiful leg and rested her bare foot on the arm of his chair, spreading herself for his viewing pleasure, teasing him with a hint of what lay beneath the denim covering the curve of her sex. He licked his lips, remembering her taste, sultry and sweet, the exquisite softness of her pussy, the ripples of her climax around his cock.

Incapable of rational thought, operating solely on instinct, he reached out and she slapped his hand away.

Denied, Jagger rumbled a warning.

"You can send some guards." She reached behind her to push his coffee cup away and her thin cotton tank top stretched taut over her breasts. A noise erupted from his throat, part growl, part groan, all desire.

Arianne gave him a cheeky smile. "Hungry?"

He licked his lips, contemplating which part of her he wanted to taste first. "Not for food."

"Maybe you could come, too." She trailed a finger along his jaw, and Jagger clasped it and drew it into his mouth. She tasted of sex and honey, and his cock throbbed beneath his fly.

"You want me to come?"

Her eyes flashed and a slow, sensual smile spread across her face. She lifted her other leg and placed her foot on his seat between his thighs, her toes only a whisper away from the bulge in his crotch. Her words came out in a sensual purr. "Yes, baby. I want you to come."

How unseemly would it be for an MC president to fuck his woman over the kitchen table while the brothers were talking outside? He drummed his thumb on the arm of his chair, considering. What if he just threw her over his shoulder and carried her upstairs? Probably better for appearances. Not that he was ashamed of his cock, but anything under Arianne's clothes was for his eyes alone.

"Upstairs. Now."

"Party. Later." She wiggled her toes, easing them closer to his throbbing erection. *Christ.* If she didn't stop, he would have her naked and over that table before she could say "saucy temptress."

"I'll set something up."

She slid her toes closer and bit her lip, her eyes darkening to forest green. "Something's already up, it seems."

He gripped the armrest of the chair so hard, his knuckles turned white. "The Sinners own three bars and a strip joint in town. You choose one, I'll close it down. You can have it all to yourselves."

"It won't be fun without any guys." She tilted her head to the side and gave him a beseeching look. "Dawn's friends are mostly single."

The chair seemed to vibrate under his body as he fought for calm. *Not here. Not in the kitchen. Not with lust raging through his veins.* "You want guys," he said, struggling to keep his voice even. "I'll get you guys. Safe guys. You tell me how many you want. I can send all the Sinners, although some will come with old ladies attached, and if that's not enough, I can call up the support clubs."

"Bikers? Dawn's friends are pretty straitlaced compared to her."

Losing the battle for self-control, Jagger reached up and cupped Arianne's chin in his palm, then pulled her down for a kiss, savoring the sweetness of her mouth. "I'll make sure the brothers know. They'll behave like perfect gentlemen."

"Yeah, right. What about drinks?" She ran her tongue along the seam of his lips, and his cock strained in his jeans as he invited her in, tangling his tongue with hers, tasting her sweetness.

"Since we can't go where we want to go," she murmured against his lips, "drinks should be free."

Ravenous, he pulled her off the table and onto his lap, nuzzling the soft skin of her throat. Her scent of sex and wildflowers made him crazed, and willing to do almost anything to get her back upstairs.

"You're pushing it, but if you ask real nice, I might consider a discount."

"How nice?" She rocked against him, grinding her pussy into his erection.

"This nice." He ran his thumb over her bottom lip, forcing her mouth open, then up over the bow before sliding his thumb inside.

Arianne closed her lips around him and sucked hard, stroking him with her tongue.

A low, guttural sound erupted from his throat, and he licked his lips, his gaze riveted on her mouth as she worked his thumb until his cock throbbed in time to her every pull. "Fuck yes. My girl's got a dirty mouth."

Arianne pulled away and smiled. "It gets dirtier if the drinks are free."

"Riders Bar?" Zane gave Jagger an incredulous look. "You want to close down Riders?"

"We're not closing it down. Just limiting admission to Arianne and her friends and any of our brothers who want to go."

"How many girls?" Cade leaned back in his chair in their new executive board meeting room, a dining room in their new and soon-to-be renovated clubhouse. The long polished oak table was large enough to accommodate twelve brothers and the room could hold at least a dozen more chairs if the board needed to bring in guests or advisors as they often did.

"About thirty. But she wanted me to point out that they aren't all lays."

Gunner cracked a smile. "They're all lays if you treat them right."

Zane tapped his pen on the polished wood table, and Jagger groaned inwardly. Zane would never challenge him in front of the executive board, but that didn't mean he wouldn't feel free to share his thoughts the minute the room cleared. And apparently he had thoughts. Lots of 'em.

Hoping to deflect Zane's concerns, Jagger pushed himself out of his chair and paced the room. "We just blew up the Jacks' ice house, claimed Viper's daughter, and injured six of his men. The Jacks will be out for blood, and things are going to get ugly. We need to celebrate when we can. Last night was just blowing off steam. We need to do something big, invite a few clubs we want to patch over. Word will get around. Viper's licking his wounds and we're boozing it up."

"I like it," Cade said. "Especially the part about thirty girls who may or may not all be lays."

Sparky's eyebrows furrowed. "I thought you were banging Arianne's friend."

"She's just interested in keeping it casual."

Gunner clutched his chest. "No. Say it isn't so. Casual? When everyone knows you're a one-woman kind of man?"

"Anyone got a gun?" Cade scowled. "Care to shut Gunner the fuck up?"

Sparky leaned back in his chair and folded his arms behind his head. "So, Jag. You gonna make her your old lady? You two were going at it so hard last night, I couldn't get any sleep."

"I'm not looking for an old lady. She's property of the Sinners, but she belongs exclusively to me."

He caught Gunner and Sparky sharing a puzzled glance and tipped his head back to stare at the cracked plaster on the ceiling and the dusty chandelier. "Like a sweet butt."

Everyone nodded. Sweet butts helped the club and the brothers in exchange for protection and a place to stay. Occasionally, a brother would claim a sweet butt for his own, with a view to making her an old lady. In those cases, although the "keep off" rule for old ladies didn't apply, the brothers respected the claim and stayed away.

Zane leaned over and whispered. "Can I be there when you tell her you've given her sweet butt status? You'll need someone to handle the funeral arrangements."

"Fuck you."

He laughed. "You're the one who's fucked."

Jagger dug his nails into his palm under the table. He was more than aware that he was walking a very fine line between duty and desire. Zane, who knew him best, saw as much. He wondered if the others saw it, too. Making her his old lady would solve the problem, but he simply wasn't prepared to go down that road. Not after Christel. And not with a woman who was still talking about leaving Conundrum. Declaring an old lady was like announcing a marriage in the civilian world. Both people had to want it. And they had to want it forever.

When no one spoke, he flipped through his agenda, searching for the next order of business, his body shaking with an emotion he couldn't even begin to understand.

"Here's how it's gonna be." He placed his hands, palm

down, on the table. "I'm not interested in another long feud with the Jacks. We're the dominant club in Montana and we're gonna stay that way. I don't care that they think they have dominant status. We need to bring them to heel."

The chorus of assent from around the table pleased him, and he relaxed back in his chair.

"We've just hit them a hard blow. Next I want to launch an assault closer to home. We're gonna pick off Viper's senior officers one by one, starting with Leo and Bear. Find them. Bring them in. Alive. Then we'll have some fun." A plausible reason for bringing them in. No one needed to know his real motive for getting Leo under his fists. And if Leo didn't survive the interrogation, the world would be a safer place.

"Damn right, we will." Zane thumped his fist on the table, and the rest of the executive board murmured their approval.

"Any news on Axle?"

"He's outta the hospital," Cade said. "Sherry went to see him. Apparently, he's even more pissed than before. Sherry thinks he's gone crazy and he's obsessed with revenge."

"Makes sense," Zane said. "Most animals are more dangerous when they're wounded. Makes them fearless."

What the fuck? Jagger slammed a fist on the table. "Sherry went to see him? Even though he's out of the club on bad terms? And no one saw that as a problem?"

The room went quiet and Jagger contemplated his next move. He'd warned Sherry to stay away from Axle. No one in the club was allowed contact with any member who was kicked out on bad terms and that included house mamas and sweet butts.

"What do you wanna do?" Cade raised his brows. "He treated her like shit, but she had feelings for him. She's a sweet girl and I'm damn sure she went to see him out of compassion, and not with any intent to betray the club. Jill said—"

Jagger cut him off with a sharp gesture, the burden of leadership lying heavy within his chest. "She knows the rules. She's out of the club. I want—"

"I didn't get to finish," Cade interrupted, his voice uncharacteristically sharp. "Jill said she showed up after her meeting with Axle with a black eye, and her arm in a sling."

Fuck. He had to kick her out of the club. It was the right thing to do. But if Axle was abusing her, Jagger couldn't just leave her out on her own. She'd had a rough life before joining the Sinners, which meant she'd put up with a lot more than most women would, and he didn't want her winding up with Axle because she had no place else to go. "Cade, send Wheels to find her. After I speak to her, she can stay in the safe house until she gets herself sorted."

More surprised murmurs around the table. Everyone had assumed he was keeping Arianne at the safe house. But the last few nights, he'd had her in his bed at the clubhouse, and he didn't want her anywhere else.

Changing the topic before he changed his mind, he looked over at Gunner. "Any luck on sniffing out our rat?"

Gunner shook his head. "I went back to the ice house and checked our position from every road. You were right. No way could anyone have known where we were unless they'd been told. And I'm wondering if the same rat called the cops at the vacant lot. Did anyone notice the cops came just as we started winning the fight?"

Jagger had noticed. He'd also noticed that Arianne had been at every location where they'd been ratted out. But he couldn't believe she was a Black Jack spy.

"Get Tank to help you and maybe another one of the junior patch. I can't believe someone slipped through our net, but when we find the bastard, we'll make him wish he'd run when he had the chance."

After business was done and the brothers had tossed around names of possible support clubs, everyone headed out to Riders. Jagger stayed in his seat, sensing Zane's impatience, and resigning himself to a lecture about things he didn't want to hear.

As expected, Zane waited until the room was clear and then launched his attack. Did Jagger realize he had become the subject of numerous discussions that bordered on disrespect? The president should be above gossip. His behavior should be exemplary. He shouldn't be fucking the daughter of the club's greatest enemy in the guise of claiming her as a blood price. If she'd been any other woman, the club would have set her to work. She should be cooking and cleaning and washing their clothes. Instead, Arianne had freedoms the sweet butts didn't have, and she slept in Jagger's bed.

Steeling himself to keep his temper in check, Jagger fired out question after question, giving Zane no time to consider his answers. Zane was a thinker, intellectualizing everything until the moment had passed to react. He wanted Zane's honest answers, his true impression.

Yes, Zane said, she did contribute to the club by fixing the brothers' bikes. And okay, she saved Bandit's ass on the hill, and probably the lives of a couple of brothers by shooting at members of her own club. Maybe she was a better pool player than anyone he'd met, and she'd drunk the prospects under the table at the party even though she was half their weight. Her shooting was good . . . okay . . . spectacular, just like her dart game. But the only reason she outraced everyone on her bike was because she didn't ride American.

And didn't that say it all.

★ SIXTEEN ★

There will be no fraternizing with rival clubs.

Arianne stood on the edge of the tiny dance floor in Riders Bar, watching Dawn's friends tangle together with a handful of junior patch bikers as they gyrated to Steppenwolf's heart pumping, "Born to Be Wild."

Lights twinkled on the faux vines twisted around pillars and hanging from beams on the exposed ceiling in the reclaimed mill house on the West Side of Conundrum. Smoke drifted upward through the semidarkness, giving the bar the look of a primordial swamp. She caught a glimpse of Dawn in the crowd and made her way over to her.

"Looking good." Dawn smiled when Arianne joined her. "That dress looks even better in this light." She pointed to the retro disco ball overhead and Arianne winced at the sight of multiple images of herself in the formfitting red dress Dawn had retrieved from the stash of emergency clothes she kept at Dawn's apartment.

The dress had attracted more than its fair share of attention, but it was clear the bikers were operating on a hands-off-or-die policy with her. No pinches, grabs, or subtle brushes of an arm over her breast in passing. No bad lines or come-ons. In that respect, it was the tamest evening out she'd ever had.

They danced through two more songs, but when the DJ spun a heavy metal ballad, Arianne's nose wrinkled. "Let's get a drink."

"I'd forgotten how hands-on bikers are." Dawn slung her purse over her shoulder and followed Arianne off the dance floor. "I swear if I have to slap another hand away from my ass or my boobs, I'm gonna scream."

Arianne pushed her way through the crowd and found them a standing space at the bar. "Not that I'm wanting to be touched, but I also don't like feeling like an outcast. Everyone stands at least two feet away when they're talking to me. When some guy stumbled into me on the dance floor, everyone scattered and he screamed and ran out the door. It's like I have a big sign stamped on my forehead that says 'Keep Off.'"

"You do." Dawn waved down the bartender. "And it's 'cause your man is Jagger, president of the Sinner's Tribe MC and expert scowler."

"He's not my man," Arianne grumbled. "If it's a relationship, it's the most confusing one I've ever had. We've never had a date. We don't hang out like normal couples. When we're together, we're either having sex or being shot at, chased, or attacked. No one can figure out where I fit into the club hierarchy, so they say things like, 'So how's the little blood price today?' or 'Yo, blood price, fix my puncture.' I don't even know where I stand with him."

"He *claimed* you." Dawn gave her a nudge. "Possession doesn't get more primitive than that. Not many people would understand what that means in the biker world, but I do. And you do, too. You just can't accept it."

"If I accept it, I'm staying in Conundrum."

Dawn laughed. "If you didn't want to accept it, you would have contacted Jeff already and made your trade."

Arianne cringed inwardly. Should she tell Dawn she'd

been in touch with Jeff? Dawn ran hot and cold with Jeff depending on how drugged up he was when he showed up at the bar or her apartment, but how could she not share with her bestie?

"I did." She waved the bartender over, not daring to look Dawn in the eye. "I texted him the phone number Bunny gave me, and he offered to drop off the passport with Jeff. But I wanted to see him again. I just need to know, whatever decision I make, he's going to be okay."

"I hope you decide to stay," Dawn said softly. "More than anything. For you and for me. You and Jagger are good together. You're different since you met him. More confident. More determined. Happier."

"Safe." Arianne twisted her mother's ring around her finger. "I feel safe when I'm with him. But that's a problem. He wants . . . no, needs . . . to protect me. And if I stay in Conundrum, I need to be able to protect myself."

They ordered their drinks. Free, of course. She hadn't been certain Jagger would actually give in, but when the bartender told them girls' drinks were on the house, a warm feeling had spread through her body.

"I think you're right that I've changed in the last few weeks." She stirred her Long Island Iced Tea. "I don't spend every minute of every day thinking about ways to escape or what Viper is going to do to me next, or even what life would be like after I leave Conundrum. For the first time, I'm kinda liking my life here."

"You have changed." Dawn sipped her margarita. "In a nutshell, you've become badass. You walk, talk, strut, ride, and shoot like a badass biker chick. I would blame Jagger, but I think you had it in you all along. You just needed a bigger badass to set you free."

Arianne laughed. "What about you and Cade? He's hunting for you. I've been watching him since he came in.

He's tapped pretty much every blonde in the place, and he's heading this way."

"He's trouble." Dawn bit her lip. "We wound up in bed together again that night he showed up at the pool hall. But I told him it had to be the last time. I mean . . . our sexual chemistry is off the charts. The minute I'm near him, all I can think about is getting his hot ass into my bed. But after we do the nasty, all I can think about is getting him out. I can't have anyone in my life right now. I have two little girls who need their mommy and I need to focus my energy that way."

"Dawn . . ." Arianne gave Dawn's hand a sympathetic squeeze. "You have to look out for yourself, too. The girls wouldn't begrudge you a little happiness."

Dawn's voice hitched, and she gave the bartender a wan smile when he slid another drink across the counter. "Cade is a distraction. One night was good. The second night . . . okay, it was epic. But I don't want him thinking there's more where that came from. How am I going to say no?"

"Like this . . . 'No.' "

"Easy to say." Dawn gave a wry laugh. "Not so easy to do. You think you could say no to Jagger?"

Arianne blushed. "Actually, last night I said no. Several times. But that's just because I didn't think I could come that many times in a row. Really, he's everything I've been running from: a biker, living in Conundrum, an MC president, dominant, possessive, aggressive, prone to violence . . . but he's also everything I ever secretly imagined. I can relax with him, be myself, laugh. He makes me feel safe. He's devastatingly gorgeous and amazing in bed. He's a great leader, and the whole protective and possessive thing—"

"My girl's stayin' in Conundrum." Dawn grinned and

then turned to chat with a couple of her friends who had spotted them at the bar.

Arianne exchanged a few words with the new arrivals, but her skin prickled with awareness. He was here. Whether it was some slight change in the vibe of the room, or the way a path cleared near the door, she just knew he was waiting.

After excusing herself from the group, she pushed her way through the crowd, back to the table she and Dawn had snagged when they first came in. And there he was, sprawled in a chair, legs parted wide, his gaze fixed on her. Intent. Carnal. Predatory. He licked his lips and her panties dampened.

"Speak of the devil." Dawn appeared at her elbow, drink in hand.

Unable to look away, Arianne just stared. He was breathtakingly gorgeous, dominating the bar with the force of his presence alone. His jeans were a feast of denim over powerful thighs, tight in all the right places. Broad shoulders covered the back of the chair and his cut hung open, giving her a mouth-watering glimpse of his black T-shirt stretched taut over his rippling abs.

Images of their night together flashed through her mind—his lips on her skin, the rough way he'd handled her, the soft whispers in her ear.

The promise she had made this morning.

Jagger's lazy gaze drifted down her body then back up to rest on the lowest-cut neckline she had ever worn—the main reason the dress had lived in Dawn's closet so long. His eyes lit with an inner glow and he crooked his finger, beckoning her over.

"Looks like your man is calling."

"Arrogant bastard." A smile tugged the corners of Arianne's lips. "Does he think I'm going to come running because he waggled his finger?"

"That would be a yes." Cade joined them and wrapped his arms around Dawn's waist. "Man sees his woman dressed all fine, looking hot as fuck, he's not gonna waste any time getting his hands on her." He nuzzled Dawn's ear and she tipped her head to the side to give him better access.

"See," she mouthed. "Can't say no."

Arianne looked up and almost melted under the heat of Jagger's gaze. So he liked what he saw, did he? Maybe the dress wasn't a bad idea after all. And if she could get him hot . . . Drawing in a deep breath, she flipped her hair and walked toward him, slow and sexy, hips swaying, her gaze fixed on his, working it with every click of her shiny black stilettos.

By the time she reached his chair, his hand was fisted on his thigh, his lips pressed together. Her eyes dropped to his neck, and she watched his pulse throb beneath his skin. What would happen if she took a little lick?

"Hey, baby." She dropped her hands to her hips and tilted her head to the side. She had never thought of herself as a sexual person, never flirted or played games, and although she liked the way she looked, she'd never considered herself pretty. But the way Jagger's eyes roved over her, as if there were no one else in the bar, naked hunger in his gaze, made her feel like the sexiest woman in the whole damn world.

"You're so fucking hot, I can't decide if I want to rip that dress off you or fuck you in it first." He slid a hand over her hip, pulling her toward him.

"You're looking pretty fine yourself." She cupped his jaw, rough with a five-o'clock shadow. "I like this look. Nothing screams 'badass' better than bristles."

He caught her hand and brought her palm to his lips. "You haven't even *seen* badass, sweetheart. I've been gentle with you so far, but seeing you in that dress and those fuck-me shoes, I'm thinking I'm done with gentle." With his free hand on her ass, he pulled her closer, between his spread legs, an entirely possessive move that was clearly meant as a message to every man in the room.

Arianne bit her lip against the arousal raging through her body. "Are you trying to turn me on?"

He traced lazy circles up the inside of her thigh, his fingers delving beneath her dress. Arianne gasped, and a slow, sensual smile spread across his face." You're already turned on. Should we see just how wet you are?" He eased her dress up an inch, and Arianne slapped his hand away.

"We're in public."

"My people." He pulled her against him, his fingers digging into her ass. "My bar. My rules. If I wanted to take you over my knee and spank you for making a man so hard he can barely think, no one's gonna stop me."

Her nerve endings tingled. The idea of giving up that much control both scared and excited her. "I'll stop you."

Jagger stilled, his gaze focused, intent. "No, you won't. You like that idea." He shifted in his chair, spreading his legs farther apart. "Jesus. My girl wants to be spanked. And I thought I was hard before." He caressed her ass, then gave her a pinch. "Tonight."

The DJ played JT's "Not a Bad Thing," and she crooked her finger and took a step back, beckoning him out of the chair, desperate to distract him from the turn of a conversation she wasn't quite ready to have.

Once she hit the dance floor, she ran her hands down her hips, dancing to the beat, her gaze fixed on him. Although he didn't move, his eyes followed every sweep of her hands as she caressed her way up her body, and his tongue darted out to lick his lips.

And then he was out of the chair and in front of her—so close, his raw, sensual scent of leather and soap, the heat of his body, and the evidence of his desire filled her with dangerous thoughts.

"We're leaving."

"It's Dawn's birthday."

"Now."

She leaned up and pressed a kiss to his throat, feeling the beat of his pulse on her lips. "One dance."

He grunted his assent, then wrapped his arms around her and swayed them to the music. She was pressed so hard against him, that she could feel the rigid line of his shaft against her hips, the pounding of his heart against her breasts.

Arianne moved trembling hands over his shoulders, tangling them in his soft, thick hair. "Is this how you dance?"

Jagger jerked her closer, thrusting his knee between her legs, forcing her dress to ride dangerously high. "Sweetheart, this is how I fuck."

Arianne softened against him, her nose pressed into the hollow at the base of his throat, her body hyperaware of every stroke of his hands down her back, the press of his thigh against the curve of her sex, the rapid thud of his heart against her chest. "What happens now?"

He twisted his hand in her hair and tugged her head back, his lips scorching a trail along her jaw. "Now, we're leaving. Soon, I'm gonna fuck you in that sexy little red dress and those sexy little heels. Later, I'm gonna take them off and you're gonna kneel in front of me and show me how sweet that dirty little mouth can be."

The press of his hard body against her was pure bliss. Lightning bolts of pleasure speared through her veins until every part of her body was hot and sensitive to his touch.

"And you will *never* do what you did tonight," he growled. "A dress like this, you wear only for me. Touching yourself, you do only for me. And you drink only when I'm with you so I can take advantage."

Drunk on his savage masculinity and his sensual promises, and maybe two too many drinks, she leaned up and nipped his ear. "I'm not afraid of you."

His fingers sank into her waist and he lowered his head, his dark eyes intense as he sealed his mouth over hers and stole her breath in a scorching kiss. Her lips parted and their tongues met, tangled, thrust together deep and wet as he took control. "Looking the way you look and dancing the way you danced in front of other men, you should damn well be afraid."

His tongue was down her throat when the first shots rang out.

Instinct sent him diving behind the low retaining wall surrounding the dance floor, dragging Arianne with him. Screams echoed around them. Glass shattered. He looked over the wall, and his blood pumped hot in his veins. *Leo.* What the fuck was he doing here, and who the hell did he have with him?

Jagger counted at least twelve men wearing cuts, six from the Black Jacks and six with patches he didn't recognize. They had secured all the exits and were herding people into the center of the bar.

"What's going on?" Arianne pulled her .38 from her purse and then rolled her eyes when Jagger scowled. "I grew up in an outlaw MC. You think I'd go anywhere without my gun? Usually I carry a .22 in my purse, but I haven't been able to go home yet to get it."

He didn't want her armed and ready to engage the enemy. He wanted her safe. Preferably hidden away in a cupboard or locked in a bathroom. "You won't be using it. Leo's out there. He's got another club with him. They might be wanting to patch over to the Jacks, so he's puttin' them through their paces. In my fucking bar."

More shots rang out. More screams. Leo's men shouted for everyone to take a seat and stay put.

Arianne peeked over the wall and huddled back down. "Road Kill. They've been trying to patch over to the Jacks for years. They'd pretty much do anything for Viper's protection."

"Like retrieving Viper's daughter?"

Arianne paled. "Yeah. That would do it. Bringing me in would win them all sorts of favors from Viper."

Jagger caught sight of Cade behind an overturned table near the kitchen door, and Zane behind the bar. Gunner and Sparky were caught in the middle and were standing with T-Rex and Tank, forming a wall between Leo and Arianne's friends. The rest of the brothers were scattered around the room, each one under the guard of one of Leo's men.

Arianne checked her clip and disengaged her safety. "Well, he's ruined yet another date for me, although your fingers are intact. This time he's not getting away with it."

"Wasn't aware we were on a date."

"I wanna hang with an MC president, I can't be expecting candlelit dinners and walks in the moonlight. Shootings and fights seem to be par for the dating course with you. And if you want to get romantic and give me a present, I could use a new clip."

Jagger chuckled, "She's my kind of girl."

Arianne rolled to her knees. "You want to take him out, or shall I?"

Jagger grabbed her wrist, his moment of humor forgotten. "You're gonna stay put until Cade signals it's clear, then I'm gonna cover you while you run for the kitchen."

She yanked her hand away. "Typical man. You want me to stay in the kitchen while the boys watch the game. No, thank you. First, I'm not leaving my friends. And second, Leo and I have a score to settle."

"Fuck, Arianne." He yanked her down. "This is no time for games."

"I'm not playing games. I'm playing to win."

"You hiding from me, Vexy?" Leo's voice rang out in the now silent bar. "Scared I'm gonna shoot you? I'm disappointed. It wasn't that long ago we were in bed together and you were screaming my name."

"Bastard." And before Jagger could stop her, she stood. "Get out, Leo. You don't belong here."

Leo sneered. "Neither do you. Once a Jack, always a Jack. No matter how many damn Sinners you sleep with."

Enraged, Jagger pushed himself to his feet, angling his body to protect Arianne as he made a quick assessment of the situation. The Sinners caught in the center of the bar had now ringed the girls, protecting them from Leo's men. Leo stood near the front door, flanked by Black Jacks, while a couple of bikers from Road Kill took up the rear. Cade and Zane were still hiding near the back and side exits. Leo's bikers patrolled the perimeter of the bar, shoving stray Sinners toward the crowd in the center.

Jagger bit his lip and tasted blood. Leo stood directly across from Arianne, not even bothering to watch the civilian roundup. "What do you want, Leo?" He kept his voice low, forcing Leo to lean in, straining to hear. "Aside from a quick death, which you're not gonna get."

Leo shot at the mirror ball above the dance floor and it exploded into pieces, raining down on the hardwood below. "Sinners blew up our ice house. We've come for a little retribution. Thought we'd redecorate your bar with bullets. And while we're here, I'll just take Vexy home."

"She belongs to the Sinners now." Jagger tensed, waiting for her usual retort that she didn't belong to anyone, but it never came. He glanced quickly to the side and saw Cade and Zane in position near the exits.

"She belongs to me." Leo sneered. "I had her first. Or did she forget to tell you?"

Crack. Arianne fired her gun and the bullet thudded into a pillar to Leo's left.

He startled and jumped to the side, his face twisting in anger. "Fucking bitch." Leo roared. "Did you just fire at me? What the fuck's happened to you?"

"I found something at the Sinner clubhouse I thought I'd lost a long time ago." Her voice shook, and Jagger placed a hand on her arm.

"Easy, sweetheart. Room's a powder keg waiting to explode. You kill him now, it will go off, and we don't want to do that until we get the civilians outta here."

"How about you get your damn hand off my arm?" Arianne grated. "I've always wanted to do that, and if I were aiming to kill, he'd be dead."

Leo snapped his fingers, and one of the Jacks grabbed a tall redhead and held a gun to her temple.

"Here's how it's gonna be," Leo shouted. "You got five minutes to vacate the bar before our shooting party starts. Anyone left inside will be considered fair game. Vexy comes with us or I'll tell my brother over there to shoot the girl."

One of Leo's Jacks opened a side door, and Sparky tried to keep order as people ran out into the alley.

Arianne leaned in to Jagger and murmured. "Look at the Road Kill president. He's not too happy with the new plan. I have a feeling Road Kill thought they were just coming to shoot up the bar and not off pretty girls."

Jagger took another quick look around. The Sinners who hadn't been rounded up were positioned near the exits and had formed a perimeter around the bar. Cade had been busy. Once they took out the exit guards, they would regain control.

"Leo's the key," he said. "And you're right. Road Kill isn't fully committed to him. You can see how they're standing slightly apart from his Jacks and the president is hanging back near the door instead of standing by his side. He's probably insulted Viper put Leo in command."

"Viper will never patch them over. This is a game to him. He dangles the carrot, gets the small clubs to do his dirty work, and then takes the carrot away."

"You need to get that message to Road Kill's president."

A smile tugged at her lips. "Leo's in my way. Think you can hit his leg at this distance? I'll go for his shoulder."

"I'd be happier if you left the bar with everyone else."

In a wry tone, Arianne said, "Prepare to be disappointed."

Jagger dropped his hand and signaled their intention to Zane and Cade, who would know to provide cover if this turned into a shoot-out. But he was banking on Road Kill not risking their lives to defend Leo or the few Jacks he'd brought with him.

"Come, Vexy." Leo snapped his fingers in a pathetic imitation of Viper then fired a warning shot that zinged over her shoulder and shattered the window behind her.

"You're not Viper. Don't even try to pretend." She pulled the trigger. Jagger did the same. The two shots followed each other in a double thunderclap. Leo screamed and fell to his knees, one hand on his shoulder and one on his thigh.

No one moved.

Arianne glared at the stunned bikers. "Anyone else want to ruin our party?"

★ SEVENTEEN ★

Only old ladies and brothers can babysit your colors.

"So, this is your apartment. It's not how I pictured it." Jagger paced around Arianne's living room, his concession to stop at her apartment on the way back to the clubhouse clearly not sitting easily with him. "I thought it would be more girly. Not all this beige furniture and brown tables and landscapes on the walls."

"Girly?" Arianne's voice shook as adrenaline continued to pound through her body. Not just from the anger and frustration at finding herself in the same situation over and over again—guns and violence and crazy bikers—but also at the thrill of finally having stood up to Leo.

She kicked off her shoes and unzipped the riding leathers Jagger had brought for her. "Notice what I'm wearing? You brought these to the bar for me. Why would you think I'm girly?"

He crossed the room in two long strides and helped her undo the snap on her leather trousers. "'Cause I know what's underneath. Hard on the outside, soft and sweet on the inside." He slid the trousers down over her hips and steadied her while she kicked them away.

Arianne looked down at him crouched in front of her, his mouth level with the juncture of her thighs. A wave of

longing suffused her body, and with it a burst of anger. Tonight was a perfect example of why she needed to get out
of Conundrum. She couldn't even go to a birthday party
with her friends without some idiot bikers shooting the
place up and threatening to drag her back to Viper. But Jagger was making it so damn hard to leave. He'd as good as
encouraged her to shoot Leo, stood by her side as she got
the revenge she had dreamed about for eleven years, and
then praised her for her accuracy.

Why? Why was he doing this to her? Why had he made
her fall for him just as the rest of her life was falling into
place?

"You keep lookin' at me like that, and we'll never make
it back to the clubhouse."

"Stop it." She stepped away. "Don't say things that make
me want you. I'm already confused. I hate being part of this
violent world, and yet it allowed me to get back at Leo for
what he did. And if I hadn't met you, I wouldn't have had
the confidence to do that much. When I'm with you, I almost like being a biker and having biker skills. And yet,
this is the life I *don't* want to lead. The life that took my
mother. The life that's taking Jeff. The kind of life where
you have a party, and your friends almost wind up dead."

Jagger stood, his face smoothing into an expressionless
mask. "This *is* your life, Arianne. You were born for this.
I don't know any other woman who could have earned the
respect of the Road Kill president the way you did tonight."

"He dropped a bandanna on the table." Her words came
out in a monotone sigh.

"It was as far as he could go. Hell, don't you appreciate
what he was saying with that gesture or what it cost him?
You're a woman. He gave you the kind of respect he would
give another man."

Her pulse quickened and she glared. "So what? I'm supposed to be grateful that he respects me? In the civilian

world, women get that kind of respect every day, and they don't have to shoot someone to earn it."

Jagger took a step toward her and she backed away. Not because she was afraid, but because she didn't know what she would do if he touched her. She was too wound up after the shoot-out. Too angry. Too excited. And too goddamned confused.

"You won't be happy in the civilian world." He kept coming, forcing her to back across the living room and through her bedroom door. Why wouldn't he respect her space? Her need to be alone? Why wouldn't he just go so she could start forgetting about him and move on with her life?

"You can't carry a gun in your purse or strapped to your leg in their world. You can't speed down the highway at one hundred miles per hour. You will struggle just as hard to earn respect from men when you try to get a job in a mechanic's shop. But this world, you know. You have power here. The kind of power Viper fears and can't control."

She forced a laugh when her legs hit the wall. "Viper's not afraid of me."

"You defy him over and over again," Jagger said, stopping only a foot away. "No matter what he does, he can't break you the way he's broken Jeff. He can't scare you or beat you or threaten you into obedience. He can't control you, and he's a man who needs control."

"Like you." Her heart pounded as his heat soaked into her body, making her nipples stiffen so much they ached.

"Like me." He cupped the back of her head with one hand and pulled her forward for a long, deep kiss.

And then he released her and walked away. "But not tonight."

Her brows drew together as she watched him stretch out on her bed, wrinkling her soft pink duvet.

"What?"

He looked around the room—its soft pastels, white antique furniture, and pink sheer curtains—and smiled. "I knew there had to be pink and girly somewhere in your place. You hide it in the bedroom just like you hide it under your leathers." He gestured to her shelves, filled with pictures of Jeff and their mom, her friends, and happier times. "You hide your heart here. These are Jeff's paintings around the room, aren't they?"

"He made the furniture for me, too." Still confused by Jagger's sudden withdrawal, she didn't move. "He bought it used and then spent months refinishing it. He said he was happy to do it and he wouldn't take any money from me. It wasn't that long ago." She gestured to the door. "I thought you wanted to get going."

"I want you," he said softly. "Here. Where your heart is. But not the way you think. Watching you in that bar, holding your own against Leo and a roomful of bikers, so fucking cool and confident . . . turned me on like nothing else. Nothing sexier than a girl with a gun except my girl with a gun." He patted the bed beside him. "You controlled that room, sweetheart, and I'm not taking that away from you."

"I don't understand."

His smile faded. "I'm a man who needs control. Always have. Always will. I need it to lead the Sinners, and I need it in the bedroom. But tonight, I'm giving it to you. I'm not saying it will ever happen again—because knowing myself as I do, I suspect it won't—but right now I want my girl to run the show." He folded his arms behind his head. "Do what you want with me."

A slow, sensual smile spread across Arianne's face as she walked over to the bed, working that goddamn skin-tight dress like there was no tomorrow. Lust soared inside him, and with it the instinctive, almost primal urge to pin his female to the bed and take her in the most primitive way to prove his dominance. But not tonight. This night he would gift her with his trust. He would rein in his need to take control. He could only hope she would understand what he was trying to say.

She stopped at the foot of the bed, and her gaze raked down his body, lingering on the bulge in his jeans. He was already hard. Hell, he'd been hard since he walked into the bar and she'd shimmied her way through the crowd. His woman. Coming to him. With the kind of confidence that could bring a man to his knees. And when she faced down Leo, squeezed that trigger, he knew he'd found the woman he'd been waiting for all his life.

He reached for his belt, and Arianne held up her hand. "No one touches what's mine."

Jagger growled, his cock throbbing beneath his fly. This had seemed like a good idea at the time but if she didn't tie him to the bed, he didn't know how long he would last.

Without taking her gaze off him, she unzipped her dress, sliding it off one arm and then the other, drawing it slowly over her curves. Blood rushed to his shaft and he shifted on the bed. When she was down to a lacy red bra and a matching pair of panties, she posed for him and twisted her lips to the side. "Hmmm. A Jagger in my bed. What shall I do?"

"You should get up here, is what you should do."

"Bossy." She turned and bent over, giving him a perfect view of the round globes of her ass and the dark shadow of her pussy swathed in red lace. "Maybe I'll just tidy up my room. There are a lot of clothes on the floor."

Jagger's body began to quake as he imagined holding her in that position, her hands on the dresser, his cock pressed against her ass. He wanted to rip those lace panties off and bury himself deep inside her. Fuck her until she came, screaming his name.

Come to me. His silent plea was rewarded with a grin when Arianne looked back over her shoulder.

"You look kinda hot. Maybe I should come up there and help you undress."

"Maybe you should undress first." He licked his lips when she kneeled on the bed, her breasts straining against the fine lace of her bra. "Or I can help you."

She crawled up his body, brushing her breasts against his shaft as it strained against his jeans. With a soft sigh, she knelt astride his hips. *Glorious.* He ran his hands along her curves, settling them on her hips.

"Tell me what you want, beautiful."

"Shirt off."

He was more than happy to comply. Pushing himself to a semi-recline, he removed his cut and handed it to her, then stripped off his shirt. When he lay down again, Arianne hadn't moved.

"Something wrong?"

She held up the cut. "Black Jack rules say only a brother or an old lady can babysit your colors."

"Same with the Sinners." And if that didn't get the message across, nothing would.

Arianne stared at him, and her cheeks flushed. Then she carefully folded his cut and placed it on a chair beside the bed. As before, he was surprised by the immense satisfaction he derived from her gesture. Nothing was more important than a biker's colors. Except maybe the woman who knew how to handle them.

She returned to her position and he lay back on the pillow and licked his lips. "Do I get a reward?"

Arianne laughed and leaned down, running her tongue between his lips before diving in deep, tangling it with his own in a hot, wet kiss that made his balls ache with pleasure.

"Good reward," he murmured against her lips.

"That was the appetizer." She slid down his chest and flicked her tongue over his nipple. Jagger groaned at the exquisite sensation and curled his hand around the back of her head, undecided whether he wanted to pull her away or hold her in place.

"Hands back." Her quick shallow breathing told him she wasn't unaffected by her sensual torture, and although he had to grit his teeth to let her go, he did as she asked.

Moments later, she was kissing her way down his stomach, nestling her soft body between his parted thighs as she undid his belt and loosened his fly.

"I think I made you a promise this morning." Slowly, painstakingly, she opened his belt buckle and unbuttoned his jeans, easing his clothing over his hips. Jagger's cock sprang free, but that small measure of relief dissipated quickly under the warmth of her breath.

"Reward for good behavior," she said, and then she licked him from balls to tip.

"Christ." Jagger's body tensed and his hips jerked, thrusting toward her hot, wet mouth. "Need to touch you."

Arianne pulled away. "No touching. You get only what I give you. Nothing more."

He growled, his fingers clenched against the back of his head, the muscles in his arms shaking with the effort of keeping still.

His brain fuzzed when she pumped him with her fist. He was already rock hard, his shaft hot and heavy against her palm. She stroked his length, and aimed it at her mouth. Jagger groaned and cursed himself for what was turning out to be a really bad idea.

"Poor baby," she whispered.

"Hard baby."

She bit her lip and looked up at him from beneath her lashes. "Let's see."

Settling herself between his legs, she took him in her mouth, just the tip, teasing him with her tongue until he was dizzy with lust. Not wanting to spend himself too soon, and definitely not before he got her off, he lay back and thought about gaskets and tires and fuel pumps and lube. Lots of lube. Slick. Sliding. Wet.

Fuck.

Arianne released his cock and then gave him lazy smile. "My work here is done."

With an impatient snort, Jagger slid his hand through her hair, yanking her forward, his hand clenched so tight, her eyes watered.

"Suck me, Arianne. Don't play."

"I thought I got to be in control." She pushed herself up and straddled him, slipping off her bra as she rocked over his hardened length. His balls lifted, throbbed, and he felt the warning tingle at the base of his spine that told him it was almost too late.

"Condom. Now."

She slowed and cupped her breasts in her hands, rolling her nipples between each thumb and forefinger. "I'm on the pill. Are you safe?"

He almost wanted to say no. Already at the breaking point, he didn't think he would be able to control himself without at least a layer of latex to dull the sweet sensation of being inside her. But the alternative, denying himself the pleasure of her slick wetness, the intimacy of being as close as two people could get, was simply unacceptable.

"Doc checks everyone once a year. Last time was just a few months ago. All okay."

"Me too." Her cheeks flushed and she gave him a cheeky smile. "Good thing, because I didn't want to stop."

She impaled herself on him, sliding her slick, wet sheath

over his erection, her hips undulating as she took him deep. They groaned together. Moved together. He captured her hips and angled her forward, dragging his cock over her sensitive inner flesh. Arianne panted, falling forward, her hands on either side of his head. Unable to resist, Jagger leaned up and captured her nipple between his teeth, giving it a swirling lick.

The low, guttural sound that escaped her lips inflamed him. He turned his attention to the other nipple, working it until it was a hard bud. Then he released her and eased her back, almost fevered with the need to take control and pump into her hot, wet channel.

She was almost regal, sitting astride him, her back straight, breasts thrust high, long hair spilling over her shoulders. So beautiful, his heart thundered for her, pride swelling his chest.

"Mine," he breathed.

Her eyes sparkled and then she bent down to kiss him. "Yours," she whispered.

She rocked over him, spreading her knees to take him deeper, driving his steel against her sensitive tissue. Sweat beaded on his brow as he strained to hold back. But when he slid his hand down her hip to her throbbing nub, her hips jerked. Slow became fast, and he lost his last ounce of his control.

"Jagger. I can't—"

With a rumbled growl, he tensed, then flipped their bodies, threading his fingers through hers, pinning her wrists to the bed, gazing into the emerald eyes that had captured him the moment they fluttered open outside his burning clubhouse.

"I have so many flaws, I wouldn't even know where to begin," he murmured. "But you are perfect. You have fire, you have soul. Your strength and resilience amaze me. Your gentleness and kindness humble me. Your beauty takes my breath away. If I could have only one thing in this life, it would be you."

"You have me, baby." She arched against him as a groan tore from her throat. "I need you."

"You need me." He dropped his weight to hold her still, just enough for him to regain control. "Next time, I'm going to spank your pretty ass to punish you for all your teasing."

"Now you're the one who's teasing."

He slanted his mouth over hers, angling his body to rub against her clit, and then he thrust deep and he thrust hard. Arianne's body bucked beneath him, and she moaned into his mouth as she came, her pussy pulsing around him, squeezing him until he was mindless with the need to move. He hammered into her, drawing out her orgasm. Pressure built at the base of his spine, and he joined her in release, tearing his mouth away to bellow as he pumped deep inside her.

After they had both come down, he rolled, pulling her over his chest. "I thought I did pretty good letting you take over. I almost made it to the end."

Arianne laughed, the sound muffled against his shoulder. "Not even close. But I appreciate your effort. I like having an MC president under my control, if only to see him suffer."

"Don't get used to it." With all the passion he felt inside, he cupped her face in his hands and kissed her.

"I could get used to this," she whispered.

He didn't know what else to say. He had given her all he had to give. Short of begging, he didn't know what else he could do to convince her to stay.

★ EIGHTEEN ★

The president shall be the sole arbiter of all
matters not covered in the club bylaws
and constitution. His word is law.

"She's not a spy." Jagger shoved the laptop across his paper-strewn desk and glared at Zane. "I thought she'd convinced you she wasn't a Jack when she fired at them to save Bandit. And shooting Leo should have sealed the deal."

He glanced up to make sure the door was closed. The study he had commandeered as an office was the only room in the clubhouse that wouldn't need significant renovation. Dark wood shelves lined the walls, a contrast to the light oak desk and matching credenza. Floor-to-ceiling windows looked out over the backyard, where the target Gunner had pinned up for the shooting demo was still visible through the trees.

Zane folded his arms and leaned back in the visitors' chair. "You can't deny the evidence in those surveillance photographs from the clubhouse fire. And it's not just me. After the incident at Riders, I had a chat with the Road Kill president. He'd pretty much figured Viper never intended to patch them over after Leo showed up at the bar instead of Viper. But he did spend a lot of time in their clubhouse, and he knew all the Jacks. I showed him the surveillance photograph, and he said he was ninety percent sure it was Jeff. Apparently, they don't have many blond Black Jacks."

"All that proves is that Jeff was there."

Zane heaved a sigh. "Jeff and Arianne were at the clubhouse together. Seems likely he's either our arsonist or Cole's shooter, or both. Given the relationship, it's possible Arianne was involved after all—a lookout, maybe, or a distraction?"

Jagger waved a dismissive hand in the air. "She hates them. She hates Viper. Her whole life has been about getting out of Conundrum. I've spent more time with her than any of you. If she were a spy, I'd know."

"I like her." Zane pushed himself out of his chair and paced the room. "The way she took down Leo, what she did at the ice house, and the work she does with Sparky . . . Hell, I almost wish there were two of her. But what if this was all a setup? She knows our men, our security systems, and our operating procedures. She's got her hands on everyone's bike and her pussy wrapped around your cock so tight, you can't even think straight. Could be you're not seeing clearly and there's nothing she won't do for the Jacks."

Jagger's gut clenched. He knew Zane was trying to protect him. "Club first" to Zane had always meant Jagger first. He had already expressed his concerns that Jagger had let Arianne get too close, and if she were betraying him, his leadership would be compromised. With the official elections still two years away, taking down a president meant taking him out—something Zane would never allow to happen.

Still, he couldn't ignore a potential threat to his club. "Club first" meant he had to put the club before anything else. Never had Jagger regretted the code more than he did now.

"She wants to meet her brother tomorrow to get her fake passport . . ." His voice trailed off as regret slid through his heart. Arianne hadn't told him what she was planning to do after she got the passport, which saved him from making a difficult decision. Did he keep her because he'd claimed her even if she didn't want to be with him, or did he let her go and risk never seeing her again? But if she was a suspect, and they took her brother, the decision would be made for him.

"Where's she going?"

"She wants to start a new life in Canada." Jagger steeled himself to hide the emotion balled up in his chest. "Since we know where Jeff will be, we could bring him in for a little fireside chat. If he's the one who torched the clubhouse and killed Cole, then we'll have him right where we want him, and we'll find out how Arianne is involved."

"I don't envy you, brother." Zane snapped his laptop closed. "Never understood why Axle wanted your position so bad. If I had to choose between our friendship and the club, I'd choose you and suffer the consequences. But you don't get that choice. You got the safety of all the brothers riding on your decisions. You always have to be a president. You never get to just be a man."

Jagger's throat tightened and it took several long seconds before he could speak. He'd tried to have a personal life with Christel, and look how that had turned out. Arianne had made him forget that painful lesson and now it was coming back to bite him in the ass.

But he hadn't become president by letting desire conflict with duty. "We'll let her go to draw out her brother. Wheels and T-Rex can guard the exits and bring a cage to escort Jeff to the clubhouse. The meet is at that East Side strip joint, Peelers. Cade knows it so well. He's got his own VIP table which he says is very private, so he'll be with me. We'll keep a low profile until Jeff arrives."

A pained expression crossed Zane's face. "So you're gonna let her go to the meet, thinking she's finally getting her ticket out of Conundrum, and then—"

"We'll bring them back here." Jagger rubbed his temples as his head throbbed in protest. "She knows she's been claimed. She understands what that means. If she leaves, she leaves only because I will it. I haven't talked to her about what she thinks will happen when she meets her brother, but if she's involved in the attack, then she's not going anywhere, and neither is Jeff."

"Fuck." Zane stood, tucking his laptop under his arm. "It's the right thing to do for the club, but if she's innocent, she'll never forgive you."

"I don't need her forgiveness." He needed her acceptance and her trust. He needed her to stay.

Zane took a few steps toward the door and then turned back. "If it comes to that . . . I know what it's like. I had a girl. . . . She was—" His voice cracked, broke. "I had to leave her. Give her up. She said she'd wait forever, but as soon as I left, she betrayed me. Fucking ripped out my heart. Never found it again."

Jagger thudded his fist on the desk after the door closed behind Zane. He didn't want to hear his thoughts on Zane's lips. He didn't want to think about how much he would hurt Arianne and how he would just reinforce in her mind that all bikers were like the Black Jacks, all presidents like the man she hated most in the world. He didn't want to think that tomorrow he was going to lose the best thing that had ever happened to him, the woman who had made him feel again, given him hope that he wouldn't always be alone.

With a frustrated roar, he swept all the papers off his desk. In the end, he would rather have her here and pissed at him than gone forever. As long as she was in Conundrum, he would have a chance to win her back.

So long as she hadn't betrayed him.

"Where's your gun?"

"I have a .22 in my purse." Arianne slid off Jagger's seat

and stepped into the shadows of the parking lot behind Peelers strip club. Trust Jeff to set up a meet in a place like this. Not for the first time, she wondered if the boy she'd known while they were growing up was truly gone.

"Make sure it's always within reach." Jagger flipped his kickstand and gestured for Cade to join them after he parked his bike.

Although Arianne had tried to dissuade Jagger from coming to the meet, he had flat-out refused. Not just because Peelers wasn't safe, he'd said, but also because he didn't trust Jeff after what had happened at the vacant lot. As far as Jagger was concerned, Jeff was a Black Jack, and he insisted on taking the same precautions he would take for any meet with the enemy.

"You don't have to tell me. I always have a weapon within reach."

His concern warmed her, as did his tacit acceptance of her skill with her weapon, especially after he'd been so cold and dismissive over the last two days. She couldn't believe how quickly things had disintegrated after their heated night together and the intimacy they'd shared at her apartment.

After returning to the clubhouse the next morning, Jagger had gone into a meeting, and when he came out, he was a changed man. He hadn't stopped her from returning to Banks Bar to take on a couple of shifts, nor had he complained when she'd told him she was meeting up with Dawn for a drink. Although she had found his protective streak stifling at times, now she wished he would show up and boss her around, just so she knew he cared.

"Get changed."

Arianne startled at his harsh tone. What the hell was going on with him? Did he think she was going to meet Jeff, do the exchange, and take off right away? Despite his change in demeanor, her heart still ached at the thought of leaving him. But she needed to see Jeff one last time. She needed to assure herself she had done everything she could to help him and that he was committed to staying with Viper. Only then would she truly be free to decide what to do.

"Maybe she shouldn't go in with a gun," Cade said. "She might get stopped and draw attention to herself. Plus, I'd feel safer being in an enclosed space if Arianne was armed with something less dangerous, like a blade."

"If I threw a blade at you, Cade, I guarantee I wouldn't miss," she said in exasperation.

"No blades," Jagger snapped, without even a glimmer of humor in his tone. "Especially if you're planning to throw them at Cade." He motioned for T-Rex and Wheels, who had been waiting patiently near the bikes, to check the perimeter.

"I wouldn't be throwing it at Cade." Arianne pressed her lips together and glared, but Jagger was distracted, checking out their secluded corner for a possible ambush.

Arianne unfastened her jacket, shivering as cool air blew through her fine silk shirt, and then tugged off her leather trousers, handing them to Jagger to put in his pack. True to form, Jagger had pawed through the duffel bag she'd packed at her apartment after giving her standard jeans and T-shirt attire a thumbs-down, given they were trying to attract as little attention as possible in the strip club.

"This." He'd tossed a black skirt and a slinky gold top, cut low and draping down the back, on the bed, then walked out of the room.

So she'd worn them. Not simply to avoid another confrontation so near the end of their time together, but also because he had been uncharacteristically subdued, almost angry when he returned from his meeting with Zane.

She traded her biker boots for a pair of stilettos from Jagger's bag and then watched as he paced around the parking lot, his muscular body fading in and out of the shadows. How could she let him go? How could she leave Conundrum when her heart was here? What if everything she had been looking for was standing in front of her, wearing a Sinner cut and an angry scowl? In her heart, she knew Jeff had made his choice. And she had made her choice, too. She just hadn't been able to accept it. Maybe now was the time.

"Jagger. I need to talk to you before we go in. I need to tell you something."

He held out his hand. "Give me your phone."

Without thinking, Arianne handed over her phone, fully expecting him to add more numbers to her address book in case of an emergency. Instead, he tucked the phone in his pocket and gestured for Cade and T-Rex to precede them into the club.

"Hey, I need that." She reached for his pocket, and Jagger slapped her hand away.

"So you can text your brother and tell him how many of us are here?"

Confused by his angry, accusatory tone, Arianne let her hand drop and gave him a puzzled frown. "What are you talking about? I came here to talk to him, and I agreed to you joining me solely on the condition that you stayed in the background so he wouldn't get scared away. We aren't a threat to you. I thought if he still wanted to go, we'd make a plan to leave, but not tonight, and—"

He drew her into the shadows beneath the west wall of the nightclub, his expression dark, almost primal with emotion. "It's so damn easy for you to walk away, isn't it? You got what you wanted from me—safety, protection, someone to watch your back. You know all about the club. All about me. You had your bit of fun, and now you're just going to turn and leave. Back to the Jacks, Arianne? With information that could destroy the Sinners? Will Viper give you a blood patch for taking out Cole?"

Stunned, Arianne took a step back, hitting the cold brick wall with a soft thud. "What are you talking about? I haven't betrayed you. I didn't kill Cole. I'm not going back to Viper. And no, it's not easy to walk away. I've been second-guessing my decision ever since . . . ever since . . ." *Ever since I realized how much I care about you.* But his fury tangled her tongue, and the words wouldn't come out.

Jagger closed the distance between them and caged her against the wall, his body quivering with pent-up emotion, eyes ablaze. "Then make another choice." His voice cracked, pain and desperation slivering through the anger.

Arianne's chin shot up. "I need to see Jeff first. I promised myself I would get away the first time mom wasn't there to protect us. Every day I woke up and made the same promise. Every job I took, everything I have done since I was nine years old has brought me here. Being with you made me look at things in a different way. It made me take off the blinders. Now part of me desperately wants to stay, but another part of me is afraid that if I don't go, he'll destroy me and Jeff, too."

"You don't think I can protect you." A statement, not a question, and uttered with such venom, she flinched.

"I don't want to be 'protected.'" Her voice quivered with emotion. "I don't want to live in a safe house and have a posse of Sinners following me everywhere I go. That isn't freedom. Freedom is never having to worry about Viper. Freedom is walking down the street and not needing to carry a gun. Freedom is being able to live where I want, and go where I want, and do what I want without being afraid someone will take it away from me."

She turned her head to the side and bit her lip as a chill seeped through her bones. No wonder he'd taken her phone. If she'd had it in her hands right now, she would be texting Jeff to run.

Jagger leaned so close, his breath scorched her cheek.

"You are not going anywhere, Arianne. You're mine until I release you. And when Jeff shows up, he isn't going anywhere either." He pulled his phone from his inside pocket, flicked to a picture, then thrust it in her face. "That's him isn't it? That's Jeff at my old clubhouse."

Nausea roiled in her belly as she stared at the blurry photograph of Jeff standing near the Sinner weapons shed, his blond hair gleaming against the dark background. Although the camera had caught him in profile, she would know her brother anywhere. But clearly Jagger wasn't so sure about the identification.

"I can't believe you would ask me that." She gave the picture a disdainful sniff and pushed the phone away. "And I'm not even going to bother to answer."

"Don't play games with me, Arianne." His eyes darkened, almost to black and his upper lip curled. "Did you make up the story about your birthday? Trying to play my sympathy as you tried to play me? Are you spying for the Jacks? Now that I see how easy it is for you to walk away, I think you just might be."

Her hand flew up before she had even considered the consequences of her actions, and she slapped him across the cheek, the crack of her hand echoing in the alley. "Bastard. I can't believe you think I would lie about something like that. I don't know what's going on with you, Jagger, or why you suddenly think I've betrayed you or why you're so angry. I've been nothing but open with you. I've told you things about my life I haven't even told Dawn."

Jagger grabbed her hand and twisted her arm up behind her back, spinning her around and forcing her cheek painfully against the rough brick wall. For the first time since they'd met, she was truly afraid.

"You're not planning to leave Conundrum at all, are you?" He pressed his lips to her ear, his voice a sinister snarl. "I don't know why I didn't see it. You haven't packed anything. You haven't given up your apartment or stored your stuff. Even your bike. Sparky said you fixed it good as new, but you never put it up for sale."

"Viper would have found out." She shuddered under his touch. What the hell had happened in Jagger's meeting with Zane? "Everything I wanted to take, I put in my duffel bag. I never lied to you."

Desperately, she tried to breathe through the tightening in her chest, the thunder of her pulse in her ears. *Jagger won't hurt me. He promised he would never hurt me.* But already she could feel the cold sinking in her emotions giving way to the armor she had built to survive Viper's wrath. Except this time it wasn't Viper that threatened her, but the one man she had thought would keep her safe.

"I didn't want it to be like this." He shoved her harder against the wall, trapping her arm between them. She tried to turn her head, and the exposed mortar sliced across her cheek.

"I wanted you to want to stay." Jagger's voice rose to an agonized shout. "I wanted you to trust me, to believe in me. I wanted you to accept that I could protect you. I wanted you to—"

"Please . . . Jagger. You're hurting me." She fought back the panic flooding through her veins. He'd said he didn't harm women. But already her cheek burned from the cut and her arm screamed in pain.

"*I'm* hurting *you*." His bitter words were poison to her heart, and the last of her hope withered and died.

He released her abruptly, dropping her arm. Even though instinct screamed for her to run, she didn't move, resting her forehead against the cool brick wall, indifferent to leaving her back exposed. She'd exposed so much already, and besides, nothing could hurt more than the pain slicing through her heart.

"Turn around."

She turned slowly, no longer recognizing his handsome face, twisted now by pain and anger. His eyes dropped to the cut on her cheek, following the blood trickling down her cheek.

"Fuck." His voice rose to a pained shout as he scrubbed his hands over his face as if to wash away the sight of her. "Fuck." He slammed both fists on the wall on either side of her head and she finally screamed, her hands shooting up instinctively to protect herself.

Jagger jerked back, eyes glazed, body trembling. He reached for her cheek, and Arianne flinched before slapping his hand away.

"Don't touch me."

"You don't have to worry about that." His voice was cool, devoid of emotion. "I can walk away just as easily as you."

Christ.

He didn't do emotions. And he most definitely didn't do emotional wreck. He'd lost it out there. Totally lost control. When he saw her dressed to kill, all cool and calm and about to walk out of his life forever, his longing had given way to fear, anger, and a determination to exert the control he hadn't had when his mother walked out the door so long ago. To stop the pain.

And he'd hurt her. Not just physically, but emotionally as well. He would never forget the look of devastation in her eyes.

He pounded the table with his fist as he cursed silently under his breath. He'd hurt her and he'd scared her away. Had she seen that potential in him? Was that why she'd decided to leave? Was that why his mother left? Because of some trait he shared with his father?

"You okay, Jag?" Cade leaned back in his chair, dragging his eyes off a pretty brunette onstage, working the pole. Their booth, a feast of red velvet cushions around a sparkling silver table, was set back in the corner, affording them a clear view of the club without exposing them to public scrutiny.

"Yeah, good." He surveyed the cheap, tawdry strip club, making sure T-Rex and Wheels were in position near the exits. A raised circular stage dominated the space, with chairs scattered in front and a DJ pounding out the tunes in a small booth in one corner. Dark and dingy, lit only by garish neon signs on the walls and the floodlights on the stage, the place was pathetic and depressing and suited his mood to a T.

Lifting his gaze, he focused on Arianne, who sat alone in a booth along the opposite wall of the club. His heart ached as he rehashed the conversation outside yet again. What the fuck had he been thinking? Even if it was Jeff in the picture, did he really think she'd give him up? And did he really believe she was part of a plot to betray his club?

Two blond frat boys stopped at Arianne's table, and Jagger glared and jerked his chin at T-Rex to shoo them away. Every fucking bastard in the place was staring at her. Not only was she the sexiest woman in the club, but her distress was like a goddamn fucking beacon. He could see her pain in the hunch of her shoulders, the tremble of her hands, and the smear on her cheek from where she'd tried to wipe away the blood. Even now he had to clutch the tabletop to keep from going over to her. No doubt he'd get another slap across the face for his efforts.

He tried to imagine what he'd put her through. How he would feel if she'd accused him of such betrayal. When had he ever lost control before? When had he ever let emotion cloud his judgment? When had he ever cared about anyone so much, the thought of losing them cut deeper than the shrapnel lodged in his heart? Not since he was seven years old, when his mom had walked away.

"That stripper's been watching me ever since we came in." Cade grinned. "I'm thinking I might be getting a private dance tonight."

"Thought you'd hooked up with Dawn." Jagger sipped his beer, letting the bitter liquid slide over his tongue, no worse than the sour taste in his mouth.

"Nah. She just wants me for sex."

Jagger's head jerked up. "Well, that's a first. Usually it's the other way round."

Cade's cheeks reddened. "She's got issues."

"Who doesn't?" He checked his watch. Jeff was already half an hour late. A few more minutes, and they'd call it a night. He'd made sure the Sinners stayed out of sight, in case Jeff caught on to their plan. Of course, the plan hadn't included Arianne trying to slap him again when he pointed her to the booth, or calling him a fucking evil bastard, or telling him she would die before she let them touch Jeff. But here they were, and pain and regret were eating a hole through his heart.

Jagger stared at the stage, unseeing. He needed to get a grip. He was the president of the dominant outlaw MC in the state; the world was his for the taking. What did it matter whether she wanted to be with him or not? Or whether their time together had meant anything to her? She was his. He'd claimed her. He could do with her as he pleased. Not that he would ever touch her without her consent, but he could make her stay.

As if she knew what he was thinking, Arianne's gaze flicked to him and then away, her lips pressing into a thin line. She leaned back in the seat and folded her arms under her breasts, pulling taut the thin material of her top and exposing the crescents of her breasts. Jagger couldn't tear his gaze away.

Christ. She was driving him fucking crazy. How could he still want her after she'd made it abundantly clear he meant nothing to her?

"You're not being very inconspicuous." Cade waved a hand in front of Jagger's face. "Anyone looking at you would know exactly what you're thinking. You look like a lion ready to pounce."

"Fuck off."

"You're wrecked. I've never seen you wrecked before. Actually, 'wrecked' isn't the right word. I think the word I'm looking for is 'heartbroken,' or maybe it's 'devastated.'"

"Fuck off again."

"That's why I keep it simple," Cade said with a wry grin. "One night, maybe two, then on to the next. No emotional entanglements. No pain. No gut-wrenching decisions about whether to let the girl you claimed as a blood price go because that's what she wants most in the world—more than you. . . ."

Damn Cade and his stupid insightful jokes. If they'd been outside, he would have punched him, wiped that smarmy grin off his face. "You don't know anything about me."

"I know everything about you." Cade shoved another beer across the table. "We served together too long not to know each other inside and out, and right now, your inside is out, brother."

Jagger had slid partway out of the booth, already committed to slamming Cade's head into the table, when Arianne left her booth and walked toward them.

"I'm going to use the restroom." Strained, quiet, her voice held none of her usual sass, and her eyes none of their usual fire. She didn't wait for him to respond, just continued on her way. Jagger looked around for T-Rex to send him to watch the door. Where the fuck was he? And where was Wheels? Jesus Christ. Had they learned nothing from their screw-up at the pool hall?

He texted them and stared at his phone, awaiting their response. But when it finally buzzed, it wasn't T-Rex or Wheels sending the text, but Zane.

Viper knows where you are. Headed your way. Will try to intercept.

"We need to get Arianne out of here." He stood abruptly and stalked over to the bathroom. How could he make up for what he'd done? How could he tell her the thought of losing her had hurt so much, he had to push her away?

"Pssst. Arianne."

Hands still under the dryer, Arianne turned to see a familiar face peering around the door to the ladies' restroom.

"Jeff!"

He held up a hand and pulled his ball cap low on his forehead. "Wait thirty seconds, then meet me out back. There's a hidden door through the storage room at the end of the hallway. The Sinners are watching, so I gotta be quick."

Heart pounding, she counted off the seconds and then pushed open the door and glanced down the hallway. She could just make out Jagger's broad form at a table near the stage. Although facing her direction, he was looking down at his phone and a waitress blocked his view. Cade's attention was focused on the stage. She couldn't see Wheels or T-Rex. Pulse racing, she slipped out of the restroom and raced down the hallway to a gray metal door marked WARDROBE.

She walked through a huge room filled with costumes, then pushed open the back door and looked out into the night. "Jeff?"

"Over here." He waved her over to a Ford battered Thunderbird parked in the shadows, and she raced across the lot to join him.

"I've been so worried." She wrapped him in a hug. "After what happened at the vacant lot . . . I didn't know if you'd be okay." And then she pulled away and her bottom lip trembled, loving and hating him at the same time. "How could you, Jeff? He was an innocent man. You're lucky he didn't die."

"He didn't die?" Jeff gaped and took a step back under the parking lot light, brushing away the lank, dirty blond hair that perpetually hung over his face. Arianne caught a glimpse of his eyes, usually a brilliant blue, but now dull and filled with shadows. Fair where Viper was dark. Small where Viper was big. Weak where Viper was strong. Jeff was the opposite of Viper in every way.

"He'll be okay. I checked with the hospital."

Jeff wrapped his arms around himself and his voice wavered. "It was killing me, Ari. Every moment of every day, I thought about him. He wasn't an innocent man like you said. He was a small-time dealer who tried to cheat Viper on a cut and then shot one of the Jacks when he tried to escape. But the idea I'd taken a life was too much for me. I loaded my apartment with crank and went on a binge to end all binges just so I could forget the pain. It was good, so good. But I've run out, and now that the ice house is gone, I can't get a new supply. I haven't slept for days."

Arianne leaned closer and studied his face. The waver in his voice and the inability to sleep usually indicated he'd entered the tweaking phase of his addiction, and if that was the case, she needed to get away from him. Fast. Tweaking made him unpredictable, delusional, and violent. But he didn't display the quick, jerky movements he always had when he tweaked. And for the first time, she wasn't sure what to do.

"What about the guy at the Sinner clubhouse?" he asked. "I shot him in the leg. Is he okay? He came out with an automatic weapon, and if I hadn't slowed him down, he would have killed us all."

"Gunner? Yes, he's fine. But Cole, the other guy you shot—"

"I didn't shoot him," Jeff said quickly. "My job was to get the guns. The other guys were responsible for torching the clubhouse and taking out anyone who saw us. I'm not sure which of them took that guy out or knocked you off your bike. They didn't know it was you, and I couldn't go to you because that guy I shot kept firing at us. We had to get out of there."

He hadn't shot them. Jeff was still her Jeff. She hadn't totally lost him to Viper. And yet, he'd left her for the Sinners to find, and it was only luck that the man from the vacant lot survived.

She looked back over her shoulder at the door. Jagger would have sent someone looking for her by now. Time to do what she had come to do. She had to find out if this was really good-bye. "Are you sure you want to stay?"

Something moved in the shadows, and she stilled, staring into the darkness. But it was gone so quickly, she wondered if she'd imagined it. "We could still go together. You could get help for your problem. Be free of Viper. You would never have to face a situation like that again."

He gave his head a violent shake. "I was in a bad place, Ari. Viper caught me and beat me for not getting all the weapons. I hadn't had a hit in days. My head was spinning. I couldn't think. And he just went on and on and on about killing that guy. He wouldn't stop talking. I just wanted him to stop talking. But it's all okay now. I've almost got the guns. I'll get my patch. He'll be proud of me the way he's proud of you."

Proud of *her*? Jeff had to be tweaking. She needed to leave.

"Do you have the passports?"

A pained expression crossed his face. "Well . . . there's a slight problem. I did a deal with the guy Bunny recommended, but I didn't have enough cash to pay for the weapons, so I tried to short him. I figured by the time he found out, me 'n' the weapons would be safe at the Black Jack clubhouse. But he caught me on the road, and said if I didn't pay him tonight, he'd kill me. So I gave him the passports to cover some of the shortfall and then I remembered I was meeting you, so I told him you were good for the rest."

"*What?*" Her voice rose to a shriek. "I worked two jobs for a year to pay for those passports. An entire year. And you just gave them away?"

Jeff scratched himself over and over as if he had bugs crawling under his skin. "He's in the car, Ari. If you've got enough to cover me, then he'll give us the passports back. But at the very least, you have to make up the difference. If I don't get those weapons, Viper will kill me. You don't want that on your conscience."

"Where is he?" She opened her purse and pulled out her .22.

Jeff pointed to his vehicle at the far end of the lot. "He's in there. You can talk to him, but don't kill him. I need those weapons."

"I don't kill people, Jeff." She spat out her words. "But I need my passports so he needs to know I mean business. They weren't yours to give. I should never have let you pick them up. If Banks hadn't offered to pay me double time to work that night because he was short-staffed, I would have gone myself, but I thought we could use that extra bit of cash. And I trusted you."

"I'm sorry, Ari. I was desperate. You know what Viper's like. You saw what he did to me. And now this guy wants to kill me. What was I supposed to do?"

What was she supposed to do?

Arianne took one last look at the door leading back to the club and felt a cold fist close over her heart. Jagger hadn't come looking for her after all. Maybe he'd decided she wasn't worth the effort. Her hand flew to her cheek, where the brick had sliced through her skin. How could she have misjudged Jagger so badly? God, she'd been seconds away from agreeing to stay, from telling him how much she cared about him. And then he'd turned around and accused her of betraying him. *So much anger.* He'd never intended to let her go. He was Viper all over again.

Time to go. And this time it would be forever.

She stalked across the parking lot, but as she neared Jeff's vehicle, he shouted and raced past her, reaching for the driver's side door.

"Quick—get in the car. Someone's coming."

She caught movement in the shadows and then a flash of blond hair under the parking lot light near the door she had just come through. Her mouth went dry when she saw the lean figure wearing a biker cut. No front patches. *Wheels?*

Arianne froze, but Wheels made no move toward her. Instead, he nodded and faded back into the darkness.

Well, if Wheels was here, Jagger wouldn't be far behind. She jumped into the passenger seat, and Jeff slid behind the wheel. Moments later, they peeled out of the parking lot and headed down the highway.

She didn't recognize the hulking figure in the backseat until it was too late.

★ NINETEEN ★

No member will disgrace the club by being a pussy.

"Where the fuck is she?"

T-Rex and Wheels paled under Jagger's relentless verbal abuse. "Two prospects and a full-patch brother should have been able to keep one woman in sight. How the fuck did she get out?"

"There's a hidden exit through the storage room," Wheels said, his voice wavering. "Leads to a secluded area of the parking lot. I was doing circuits of the building and musta been around the front when she came out. There's no way anyone could have known there was an exit back there, and we'd already checked that the windows in the restrooms were secure."

"There is a way we could have known about the secret exit." He grabbed Wheels by the collar and shoved him against the brick wall where only an hour earlier he'd held Arianne. "You could have fucking asked."

"I did ask." T-Rex put a firm hand on Jagger's wrist. "The owner assured me there was no way out from the bathroom corridor. I've dealt with him."

Slightly mollified, Jagger released the trembling Wheels. "Go pull the security tapes. We have to find out who has her. Zane lost Viper on the road, so it might be the Jacks caught her outside. Or it might be her brother came after all, and they're gone."

After they had departed, Jagger slumped against the wall. He doubted Viper had snatched her. What would be the point? He hadn't been able to keep her before, and nothing had changed. And if he wanted her dead, she would be lying in the parking lot. It had to be Jeff. So why was he wasting time and energy looking for a woman who didn't want to stay? And wasn't this the best result? She would find the happiness she wanted, safe from Viper and from him.

Cade clapped a hand on his shoulder. "We'll find her."

"What if she doesn't want to be found?" He pushed himself to stand. "She came here to meet her brother and leave with him. I made it easy for her to do just that. My guess is they're long gone."

Probably the best result for him, too. If tonight was any evidence, he had lost his objectivity, and his emotional involvement had almost compromised the club. The old ways were the best ways. No attachments. No strings.

No Arianne.

"I have died and gone to heaven."

Arianne stilled when a knife slid across her throat. She knew the voice coming from the backseat. Remembered the cool feel of a blade on her skin. She glanced up in the rear view mirror, and her mouth went dry.

"Axle." She lowered the .22, still in her grasp, down by her side, praying Axle wouldn't notice.

"The one and only. Still alive and kicking after Jagger and his boys got a blowtorch and burned my Sinner's Tribe tat off my shoulder blade. Lucky for me, I didn't get the full version across my back, or I would have died in that fucking clubhouse basement."

"You know my sister?" Jeff met Axle's gaze in the rear view mirror.

"Your sister?" Axle spat. "She's your fucking sister? So who are you? Bunny never gives out personal details. So spill. Are you Viper's boy?"

"Yeah. The weapons are for him."

"Well, damn." Axle barked his delight. "Things were looking pretty bad for me for a while there, but fortune has smiled on me at last. Price just went up, J-Boy 'cause the weapons I have to sell are the weapons Viper tried to steal from the Sinners. I got them this evening with the help of a sexy redhead."

"Sherry?" The name dropped from Arianne's lips before she could catch it.

"So clever." Axle pressed the knife against Arianne's throat. "Yeah, Sherry got me into the storage shed behind the safe house where she's stayin'. Jagger kicked her outta the club, but he let her stay at the safe house because someone roughed her up real bad, and Jagger just can't deal with seeing a woman in pain. I had to hit her quite a few times to make it look authentic enough for him to want to help her, but I never expected he'd put her in the safe house, right near the shed. Never thought it would be so easy for her to get the code. But a man will pretty much give up anything for good head, and Sherry's the best."

Her lip curled. "You're disgusting."

"And you're gonna suffer so much worse than she did when she first told me she wouldn't do it."

Jeff's hands convulsed on the steering wheel, and the car veered to the side of the road. "That wasn't our deal. She's not part of this except to get the extra cash."

"Consider her a surcharge." Axle laughed. "I gotta say, I was worried about how to make a living after I got kicked outta the Sinners, but getting into bed with Bunny, using my connections to get shit he needs, has more than made up for my loss."

Arianne fingered the trigger on her gun, weighing her

chances of avoiding the blade if she could shoot Axle across her opposite shoulder. "How much more does he owe?"

"Eighty grand. And hand the gun over to Jeff, love. Nice and slow. I know you got it, and I don't got any problem cutting you tonight, because every day you've been alive since we found you at the clubhouse has been borrowed time."

Muttering a curse, she held the gun out for Jeff, who took it with his right hand, and lowered it carefully to the floor beneath his legs.

"Nice piece," Axle said. "I always carry a .45. Much more effective. But maybe I'll add your toy to my collection."

"Fuck off."

"Don't antagonize him," Jeff whined. "We just need to get the money and—"

"Eighty grand?" She cut Jeff off and glared. "Why the hell did you tell him I would give him the money? I don't have eighty grand. I spent everything on those passports."

"You must have some cash, Ari." He scraped a hand through his hair. "I'll drive you to the bank and you can check."

The car veered to the right, and Arianne sucked in a breath. "Are you okay to drive?"

"No. I'm not okay." Jeff wrenched the steering wheel in the opposite direction. "I'm outta meth, and there's a shortage since the ice house blew up. Axle wants his money. Viper wants his guns. You want to fucking run away to Canada. I can't take anymore. I can't take the pressure. I need one thing to go right." His voice rose and his hands jerked on the steering wheel. *Oh God.* He was tweaking. She had to get him out of the car or he'd kill someone.

"My bank is five blocks to the east," she said. "I might have some cash in my savings account."

"Lucky for you." Axle eased the pressure against her throat.

Arianne scowled at him in the rear view mirror. "Lucky is winning the lottery, falling in love, or being the only person to survive an airplane crash. Lucky is not riding around in a decrepit vehicle with a tweaking brother while some low-life scumbag holds a knife against my throat and threatens to steal my money."

"You forgot the part where I'm going to kill Jeff if I don't get my money tonight," Axle said. "And then there's the fun you and I are going to have after the deal is done."

Fear and anger curled through her belly. This wasn't happening. After all they'd been through together, Jeff wasn't betraying her when they were so close to the life they had dreamed about since the day they huddled on the roof all night, praying for the sun to come up.

Jeff pulled up outside the bank, and Axle switched out his knife for a .45, concealing it under his jacket as he marched Arianne over to the bank machine with Jeff trailing after. Her mind raced as she put her card in the slot. She knew the balance would show as zero. She had emptied her account the night she thought they were running away.

But what to do? No damn way was she getting back in that car. As she punched in her numbers, she glanced up at the security camera and mouthed the word "help." Then she cast a glance down the street, but at this late hour the sidewalk was deserted and the few cars on the road drove past without slowing down.

The machine flashed the zero balance, and Axle smashed his hand into the wall, then motioned them both into the alley with a jerk of his gun.

"Fucking hell," he spluttered as he marched them into the semi-darkness. "You said she had the cash."

"I thought she did." Shaking uncontrollably, Jeff turned

to face Axle when they were mid-way down the alley. "Maybe she can get it from someone else. She could give you her bike. Maybe—"

"Shut the fuck up. I'm trying to think." Axle's gaze raked over Arianne, making her skin crawl.

"Fucking bitches are good for only one thing."

"While we're thinking, let's go see Bunny." Jeff paced up and down the alley, rubbing his hands over his thighs. "He'll have some meth. He can give me a hit, and I'll be able to think clearer."

Axle rolled his eyes. "You can't pay me. How the heck are you going to pay Bunny? You got nothing 'cept a beat-up car and a fucking hot sister."

Hot sister? She could see where the conversation was headed, and if she didn't run now, she might not get another chance. Taking advantage of their distraction, Arianne bolted, pounding her way down the alley, cursing the shoes that were slowing her down.

"Fuck. Get her."

Arianne kicked off the shoes and ran barefoot, her cry for help echoing in the confined space. But although she was fast, the stilettos had slowed her down.

Jeff caught up with her just a few feet away from the sidewalk and yanked her back into the alley with an arm around her waist. "Stop. Please. We won't hurt you."

But she didn't trust him. This wasn't Jeff. Not the sweet boy she'd pushed on the swings and protected from Viper's wrath. Not the boy who had almost died trying to save her from Leo. He was a stranger. An addict. And although she had desperately wanted to save him, she realized now it was far too late.

Kicking and screaming, she writhed in his grasp until he flung her against the wall. Her forehead cracked against the brick, and she stilled, stunned.

"Don't fight me, Ari." Hearing his pet name for her on

his lips sickened her. If he was doing this, knowing who she was, then he wasn't tweaking at all.

Turning, she kicked him in the stomach. Jeff doubled over with a groan, but recovered quickly and shot up and punched her, his fist grazing her cheek and over her eye. Gravel crunched behind them.

"Christ. She's a fucking girl. How hard can it be to take her down?"

But before she could turn to face the new threat, something slammed into her head.

And then there was darkness.

"You've watched it five times, Jag. You're not going to see anything you didn't see already."

Jagger scrubbed a hand over his face as Zane took a seat beside him in the clubhouse meeting room and peered at the image frozen on the laptop—the image he couldn't get out of his mind. The long moment when Arianne stared at the back door to Peelers, pain and longing etched on her beautiful face.

Pain he had put there. And the longing—could he even hope it was for him?

He assumed the blond-haired driver was her brother, Jeff. From what he could see on the tape, she knew him well enough to hug him when she'd joined him in the parking lot, and he resembled the man he'd seen in the vacant lot, although even thinner and looking more strung out.

"Did you ask Sheriff Morton to run the plate?" Having the sheriff at their beck and call was more than worth the monthly expense.

Zane stretched his long legs under the table. "Stolen. The police have it in their system, but no patrols have spotted the vehicle yet. He wanted to know if we could do a protection run for him tomorrow. Coupla boxes of handguns heading south."

"Get Gunner on it. And T-Rex, so he can get some experience." He stared at the screen. "What about the owner of Peelers? Anyone talked to him after T-Rex took him out back?" He checked his cell out of reflex, but of course, he'd taken Arianne's phone, so she couldn't call him.

"He remembered Arianne but didn't see her leave. He didn't know anyone matching the descriptions I gave him from the surveillance footage."

Jagger tilted his neck from side to side, trying to alleviate the tension that strained his body. If she had left, he would deal with it. If she'd been taken, he'd find her. But not knowing was killing him as much as sitting still. He shoved his chair away from the table and slammed the laptop closed. "I'm going out again. Tank can come with me, and—"

"Why don't you just let her go?"

Jagger whipped his head around. "What if she was coerced into that vehicle? I gave my word I'd keep her safe."

"You saw the tape, same as me." Zane said. "She ran out the door and hugged him. There was no coercion going on. Odds are that was her brother and he was scared to come inside. She's gone, Jag. Although I didn't completely trust her, she was always up-front about what she wanted. And what she wanted was out. I know you cared about her. Fucking blew my mind after all the years you said you didn't want to get involved, but it's best for her and it's best for you. So just let her go. If she feels the same way about you, she'll come back."

"Like you did?"

Zane had the good grace to grimace at Jagger's reference to a time in their lives they never discussed. Zane had disappeared when Jagger needed him most, and although they had mended their friendship, the hurt remained.

"You never told me where you were all those years I was in the army, or where you went that day after you came to see me in the hospital." Jagger rubbed at the back of his neck, trying not to let his disappointment show. "You asked me to let you go, and you never came back."

"I'm here now."

"I needed you then."

"You wanted me to help you die," Zane said. "And God help me, I would have because I couldn't watch you suffer like that. We all thought it was only a matter of time. That's why I asked you to let me go. I knew if I did what you wanted, I would regret it for the rest of my life. I'm sorry I wasn't there for you, but it was the best decision I ever made."

He pushed himself to standing, his voice thick with emotion. "I kept tabs on you, brother, and I came back as soon as you had yourself sorted out. I came when I knew you wanted to live again. I came back 'cause you're like a fucking blood brother to me."

"Then help me find her," Jagger pleaded. "The Arianne I know wouldn't leave without saying good-bye."

Arianne awoke with a headache.

No, not just a headache. Her skull was splitting—the pain so intense, she could barely think. She took in the dark, cold room, her body lying haphazardly on the concrete floor, one eye swollen shut, and was that a chain?.

Startled, she tried to move, and the chain rattled, jerking her leg as she pulled away. Her arms, tied behind her back, encountered similar resistance, and she opened her mouth to scream, then closed it again. Why let her captors know she was awake? Whoever they were.

"Don't waste your breath. They won't hear you. And even if they do, they won't care."

She craned her neck in the direction of the voice—a female voice. Light filtered through the bottom of the door, and in the darkness she could make out two distinct shapes. Both women. Both tied and chained as she was.

"Where are we?" Arianne's voice was no more than a croak but they understood her.

"Basement of Bunny's pool hall." The woman—no, girl—who answered was small and slight, no older than eighteen, her long blond hair matted and stuck to her cheek. She wore a light-colored dress, soiled and torn, and a pair of four-inch heels.

Memories flooded back. Axle. The alley. And Jeff. Pain sliced through her heart at his betrayal. She was here because of Jeff.

"Did they process you yet?" The second girl was all harsh planes and angles, her sparkly silver dress torn away from her chest to reveal the crescents of her breasts. She looked to be about the same age as her friend, but her voice was that of a much older woman.

"I was in an alley. Then I was here. I don't know why."

"She doesn't know why." The girl in the silver dress gave a bitter laugh, and her companion admonished her with a nudge.

"Ease up on her, Sheila. She just woke up."

Arianne pushed herself with her feet until she was sitting, facing the women. "Why?"

Sheila shrugged. "Bunny."

"What about him?"

"This is what he does." Sheila stared at Arianne, but when Arianne gave her a blank look, her face softened. "You never walked the streets? You never heard of Bunny?"

"I met him. I thought he sold things."

"He sells people. Women, mostly. He runs the biggest human trafficking ring in Montana."

Her blood chilled. "In Montana? Seriously? Does that kind of thing really go on here?"

The girl with the heels leaned forward. "You don't look like his usual type. Usually he grabs girls off the streets, around our age or younger. Homeless kids . . . hookers. People who don't have anyone to ask after them. Usually the pimps pay him to leave us alone, but our man, Walker, took a bad hit and wound up in a ditch. He wasn't dead more than an hour before Bunny sent his people to find us."

"Sometimes, though, he has special orders. You must be one of them." Sheila sucked in her lips. "Worse for you. Buyer will expect more. Mostly we've heard the girls are sold to brothels around the country. Some shipped overseas."

Her friend let out a sob and dropped her head to Sheila's shoulder.

A sickening wave of terror welled up in Arianne's throat. For all the abuse she had suffered at Viper's hands, under no circumstances would he have done anything like this. She was his, and he never let her forget it.

The door slammed open, flooding the room with light. She craned her neck over her shoulder, freezing when she saw three men silhouetted in the doorway. She recognized Jeff at once. And Bunny from his girth. The third man had to be Axle. She shuffled around to face them and straightened her back. No way would she let them see her fear.

"So what did you bring me that's worth eighty grand and a kilo of meth?" Bunny flicked on the light and leaned against the doorjamb. Axle entered the room, grabbed Arianne by the shoulder and pulled her to her knees.

"This. Jeff's tied her up and chained her. She's a bit of a hellcat."

"Don't touch me." Rage, fierce and unexpected, shot through her veins. She tried to shake him off, heedless of his hand swinging—until pain exploded across her cheek.

"Shut the fuck up."

"Don't damage her anymore." Bunny joined Axle and then crouched down in front of Arianne. "I can't sell her if she's marked up too bad, and you've already lowered her price by giving her all those bruises."

Although her cheek throbbed and her vision was hazy, she met his gaze, staring into his cold, black eyes. "You can't seriously think Viper will let you get away with this."

Bunny tilted his head to the side. "Viper? I'm not afraid of Viper. But why would he care about a piece of trash like you?" He twisted his hand through her hair and yanked her head back.

She drew in a shuddering breath. Bunny didn't recognize her. And how could he, with her face swollen and bruised? And if neither Jeff nor Axle hadn't told him who she was . . .

"You don't recognize me, Bunny? After I whipped your boy's ass at pool? And I thought we had a deal. I won. Jeff's debt was wiped out. Although now I'm thinking you should break his legs like you said you were going to do, because he's no brother of mine."

Bunny stiffened and shoved her back. "Jesus Christ. You're Jagger's girl." He pushed himself to his feet and glared at Jeff, his face a mask of fury. "You brought me Jagger's girl? Your fucking sister? I knew you weren't right in the head, but that's fucking twisted. You're selling your sister for eighty grand and a kilo of meth?"

"You want her or not?" Jeff said, his tone flat. And just like that, she knew she was alone. His voice was devoid of everything that had made him her little brother: compassion, emotion, warmth . . . love.

Bunny grabbed Jeff's shirt and shoved him against the wall. "She's Jagger's girl. You got that?"

"What the fuck are you talking about? "Jeff shouted. "Jagger claimed her as a blood price for the shit that went down at his clubhouse. He's gonna kill her, not fuck her. I'm saving her life, bringing her to you."

"That's not what I saw." Bunny thudded him against the wall again. "She came here for you and he came looking for her. Brought his boys with him. But did he drag her outta here? No fucking way. He was all over her. And I mean *all* over. I thought they were gonna go at it right on my damn pool table. I got it all on tape. When I say she's his girl, I don't mean she was gonna blow him for the night, or she was being forced into it. I mean. She. Is. His. Girl."

Jeff's eyes narrowed and he glared at Arianne. "No fucking way."

"Yes fucking way." Bunny grabbed the neck of his T-shirt and tugged it down. "And just so I got the message, Jagger had his boys beat the fucking crap outta me and my crew. Two of them are still in the hospital. They broke a couple of my ribs and they did this."

Arianne couldn't see what he showed Jeff on his neck, but she could guess.

"I thought I'd fucking bleed out on the street," Bunny spat, his voice thick with venom. "If Peter hadn't found me and called an ambulance, I woulda died in the alley. Gonna have a scar across my neck for the rest of my life. And all so I wouldn't forget she was his girl."

Jeff's lips curled in disgust. "You sold out, Ari? You're sleeping with the fucking enemy? You betrayed our club? Our family?"

Blood roared through her ears drowing out every sound except the thunder of her own rage. "Seriously? How can you accuse me of betraying our family when you're trying to *sell* me to pay a debt to Axle and buy yourself drugs? You don't understand what family means."

"*You* don't understand." Jeff's voice rose to a shout and he shoved Bunny to the side. "You never did. Little Miss Perfect. Viper's fucking pet."

Pet? He *was* delusional.

"You two shut the fuck up." Bunny's mouth thinned in a stubborn line. "I'm not interested in getting involved in a family feud. I'm also not interested in anything to do with Jagger's girl. I want her outta here. Now."

A spasm of irritation crossed Axle's face. "Christ. It's not like he's ever going to find out. And I want this, too. I want her gone. I want her to suffer. I want her to pay for getting me kicked out of the club. This is the perfect solution."

"Yeah, if I'm tired of living." Sarcasm laced Bunny's tone.

Jeff gave a disdainful sniff. "If you aren't afraid of Viper, why the fuck are you afraid of Jagger?"

"If you gotta ask that question, then you don't know nothin' about business," Bunny said. "I got such powerful backers, I'm not afraid of any local MC. I coulda had them wipe out Jagger's MC in one night as payback for what he did. But I'm not stupid. Lotta bikers in Montana who look up to Jagger and they give me good business. I don't want to damage my reputation. He made it clear that this is his woman. I respect that. And no way will I touch her."

Arianne swallowed past the lump in her throat. She'd seen how Jagger reacted when she'd told him she was leaving, felt his anger. And she'd seen his rage when Axle threatened her, watched him let that anger loose. Bunny knew as well as she did that if anything happened to her, he would pay with his life. Which gave her no small amount of power, and she knew exactly how she was going to use it.

"He almost had me killed as a warning." Bunny continued to rant. "What do you think he would do if he found out I had his girl down here? It won't just be bad for business, it'll be bad for my health. He'll go after my boy, my family . . . Hell, if he finds out you were the one who made her face look like that, your life won't be worth living. Now, get her—"

"They walk out of here with me." Arianne cut him off and pointed to the women behind her. "I'm not leaving here without them."

"Sorry, love. They've been contracted already." Bunny turned away.

"I'll give your regards to Jagger when I see him again, shall I?" Arianne bit her lip. Might as well play the old lady card while it was still fresh. "He'll be happy to hear about your hospitality."

Bunny whipped around to face her. "I didn't touch you. I didn't know you were here until I walked into the room. And when I found out it was you, I told them to let you go. You tell him that. You tell him Bunny did the right thing. I helped you out. I saved you."

Arianne met his gaze. "We live in the same world, Bunny. I think we understand each other. What I tell Jagger depends on what happens to the two women behind me. And I'm thinking the value of Jagger's gratitude would far outweigh any money you'll get from selling them. Unless, of course, you're wanting to make your pretend necklace real."

His lips curled in a snarl. "Fucking hell. No wonder Jagger wants you. You're just like Viper. Beaten, tied up, chained to my wall, and you're negotiating with me like you've got a gun to my head."

"I'm nothing like Viper."

Bunny laughed, showing a mouth full of chipped, broken teeth. "That's were you're wrong. You're your daddy's girl to the bone."

"Fucking useless piece of shit." Axle shoved Jeff aside as they headed across Bunny's parking lot toward Jeff's vehicle.

Arianne winced when the .45 pressed into her back. She'd assumed Bunny would make sure she got out safely, but he disappeared after Jeff unchained her, and she'd found herself once again at the wrong end of Axle's gun.

"I should just shoot you now and put you out of your misery." He glared at Jeff.

"I'll get the money," Jeff said quickly. "Just . . . how about you give me the guns to give to Viper, and I'll pay you the rest as soon as I have it?"

"Not the way I do business." Axle leaned against Jeff's vehicle, his gun pointed at Arianne's chest, while Jeff fumbled with his keys. Across the street, Sheila and her friend tried to flag down a cab.

"What about Arianne?"

"I'm gonna have some fun with her." Axle poked her again, and her lips pursed with suppressed fury.

"Nothing will piss off Jagger more than knowing someone else fucked his girl. And I'm not gonna just fuck her. I'm gonna use her and break her. And then I'll drop her off at the clubhouse like the Wolverines MC did to his last girl. That will be a message he'll never forget."

A cab crawled to a stop across the street. Sheila bent down to talk to the driver. Arianne looked at Axle's .45, her heart drumming in her chest. After Leo's attack, she'd spent years in therapy, and as part of the recovery program, she had been required to take self-defense classes. Given the world she lived in, she hadn't gone for the regular classes that taught basic twist-and-run techniques. She'd taken the courses about disarming attackers wielding knives, handguns, steel pipes, and brass knuckles. Although she'd never really had the chance to put some of the more extreme moves to the test, given that the alternative was getting into the car with Jeff and Axle, she deemed the risk worthwhile.

While Axle was distracted, talking to Jeff, she took a

step toward him and grabbed his gun hand at the wrist. Before he could react, she clasped the barrel of the gun and pushed it toward him, rolling it against his thumb until it pointed at him. Another roll and he involuntarily released the gun into her hand. Although it took only moments, the delay seemed like a lifetime, but once she had the gun, she didn't waste a second. Sprinting across the street, she shouted for Sheila to open the cab door.

Her heart pounded against her ribs as she ran toward the vehicle. Sheila flung open the door and stretched out an arm toward her. Arianne's bare feet thudded across the pavement. She was close. So close, she could see the chips in Sheila's red nail polish, the gold ring on her finger with a brilliant blue stone.

And then pain exploded across her arm, and she fell forward, the blue stone fading to black.

★ TWENTY ★

*The president shall defend club members,
property (including chicks), and territory
from outside threats.*

"Where is she?"

Jagger trod over the broken door and glared at Banks and Dawn. Banks had a gun pointed at his chest and held Dawn protectively behind him.

"You said he'd find her," Dawn muttered behind Banks back. "You didn't say he'd kick down my door."

"I thought he'd knock."

"Where—is—she?" Jagger stalked toward Banks, disregarding the weapon. He hadn't paid much attention to the bar owner before, but from his stance and the way he held the gun, it was clear he'd had military training. And that told him Banks wouldn't fire on him because he wasn't a threat. At least not if the man told him where to find Arianne.

"She's asleep in my room." Dawn gestured to the hallway behind her. "Two women brought her to to the bar in a cab. They said someone had been shooting at her and she'd fallen and hit her head while trying to escape. She wasn't making much sense, but she was able to ask them to bring her to the bar. The women who brought her gave Banks the full story."

Safe. She was safe. Jagger just managed to keep himself from sagging against the wall. "Appreciate the call."

Dawn smiled. "Had a feeling you might want to know."

"Word of warning." Banks lowered his weapon when Jagger took a step toward the hallway. "She's been roughed up a bit. Dawn and I looked after her, but you might want to prepare yourself. Try not to break anything else. I don't pay Dawn enough for extensive repairs."

His tension returned tenfold. Rubbing the back of his neck, he stalked down the hallway. But when he reached the bedroom door, he paused. What if she didn't want to see him? He'd failed her. He had promised to protect her, and instead he'd hurt her, chased her away, and when she needed him most . . . He clenched his fists. *Fuck it.* He'd take his chances.

Jagger pushed open the door and stepped into the dimly lit room. Arianne lay asleep on the bed, her hair spread over the pillow in a chestnut wave. From his position in the doorway, she appeared okay. And then he saw the bandage.

With a growl, he flicked the lights on and slammed the door closed. Arianne startled and shot up in bed. "Jagger. God, you scared me."

No. No. No. As his eyes adjusted to the light, he didn't think he would be able to contain himself. Her face was bruised on one side, her eye black, a thick white bandage plastered to her temple. His lungs constricted, and although he tried to speak, no words came out.

Soft and sleepy, Arianne gave him a wry smile. "I guess I must look pretty bad. You look like you're about to explode."

He pointed to her arm, knowing from the size and shape of the bandage what she would say before he even asked. "What?"

"Bullet."

A maelstrom of emotions threatened to rip him apart. Needing an outlet, he turned and punched his fist through the door. Could he have failed her anymore?

"Always with the drama." Resigned amusement tinged her pain-ridden voice.

He whirled back around to face her, his heart pounding so hard, he feared he would break a rib. "Someone shot you?"

"Yeah. That's usually how someone gets a bullet wound." Her trembling hands belied her light tone and his voice rose almost to a shout.

"Who?"

"It doesn't matter. . . ."

Doesn't matter? He had only two thoughts in his head: first make sure she was okay; and second, make sure whoever had done this never hurt her again.

"It matters to me. Tell me. Now."

"You can growl and shout and threaten me all you want tomorrow, but right now, I just want to be alone." She scrubbed her hand over her face. "I should just have gone with Banks to his place. He's got a triple steel door. No Jaggers would be able to get through."

"You should have come to me."

She lay back on the pillows, seemingly unaware that the flimsy piece of satin she wore had slid to the side, exposing the crescent of her breast. His groin tightened painfully, and he dug his nails into his palm. *Damn.* Not now. Not when she was injured and looking at him like he was the last man on earth she wanted to see. But with adrenaline still pumping through his system, he was almost overwhelmed with the primal need to take her, hold her, make her his again. And then he would hunt down and kill the bastard who had hurt her.

"After what happened outside Peelers, you weren't on the top of my list."

His shoulders tensed. Not just because he had hurt her, but also because he'd never even considered she would look to another man for comfort or protection. And what if she had gone to Banks's house? What if he'd found her lying in his bed? He'd have killed the bar owner most likely. Just the thought of her with another man sent rage coursing through his veins. "It's *my* job to protect you."

"You took my phone. Oh . . . and you betrayed me. Accused me of betraying you. Hurt me. So forgive me if I didn't think of you when I needed protection." She shifted in the bed and winced.

"You need medical treatment." Jagger pulled out his phone. "I'll call Doc. Take you back to the clubhouse."

"I'm not going anywhere with you."

Goddamn it. Didn't she understand she needed proper medical treatment and not a waitress and a bar owner fumbling with her wound, no doubt leaving her with an infection or a scar or worse? His hands fisted at his sides as he fought back the urge to throw her over his shoulder and carry her out the door. "You're hurt."

"I'm fine." Her voice softened. "Dawn had a full first aid kit that she brought from the bar after the fight. And Banks knew what he was doing."

But she wasn't fine. He'd never seen her so pale, bruised, beaten. Even now, her hands shook and the spark was gone from her eyes. But instinct warned him not to push. He was lucky she was talking to him at all.

"I'll check to make sure." He found the bathroom down the hall and washed his hands, barely recognizing the strained, anxious face that looked back at him in the mirror. When had he last been so emotionally volatile? Not since Christel died.

When he returned to the room, Arianne had pulled the covers around her. She edged away when he sat on the bed and winced when he lifted her arm.

"What does a biker know about treating bullet wounds?"

"Field training in the army. Everyone was taught how to treat a bullet wound."

She tilted her head to the side. "You were in the army?"

"Fourth Infantry Division. Two tours of Afghanistan."

When she didn't respond, a niggle of doubt worked its way through his mind. By way of distraction, he carefully removed the bandage and examined the wound, testing the edges with his thumbs for tenderness or infection. "I've rendered you speechless."

"Why did you quit?" She blurted out. "How did you go from the army to being an outlaw biker?"

"I didn't quit." He felt a familiar heaviness in his chest. Although he had never regretted his decision to join the Sinners, the circumstances that led to the end of his military service still pained him. "I was honorably discharged. Shrapnel from a rocket-propelled grenade got lodged in my heart during a raid. Doctors said it was too risky to take it out and an even bigger risk to have me in the field. Couldn't handle a desk job, so they booted me out."

Concern replaced her curiosity, and she lightly stroked his forearm with her free hand. "You have shrapnel in your heart? Aren't you worried that one day—?"

He waved a dismissive hand. "Only a problem if they have to open up my chest. That's when there is a risk of it dislodging. Otherwise, there isn't anything I can't do. But despite all the medical reports, the army didn't see it that way. They thought it was too much of a risk."

"I'm sorry."

He looked up and met her gaze, warmed by her genuine sympathy and moved to tell her more. "Found a place with the Sinners. Lots of ex-military, discharged 'cause of injury like me. Some just lost in the civilian world. Others unhappy with people's lack of understanding of the sacrifices we made for our country. Same core values of brotherhood, trust, and honor . . ."

"I can't believe I had to get shot to hear the story behind your scar," she said as he wrapped the wound. "I should have made you get shot before I told you about the belt." She flinched when he finished the wrap, and Jagger stilled.

"I hurt you."

"No . . . you've been surprisingly gentle."

He clasped her hand, twining his fingers through hers. "Surprisingly?"

"From what I've seen so far—Axle, the bar brawl, pounding Leo's face into the counter, putting your fist through the door—'gentle' isn't the word I would have used to describe you."

She was right about that. He wasn't a gentle man. And yet with Arianne, it was no effort to hold back.

"And this." He brushed his thumb over the cut on her cheek. "I did this." He cupped her jaw and stroked over the cut again as he fought back a wave of remorse. "I didn't want you to leave." Jagger clasped her hand and ran his thumb over her knuckles. "When we got to Peelers, all I could think about was that I might not see you again. I didn't want to care. I didn't want it to affect me, and I was angry at myself that it did. I took it out on you."

A smile ghosted upon her lips. "You grovel well."

He brought her hand to his mouth and lightly kissed each finger, tasting the salty sweetness of her skin, breathing in her scent. It was as close to an apology as he had ever come, as open as he had ever allowed himself to be.

"You need to be held." Even as he spoke the words, he knew they were for him, as much as for her. He checked the bandage, then pulled her onto his lap.

"I'm not a child, Jagger." But her body softened when he put his arm around her, and she leaned against his chest with a gentle sigh. Perversely, the ease with which she gave up the fight increased his agitation. Whatever had happened tonight had taken the fight out of his fighter, and damned if he wasn't going to ensure that never happened again.

"What happened tonight? Who hurt you?"

She went rigid against him. "I don't want to talk about it right now. Please."

Torn between the urge to hold her and the need to get the necessary information to hunt down and eliminate the threat, he enfolded her in his arms, listening to the steady rhythm of her breathing and the rapid thud of her heart against his chest.

"I always tell the boys, you aren't a real biker until you get shot." He kept his tone light, teasing. "I guess you're a real biker now."

"Maybe I always was a real biker."

"My biker," he said. "And I'm taking you where bikers belong."

She gazed up at him, and the defeated expression in those beautiful green eyes stabbed him in the heart. "No, Jagger. I just want to go home."

Caught in the last remnants of her nightmare, Arianne sat up so fast, her head spun. But Viper wasn't beating her in the Black Jack clubhouse. And Leo wasn't pinning her to the bed with his heavy body. And Jeff wasn't in a parking lot, shooting her as she ran.

But she was alone for the first time in two days.

After reluctantly taking her home, Jagger had called the club doctor to come and check her over, and then he'd held her all night long, his arm around her, his body tucked against hers. He'd stayed with her the next day, hanging out in the shop with Sparky, fiddling with his bike, and shutting down all the gossip—to everyone's disappointment. And last night they'd made love for hours. But they hadn't talked. And it was clear from his unnatural silence and haunted expression, there were things he wanted to say.

Pulse racing, she walked over to the window and rested her forehead against the glass, looking out over the calm, still night. Peaceful. Moonlight filtered through the dark clouds overhead, chasing shadows across the street. Just as the nightmares chased her. She knew now she would never escape them. They were part of this world. A world where she could never be safe. She had to leave Conundrum to truly be free.

The front door opened and closed. She heard the whisper of leather and the rattle of steel out in her living room as Jagger removed his cut and the heavy chain he wore around his belt. What time was it? Three? Maybe 4 A.M.? Where had he gone? But before she could ask, she felt his heat behind her, his body pressed against her own. Arianne's bones turned liquid.

"You should be in bed." He swept her hair to the side and kissed the sensitive dip between her neck and shoulder, his lips whispering over her skin.

"I couldn't sleep. I keep thinking about being shot at when I ran for the cab." She shook herself, changing the topic. Enough she had to deal with the nightmares in her sleep. "What about you? It's late to be working."

He pressed his lips to the back of her neck, and her stomach fluttered with awakening desire.

"T-Rex, Gunner, and some of the boys got ambushed by the Jacks on a protection run. Four men hurt, and we lost the weapons. T-Rex managed to get them help and rode to the clubhouse injured and alone. He just got back an hour ago and he brought this message." He handed her a crumpled picture, but before she could open it, he covered her hand.

"Usually I lead the protection runs, but I wanted to stay with you, make sure you were okay, so I sent Gunner in my place. They'd been tipped off that I would be there, and Gunner took two bullets because they thought he was me. They didn't just want the weapons, they wanted me dead."

Her breath caught. "Is Gunner okay?"

"Thanks to T-Rex's quick thinking, yes. He flagged down a trucker and had him take Gunner to a hospital. They left that picture in Gunner's cut."

Hands trembling, Arianne unfolded the picture. She couldn't remember the last time she'd held an actual photograph. Even Jeff rarely used his darkroom. She stared at the photo, and her heart seized in her chest. Someone had taken a picture of her, beaten and chained in Bunny's basement. Although the light was poor, she was easily recognizable. She flipped it over, and written on the back was the word, *Traitor.*

Her blood chilled as Jagger tensed behind her. Although she'd managed to put him off for two days, there was no way he would let this go. Not as a man. And not as president of the Sinner's Tribe.

"Tell me what happened. Who shot at you? I can promise it will never happen again."

She recognized the fury in his voice from the night at Peelers, but this time every word was cold and calculated. Determined. He would not be so easily put off. And yet, she had to try.

"I told you before. I just want to forget about it." Not only was she still reeling from Jeff's betrayal, or the fact he'd shot her with her own gun, but she also mourned the loss of the brother she had loved so dearly. Even the drugs were no excuse. Somewhere along the road, he'd become his father's son. And this picture—it had to be Jeff's picture—proved it. Viper would never do anything as childish. Or as personal. And she betrayed him, too. "Let's talk about something else."

Wrong thing to say. Jagger fisted his hand in her hair

and jerked her neck to the side, a shocking contrast to his gentle touch only a moment before. "You don't understand what it does to me, seeing you like this, Arianne—the cuts and bruises, the bandages, the fucking ropes and chains, knowing someone hurt you, shot at you, and I wasn't there to protect you."

"Jagger . . ." She tried to pull away, but he held her firm and scored his teeth down her neck, sending a pulse of electricity straight to her sex.

"Tell me who it was. I need to find the bastard or I'll go fucking crazy."

"Please. Let me go."

"I let you go once, Arianne. I won't make that mistake again." He grasped her breast in his broad hand, squeezing roughly until she gasped, more at the shock of his sudden change in demeanor than at the bittersweet pain that made her sex ache to be filled.

"What are you doing?" She tried to look back over her shoulder, but he gripped her hair harder, keeping her still. "Why are you being like this?"

He ground his pelvis against her, pressing his arousal along the cleft of her buttocks as his free hand tightened on her stomach, pinning her to his body. "I gave you time. I was patient. And while I was being patient, I sent my boys out to find out who hurt you. They came back with nothing."

Was this his game? Seduce the information out of her? Well, no seduction needed. She could give him enough information to keep him satisfied. And then he could satisfy her.

"Jeff was at Peelers." She scrambled to come up with a plausible story that wouldn't implicate Jeff. But not a lie. She couldn't lie to Jagger. "He saw one of the prospects when we arrived, so he hung around outside and caught me when I was in the restroom. He said he had given my passport to someone who was in his car. I couldn't let you take him, and you suspected me of betraying you anyway, so I went to get it. A guy in a cut came around the corner, so we jumped in the car and drove away."

She could feel the wave of anger ripple through his body as his fingers dug painfully into her flesh. "You got in the car because of me. You were going to leave."

"I got in the car because I wanted the passport." She trembled beneath his touch. "Not because I'd decided to go that night, but because I wanted the option. I wanted to have it in my hand so that I'd know if things went bad, I had a way out. You just . . . made it easier to get in the car."

Her words inflamed him. With a growl, he spun her around, backing her up to the wall. She shivered as the cool surface pressed against her bare skin, her nightie providing no protection from the chill.

"I won't make it easy again." He bracketed her wrists with one strong hand, lifting her arms and pinning them above her head. "What happened after you drove away?"

Anger and arousal roared through her blood. She writhed in his grasp, but her struggles only heightened her desire, her nipples hardening as they brushed over his solid chest. Jagger forced her legs apart with a thick thigh, the rough denim of his jeans scraping over her sensitive flesh as he held her in place. "Tell me."

Ah God. How could she save Jeff from Jagger's wrath? He was lost to her, but she couldn't be the instrument of his death. "Axle was in the car. Jeff owed him money. He was tweaking and needed a hit. We wound up at Bunny's."

"Jesus Christ. Axle." Jagger spat out the name. "I should have finished him when I had the chance."

His eyes blazed so hot, she could almost feel the burn, and his pulse throbbed rapidly in his neck. With his gaze fixed firmly on hers, he brushed his fingers along her throat, feathering his way to the top edge of her nightgown.

Then, with a brutal yank, he tore it away.

"Jagger!" Vulnerable, inexplicably ashamed, she tried to turn, hide herself from him, but his hands kept her pinned against the wall, and his thigh held her immobile.

"I thought I made it clear: You don't go to see Bunny. Ever."

She bit her lip, her heart pounding in her chest. "I didn't have a choice. Axle had a gun."

He gave a satisfied grunt, then leaned down and nipped her lower lip, sucking it into his mouth. Confused by his unpredictable shifts between hot and cold, rough and gentle, she pulled away.

"Is he the one who hit you?" With his free hand, he cupped her breast, kneading it until she physically ached to have him inside her. He brushed his thumb lightly over her nipple, then gave it a rough pinch.

Her body heated, burned for him. And he was hard—so hard, she could feel his arousal against her stomach, smell his hunger thick and hot around her. She rocked her hips, grinding her wet sex against his thigh, hoping to distract him from his questioning, making him lose control.

"Answer."

Her stomach clenched. He wouldn't kill Jeff for hurting her, but he wouldn't let him get away with it either. "They . . . both did."

He reacted as she knew he would, his body going rigid, his face smoothing into an expressionless mask. "Jeff hit you, too?"

"I was trying to run away. He was tweaking."

"Fuck." He pounded his fist against the wall beside her head. "Jesus Christ, Arianne."

Torn between fear and arousal, she tried to pull away, but he slid a hand between them, his fingers reaching inside her panties to stroke her wet curls. Arianne's body arched and trembled, but when she licked her lips, a bitter taste coated her tongue. "I don't want to play this game anymore—"

Her words choked off in a gasp as he lowered his thigh and pushed one finger deep inside her. Her inner walls clenched around him and she bit back a groan.

"What happened at Bunny's?"

"Bunny wasn't involved," she murmured, leaning her forehead against his shoulder as he drew his finger out, then thrust deep again. "He recognized me and let me go. He said he didn't want to get on your bad side."

Jagger added a second finger, rubbing along her sensitive inner walls as he penetrated her. Moisture flooded her sex and she rocked shamelessly against his thrusts, seeking a release from the tension coiled through her body.

"I want you, baby," she whispered.

"I know, sweetheart." His deep, husky rumble reverberated through her body. "I can feel your heat. I want you, too. But I want something more."

"What? What do you want?" Her hips pushed against his hand, but his rhythm didn't change. Too slow. Too shallow. He was in control, and his dominance served only to heighten her arousal.

"I want to know who beat you, tied you up, shot you, and chained you to the wall."

Dazed, on the precipice of orgasm, her body pulsing and throbbing with need, she almost gave the game away. Almost. "It doesn't matter. I got away."

"It matters." He added a third finger, filling her, stretching her, pounding inside her with an exquisite, brutal intensity. "It's killing me, sweetheart, because I wasn't there, and if you don't tell me who did it to you, I'm gonna lose my fucking mind."

"Please . . . don't do this, Jagger. Not now."

"*Who?*" His voice rose to a shout and he pressed the

base of his palm against her clit, sending her arousal spiraling out of control. "Was it Bunny? Axle? Who else was there? Jeff?"

"I was in an alley and then I was tied up." Her head pounded with the effort of trying to skirt over the critical piece of information that could end Jeff's life and destroy what she and Jagger had together while at the same time, endorphins flooded her brain and her body quivered with need.

"How did you get away?" He renewed his assault, his thumb flicking over her sensitive bundle of nerves as he drove his fingers deeper inside her, his lips a feather-light contrast as he pressed tiny kisses along her jaw.

"Bunny made them untie me. We went outside. Axle had a gun. They were talking about how Jeff could get Axle's money. I disarmed Axle and ran."

"Who shot you, Arianne?" Clearly at the end of his patience, his words came out in a sharp bark, and her brain fuzzed, no longer able to separate fear and arousal, torn between pushing him away and begging him to make her come.

"I can't—"

"I need to know like I fucking need to breathe. I. Need. To. Know."

Her heart sped up double time. Despite everything Jeff had done, she could never give him up, especially not to a man she suspected would kill him. She hated her brother, but she didn't want him dead. She owed him for the night long ago when he had saved her, and for the past they shared.

This has to end. Now.

Drawing on the skills she had learned to survive Viper's wrath, she allowed her anger to rise sharp and fast burying her emotions in a protective burst, burning away her confusion. "Don't do this, Jagger."

"Tell me."

Bastard. How could he use their intimacy as a means to get information from her? His actions were as much a betrayal as her failure to tell him that the bullet Banks had pulled from her arm was a .22, the gun Jeff had taken from her. Axle had the .45.

"The bullet came from behind, and that's all you'll get from me."

Jagger pulled away, releasing her wrists as he slid his fingers from her dripping sex. Arianne staggered back at the sharp pain of abandoned arousal. And then shame washed over her in an acid wave. Shame at having let the game go so far. Shame at leaving herself so vulnerable and exposed. Shame at wanting him so much, she had forgotten the most basic rule: Do not trust.

Nausea roiled in her gut. She took a step toward her clothes, and Jagger stepped in her way.

"I want you so bad, I fucking ache with wanting you." His voice shook with emotion. "I would do almost anything to have you right now. But more than that, I want you to be safe. I can't honor my duty to the club or honor my promise to you if you don't give me a name. I know you know who it is."

Fury scoured away the shame. She took a step into his space, determined to get her clothes, silently daring him to stop her. "No one is going to die because of me."

Jagger stood firm. "No one touches what is mine, Arianne. No one hurts my girl. No one shoots a woman under my protection and lives. And no one fucks with the Sinners or what belongs to us. I will get that name, and when I do, I will show no mercy."

"You did this for a name?"

He turned and headed for the door. "I did this because I love you."

★ TWENTY-ONE ★

No fighting or violence on club grounds.
Penalty is an ass-kicking.

Tap. Tap. Tap.

Arianne awoke to a gentle rapping on the front door. Soft morning light filtered through her curtains. Jagger? She quickly dismissed the thought. No way would Jagger ever knock. He would just barge in.

Wrapping a blanket around her shoulders, she threw on some sweats and called out. "Who is it?"

"Wheels."

With a sigh of both relief and disappointment, Arianne opened the door to the pinched expression of a clearly agitated Wheels.

"Jagger asked me to come and get you. He's got something he wants you to see." He shifted from foot to foot, avoiding eye contact, and Arianne frowned.

"What's the matter?"

"Nothing." He stuffed his fists in his jeans pockets and looked away. "Just . . . don't like to keep Jagger waiting. You know how it is. He says now, he means yesterday. He says yesterday, he means last week."

Still disconcerted by the events of last night, Arianne grimaced. "Come on in. I'll just be five minutes."

Five minutes became ten as she scrambled to wash up and tidy her hair before throwing on her jeans and T-shirt. All the while, she agonized over whether to ask Wheels about the night at Peelers. Had that been him by the door that night? If so, why had he let her go?

By the time she joined him in the living room, she had resolved not to raise the issue unless he did. The consequences for him were severe, and she couldn't risk anyone overhearing their conversation. Plus, he was already in full anxiety mode, muttering to himself as they walked down the stairs.

Wheels' Harley Sportster was small and compact, not designed for the comfort of a pillion rider, and she shifted in her seat as he raced through Conundrum, blowing through red lights and careening through back alleys. By the time they arrived at the clubhouse, she knew something was seriously wrong. Even a senior patch wouldn't take the kind of risks he'd taken on that ride unless he'd been threatened with death.

He led her through the clubhouse in silence, his hand pressed against her lower back as if she might suddenly turn and run. But she stayed on course, curious about what could rile the easygoing Wheels and make Jagger demand her presence instead of coming for her himself.

They descended the stairs to the basement, and Wheels led her down a long narrow hallway, and through a spacious games room, his fingers twitching against her.

"What's got you so agitated?" She skirted around the pool table, and eyed the well-stocked bar with appreciation.

Wheels stared straight ahead and mumbled. "Sometimes I forget."

"Forget what?" she said in an uncertain tone.

"Who he really is and how careful I have to be."

She didn't have to ask what he meant. They walked into a small room with blacked-out windows, and she knew.

"Banks!" A sudden coldness hit her core, and she flung herself forward, her cry echoing through the small space.

Tied to a chair in the center of the room, his left eye swollen shut, blood trickling down his temple, and his face a mass of cuts and bruises, Banks regarded her with a resigned expression. His eyes flicked to Jagger standing to his right, fist raised to deliver another blow.

"Bastard." Banks growled. "Did you have to bring her down here?"

"No." Arianne threw herself in front of Jagger and held up her hands, palms forward, taking in Cade and Sparky, leaning against the wall and Zane behind the chair. "Don't touch him. Don't you dare touch him."

The room, pungent with the scent of blood and sweat, stilled. Jagger turned to her, his eyes cold, hard, and resolute. "He has information I need, and so far he's been reluctant to give it up. Apparently, the women who took you to him told him the whole story, and it's a story I want to hear."

Seized by an unbearable fury, heedless of the muttered warnings around her, Arianne turned on Jagger. "You're doing this to get information I did not want you to have. This is between you and me. Let him go. *Now.*"

Jagger's eyes narrowed. "Careful, sweetheart. There's a line you don't cross, and you're standing on the edge. I'll tolerate only so much disrespect, and right now my patience is at its end. I want a name and I'll do what has to be done to get it. He knows who fired the gun."

Her face twisted in revulsion. "So you're going to beat him up? He looked after me, Jagger. He took a bullet out of my arm. And right now he's suffering for being a good friend to me. And this is the thanks he gets? I trusted you—"

"You don't trust me." He said through gritted his teeth. "You told me last night. What would the Jacks think if they found out was a woman I had claimed had been shot and

I did fuck-all about it? Or the Triads? Or the Mafia? Everything we do or don't do sends a message. Everything is a power play. I have one hundred men depending on me to keep them safe. We are the dominant club in the state, and we stay that way because we make sure no one fucks with us. And beating my girl, tying her up, chaining her to a floor, and shooting her goes way beyond that."

"I'm not your girl." She couldn't hide the bitterness in her voice. "I'm your prize. Your finger to Viper. The life you took for Cole's life. If I were anything more, you wouldn't be doing this."

"You were mine the second you drove onto Sinner property." His flat, toneless voice sliced through her heart. "You will be mine until I let you go."

He sidestepped Arianne and looked down at Banks. "Name."

"Fuck you."

Without warning, Jagger punched Banks in the jaw. Banks's head snapped to the side and he let loose a string of swearwords.

"Oh God. Stop." She grabbed Jagger's T-shirt and yanked him toward her. "Stop."

His face twisted with rage. Stark, raw, and almost unrecognizable as the man who had been so gently cruel with her last night.

"I want a name."

"Don't fucking tell these bastards anything." Banks spit blood on the floor. "Told you bikers were nothing but trouble. You keep your secrets to yourself and know they are safe with me. I'm not gonna break 'cause some pussy with marshmallow hands is pattin' me on the cheeks."

Jagger looked over at Sparky and dipped his chin. Sparky picked up an iron bar from the floor and tapped it in his hand. Wheels paled. Arianne took a step toward Banks, and Jagger grabbed her arm.

"Don't interfere."

Her stomach sank, and a wave of nausea washed over her. Wheels was right. She, too, had forgotten who Jagger was: not a friend or a savior, or even a lover, but a ruthless MC president who put his club above everything else. Just like her father.

Softening her expression, she swallowed her pride and dropped her voice to a pleading tone. "Please, Jagger. Don't hurt him."

But he wouldn't be moved. "I'm tired of playing these fucking games, Arianne. You know I won't hurt you, but I have no problem hurting him. None whatsoever. I want the name of the guy who did those things to you, or I'll start at his ankles and work my way up."

She cast one last, frantic glance at Sparky, but he just gave her a sympathetic shrug and looked away. Zane snorted, amused. Wheels's face contorted in shared anguish and he looked away.

Damn him. Damn them all. Damn stupid biker culture. How had she misjudged him so badly? How had she fooled herself into thinking he wasn't like the other bikers she knew? He was as bad as Viper. Maybe even worse.

She spun around and stormed out the door, searching for a weapon. She had her .38 strapped to her leg, but she wasn't prepared to go that far. Not yet. She grabbed a pool cue from the rack and raced back into the room. Jagger was still in front of Banks, his back to her. She moved quickly, swinging the pool cue before anyone could bark a warning.

"No." The pool cue whipped over Jagger's back and split in two with a loud crack, leaving her holding a splintered piece of wood.

Jagger reacted so fast, she barely registered that he had moved. One moment his back was bowing under her strike; the next she was against the wall, the broken pool cue against her throat. His chest heaved, eyes glittered, unseeing.

"Goddamnit." Banks struggled against his bonds. "Leave her alone. I'm over here if you want a punching bag."

Arianne glared as the stick pressed against her throat. "That's right," she gritted out. "Hurt *me*. I'm the one who won't tell you what you want to know. And I can take it. I've taken it all my life. There isn't anything you can do to me that Viper hasn't already done. Hit me, Jagger. Show me how wrong I was about you. Show me you're all the same. Do it for the club."

A curious mix of emotions flickered across Jagger's face—shock, fear, self-loathing, torment—but no compassion, no love. He hadn't meant the words he uttered last night. And even if he had, he clearly didn't know what they meant.

"I will protect you, Arianne. Whether you want it or not."

Without another glance, he walked over to Sparky and took the bar from his hand. Holding it like a golf club, he touched Banks's ankle, then raised the bar over his shoulder.

If she had been in that chair, she would have let him hit her. Viper hadn't just used his fists, and she'd survived, she knew she could survive whatever Jagger dished out. But it wasn't her in the chair. And just as she couldn't be the instrument of Jeff's death, she couldn't watch someone she cared about suffer on her behalf.

"Jeff." She screamed the name and ran over to the chair, blocking the bar with her body. "Jeff chased me and hit me. Axle knocked me out. It was Jeff's idea to go to Bunny. They both took me there. Jeff's the one who tied me up and chained me to the floor."

"Who shot you?" His voice held no emotion, no anger, no disappointment. Nothing.

"Jeff had my gun." Her chin and lips trembled as she gave him away. "He didn't know what he was doing. He's an addict. He gets psychotic when he's tweaking."

But for the first time, she didn't feel any conviction for that excuse. Had he been tweaking when he picked her up or decided to sell her for a kilo of meth, or when he caught her in the alley and punched her in the face? There were moments when he'd seemed like himself, when she thought he knew exactly what he was doing. But in the end, did it matter? He was responsible for his actions, and his actions had led to her being tied up in the basement of Bunny's pool hall.

Jagger made a disgusted sound. "And yet after everything he did, you protected him right to the very last second."

"I don't want him dead. He's my brother. I owe him my life."

"And my clubhouse? Cole? He was my brother."

"Jeff said he wasn't the shooter."

Jagger tapped the bar in his hand, and the skin on the back of her neck prickled. He wasn't finished with this. What else did he want?

"Maybe it was you. You're good on your bike, good with a gun. Hard to believe someone could knock you off. Easy to believe you could take someone out while riding."

"You fucking bastard." Banks snarled and struggled against the ropes. "Arianne, get me the hell outta this chair and I'll teach this betraying piece of shit about honor and loyalty and how to tell a good person from a piece of fucking Sinner crap."

She didn't feel Banks's anger. Or his indignation. Although she was grateful he believed in her. She felt nothing but a deep aching sadness for the loss of something she had known in her heart was too good to be true.

"If you really believe that," she said to Jagger. "If you

really believe I could do those things, then do your duty. Give your club justice. Revenge. Show us what you're made of, Mr. President. Use that bar on me." She spread her arms and stood in front of him, fully prepared to die.

And in that moment she was sixteen again and determined to win her freedom, even if she had to die for it. But that time, she'd been holding a gun.

His jaw twitched and he held her gaze, his face an expressionless mask. They both knew she had left him with only two choices: He could kill her, or he could release his claim. Either way she would be free.

The seconds passed in interminable silence. Finally, Jagger handed the bar to Zane. "Find Jeff. Bring him here. Take as many brothers as you need. I don't care how many Jacks you have to go through to get him. Then go deal with Bunny. He should have called me the second he saw her, and he never should have let her go."

Zane gave him a curt nod. "Axle?"

"Spread the word through the underground: Mafia, Triads, Russians, every MC, and our law enforcement contacts. He's an enemy of the Sinners, and we've put a price on his head."

"You want me to take Arianne home?" Wheels took a step forward, his face stark, brows deeply furrowed. He looked like he'd aged ten years in the last ten minutes.

Jagger leveled his gaze at Arianne. "I can't protect you if you aren't honest with me. I can't keep you safe if you choose to protect the very people who mean you harm. And I can't trust you if you keep secrets from me. I release you from the Sinner claim. We're done."

And then he was gone.

Leaves crunched beneath Jagger's feet as he pounded his way through the forest. Max ran by his side, unusually quiet, as if he could sense Jagger's torment.

His sweat-soaked shirt clung to him and his thighs burned in protest, but he couldn't stop, couldn't go back, couldn't think about Arianne's face when she walked into the room and saw Banks tied to the chair.

Shock. Devastation. Betrayal.

Nothing had ever cut him so bad, except making the decision to push her away in the first place. He'd never be able to tell her he'd done it to protect her. That it was partly a charade.

He stumbled. Caught himself. Pushed on. She should be gone by now. Someplace safe. Away from him. Away from Viper, Jeff, and everyone who meant her harm. She would find the happiness she had been looking for. She would be free.

Max stopped suddenly and barked. Relieved to have an excuse to stop punishing himself, Jagger slowed to a walk and greeted Zane, who waited for him near the low stone wall surrounding the property.

"Hey." One word. A host of questions. But mostly Zane wanted to make sure he was okay.

He didn't answer. No, he was far from okay, but he couldn't admit that weakness, even to his best friend. Instead, he paced along the wall toward the house, cooling down, wondering if self-loathing could kill, determined not to talk about the real reason Zane was here. "What's up?"

"Sherry wants to come back. She's hounding everyone."

Max bounded over to them and Jagger picked up a stick and threw it far into the trees. "I don't kick people out so I can bring them back. She made her choice. She chose poorly. I can't undo her mistake."

"If you say so. But she came clean about helping Axle steal the guns, and I believe her when she says he forced her to do it."

Jagger bristled at the implicit admonishment. "Anything else?"

"Gunner thinks the same person who tipped off the Jacks at the ice house also tipped off the Jacks about our party at Riders. He's gonna recommend an information lockdown regarding future missions and gatherings until we flush the bastard out."

"Christ. Everything's falling apart. How did a rat get into the club? We fucking screen them to death."

Zane lifted a shoulder. "Could be someone turned, like Axle did. He's gone underground, by the way. No one can find him. I've doubled the reward and made it clear we'll take him alive or dead. If I was him, I'd get out of the state as fast as possible."

"I hope he leaves our fucking guns behind."

"Lotta guns floating around," Zane said. "T-Rex ID'd Jeff as the leader of the protection-run ambush, which means Viper has Sheriff Morton's guns, too."

Jagger slapped at a tree branch in his path. "We'll have to offer Morton the money we picked up from trunking a few weeks ago, smooth his ruffled feathers. Christ. If we can't get at least one stash back, we'll have a hard time getting new contracts."

"Viper must be suffering from the loss of the ice house if he's trying to take over our arms trade." Zane swatted at a branch overhead. "You know what the dealers are like when they don't get their stuff."

"Small consolation." Jagger kicked at the leaves as they passed a broken fountain, two cupids entwined, their bows broken, bodies covered in moss. "What about Banks? Did you offer him a place as a prospect?"

"He told me to shove my head up my ass."

Any other time he would have chuckled. Instead, he scraped a hand through his hair and sighed. "I'm not giving up. I want him in the club. He said he was Special Forces, and Sparky told me he had six of our boys groaning on the floor of his apartment in under five minutes. I think he let them take him, just so he could check up on Arianne. He's not a man who goes anywhere he doesn't want to go."

"So how are you going to change his mind?" Zane whistled and Max bounded over to them. Jagger bent to ruffle Max's fur before continuing down the path.

"I told Cade to call in a coupla marks and send a construction crew over to his bar to fix it up. And I'm sending Doc Hegel over to check him out after he's finished with the six Banks beat up."

"He's a fucking fighting machine," Zane said, his voice laced with admiration.

"And I want him." Jagger rubbed his brow. Banks wasn't going to come to them easy, especially after what he'd done, but with the truce broken, he needed good men and Banks had skills beyond those of the average biker. "I'm going to lean on him until he caves," he said, with a confidence he didn't feel in the least. "Man like that would be an incredible asset for the club. He knew what was going down with Arianne the first time I hit him. He knew it was all for show. He played the game because in the end, we both wanted the same thing."

They paused at the steps to the clubhouse and Zane twisted his lips to the side. "You ever wonder what a guy from Special Forces is doing running a bar in Conundrum?"

"Already checked him out. The car, bar, and his apartment are all in the name of Joe Banks, but except for those three records, Joe Banks doesn't exist. He has no history, pays no taxes, and has no bank accounts."

"And soon he'll have no bartender."

Jagger gave his friend a cool warning glare. "Don't go there, Zane. It fucking killed me to do what I had to do, but it was the only way to keep her safe. I had to make her hate me enough that she'd leave Conundrum and never look back. That picture T-Rex brought back did it for me. With the Black Jacks putting a mark on her, it was Christel all over again."

Zane sat on the top step, resting his elbows on his thighs. "This situation is nothing like what you faced with Christel. She was a sweet girl, but she wasn't cut out for this life. She didn't have the edge or the street smarts to stay alive. She needed someone to take care of her, but you were already spread too thin. I'm sorry you lost her, but there was a reason you never made her an old lady, and that's because you knew she wasn't right for you."

"Zane . . ." But the usually reticent Zane was on a roll and didn't heed his warning.

"Arianne isn't anything like her. She can take care of herself. Would Christel ever have tried to escape out a window, stand up to Viper, or shoot Leo when he busted up her party? Would she have hit you with a pool cue when she thought you'd crossed the line, and fucking dare you to take her life? Arianne's the kind of woman who will always have your back. If she thinks someone's sneaking outside her house at night, she's not gonna call you a hundred times, sobbing into the phone. She's gonna pull out her gun and shoot the fucker in the nuts. She's an asset, not a liability. She's probably the only woman I've met who is worthy of you. A woman to stand by your side instead of in your shadow. She makes you stronger, not weaker."

Jagger sat heavily on the step beside his old friend. "I thought you didn't like her. You accused her of being a spy. You've spent the last two months trying to push her out."

Zane shrugged. "I changed my mind. Seeing her today, all bruised up, her arm bandaged, and she's still telling you off, whacking you with a pool cue to knock some fucking sense into you, doing everything she could to protect the people she loved—even you. She changed my mind."

Max trotted over and settled beside Jagger, resting his head on Jagger's shoe. He felt another tug on his heart.

Loyalty. One of the fundamental tenets of biker culture. Arianne had it in spades. But he hadn't been loyal to her. Yes, he'd wanted to protect her, but he hadn't given her his faith or support. He hadn't trusted her judgment or respected her wishes. Instead, he had pushed her away, long before this latest plan to keep her safe.

Just as his dad had done to his mother. He was his father's son, after all. Ironic how history came full circle.

He rubbed Max's back, brushing out the leaves and twigs with each long stroke of his hand. "The Jacks have marked her because of me and the choices I made. She'll be safer if she leaves Conundrum."

"Christ." Zane gave an exasperated groan. "What does she have to do to prove herself to you?"

The opposite of what his mother had done.

Stay.

★ TWENTY-TWO ★

> *Members wishing to leave the club must have
> served five full years and turned their colors
> over to the president.*

"So . . . you're leaving Conundrum?"

"Yeah." Arianne stared out the window of the Sinner SUV as Wheels pulled away from the curb outside Banks's Bar. Banks waved from the doorway, and then disappeared inside, but she'd caught his slight wince as he raised his arm. He was injured because of her. If she'd just left when she'd planned, none of this would have happened.

But then she would never have met Jagger. And she wouldn't have known the truth about Jeff.

"Hey." Wheels reached over and squeezed her hand. "You okay? That wasn't good-bye forever, was it?"

Her chin dropped to her chest, and she crumpled under his scrutiny. "I promised I'd stop by the bar and say good-bye to him and Dawn before I left. It's just . . . when I look at him . . ."

Sympathy creased his face. "It's not your fault."

"Of course it's my fault." She wrenched her hand away. "I should have thought about what would happen if I got anyone else involved. Once Banks heard the whole story, what happened this morning was a foregone conclusion.

And that's what kills me. I understand why Jagger did what he did. It was a matter of honor for the club. That's our . . . their way."

"You don't think of yourself as a biker?"

"Do I look like a biker?"

Sweat trickled down his forehead and he wiped it away. "Frankly, yes. You walk with the same confidence. You share the same attitude. You've got the same edge. You've got a kick-ass bike. You ride and shoot better than most of the guys. Everything about you gives your biker roots away, just like someone would know I was American if I went to France."

She gave him a sidelong glance. Wheels sure didn't talk like any biker or prospect she knew. He talked like someone who'd spent a lot of time in the biker world. Maybe he had biker roots, too. "Just because I was born into it and forced to live the life, doesn't mean I have to embrace it." She twisted her mother's ring around her finger. "We have a choice. I chose to turn my back on biker life and find a place where I can be happy and not afraid. I just never thought I'd be going alone."

"If my dad and brother threatened to kill me, I'd probably run, too." His hands jerked the steering wheel and he muttered a curse. "I mean, if I had a brother." He cast her a sidelong glance and then looked back at the road. Arianne tilted her head to the side, trying to reconcile the odd tremor in his tone and his even stranger reaction, with what she had first taken to be an innocuous statement.

"Viper never threatened to kill me."

"But he put that picture in Gunner's cut," Wheels said. "Jagger took it as a death threat. He went crazy. You saw the result."

Indeed she had, and she would never forget the sight of Banks tied to that chair. But as for Viper . . . She scoffed.

"That was Jeff. Viper doesn't threaten. He doesn't do furtive. And he doesn't know his way around a dark room. He'd see an action like that as cowardly. If he wants someone dead, he kills them. No messing around. That's why the members of his club follow the rules. If they screw up, there is no warning. There one day. Dead the next."

Wheels stared at her with a scrutiny that was unsettling, particularly because his eyes were supposed to be on the road. "Do you wonder if maybe Jagger released his blood claim because he wanted you to leave? So you could go somewhere safe?"

"Maybe you should watch where you're going." She pointed to the windshield, even as she shook her head. Jagger was protecting the honor of the club, not her. Love wasn't part of the "club first" equation.

When they reached her apartment building, Wheels pulled over to the side of the road and turned off the engine. "What are you going to do now that you're free?"

Free. She'd dreamed of being free, but not like this. "I'm leaving town before Viper hears Jagger released me from his claim. If I don't, I'll never get away. I'm almost at the point where I've exhausted all my escape options. This tiny window, where he thinks I'm with the Sinners, is pretty much my last hope."

"So you're leaving the biker life?"

Arianne gave him a half-hearted smile. "I'm going to be normal . . . happy." But for the first time since she'd made up the little speech that had seen her through the worst of times, she didn't feel any conviction behind her words.

Wheels clicked his fingernails against the steering wheel and shifted in his seat. Puzzled, and no small bit apprehensive, Arianne pushed open the door.

"Wait." He scrubbed his hands over his face. "It's just . . . I like you."

"I like you, too, Wheels." She forced a smile and stepped out of the vehicle.

"Maybe you should leave tonight," he said. "You know . . . just in case Viper finds out."

She breathed out a relieved sigh. Ah. He wasn't crazy after all, just a nice guy looking out for her. "I need to get stuff ready and say good-bye. I'm going to be leaving for-ever, and forever is a very long time."

Two days after Banks's beating, the Sinners held a party. Partially in honor of all the brothers who had been injured recently, and the brother they had lost, but mostly to keep up their spirits, because the war with the Jacks had just begun.

By the time Jagger arrived at Riders, Cade had taken over the DJ booth by the window and was spinning his fa-vorite blend of heavy metal and thrash, interspersed with the odd Irish jig. The vines and palm trees from Dawn's party had been cleared away, the bullet holes filled, glass repaired, and the bar was back to looking as a biker bar should: rough and gritty, with worn tables, wooden floors, and metal band posters plastered over the walls. The sweet butts laughed it up with the brothers, and old ladies helped the staff serving snacks and pouring beer. Gunner stood at the corner of the room, arms folded, trying to keep order with the fierceness of his scowl.

Jagger nodded a few greetings and then threw himself on the couch at the back of the bar. He was here for ap-pearances and nothing else.

"Hey, baby. You're not lookin' the way a man should look at a party." Sherry joined him on the couch, tug-ging the bottom of her skin-tight black dress over her ass. The damn dress was cut so low, the only part of her tits not showing were her nipples. But then, Sherry had nice tits and she liked showing them off. Tonight, however, he didn't take up the invitation when she leaned across his body, ostensibly to brush something off his shoulder.

Instead, he turned away. "You're back on probation on the recommendation of the executive board," he said abruptly. "And not just because you've been feeding us info on Axle's whereabouts, or because we found out you acted under duress and no small amount of abuse. If it were up to me alone, you'd still be gone, especially after you helped him steal our weapons."

"You looked like you needed some cheering up," she said softly. "And I know where you sit on me coming back. I also know you could have vetoed the vote, so thank you for not doing that. Axle was a mistake. I was messed up after you broke it off, and he was there for me. He told me he loved me, and I believed him. But after you kicked him out, and he started making all sorts of demands for information about the club, and forcing me to do things I didn't want to do, I realized he never really loved me at all. He was using me to get to you. You're a wanted man, Jagger. In more ways than one."

She settled by his side and leaned her head on his shoulder. His nose wrinkled at the sharp scent of her cloying perfume, but he put an arm around her for the simple comfort of her familiarity and the fact she didn't want anything from him, at least for the moment. They always wanted something. The sweet butts and hood rats wanted in his bed. Sherry had wanted to wear his patch. The brothers jostled for position or favor. Even Max would nudge his leg or nip his hand when he wanted to play or go for a walk. Everyone needed a piece of him.

Except Arianne.

Damn, the woman had made it clear she wanted nothing from him. Didn't need his help or his protection. Hell, she took independence to a whole new level. Jagger didn't know if he liked that or not. How could he control her if there was nothing she needed from him? Not that it mattered now.

"I knew you couldn't stay grouchy for the entire party." Sherry slid her hand over his thigh and his cock twitched—an automatic response, given their history together.

"Sherry . . ."

"You're thinking about her." Sherry gave his leg a chaste pat. "You only smile when it has to do with women or Max. So don't worry. I won't try to seduce you, although you're looking mighty seduceable, all glowering and moody here in the corner. Some girls go for cheerful guys. I go for the dark, sullen type."

"Well, then, Zane's your man." He jerked his head at Zane, who was chatting with Gunner in the corner.

Sherry laughed. "I think I'll pass. You might be scary, but you've got heart. Zane is cold all the way through."

"He has heart," Jagger said. "He's just hidden it away."

"And yours is on your sleeve."

"She's gone, Sherry." He stood so quickly, she had to throw out an arm to catch herself. "I withdrew the Sinner claim, and kicked her out. She's nothing to the club."

Sherry squeezed Jagger's hand. "She's something to you. Even though you pretend you don't—you do care, Jagger. And if you let *me* come back, how can you do less for her?"

Less? Hell, he'd done more. He'd released his claim and given her the freedom she desired. *He'd let her go.* Damn Sherry for stirring things up when he'd already settled everything in his mind. He'd done everything he could do. Time to move on.

"I'm outta here. Not in the mood for a party." He took a step away, and then looked back over his shoulder. "You okay getting home?"

Sherry smiled. "I am home. You know the brothers will watch out for me."

And they would. Which meant he could get on his bike and just ride. Away from the crowds and the memories, away from the hope Sherry had planted in his heart. He needed his bike, and the afternoon sun in his face. He needed the rev of the engine and the wind in his hair.

He needed his girl. *Arianne.*

"You aren't leaving tonight." Banks scowled at Arianne as a worker narrowly missed running a two-by-four through the mirror behind the bar. "Don't even think about it."

Arianne stared at Banks's bruised face. He looked worse than when she'd seen him three days ago, the bruises now a motley collection of blue and green. She turned away and swept broken glass from the bar counter into a container. Renovations were almost complete, and Banks had called her in to help get ready for the big reopening.

"Tomorrow," she said. "And after I go, I won't ever have to worry about Viper hunting me down or beating me again. I won't be kidnapped, shot at, or claimed as a blood price. I'll be normal."

Dawn slid onto a stool and out of the way as two workers carried a new table to the center of the bar.

"Is that what you really want? I mean, you're not going for Jeff anymore, and the people who love you most are right here." Dawn hesitated. "Me and Banks. Your friends. Jagger's here."

"Jagger will be hunting for Jeff. He knows everything now, and there's no way he's going to let it go." Arianne grabbed a wet cloth and scrubbed the counter so hard, the cloth squeaked across the surface. "I've left messages on Jeff's phone and with some of his friends to warn him. But that's all I'll do. I'll never give up hope that he might change or reform, and he won't have that chance if he's dead."

"You're loyal to a fault." Dawn's sympathetic look sliced through Arianne, shaking her resolve. How could she leave her bestie? And yet, how could she not go?

"That's the problem." She rinsed out the cloth in the bar sink and hung it to dry. "How can I be with the man who kills my brother? How can I love someone who lives by a code that puts the honor of his club over Jeff's life? Jagger and I share the same values, but for me they lead to forgiveness, and for him they lead to revenge. It's a conundrum."

Dawn laughed. "Then you're living in the perfect place."

Banks joined them at the bar and hefted a box of liquor on the counter, a scowl on his face. "Not working as usual, I see."

Arianne pulled a bottle of whiskey from the box and put it on the shelf behind the bar. The entire display stock had to be replenished. Not one bottle remained unbroken after the fight.

"That's 'cause you're under renovation until the doors open. You were lucky to get a crew out here so fast to fix the place up."

"Wasn't me." Banks handed Arianne another bottle. "Didn't recognize the name of the company on the work order, but I'm pretty sure Jagger sent them."

"Jagger?" A knot formed in Arianne's belly. "Is that his way of saying sorry?"

"Man like that doesn't say sorry." He nudged her until she'd put the bottle on the shelf and then gave her another one. "The work crew . . . they're here because he wants something from me."

Arianne froze. "I gave him what he wanted. If he hurts you again—"

"He didn't hurt me."

"Look at your face." Her voice rose above the cacophony of sound. "Of course he hurt you. It's just another reason why I'm leaving. Normal people don't tie up your friends and beat them up to get information. They ask. And if the information isn't forthcoming, they might get angry, but then they walk away."

"He didn't hurt me, Arianne." Banks's face softened. "What he did was all for show. If he really wanted information from me, he would've broken a coupla my bones. He woulda picked up that iron bar and used it first, or he would have used a knife. And he wouldn't have done it in front of you. There's a big difference between hitting someone to make a point and hitting with the intent to harm."

"What point?" The bottle dangled from her fingers as her brain tried to process Banks's words. "It was about the club, Banks. You don't understand. He has to avenge the club."

"I got that about the club." Banks dropped his hands to the box and leaned toward her. "But he also had a duty to protect you, and he couldn't because you wouldn't let him. People were beatin' on you, tyin' you up, shootin' at you, and you wouldn't give him the information he needed to stop them. So what's he gonna do?"

Her lips pressed into a thin line. "Beat up my friend."

"Nah." Banks stepped behind the bar to avoid two workers carrying a plate-glass window. "I took down six of his guys in under five minutes. He got the message I wouldn't be talking. He brought me in anyway because he had only one option left."

Just as Wheels had said. "Make me leave town." She slumped against the bar and covered her face with her hands. Why hadn't she accepted it before? Jagger was capable of much more than bruises. She'd seen him with Axle and Leo, and she was intimately familiar with the difference between hurt and harm.

"He's at Riders." Banks pulled out another bottle of whiskey, then twisted off the cap and poured himself a shot.

"He invited me to their party. They want me to join the MC."

Wide-eyed, Dawn grabbed the bottle from his hand and poured another glass. "Seriously? They beat the crap out of you, drag you out of your bar, tie you up, beat you some more, and then invite you to join the club?"

Banks grinned. "Yeah. But I turned them down. Zane told me if I changed my mind, or wanted to get to know the guys, they'd be at Riders tonight." He looked at Arianne and his voice roughened. "Thought you should know. Just in case you want to say good-bye."

Jagger didn't know how far he'd ridden, or for how long. He didn't feel the cold, although his visible breath told him the temperature had dropped below zero. He couldn't remember the last time he'd eaten, and the only reason he'd had a drink was because at some point during his ride he had to stop for fuel. He knew only that the sun had set long ago, and he was being torn in two.

Life hadn't equipped him to deal with divided emotions. Duty had defined his world since he was old enough to say the word. In an attempt to curb his rebellious nature, duty had been drilled into him by his military family over and over again until he knew only duty and nothing of desire. He had never allowed anything to conflict with duty. And yet, despite his best intentions, it had happened anyway.

Arianne.

He wanted her with an ache that burned into his soul. He wanted her more than anything he had ever wanted in his life. Desire was tearing him apart, mercilessly ripping through his body like the shrapnel that had pierced his heart. And still, he clung to duty, his life raft in the tumult of emotions that rocked his world.

His phone buzzed in his pocket as he filled his tank. Would they never leave him alone? For once, he wanted to be free from duty. He wanted to ride until his body and brain were numb and Arianne was gone from his heart.

Buzz. Buzz. Buzz.

He pulled out the phone, intending to turn it off until he saw Sherry's name on the screen. With a sigh, he answered the call.

"Arianne came here looking for you." Sherry shouted above the music at the bar. "Thought you might want to know."

A wave of longing crashed through him, and he mentally patted himself on the back for leaving the party early. How much harder would it have been to see her again, knowing for certain it would be the last time? "I'm riding, Sherry. I'm not coming back."

"I asked Zane to take her to the clubhouse. She's waiting for you."

"Why the fuck did you do that?"

Her voice dropped so low, he barely heard her next words. "Club first. I loved you, Jag. I would have been proud to be your old lady. But the first time I saw you with her, I finally understood why you broke it off. It had nothing to do with Christel and everything to do with the fact that I wasn't the right girl for you. But she is. And this whole thing is tearing you apart. I need you, but the club needs you more. This thing with Arianne is taking you away from us. You gotta settle it. Either say good-bye and finish it, or tell her how you feel and convince her to stay."

"Sherry—"

"You can thank me later," she said softly.

"I thought you were afraid of Zane." He replaced the gas nozzle and straddled his bike.

"I am, but I'm more afraid of what will happen to you if you lose her, so I took one for the club. Turns out, he's not so scary after all. He was right choked up when I told him what I wanted."

Jagger smiled. "You did good, Sherry."

"You saved me once," she said. "You gave me a home in the club when I had nothing, a reason to live when I just wanted to die. And you did it again after I screwed up so bad with Axle, although you like to pretend it was all the board's doing. Thought it was time I returned the favor."

The drive took forever.

But not so long as the walk through the clubhouse. Room by room, he searched for her, his anxiety increasing exponentially until he reached the top floor. Was she still here? Or had she changed her mind?

Heart beating an erratic rhythm in his chest, he pushed open the door to his room.

Moonlight streamed through the window overlooking the grounds below. His gaze followed the soft light as it washed across the hardwood floor. And then he saw an angel.

Long dark lashes rested on creamy cheeks, and her T-shirt caressed the sweet curves of her breasts. His hands trembled as he remembered the softness of her skin beneath his palms, and when he finally drew in a breath, he caught her scent of wildflowers in springtime.

He had never before watched her sleep. Never realized how much softer she looked in repose, younger, unburdened.

Under his scrutiny, she awoke, stretched, her breasts straining against the thin fabric of her shirt, and then she caught him with her gaze.

"Hi, baby."

His throat seized and he pressed himself against the door jamb to keep from walking toward her, taking the one thing he longed for most in this world. The only thing he had ever truly wanted.

"Why are you here?" His words came out harsh, abrupt, but she didn't flinch.

"I wanted to see you."

His siren beckoned. An arm outstretched. Inviting. Beguiling.

Jagger remained resolute by the door. Duty before all else. Duty before desire. Duty silenced the keening of his heart. "I can't." His voice cracked, broke. "I can't do this. You need to leave."

"I've lived this life," she said. "There aren't many people who could say this to you, but I understand. Truly I do. I'm not saying what you did to Banks was right, and I'm not saying I agree or even that I forgive you, but I know you were trying to protect me and uphold the code, and the code says 'Club first.'"

She threw back the covers and slid off the bed, her only clothing a T-shirt and a tiny pair of panties. He dipped his gaze, trying not to notice her beautiful, long, supple legs, or the tiny frills peeking out from beneath her shirt. But his cock swelled and his heart pounded and by the time she reached him it was all he could do to stay still.

"I also know you're hunting for Jeff. Any MC president would do the same." She leaned up and kissed his neck. "I've warned him. Despite what he did to me, I'm still his sister and I owed him that. I understand what you have to do, but I can't condone it, and I can't stay. I'm leaving tomorrow, so tonight I came to say good-bye."

He closed his eyes and fisted his hands by his sides, but her scent surrounded him, her voice warmed him, her touch inflamed him, and his heart squeezed in his chest when she leaned closer and brushed her lips over his.

"Say it, then."

Her lips whispered over his cheek. "Not just words. When I'm gone, it will be forever, and I didn't want to leave the way we ended things. I want to spend the night with you. And in the morning, you'll do what you have to do, and I'll do what I have to do, and we'll say good-bye and never see each other again, but right now those choices don't have to be made. Right now, it's just you and me alone in this room, and I want you so much it hurts."

She unbuckled his belt and then slid it through the loops, doubling it before she placed it in his palm. "I trust you, Jagger. I want to give you everything. Make this beautiful for me so I never have nightmares again."

He broke. Split wide open, his damaged heart drawing him down to the angel in front of him with the power of a desire that had waited a lifetime to be fulfilled. As he took her in his arms, cleaved to her warmth, he knew with a certainty that shook him to the core, she was wrong.

He would never say good-bye.

"Clothes off. On your knees. Back to me."

She stripped off her shirt and panties, then knelt on the bed and positioned herself as he directed, her body trembling under his scrutiny.

"If you feel uncomfortable or afraid; you want me to stop or slow down, just say the word."

"Okay."

Jagger gently eased her hands back and then bound them together, tightening the leather around her wrists. Her back arched ever so slightly, her ass on display. He ran a hand over the creamy cheeks and steeled himself to restraint.

"Too tight?"

"No."

"Feel me, sweetheart." He swept her hair away from her neck and pressed his lips to her nape, slow and tender, fanning the flames of her desire. "Don't think about anything except my lips, my hands, my body on yours."

He eased her down until her cheek pressed against the cotton sheet and her ass was up in the air.

"Love your beautiful ass." He smoothed his hand over

each cheek and then leaned forward and feathered kisses down her spine. She shivered as his lips whispered over her skin, but when he reached around to cup and caress her breast, her body softened.

"Love these beautiful breasts. I could play with them all night."

"Please don't."

Jagger chuckled. No real chance of that. Already he was rock hard and ready for her.

Sliding his fingers between her thighs, he forced her legs apart, then spread her open, parting her folds to expose the delicate heat beneath. He was tempted to slick her moisture up around her clit, tease her until she writhed beneath him, but he wanted to build sensation on sensation until she knew only desire and nothing of fear.

Gently, he pressed a finger inside her moist, wet heat, his cock pulsing in time to his strokes. She tensed and quivered around him, sliding her knees wider to give him better access. If it had been any other night, he might have smacked her ass for moving without his permission. His dominance aroused her, and he suspected she would get even hotter if he exerted more control. But not tonight. Tonight was about pleasure. Not pain.

He added a second finger, spreading them inside her, pumping long and deep, delighted when he'd stimulated her sensitive inner tissue to the point that moisture gushed from her sex and she shuddered and moaned.

"Good girl." One hand deep inside her, the other tweaking her nipple, he feathered kisses down her spine to her bound hands, and then he kissed each open palm, reminding her that she was bound but cared for. Restrained but loved.

No part of her body went untouched as he awakened her senses with soft kisses and sweet caresses, while he continued to drive his fingers into her channel, controlling her arousal with a rhythm that would keep her on edge but not let her go over.

"Oh God, Jagger. I'm so close." Her hips rocked in time to his thrusts, her pussy grinding against his fingers as she sought the release he was withholding.

"My little Sinner." He pressed his lips to her lower back, just below her bound hands, brushing kisses down to the cleft of her buttocks. "One day I want to show you what it truly means to sin."

She gasped, moaned, her hands straining against the bonds, but she was aroused, not afraid, trembling beneath his palms.

"You want to come, sweetheart?"

"Yes," she whispered.

"Tell me." He shoved his jeans past his hips, sheathed himself with a condom from his wallet, and then stroked the length of his cock. Once. Twice. But instead of relieving the pressure, his touch increased the pain, and he felt the beginning tremors in the base of his shaft that signaled his imminent release.

Arianne groaned and shuddered, stilling only when he added a third finger, readying her for him.

"Please. I want to come."

He gave a satisfied grunt and then withdrew his fingers and spread her moisture up and around her clit. "I'm going to make you come like this, sweetheart, with your beautiful ass in the air, and your hands tied behind your back. And I'm gonna hold you so all you'll be able to do is feel the pleasure I give you. I have control, sweetheart. You don't have to fight and you don't have to fear. And when you let go, you'll know you're coming because I want you to come, and you'll know I'm there to catch you. Are you ready for me?"

"God yes."

With a tortured groan, he spread her wide with his thigh

and then he thrust, stretching her, parting her swollen flesh as he drove his cock deep inside her.

Fucking heaven.

Arianne whimpered and her pussy clenched around him. Heaven became hell and he had to move, pulling out and driving in as far as he could go. Mindless, she rocked her hips against him, begging him to give her what she needed. Hard. Fast.

Now.

With powerful, relentless strokes, he pounded into her, until his brain had fuzzed with lust and he was only seconds away from the oblivion of release.

"Come with me." He slid his hand around her hip and teased her clit until her muscles tightened, coiled like a spring. And then he let her go.

"Now, sweetheart. Come for me."

And she did. A scream ripped from her throat, and her sex pulsed around him, drawing him so deep inside her. When he couldn't fight it anymore, he grabbed her hips and pounded into her, his cock hammering in a frantic rhythm. He climaxed hard and fast, her name a roar on his lips as he pumped his seed inside her.

Before she had fully come down, Jagger released her hands and settled her on his chest, enfolded in his arms. She had given him her trust tonight. She had let him protect her. He could only hope he was worthy of her gift.

"I love hearing you scream." He pressed a soft kiss to her forehead.

"I didn't scream." She looked up, mocking a frown. "I'm not a screamer."

A satisfied smile spread across his face. "You did. You screamed my name."

Arianne pushed herself further up and glared. "I think I would know."

"I think you wouldn't. You were too far gone."

Because she had let herself go. When her body finally accepted she had neither the strength nor the will to defeat him, she had yielded, trusted he would keep her safe. And he had kept his word. But would it be enough to convince her to stay?

"Whatever you want, whatever you need, sweetheart, I will find a way."

"Thank you." She rested her cheek on his chest, and his lungs seized with emotion. "For everything."

★ TWENTY-THREE ★

No vigilantism and no heroics. Threats to the club
and its members will be dealt with by the club
as a whole. No one goes it alone.

Last night in Conundrum.

Maybe.

Arianne sat at the counter in Banks's newly renovated bar and fiddled with her bike key. Slipping away in the early hours of the morning while Jagger slept was the hardest thing she had ever done, but she needed time to think. Last night hadn't been planned. At first, she'd just meant to say good-bye, but when Jagger walked into the bedroom, and she'd seen her own hurt and confusion reflected in his handsome face, she realized parting ways wouldn't be so easy.

So she'd given him her trust. A test. And she'd never felt safer in her entire life than when she'd been bound in his arms.

"You gonna stare at that key all night, or you gonna do something useful like work the bar?" Banks threw an apron on the counter. "I have thirsty customers who need drinks. If you don't get back to work in ten seconds, you're fired."

Arianne laughed. "You can't fire me. I already quit." Then her smile faded. "I'm going tonight. I called my trucker friend, and he's meeting me in Whitefish. I'm going to hide in the secret compartment of his truck, and he'll take me right across the border. Not as good as a passport, but he's smuggled people before, and this is going to be his last run because he's retiring next month. He even has a friend who can sort out some paperwork for me in exchange for some mechanic work."

Banks looked unimpressed. "Thought you were made of stronger stuff."

She shoved the apron out of the way and glared. "I thought you, of all people, would understand. I'm leaving my friends, my life, my job . . . everything."

"Runnin' away."

"I am not running away." She slapped the counter, startling herself at the intensity of her emotion. "Leaving Conundrum has always been my dream. You know that."

Banks slid the apron over her neck. "It was your dream when you had no options. Now you do. Jeff is outta the picture and you got Jagger to watch your back. Your friends are here. Your work is here. That tiny place you call an apartment is here. What are you looking for out there that's so much better?"

"You aren't a biker like me. You couldn't possibly understand." She slid off the stool, pushing past him as she rounded the bar. She had some time before the rendezvous. Might as well earn a little cash. Better than having an uncomfortable discussion with someone who hadn't lived the life.

He looked up and his lips twitched in a smile. "I understand that's the first time you ever called yourself a biker." Seemingly pleased with himself, he winked and headed past the bar toward the stockroom.

"By the way, I'm only working the bar 'cause I feel sorry for you with your bruised-up face," she called out as he pushed open the door. Her fault. Banks was hurt because of her. Another reason why leaving was the right thing to do. So why wasn't she already gone?

He looked back over his shoulder. "Fired again. I'll be up to my eyes in damn paperwork 'cause of you."

"Someone is in a bad mood tonight." Arianne looked up when Dawn slid her tray across the counter and handed her a drink list.

"He's upset you're leaving." She forced a smile, but her voice wavered. "So am I, but I'll just tell you to your face."

"I have to leave, Dawn. What Jagger did to Banks was pretty unforgivable. I know he did it to protect me, but that's the kind of protection I don't need."

"You still don't get it." Dawn ran a hand through her soft, blonde curls. "Yes, Jagger would do anything to protect you. But he'll also stand with you. That night Axle crashed my birthday party and you pulled your gun on him, Jagger was beside you. He could have taken over, but he didn't. And that was a hell of a message. You had his support and he would kill anyone who hurt you, but it was your damn show."

Arianne smiled. "He was furious because I wouldn't hide in the kitchen where it was safe."

"But he respected you for taking a stand," Dawn said. "You're his equal and he knows it. Viper knows it, too. You and Jagger together must be his worst nightmare. He could barely deal with each of you alone. Now you've found the part of yourself you lost chasing after something that was always here. You always had the strength to carve out any kind of life you wanted. Jagger just makes it that much easier. Having him by your side only makes you stronger; it doesn't take anything away."

"When did you get so smart?"

Dawn's eyes lit with a warm glow. "Observant, not smart. And I've got a particular weakness for watching people fall in love."

Love? Arianne didn't know much about love but she did know Dawn was right about one thing. She was stronger, physically and emotionally. Only a few months ago, she would never have had the confidence to stand up to Viper, shoot Leo, or hit the president of the Sinner's Tribe MC with a pool cue to save her friend. At sixteen years old, she'd found her way around the biker code and forced Viper to let her go. If she really wanted to be with Jagger on equal terms and spare Jeff's life, she'd find her way around those rules again.

Whatever you want; whatever you need, I'll find a way. Jagger's words drifted through her mind. Maybe he'd been telling her he would find a way, too.

A cough drew her attention, and she looked up and smiled. "Wheels."

He didn't return her greeting. "I gotta talk to you. It's important." He glanced around the bar, and then gestured to the stockroom. "You got a minute? Can we talk back there?"

"Sure." Her pulse kicked up a notch as she led him into the stockroom. Was this a trap? An ambush? Had Jagger sent Wheels and his men to take her back? She felt the familiar weight of her .38 on her lower leg and her tension dissipated. Although not an easy draw, the gun was there if she needed it.

"What's wrong?" She turned to face Wheels, carefully positioning herself with her back to the wooden shelving, and within steps of the door.

Wheels raked a hand through his blond hair, his face haggard with worry. "It's Jagger. Viper's got him. I know you're leaving tonight, but I thought you should know."

Her hand flew to her mouth. "Have the Sinners gone after him? Do they know where he is?"

"They know." Wheels exhaled an irritated breath. "The executive board is getting the brothers together for a rescue mission, but they're taking so damn long. They wanted to hold a meeting first to decide on a plan."

"A *meeting*?" Her voice rose to a shriek. "Viper's not going to keep Jagger around long enough for them to have a meeting. And that doesn't sound like Zane. When it comes to Jagger, he acts quickly, decisively. Maybe I should call and tell them there's no time to waste—"

She cut herself off, her head jerking to the side when she heard a sound behind the shelving near the door to the parking lot. But before she could investigate Wheels coughed, and she turned away.

"Phones are turned off during meetings," he said. "But I'm sure they'll get going soon. I just thought . . . maybe you'd want to know before you left. Not that you can do anything . . ."

Not that you can do anything?

There was a hell of a lot she could do: She could ride faster than any of the damn Sinners; she could shoot better than most of them, too; and she knew Viper. She could offer herself up if he let Jagger go.

But that meant she would miss her chance to escape. And the Sinners were probably already on the road.

She looked through the window of the stockroom door to where Dawn was serving drinks to a table of rowdy college kids in the corner. The same table where Jagger had watched her and almost stabbed a Devil Dog for pinching her ass. Even now she remembered the thrill of seeing him, the take-your-breath-away moment when he'd winked and she realized he wasn't there by chance. He'd come to see her.

Banks was making the rounds, weaving his way among the tables as he greeted the regulars. When anyone gestured to his face, he just shrugged, seemingly unconcerned that he looked like he'd been in a car wreck.

Just for show.

Jagger had hurt Banks to protect her. Claimed her to keep her out of Viper's clutches. Professed his love, then broken her heart to keep her safe. If she asked him to spare Jeff's life, he would find a way.

Memories came back, all in a rush—Jagger's warmth and gentle teasing, his protectiveness, his body so strong and hard and firm against her. And the indescribable feeling of being safe and cared for in his arms.

Mine.

Last night he'd bound her hands the way Leo once bound them, and then he had made love to her. Sweet, tender love, driving away every fear and every thought except how much she wanted him, needed him, loved him.

Mine. From the moment they met, he had been hers as much as she had been his, but it had taken her until now to understand. Just as it had taken her years to realize she was a biker. And the sooner she stopped denying who she was, the faster she would be able to save Jagger's life.

"Do you know where he is?"

"I'll get in a shitloud of trouble, but I can take you there." Wheels's eyes glittered and he licked his lips, smiling, a curious reaction given they were likely riding into a situation they might not survive, but one she put down to his lack of experience. Well, she wouldn't put him at risk. She would send him back as soon as they reached their destination.

And then she would face Viper one last time.

"How was your meeting with the sheriff?" Jagger watched a heavily bandaged Gunner ease himself into a chair in the meeting room. Last fucking place he wanted to be after hunting for Arianne all day. He'd posted T-Rex at Banks Bar in case she showed up and sent a few brothers to her apartment and Dawn's place, but so far no one had called. Where the hell was she?

"Good. Gave him the money we got from trunking to smooth things over. Told him we'd get those weapons back or replacements in the next two weeks."

Sparky laughed, gesturing to the bandages covering Gunner's shoulder, chest, and arm. "Gunner played the suffering martyr so well, sayin' he took the hits to protect the weapons, the sheriff forgot to be pissed off and offered to buy him lunch."

Jagger couldn't even force a smile. He had a Mexican cartel riding his ass for the weapons they'd been promised and the reputation of the club was at stake. "We need to get our weapons back. Word on the street is that Axle sold them to the Jacks, which makes two loads of weapons they've taken from us. Anyone got a line on a fresh supply to keep our buyers happy?"

"I called in favors two states over but no one has weapons to spare." Zane leaned back in his chair. "The Koreans aren't getting a shipment in for at least four more weeks so they can't help us out."

"And the Irish have had to cool things off because they're being watched by the ATF," Sparky added.

Cade huffed his frustration. "How about the Mexicans?"

"The Pueblos Cartel were our buyers," Jagger said. "They've expanded their drug operation to include the fruit trade and have gained a foothold in Michoacán. They're trying to control the entire supply of mangoes to the U.S. and they needed the weapons to scare off international importers."

"Don't like mangoes." Gunner wrinkled his nose. "Gimme an apple or banana any day. I eat simple, but tasty."

"I thought you only ate pussy." Sparky jabbed him with his elbow and Gunner was already halfway out of his seat before Jagger shut them down with a scowl.

"Enough. We have more important things to discuss than Gunner's eating habits."

"Yeah. We also gotta talk about this." Zane flipped his laptop around, and a picture flashed on the screen. "I have a friend who's got experience with digital photography. I got him to fill in the missing detail on the surveillance tapes from the night the Jacks burned down our old clubhouse. He did a bang-up job." He clicked and zoomed in on the scene. Four men were now clearly visible. A blond near the weapons shed, two tall dark-haired Jacks with gas cans near the truck, and another blond-haired man with a load of Sinner weapons in his arms.

"I'm only showing you a few pics. But basically it looks like the truck drove into the yard through the trees. Jeff stayed at the weapons shed and loaded the guns into the truck. He's the one who shot Gunner. The two tall guys were guards and one of them shot Cole. And this bastard blew up the clubhouse." He zoomed in on the blond with the gas can. "Anyone recognize him?"

"Wheels!" Gunner spat out the name. "Goddamnit. He's the fucking rat I've been chasing around. I've been going through all our data on the brothers, but I hadn't gotten to him, 'cause he was new and I figured our screening systems are tighter now than they were before."

A Black Jack rat. In his club. Jagger's gut twisted. He wasn't surprised so much as outraged. He'd known something about Wheels wasn't right, but he'd been too preoccupied with Arianne to heed the warning niggle in his mind. *No wonder Viper was always one step ahead of the game.* With a roar, he rose from his seat and slammed his fist into the table.

"I want every brother in the club on the road and looking for him." He gritted the words through clenched teeth as rage suffused every cell in his body. "I want every mark pulled, and word spread to every gang or club we know. But tell them I want him alive. He is going to fucking curse the day he was born when I get my hands—"

A sharp rap on the door cut him off and Jagger scowled. Everyone knew they weren't to be disturbed during official board meetings.

"Come."

The door opened and T-Rex stumbled into the room, his face a mask of horror. He stared at Zane, who was seated across from the door. "They have him," he panted. "The Jacks got him."

"Who?"

"Jagger."

Zane motioned to the head of the table. "He's standing right there."

T-Rex glanced over at Jagger and jerked back, reaching for the open door to support himself. "You're okay."

"Of course I'm okay." Jagger shot Zane a puzzled glance and then his gaze slid back to T-Rex. "But I thought I assigned you to Banks Bar. Clearly that job isn't being done if you're standing in my boardroom interrupting a meeting."

T-Rex sagged against the door frame and let out a breath. "I was there like you asked. Arianne came in to say goodbye and Banks got her doing some work. I told Banks you wanted me to keep a low profile, so he said I could hide out in the stockroom. I texted you a coupla times and Banks called . . ."

Jagger reached beneath his cut for his phone. "Went for a run when I got back to the clubhouse and then came straight into the meeting so I haven't checked my messages." He saw four messages from T-Rex and a missed call on his screen and gestured for T-Rex to continue.

"Wheels came in. He brought Arianne to the stockroom and told her Viper had kidnapped you. He said the executive board was in a meeting deciding how to rescue you. Something didn't feel right, so I stayed put. I figured if you were gone, Zane woulda been in charge, and everyone knows he hates meetings. I just couldn't see him hearing

Viper had you and then sittin' around the table, trying to decide what to do."

"Damn right." Zane thumped his fist on the table. "If that *had* happened, I woulda be on my bike and halfway to hell before you'd even finished saying what you had to say."

T-Rex grimaced. "That's kinda what happened with Arianne. She didn't hesitate. When Wheels said he knew where Viper was holding you, she told him to take her there right away. I was torn whether to go after them or come here, but when I heard Wheels tell her where they were going, I thought I'd better come straight here. I couldn't believe anyone could take you, Jag, and since no one was answering the phone, I wanted to see with my own eyes if Wheels was telling the truth."

"You did good."

T-Rex scrubbed his hand over his face. "I was thinkin' all the way what would we do without you, Jag? Nothing would be the same. And then when I walked in the door—" His voice broke. "Fuck. It's good to see you. But we gotta go get her, man. Wheels betrayed us. It's a trap."

Stay strong. Stay strong.

Arianne carefully worked the lock on the handcuffs binding her hands behind her back. Bear had tied her to a chair in the center of the dimly lit warehouse, and she had to take care that no one realized she'd grabbed a loose nail when he'd thrown her to the floor.

Jeff was hunched against the wall a few feet away, clearly suffering the effects of withdrawal. "You got anything on you, Ari?" He spoke in a low whisper. "Even a joint? Or a prescription? Painkillers?"

"Unlock these cuffs, and I'll take care of you the way you took care of me at Bunny's." She couldn't keep the bitterness from her voice. Trusting Wheels, desperate to save Jagger, she'd walked right into a trap. Although she'd had her gun ready when she walked into the warehouse, Bear and Jeff had been waiting for her. Taking her by surprise, they'd grabbed her from either side, disarmed her, and thrown her to the floor.

She glanced around, assessing her best route for escape. Light filtered through dirty, broken windows dotted around the perimeter of the ten-thousand-square-foot space. Concrete floor. Boxes and barrels in the corners. Delivery truck in the far corner, back open, crates of guns on the floor. A second door at the back. Her weapon lay on the floor, only a few feet out of reach.

She had to get out before Viper arrived, because she knew what was going to happen. This wasn't meant to be a family reunion. It was an execution.

A pained expression crossed Jeff's face. "I'm sorry, Ari. I was tweaking and I couldn't think straight. I just wanted to go to Bunny's place to get some meth. It was Axle's idea to sell you."

"You could have stopped him. You could have taken the drugs and gone." She made no effort to hide the bitterness in her tone. "But you couldn't, could you? Because you didn't have any money to pay. But you had me."

"I was trying to save you." Jeff scraped a hand through his hair and whined. "Viper wants you dead. I figured at least you'd be gone and alive that way. I did it for you and I paid the price. He punished me for it. He beat me so bad, I was coughing up blood, and he cut off my supply. He cares about you more than he cares for me."

Her lip curled. "He punished you because you tried to sell his property. That's how he thinks of me. Property. And you're pathetic. You've let the drugs and your need for his approval destroy your life. If you'd come with me that night you picked up the passports instead of going to the Sinner clubhouse, you'd be clean by now, and we'd be in Canada, living a better life."

"I don't deserve a better life." He slid farther down the wall and moaned. "You don't know what I did, Ari. I'll never forgive myself, and the drugs are the only thing that takes away the pain. That and Viper's approval."

"Well, you're going about it the wrong way." The lock released with a soft click, and she stilled. If the cuffs slipped off her wrist, her efforts would be wasted.

The door opened and closed, and the air chilled. She didn't need to look up to know Viper was in the building. His hulking presence sent a shiver down her spine, and she had to swallow back the bile that rose in her throat when he stalked across the warehouse toward them.

"Shut the fuck up." Viper cuffed Jeff on the head. "Don't get too cozy with your sister. She's done. And you're gonna be the one holding her down when I slice up that pretty face as a message to Jagger when I dump her body at his fucking gate."

He grabbed Arianne's hair and yanked her head back. "You disappointed me, girl. Thought you had balls, but it turns out you're as weak as your brother. A man waves his dick in your direction, and you drop everything and run. Honor. Loyalty. Family. They mean nothing to you. Before you dishonored our club, if I had to choose between you and Jeff, I woulda chosen you 'cause I thought you had a spine of steel like your old man. But now I know you're just like your whore of a mother, willing to throw everything away for a bit of cock."

"Fuck you." She braced herself for a blow, but Viper just laughed.

"Not me. But Bear's earned a reward, and I gave him my word: You're his after I've marked you until he doesn't want you anymore."

Her heartbeat thrashed in her ears, and her defiance trickled away. No one knew she was here. Wheels had betrayed the Sinners. Dawn and Banks would have thought she'd gone. Jeff was totally lost to her. And after last night, Jagger wouldn't be looking for her.

She had never felt so alone.

He ran.

Up the stairs, through the house, and then he was outside. *Arianne*.

Heart thudding. Lungs burning. Thighs aching. *Arianne*.

He couldn't remember the last time he had run—really run. Not the casual jog he took every morning, but a full-out sprint, his feet barely touching the grass as he raced toward his motorcycle.

Even as his mind screamed for him to go faster, and his heart pounded against his ribs, memories assailed him. A barren desert. A helicopter hovering just outside the range of enemy fire. The crack of weapons. Bullets pinging around him. But he wasn't in Afghanistan now. And he wasn't carrying an injured man on his shoulders. And the enemy fire . . . it came from within. But this time he drew strength from the past, from the pain. This time he would not fail.

Pounding his way over the grass, he heard shouts and yells behind him. And he knew. *Knew.* Every brother in the house would be behind him, streaming to their bikes as if they tasted his urgency, felt his despair, heard his heart thundering in his chest. His brothers. His friends. They would have his back the way he should have had hers.

Arianne.

Without slowing down, he threw himself on his bike, punched the ignition, and peeled out of the yard. For the first time in his life, he wished he had a foreign bike. Nothing matched them for speed—and speed was what he needed.

The roar of bikes starting up followed him down the long drive, but when he hit the highway, he kicked into gear and left the rumble behind. Too many speeding bikers would attract trouble. One would escape detection.

Arianne. Arianne. Arianne.

Her name was the beat of his weakened heart, the rev in his engine, the light in his soul. Nothing in his life had prepared him for the powerful emotions raging through his body. Not Christel, not the wars he'd fought, not the devastation he had felt upon being discharged and discovering he had nowhere to go and no skills beyond what he'd learned in the army.

No one to help.

No one at his back, until the Sinner's Tribe took him in. Even now he could hear the thunder of their bikes, the rage in their souls.

Family. Freedom. Brotherhood. Loyalty. Honor. This was his world. Their world. Arianne was part of them—part of him. And he would move hell and earth to protect her.

He would not fail.

By the time he turned off the highway, he was running on pure adrenaline, liquid rage sliding through his veins. If they so much as touched her, he would rain down a fury like the world had never seen.

But first, he had to find her.

★ TWENTY-FOUR ★

Traitors shall die.

The warehouse door opened and hope flared in Arianne's chest. But when she saw the two Jacks silhouetted in the doorway, she sank back in her chair. No one was coming to rescue her. She would have to figure a way out herself.

Viper waved them over to the truck. "We gotta get the weapons outta here in case someone comes nosin' around. Load them into the truck and hurry it up 'cause I got business to finish here."

"You did this to yourself," Jeff said, pushing himself up. "If you hadn't kept defying him, just like mom did, things would have been different."

Arianne slid her hand out of the cuff. "All I've ever wanted was for us to be free and to get you help. I wanted us to be happy, the way we used to be."

"We were never happy." His voice dropped, devoid of emotion now. "Happy is not hiding on the roof while your mother takes a beating meant for you. Happy isn't being a constant disappointment to your father because you're always being measured up against your fucking perfect sister."

Perfect sister? How could he begin to think Viper would

compare them? She had dared to be born a girl. "I could have gotten us out."

Jeff walked toward her, his face blurring into the shadows. "You don't get it, do you? I don't want out. I never wanted out. I want to make him proud—" His face twisted in anger and his voice rose to a shout. "—I wanted us to be a family. But you left when I was sixteen, and you've betrayed us again, just like mom. You're a traitor. And now you'll pay the price mom paid."

Puzzled, she frowned. "What are you talking about? What does mom have to do with this?"

"She was having an affair." His voice wavered. "Viper told me. He said sometimes a man has to do things he doesn't want to do because there is nothing more important than honor. He knew about that bald-headed guy with the glasses who came to the house all the time. He killed her because she was cheating on him. She didn't want us to be a family. And neither do you."

Arianne looked at him aghast. "Oh God, Jeff. He was a doctor. Mom's best friend's husband. He came over to look after her every time Viper beat her up. She wouldn't go to the hospital in case Social Services took us away, and he couldn't bear to let her suffer. She took those beatings and she didn't go for treatment, *because* she wanted us to be a family. Just like I wanted to leave so we could be a family, too."

Jeff's face froze in a mask of horror. "I didn't know." He slumped forward, clutching his head in his hands and his voice dropped to a whispered rasp. "I didn't know. I was the one who told him, Ari. I was too young to know he would think she was having an affair, but I told him she'd broken the rule about visitors in the house, because I wanted him to be proud of me. He was always so proud of you because you did everything right."

She gritted her teeth. "If he was, he never let me know."

"Even when we were older"—Jeff fisted his hands against his knees—"he said the day you put the gun to your head and told him you would rather die than live with him was the proudest moment of his life. He admired your grit and determination. He admired how you never gave up, no matter how hard he beat you. He said I would never live up to you. I loved you, but I hated you for that. And I hated needing your love. The only peace I ever had was when I was high. Then everything would go away. I just want it all to go away."

When the warehouse came into view, Jagger pulled over and pushed his bike along the side of the road to the building. No point alerting the Jacks to his presence if the distant rumble of his bike hadn't done so already.

After parking at the side of the warehouse, he plastered himself against the wall under the window, straining to hear through the corrugated metal.

Nothing.

Weapon unholstered and heavy in his hand, he stretched up to peer through the grimy window. There. A light in the darkness. He glanced over at the door and fought back the urge to kick it in, but he had no idea how many Jacks were inside or whether they were armed—or whether Arianne was even with them.

Jagger gritted his teeth and ran a quick reconnaissance around the building. Windows, mostly inaccessible. Front door. One rear exit. But without a visual, he would be going in blind.

Side exit, it would have to be. He reached for the handle, turning it slowly until it clicked.

"Don't move."

He froze and then looked over his shoulder.

Wheels. And with a weapon pointed at Jagger's back.

"I figured you might be coming to join the party,"

Wheels sneered. "I only remembered you'd asked T-Rex to watch the bar after I got here. Didn't want to bother Viper with a detail I could clean up myself, so I've been waiting. Turn around, throw me your phone, and drop the weapon."

Blood pounded through Jagger's veins so hard, he could barely see. "Fucking traitor." He spat out the words as he turned, dropping the gun at an angle that would make it easy to retrieve if he had a chance to bend, and then tossing his phone at Wheels's feet. "Were you working for the Jacks when you first started hanging around the club?"

A movement in the trees behind Wheels caught Jagger's attention. A shadow in the darkness. And then a hand. A signal.

Zane.

Keep him talking.

"Right from the start." Wheels laughed. "Viper's been planning to break the truce since it began. He orchestrated everything. My fake background, paperwork, the way I look, the way I talk. All planned to bring you down. And it went like clockwork. The knowledge I've got in here." He tapped his head. "Is going to destroy the Sinners forever. Only thing that will disappoint him is that you won't be around to see Vexy die."

Arianne.

He could not fail.

"We were on to you," Jagger said. "We caught you on the surveillance tapes outside the old clubhouse. If you hadn't picked this evening to take her, I would have had you down in my dungeon, begging for your life."

Wheels smirked. "Wasn't ideal for us either, but she was planning to run that night, and Viper was done with her. To be honest, I can't believe you came to save her when she had no interest in staying with you. She was all packed and ready to go and start a new life without you. And you know what? I liked her, too. I even had a moment of weakness and tried to give her a push to leave before Viper set the wheels in motion."

"But she didn't go." Jagger flexed his hand as Zane took up his position behind Wheels. "She stayed to save me."

Crack. Zane's shot echoed in the stillness. Wheels dropped to his knees, his face frozen in shock. Jagger dived for his gun, rolled, and pulled the trigger, pumping two bullets into Wheels's chest. With a soft grunt, Wheels fell sideways, the gun falling from his hand.

"Halfway to hell . . ." Zane rasped as he stepped out of the shadows.

Jagger nodded, emotion welling up in his chest. "Halfway to hell, brother."

"Gonna have a good time with you." Bear trailed the barrel of his gun along Arianne's jaw, making her flesh crawl. "Gonna have some of the sugar Leo's been panting after all these years."

Arianne slid her other wrist out of the cuffs and doubled them together, holding them around her knuckles in a fist behind her. "There's no sugar left in me. Viper beat it out." She shot out of her seat, hitting him in the solar plexus with her brass knuckle handcuffs, knocking the wind out of him, before she angled to the side and bolted.

"Fucking bitch is loose." Viper shouted from the far end of the warehouse. "Catch her."

Gulping air furiously, Arianne ran for the rear exit door. A sliver of light appeared, slicing through the darkness. Feet thudded behind her and the light grew brighter, then dimmed as a shadow filled the space. Her chest constricted. She knew that shadow. She had memorized every line and plane of that body, kissed that broad chest, held those massive shoulders.

"Jagger!" She screamed his name, because if she could

see him, the others could see him, too, and if she was going to die, she wanted to go with his name on her lips.

"Fuck. Stop her." A shot rang out, the bullet pinging off the concrete beside her feet.

"Arianne." Jagger's roar echoed through the warehouse, his rage evident in every taut line of his body.

She hit him at full tilt, knocking him back, and he immediately spun around, protecting her with his body.

"Go." He pointed to the door.

But before she could protest, she caught movement in the shadows, and then Bear was beside them, his gun raised at Jagger's unprotected left side.

No. She wasn't going to lose him now. Her arm flew up and she aimed at Bear's shoulder, but she was a second too late. His shot echoed through the warehouse, thudding into Jagger's side. Jagger's hand dropped to his cut, and he staggered back.

"Jagger!" Arianne pulled her trigger and Bear dropped to the ground with a loud thud. Horror washed over her in a suffocating black wave. "Oh God, I shot him."

But she had no time to dwell. Another bullet thudded the concrete beside them, sending up a little puff of smoke. Jagger shoved her toward the side door. "Get out."

"I'm not leaving you."

"Dammit, Arianne. This isn't the time to argue. Viper and I have a score to settle."

She grabbed his arm and tugged him back. "You've been shot. And it's not just Viper. Jeff is here too."

"And he's about to restore the family honor." Jeff stepped out of the shadows.

"Jeff. Please. Don't do this." She stood in front of Jagger, protecting him with her body. Jagger muttered a protest and then dropped to one knee with a groan.

"Out of the way, girl," Viper bellowed, coming up behind Jeff. "Let your brother show me he has what it takes to be a Jack, or I will be the last fucking thing you ever see."

"Never." She leveled her gaze at Viper and a calm settled over her body as she raised her weapon.

"Then die like your betraying mother did." The barrel of his gun gleamed in the darkness.

"Don't do it." Jeff spun and pointed his weapon at Viper. "You're the reason our family has no honor. You killed mom. You drove Arianne away. You destroyed our family. I was never good enough for you. No matter how hard I tried, I was never as good as Arianne. You beat me until I couldn't take it anymore, until the drugs were the only thing that made life worth living. This is all your fault."

"Don't be a fool." Viper growled. "Lower the gun and look to the real enemy. Your betraying sister and the bastard who dishonored our club." His eyes lifted to Arianne. Cold. Black. Soulless. "It's over, girl."

"Not Arianne." Jeff threw himself in front of Viper's gun. The bullet hit his chest with a sickening thud, and his momentum carried him to the ground.

"Jeff!" Arianne screamed and dropped to her knees beside his body.

Viper roared in anguish and aimed his weapon at her head. "This is because of you, girl. You killed my son."

Two shots rang out in the darkness. Viper stumbled back and fell. She glanced over and saw Jagger half sprawled on the floor, his gun still pointed where Viper had stood only moments ago.

The door burst open, flooding the warehouse with light. Zane raced to Jagger's side, and Arianne bent over Jeff and checked for a pulse. But from the blood pooling on the floor beneath him, she knew she wouldn't find one.

"I'm sorry." A sob ripped from her throat and she smoothed his hair back from his pale, still face. "I'm sorry

I couldn't protect you. I'm sorry I left you behind, but he said he would kill you before letting you. I didn't know he loved you. Tears trickled down her cheeks. "Thank you for saving me, and for being there when I ran away. I tried to be a good sister to you. I'm sorry I failed. But I hope you finally have peace."

Zane knelt beside her and pressed his finger to Jeff's throat. "He's gone," he said softly. "Viper's unconscious, but still alive. I don't know if he'll make it. And we got a problem." His voice tightened. "Jagger wasn't wearing a vest. The bullet hit close to his heart—"

Her breath left her in a rush. "The shrapnel. We need an ambulance."

"Stay with him. My phone's outside."

She made her way over to Jagger, trying not to look at the hulking form of Viper lying still on the floor. Her father. But she felt nothing for him. No urge to help him. No sadness. No regret. No urge to help him. No remorse. If he died, he deserved his fate, and the world would be better for his absence.

"Baby . . ." The hair lifted on her nape when she crouched beside Jagger and took in the blood-soaked bandanna pressed against his chest. "Zane's calling an ambulance."

"I'm okay. Just a flesh wound." He reached out to stroke her hair. "I'm sorry about Jeff."

"He died doing something good." She wiped a tear off her cheek. "I never knew how much he'd been suffering. He'll have peace now, but I'll miss him so much."

The rumble of motorcycles filled the air and the warehouse trembled. Jagger gave her a half smile. "Sinners are here."

She covered his hand with her own, pressing the bandanna harder against his chest. "They'll look after you. Maybe they brought a cage."

"No cages." He coughed, and her gut twisted. They didn't have time to wait for an ambulance. He needed medical attention now.

"If your girl says you're riding in a cage, then you're riding in a cage."

Jagger gave her a weak smile. "My old lady."

"Yes, and she's prepared to defy you to save your life."

Gravel crunched outside the front door and Arianne's head jerked up, but hope died in her heart when she saw Zane's grim face. "We gotta move him. It's the Jacks."

Bracing himself on the floor, Jagger pushed himself to sitting. "My bike's out the side door."

Arianne looked at him aghast. "You can't ride."

"Gotta ride, sweetheart, or we're gonna die."

She and Zane helped Jagger to his feet. Weapon ready, Zane pushed open the door, holding Jagger and Arianne back with his hand.

"Clear. You two go. I'll try to head them off. Sinners will be coming from the south, so we should have backup soon."

Arianne staggered under Jagger's weight as they crossed the gravel toward his bike, but when she slid onto the driver's seat, Jagger waved her back. "My bike. My ride."

"You're shot. Bleeding. I'll drive."

"Man can't ride. Man can't live. No time to argue. Now, move back."

She slid back in the seat and threw her arms around his waist. "Stubborn ass. You might just get your wish."

He revved the engine and looked back over his shoulder. "We'll head back to the clubhouse from the north, avoid the conflict."

"Go straight to the hospital." She leaned up and pressed her lips to his ear. "Hospital."

"No hospital. Doc Hegel will fix me up."

"Jagger—"

But her protest was drowned in the roar of the engine as he pulled away.

Arianne looked back over the shoulder as they headed down the road. The Jacks had just crested the rise, and Zane was headed toward them, a lone soldier against an army.

"Zane."

"He'll be fine." Jagger chuckled, then winced. "He rides almost as well as you."

The world blurred past, and for a few minutes she thought everything would be okay. But only five miles into the ride, Jagger keeled to the side and the bike pitched. Arianne screamed and jerked him upright. "What's wrong?"

He shook his head and kept driving, but a few miles later they pitched again. "Stop." She yelled over the roar of the engine. "Stop. You can't drive."

Jagger glanced at her in the rear view mirror and dipped his chin. She looked back over her shoulder and spotted the flash of multiple headlights in the distance, still far away but slowly gaining.

"I'm fine. I can ride."

After another two miles, the bike dipped again. Her heart pounded so hard, she thought she'd break a rib. Pressing herself against Jagger's back, she tried to support him with her arms. Stubborn man. Would they have to crash before he would accept her help? "Please, Jagger. Please let me drive."

The foothills gave way to flatlands, but as they descended the rise, Jagger keeled forward and then slowed the bike, pulling into a turnoff at the side of the road.

"I . . . can't . . . ride." He choked on his words as he looked over his shoulder. "Take the bike. You'll be able to outrun them. I'll wait in the bushes over there. Call the Sinners, and someone will come for me."

"Are you serious?" She slid off the seat and shoved him back to the pillion seat as fear and anger flooded her veins, a potent cocktail that gave her a strength she'd never known she had. "I can drive your bike, Jagger. Probably better than you, as you just pointed out. And there is no way in hell I'm leaving you out here. So just get over your damn masculine pride and get on that fucking pillion seat. I'm packing a Jagger package tonight."

His lack of protest scared her even more than the blood seeping through his shirt. He eased himself back, and Arianne slid in front of him. "Hold on to me and prepare yourself for the ride of your life."

He gave a weak chuckle and wrapped his arms around her, leaning his weight against her back. The thunder of motorcycles filled the valley, and she caught a sea of headlamps coming down the mountain toward them. "We're going to a hospital."

"No hospital. Take me to the clubhouse. Doc knows what to do. I promise you."

Sweat beaded on her brow as she accelerated away from the turnoff and back on to the highway, trying to adjust her balance to accommodate his weight. The world flew past but she saw nothing except the road in front of her. Heard nothing but Jagger's tortured breaths, felt nothing but his weight getting heavier and heavier behind her, his grip around her waist loosening.

"Hold on." She turned a corner and recognized the road and forest. "Only a mile to go. And I don't see them behind us, I think we've lost them."

But although she was fast, she wasn't fast enough. When his hands trembled around her waist, and slipped to her thighs, his weight almost fully coming down on her, she pulled off the road. By the time she'd come to a full stop, she was bearing almost his full weight against her back.

"Jagger." She panted as she struggled to hold the bike upright and keep Jagger from falling, but it was too much.

The bike dropped to the ground, and Jagger fell, rolling into the ditch.

"No." Scrambling over the fallen bike, adrenaline coursing through her veins, she slid down the ditch after him. "Talk to me. Say something."

She eased him onto his back and watched his chest rise and fall. Still breathing. Relief flickered through her.

With a soft groan, Jagger lifted his head. "Call Zane. Let him know where we are."

"Well, that's a problem, because Bear took my phone when I got to the clubhouse. Where's your phone?"

"Wheels got it."

"Bad planning on your part."

"Don't . . . make me laugh, sweetheart. Hurts too much. You go. Please. They're not far away."

"Not that I would ever leave you," she said, her voice thick with derision. "But I can't lift the bike on my own. It must weigh at least one thousand pounds. Your fault for buying American. Wait here while I go hide it."

With one last look back at Jagger, she climbed up the ditch and gathered branches to cover the bike. She had just thrown the last few boughs over the top and slid into the ditch when the Black Jacks raced past in a thunder of dust and metal.

"They're gone," she whispered. But when she looked down, Jagger's eyes were closed.

"Wake up." She shook him. "Wake up, Jagger."

Terror burst from her chest in a long, plaintive wail, and she grabbed the fallen bandanna and pressed it to his wound. "Please, wake up."

Stay and staunch the bleeding or leave him and run for help? Her brain froze with indecision and then she bent down and pressed her lips to his. "I'm the one who is supposed to leave. Not you."

Lips. Fingers. Mouth. Whistle. Max.

Max.

Jagger had said he could hear a whistle a mile away. Licking her lips, she stuck her two fingers in her mouth and blew. But her lips were quivering and tears were running down her cheeks and she couldn't take a deep enough breath to make a sound.

Calm. Stay strong. She squeezed one of Jagger's hands and thought of the night he'd caught her as she tried to run away. She thought about his warm arms around her, his soft lips the first time he kissed her, his hard body against hers. She imagined his deep voice, his dry humor. Her heart thumped softly in her chest, and her body relaxed.

"I love you." She pressed a kiss to his cheek and then she whistled.

Loud and clear. Again and again. One perfect whistle after the next. Until she had no breath and the night grew still, and his cheek grew cold to touch.

★ TWENTY-FIVE ★

Property patches are optional for old ladies.

White.

Everything was white.

For a moment he wondered if he'd died, but when he glanced to the side and saw Arianne asleep in a chair, he knew he'd made it to heaven.

Unwilling to wake her, he looked around, taking in the bright, sterile room, machines beeping around him, wires protruding from his chest and arms. All the signs of a hospital.

Jagger's stomach clenched. He'd spent the last ten years blocking the memories of his last hospital stay: the IV that pulled at his hand; the cloying scent of disinfectant; the tubes in his throat, stents in his heart, and lungs; and pain so bad, they had strapped him to the bed and dosed him up with morphine and ketamine. Four weeks of agony. Four weeks before they'd told him it was too big a risk to remove the shrapnel from his heart and his career in the military was over. Of all the memories, that one was the worst.

"You're awake. I'll ring for the nurse."

He looked over at the angel beside his bed. Deep shadows circled her eyes, and her face was pale and drawn, but he'd never seen a more beautiful sight.

"Arianne." His voice was a hoarse rasp, almost unrecognizable. She poured a glass of water from a pitcher on the table and held the straw for him to drink.

"I've been waiting so long to hear your voice." Then her face crumpled. "You were supposed to wake up days ago . . . after the surgery . . . the doctors didn't know what was wrong."

"Doc Hegel didn't—?"

She shook her head. "He couldn't. Not with the shrapnel. So I made a few arrangements—"

"What arrangements?"

Arianne patted his hand. "Shhhh. Nothing for you to worry about. It's all taken care of."

"Shhhh?"

She laughed at his incredulous look and leaned over to kiss his cheek. "You didn't hook up with a soft civilian princess, Jagger. You got yourself a badass biker chick, and there was no way she was gonna let her old man die. I found the best heart surgeon in Montana, arranged for an ambulance to take you out here to Helena, and Zane made sure the club paid your bills."

He turned away to hide the emotion that thickened his throat. "I'm going to want a full detailed report and accounting—"

"Don't you want to hear the good news before you start bossing me around again?" She clasped his free hand between her own, and Jagger turned back to face her.

"You're here. Safe. I'm alive. Can't think of better news than that."

"They removed the shrapnel." Her eyes sparkled and she twined her fingers through his. "Your heart will be as good as new. You can get shot as many times as you want in the chest and not have to worry about dying of anything but the bullet itself or my anger if you put yourself in danger again."

Shrapnel gone. How many times had he wished to hear those words? And now he heard them from an angel. His angel.

"You saved me."

"Actually, Max saved you. He heard me whistle and was on the road when Zane came by looking for us. And for the record, you saved me."

Jagged laughed. "I protected you. Finally. Can't believe what it took before you let me keep my promise."

A blush spread across her cheeks. "I won't make it that hard again."

"What happened to the Jacks?"

Her smile faded. "They backtracked when they got to the clubhouse. I guess they figured we'd made it inside and they weren't prepared to take on the whole club. But a couple of miles up the mountain, they met the Sinners." She swallowed hard. "The Jacks were outnumbered. There was a shoot-out and you lost a man, Tinker. I sent Cade and Gunner to get your guns out of the warehouse before the police found them, and they squared things away with whoever was meant to have them."

"Jeff?"

A tremor ran through her, and she looked away. "I arranged a funeral. He's buried beside our mom."

Jagger stroked her cheek, his throat aching when he saw her eyes tear up. "I would have liked to have been there to honor him for saving your life."

"Zane and Cade stood in for you," she said softly. "They said you would have wanted that."

They sat in silence, and then Jagger brought her hand to his lips. "Are you still planning to leave?"

She ruffled her fingers through his hair, then smoothed it down. "You want me to leave Conundrum?"

Too tired for games or pretense, his head still fuzzy, he answered honestly: "No."

"Then I'm not leaving." She mocked a frown. "But I'm warning you, prepare yourself for the ass-kicking of your life when you get out of here. A man in your condition should not have put himself in the line of fire to protect me and then tried to ride with a bullet in his chest."

He chuckled, trying to fight the exhaustion that threatened to take his angel away. "That's what men like me do."

Arianne's face softened. "Good thing I like men like you."

"How much?" He began to drift, but awakened when she kissed his cheek.

"Enough to stay. Forever."

They waited in breathless anticipation.

Every brother, old lady, sweet butt, hanger-on, hood rat, and house mama had been ordered to show up at Riders Bar by 8 P.M. Mandatory.

When the sound of a motorcycle engine outside cut the silence, a murmur rippled through the crowd.

Jagger frowned. "Shhhhh."

"Don't *shhhh* them." Arianne wiggled to rebalance herself on his lap. "He'll know something's up if he walks in here and everyone is staring at him. It would be better if they just do what people normally do at the bar."

His eyes narrowed. "I said *shhhh* and I meant *shhhh*. Don't contradict your president."

"You like it when I contradict the president." She kept her voice to a whisper. "But only when no one else can hear."

He stroked his hand through her hair. "Might have to rethink that concession. You're getting ideas."

"I have lots of ideas. Naughty ideas. But right now the only idea I'm having is that if you keep everyone quiet, you'll tip him off." She nuzzled his neck and Jagger growled, a deep low rumble that sent quivers of lightning straight to her core.

"I got club business to deal with, Arianne. Don't start something you can't finish."

She jerked away and laughed. "I can't finish? You mean *you* can't finish. You're the one who had heart surgery."

He tightened his grip around her waist and hauled her against her chest. "Nothing wrong with the rest of me, sweetheart. Thought I proved that to you last night and several times every night for the last coupla weeks. So like I said, you keep that up and I'll take care of you right here, right now, and I won't give a damn how many people are watching."

Arianne licked her lips and looked over at Dawn, sitting beside her, who was studiously trying to ignore Cade's attempts to attract her attention. "Hmmm. My biker boyfriend has a kinky side."

"I'm not your boyfriend."

A smile tugged at her lips. "What are you, then?"

The door opened and the dull roar faded to a murmur as T-Rex entered the bar. Jagger eased her off his lap and motioned for T-Rex to join him at their table.

"You're gonna find out soon enough."

Dawn leaned over to whisper in her ear. "Jagger loves this. Lookit him trying not to grin. You picked the only MC president with a wicked sense of humor."

"I think it's cute."

"Cute?" Dawn jerked back. "The man's a badass danger to society, just like Cade. That's why I told Cade we're done. I've had enough badass in my life. I need someone good. Someone who can help me straighten out my life. Clean, simple living. That's me."

"That's not you." Arianne lowered her voice as T-Rex approached the table. "You're as badass as him. That's why you're so good together."

Jagger scowled and put his finger to his lips. Arianne turned her attention to poor T-Rex, making his way gingerly through the bar, his gaze sliding to the side as he passed the club members, unusually somber and quiet. Even Jill and Tanya, seated beside Tank and Gunner, managed to suppress their smiles.

By the time T-Rex reached Jagger's table, sweat had beaded on his forehead and he'd picked up a noticeable tremble.

Jagger held out a hand. "Package."

T-Rex paled. "I went to the address you gave me on the other side of town, but the building was empty. I walked around, checked with the neighbors, but no one was there. I called and texted you and Cade and Sparky. No one answered. I'm sorry, Jag. Maybe the guy pulled a runner."

"So you didn't bring the package?"

"No, sir."

Jagger leaned back in his chair and folded his arms, raising his voice to be heard by the crowd. "I think we have a serious problem here, T-Rex. You don't seem to be able to follow simple instructions." He reached under the table and pulled out a package wrapped in brown paper. "Our contact got tired of waiting for you when you didn't show up at six o'clock and dropped the package off here."

T-Rex's mouth dropped open. "Six? I thought you said seven."

Admirably maintaining a stern expression, Jagger looked over at Arianne. "You were there. Did I say six or seven?"

"Six. Definitely six."

Jagger slapped the package down on the table. "So you were late. And this was time sensitive. What the fuck kind of prospect are you? Do you think we'd patch in someone who can't tell six from seven?"

Arianne looked around the bar at the sea of smiling faces poor T-Rex couldn't see. Prospect hazing aside, she still wasn't used to the Sinners' teasing or the jokes they played on each other. MCs were supposed to be serious, no-nonsense, and all about sex, drugs, violence, and women. Or so she'd thought.

T-Rex's shoulders slumped. "No, sir. I guess not."

"Hand in your cut."

Shoulders sagging, T-Rex shrugged off his prospect cut. "I'm sorry I let you down."

Arianne dug her nails into her palm. How could Jagger do this with a straight face?

Jagger took T-Rex's cut and threw it on the table. The crowd drew in a collective breath of anticipation.

"Open it." Jagger pointed at the package. "I want you to see firsthand the consequences of what you've done."

He was a master performer, Arianne decided as her gaze traveled over his impassive, slightly annoyed face. But not with her. She already knew to look for the softness in his eyes that would tell her he was teasing. And he enjoyed teasing her. Maybe too much.

Hands shaking, T-Rex tore away the paper. Then he stilled and looked up at Jagger. "Is this—?"

"Your cut. Three patches on the back. Welcome to the club, brother."

T-Rex's eyes moistened and he cleared this throat several times as he stroked his hand over the patches on his new cut. "Well, damn."

"You showed real courage and bravery in that ambush. A man who would do what you did to save his brothers is deserving of that patch, but you also showed good judgment when you came to warn us about Arianne. You've done a hell of a lot for the club over the last year. That patch is long overdue, and I'm proud to call you brother."

The bar erupted in cheers as Jagger unfolded the cut, then stood to slide it over T-Rex's shoulders. After a manly hug and a thump on the back, he released T-Rex into the crowd all primed and ready for a nightlong patch-in party.

"You're not supposed to be jumping up and down," Arianne said as he settled on his chair and pulled her onto his lap. "Slow and easy. That's what the doctor said."

He brushed the hair away from her neck and feathered kisses along her throat. "Good plan. I'll do you slow and easy first when we get home tonight. Then hard and fast. After that I'm gonna spank you for contradicting me." He slid one hand between her thighs. "And you're gonna like it 'cause I know what makes my girl wet."

"Jagger." She slapped his hand away, but not before he managed to slide his finger up the skirt he had insisted she wear, and flick a finger along her slick folds.

"Good girl." His breath was hot and moist in her ear. "Wasn't sure if you'd gotten my message about not wearing panties."

Arianne pressed her lips together and glared. "How could I miss it? You texted, left a message on my phone, sent Bandit with your message in a sealed envelope, and then used my best lipstick to write 'No panties tonight' on my bathroom mirror. It was almost like a scene from a horror movie. When we move into our new house, I'm going to remove all the mirrors."

Jagger chuckled. "It would only be a horror if you didn't listen." He reached under the table and pulled out another package. "But since you did, you get a present."

"What's this?" Arianne stared at the parcel, and the skin on the back of her neck prickled.

"Open it."

Vaguely aware that the crowd had hushed around them, Arianne reached for the package. The paper crinkled in her hand.

"Jagger . . ."

"Open it, sweetheart."

Arianne tore away the paper and pulled out a leather vest.

"A Sinner's Tribe cut." She let out a relieved breath and kissed him on the cheek. "I'll be proud to wear it." She spun it around amid the cheers, and then her smile faded. "Property of Jagger?" She read the lettering stitched on the back out loud, and then lowered her voice below the excited murmur of the crowd. "You know how I feel about being property."

"I know how you feel about me, so I know you'll wear it." A self-satisfied grin played across his lips.

Arianne lifted an eyebrow. "How do I feel about you?"

"You love me."

She wanted nothing more than to wipe that grin off his face, but she couldn't deny he was right. "Usually people wait until they are told they're loved. They don't make the declaration themselves."

"Why waste time? You've loved me since the moment you laid eyes on me."

A smile tugged at her lips. "And how would you know that?"

"Because that's when it happened for me."

Read on for an excerpt from the next book by

SARAH CASTILLE

★ BEYOND THE CUT ★

Available from St. Martin's Paperbacks

Dawn bolted awake when someone banged on her door.

Heart pounding, she reached under her bed for the .22 Arianne had given her as a birthday present. Trust Arianne to give her a gun. Although she had often talked about living in the civilian world, Arianne was a biker through and through. And no American biker would ever leave his or her house unarmed.

Well, Dawn wasn't a biker. And the two weeks of lessons at the shooting range with Arianne hadn't changed her mind. Still, it was a comfort to know that she'd be able to defend herself from the crazy person trying to break down her door at three in the morning. Or, at least threaten them. She never loaded the gun because she wasn't prepared to kill anyone.

Weapon in hand, she raced through the living room and stood on tip-toe to peer through the peep hole.

At first she didn't recognize the man standing in front

of her door, his face all swollen and bloody, his shirt in tatters but it was his hair, golden strands matted with blood, glinting in the semi-darkness, that made her look again.

Her breath caught. She undid the dead bolt and threw the door open.

"Oh God, Cade. What happened?"

"Jesus, Dawn. Put the gun away." He pushed her aside and stalked into her tiny apartment, his clothes rank with blood and covered in dirt. "What the fuck were you doing with a piece of shit like him?"

Stunned, Dawn could only stare. "You almost break down my door at three in the morning, looking like you need to get to a hospital, to ask me that?"

"Yeah."

"If we knew each other better," she said, her voice tight. "If we were friends, or actually seeing each other, maybe I wouldn't be so pissed off at being pulled out of bed and ordered to explain my life choices. But we're not. We've slept together twice. We've never had a conversation that lasted more than five minutes, four minutes of which consisted of deciding where we were going to have sex next. So you don't have the right to ask me that question, and unless you're in dire need of medical attention, I suggest you leave."

By way of answer, Cade took a step forward, staggered to the side and grabbed the back of her sofa for support. "Damn. Gimme a minute."

With a sigh, Dawn closed and locked the door, then put the gun in her purse. "I see you've chosen door number three, 'dire need of medical assistance.' You want me to call the Sinners's doctor or take you to the local hospital?"

"No hospital."

Dawn snorted. "Right. I forgot. Too manly for the hospital. You got a number for the club doctor?"

Cade shook his head. "No doctor. Just . . . water . . . bandages . . . maybe some whiskey. I'll be fine."

Hmmm. Fine was obviously a relative word. To her nonmedical eye, he certainly didn't look fine. In fact, he looked like he was about to collapse, and from the way he was holding himself, he was clearly injured far beyond the cuts and bruises she could see on his face. But that was always the way with biker beatings. Why go for the small target when you could go for the big one?

"Kitchen. Now." Dawn gestured to the small kitchen area visible through the open breakfast bar behind the couch. Living on her own, the cozy space suited her fine although the pastel décor and white rattan furniture was not really to her taste. But the rent was cheap for a two bedroom bungalow, so she really couldn't complain, and there was an extra bedroom if . . . No . . . when the girls came home.

Cade followed her to the small kitchen, decorated in country chic pink and mint green tiles, and pulled out a white wicker chair from the breakfast nook. As he lowered himself to sit, Dawn grabbed a tea towel and threw it over the seat.

"Lotta blood on you," she said by way of explanation. "Not sure how much is fresh."

"None of it since I was fighting a buncha deadbeats." Cade grimaced. "Six of them to one of me. They'd tied my hands, but your Mad Dog is quite the talker and while he was yammering on I managed to get free and suss out the weaklings in the group. Used the advantage of surprise to take them down, then went after the better fighters. When they were all moaning on the ground, I grabbed a weapon, and took off in their van. He placed a niclel-plated .38 on the table and Dawn laughed. "Barbecue gun."

"You know your guns?"

"Just the basics, cowboy, shooters, and some of the big, scary ones. Where's the van?"

"Parked it out front."

"Excellent. Now the sherriff will know where to find you." Dawn pulled out her first aid kit and washed her hands in the sink. Even though he was battered and bruised, his eyes full of questions she would never answer, his presence soothed the nervous flutter that was always in her stomach.

There was just something about him beyond his obvious physical strength . . . Maybe it ws the way he filled a room with his sheer, papable presence. Or maybe it was the way he looked at her: Like there was no one else in the room. Like she was his and woe betide any man who dared hurt her. Or maybe it was all in her imagination.

She eyed his bloody clothing and grabbed a plastic bag from the cupboard. "You'd better strip. I'll throw your clothes in the wash. Looks like you get to spend the night in your undies on my couch."

A smile tugged the corner of Cade's battered mouth as he undid his belt. "Will I be alone?"

"Condition you're in, you will most definitely be alone." She eased herself between his parted legs to help him take off his T-shirt, freezing when he winced at her touch. "Well, that just settles it." She carefully pulled the shirt up his body. "I'm not about to take advantage of an injured man."

"I'm not injured everywhere." The deep rumble of his voice made her skin tingle.

"Christ, Cade." Dawn swallowed hard as her hands followed the shirt up his torso, her fingers brushing over heated skin and hard muscle. God, he was magnificent, all taut pecs and rippling abs. Even the bruises couldn't mar the perfection of his body. "How can you be thinking of sex at a time like this?"

His voice dropped, husky and low. " 'cause you're standin' between my legs wearing a tiny pair of shorts that only cover your ass cheeks, and a damn tight top that doesn't hide what you're thinkin." He leaned forward in the chair, so close she could feel his breath on her skin.

"And nothing underneath."

Dawn's breath caught in her throat and her blood heated, thundered through her veins. Until this moment, focused on Cade's injuries, her attire had been totally irrelevant. "How do you know I have nothing underneath?"

Cade traced lazy circles up the sensitive skin of her inner thigh, pausing at edge of her cotton PJ shorts. Dawn stilled, her breaths coming in quick shallow pants as her brain clouded with desire. It was always this way with Cade. A chemistry so potent she was surprised they didn't combust.

"Let's see." He slid his finger inside her shorts and stroked along the sensitive crease at the top of her thigh, sending a zing of electricity straight to her core.

"Hmmm. Can't tell. Spread for me, babe. Let me in."

Her face flushed. God, the things he said did all the wrong things to the right parts of her body. "Cade . . . this isn't the time. You're hurt. Let me look after you."

He grabbed her hips, pulling her close she could feel the heat of his breath through her clothes. Dawn breathed in his scent of blood and grass, mixed with the heady aroma of leather and manly musk, and a delicious shiver ran up her spine.

"You are taking care of me," he said. "Man gets in a fight. Hurts all over. He wants to feel good. He wants something to make him forget the pain. And you—all soft and sexy and smellin' like flowers—will do the trick."

"I thought you came here for help." Dawn made a token effort at resistance and raised an eyebrow. "I didn't realize it was a booty call."

Cade slid a hand down her hip, and then his finger was

inside her shorts, stroking over the bare skin of her folds. Moisture flooded her sex and her nipples tightened beneath her thin cotton tank. Had she really thought things would be different from every other time they'd been together when he walked in the door?

"Naughty girl," he whispered. "You go to bed without your panties and someone might take advantage."

"Cade." She pulled back just enough to dislodge his questing finger, at once disconcerted and aroused. "Why did you come here?"

His shoulders slumped and he leaned back in the chair, his easy capitulation more disturbing than his injuries. "The minute I got outta there, I called Jagger. Told him what had happened. The Wolverines are planning to patch over to the Jacks. You know what that means."

"They'll destroy the Sinners." She pulled the shirt over his head, biting her lip when she saw the extent of his injuries. Not an inch of his torso had been spared, his skin a mass of swelling and bruises, with a few surface knife slashes across his abdomen, below the fabulous tat of blue wings and twin pistons across his chest. And were those boot prints on his side?

Dawn steeled herself to calm. She couldn't help him if she panicked. And she'd seen worse injuries when she'd been with the Wolverines. Hell, Jimmy had given her worse injuries, and she survived. "What did Jagger say?"

Cade stiffened when she reached for his belt. "He called a church meeting for eight o'clock tomorrow morning."

"I'm not surprised." Biker "church" meetings were usually held once a week in most MCs, or in extraordinary situations. Attendance of all full-patch brothers was mandatory. Anyone without a patch wasn't allowed in the door.

Cade pushed himself to standing and unzipped his fly, but when he tried to push off his jeans he winced. Dawn gently moved his hands off his hips, giving him a moment to collect himself, before she said, "Let me."

Licking her dry lips, she eased his jeans over his narrow hips, dropping to her knees in front of him to slide them over his powerful thighs and muscular calves.

Without taking his gaze off her, Cade stepped out of his jeans, seemingly unconcerned to be standing in her kitchen, wearing only black boxers and sporting a sizeable erection.

For the briefest, most inexplicable moment, Dawn wanted nothing more than to pull off his boxers and take him in her mouth. He'd never let her take him that way when they'd been together. She'd held him, marveling at the feel of silky smooth skin over hard steel, and teased the tip of his cock with her tongue, but when she tried to go further, he had pulled away, saying he had a better idea. And he always did.

"Dawn . . ." Cade's voice cracked, even as his gaze burned into her, focused, intent.

She should get up. Kneeling in front of him like this was sending all the wrong messages. He was hurt. Badly. His injuries needed tending and he needed to rest. And she didn't want this. Didn't want to open this door again. Especially not now, with Jimmy on a tear. And yet she couldn't pull herself away.

"You still haven't told me why you came here," she said.

Cade sifted his hand through her hair, his touch more soothing than erotic. "I needed to tell you something . . . Fucking bastard's gonna make you choose between going back to him or losing your kids. And it's all my fault."

"Your fault?" Dawn looked up and frowned. "It has nothing to do with you. It's because of me. I knew the risks, but I couldn't help myself. Three hours a week just isn't enough. I miss them so much I ache inside every minute of every day." Her throat tightened and she looked away. "But thanks for coming to tell me."

His hand stroked down her hair. "That wasn't the only reason I came here."

"Oh?" A sliver of anxiety wound its way through her heart but she forced herself to meet his gaze.

"I wanted to see you."